FAWNED

Content Warning

This book contains explicit sexual situations and is intended for mature readers only.

Situations involving self-harm, suicidal ideation, and implied suicide attempt are also included.

Chapter 1

It wasn't the first time he'd invited a match from a hook-up app to spend the night in his dorm.

It wasn't the first time he'd taken extra pillows out from the closet to accommodate another for a bed that'd seen its fair share of visitors.

Condoms and strawberry-flavored lube? Right where they'd always been, in the top drawer of his nightstand, still plenty of each to last a few rounds. He kept his toys in the bottom drawer, not as easily accessible. But should his date feel so adventurous—

Gil Connolly sighed as he paced around the room.

His date.

Re-reading their Direct Messages - ones that had persuaded him to swap his typical grunge flannel for a black, wrinkle-free dress shirt - he suspected his toy box might be better unmentioned.

Reasoning: when Gil offered to get them a bottle to drink, he expected the other to answer with a type of wine, or vodka, or champagne -

> Sparkling Cider, thank you.

It'd been a while since he'd performed sober.

There wasn't much else to their conversation besides a time and day, either. No promises or plans, only "let's see where things go."

His date's profile told him all he needed to know: he was, in his own words, "vanilla." He wore a polo in every photo with his ash blond hair styled the same with each outfit, like a Mormon boy ready to go out on his first mission.

He was the opposite of Gil, who was topless in half of his own pictures and whose raven black hair could hardly be tamed, constantly needing to be brushed back from his dull, grey eyes.

His date's eyes were what stood out to him the most - two brilliant, hazel gems on a round, youthful face. They nearly distracted him from his lips, plump and pink.

His name was Barnaby.

He wasn't the type that Gil was used to, but he wasn't opposed to trying something new.

A controlled knock at the door snapped the man into focus. Brushing his hair behind his ear, he discarded his phone to the pocket of his leather pants and took a deep breath.

Showtime.

Opening the door revealed a boy that was half a foot shorter and a few pounds heavier than him. He stood as far away as possible while still being seen, beet red and fidgeting with the collar of his green polo.

With a visibly strained smile, he pried a trembling hand away to offer a small wave. "Hi."

Gil almost forgot to plaster on his routine smirk. "Hey, Barnaby—" He stepped aside, leaving the door open for him. "Come on in, you look great."

Despite the apparent nervousness, that much was undeniable. He was curvier than Gil expected him to be, wearing clothes that may have been a size too small. Not that Gil was complaining, of course. His hips were wide and girlish, and his khakis did a fantastic job of accentuating it.

Barnaby shuffled into the dorm, mumbling a "thank you", and Gil closed the door behind him. Expecting to turn around and face him, he found the boy's back instead. First, Gil noticed he was looking around the room, at blank white and brick walls. Then, Gil noticed his ass.

Jesus Christ.

Bent over, he wondered if those khakis would rip apart on their own.

"You can sit on the bed or the chair—" Gil gestured vaguely at the room. "Whichever."

Or my lap. Or my face. Whichever.

He made himself useful, going to his kitchen area to pour sparkling cider into two champagne glasses.

Barnaby claimed a seat at the edge of his bed, smoothing his hands along his thighs.

Crossing to his desk chair, Gil handed the boy his glass and sat down. He swirled his own glass, watching the bubbles disappear, and commented for conversation's sake, "I hope I got the right kind. I thought sparkling cider was just, *y'know*...sparkling cider. I didn't realize there were so many different flavors."

A hand flew to Barnaby's mouth after he'd taken a sip, still too late to muffle his snort. "*It's,*" he croaked, struggling to recover. He cleared his throat and managed a steadier smile at his host. The red in his face had begun to fade. "It's fine. Thank you. All flavors are good flavors."

"I'll take your word for it," Gil muttered, amused. He downed half of his glass in one gulp and proceeded with the obvious question, "So, I'm guessing you don't drink?"

"I can't—" Barnaby's grin widened sheepishly, and he fidgeted in his seat. "I'm not twenty-one yet, so...No." When Gil dramatically rolled his eyes, he sputtered, "I don't want to risk it! At least not on campus. Like, when I'm at home, I usually have wine with my mom."

"Aw, you *are* a rebel," Gil snickered. Barnaby's profile had said he was twenty, and based on the Everything Else About Him, it came as no surprise that he'd want to play it safe. "Might let the dean know about that."

"Please," Barnaby scoffed, being the next to roll his eyes, "I bet you've done much worse."

Gil blinked in surprise, quirking a brow. He didn't know whether to be insulted or impressed. "Oh yeah?" he tested the boy, a careless lift in his tone, "And what exactly do you think I'm capable of?"

Barnaby's expression faltered, eyes slowly widening as he stammered, "I mean...Not...*Not* like you're a bad person, just...with the, uhm...the drinking..."

"You think I'm an alcoholic?"

"No!"

"Then, *what*?"

"*Just—*" Barnaby's voice cracked, and the glass in his hand began to shake.

Gil sighed, remembering why he always tried to keep conversation to a minimum. "Wait—"

"*Sorry.*" It was already too late for the boy to stop himself; his leg began bouncing a mile per minute. "I just...meant that...You've probably done worse than *me*. Which is fine! Because I...I don't really do anything...at all? I've never met up with anyone, and I know I'm like, *freaking out*, and you're all cool and calm and *hot*, and you offered to get me alcohol, so I'd assume you'd have experience, but I'm..." He paused to catch his breath and place his glass on Gil's nightstand. "I'm really bad at words, s-so I'm sorry if I insulted you, I, I promise I don't mean it that way, I...admire it, actually."

Gil made sure he was done before pinching the bridge of his nose. He closed his eyes, then rubbed his forehead.

It was a first for him as much as it was his date's.

"*I'm sorry*," Barnaby pleaded, "If you still want to do anything, I can, I can shut up. I won't say anything else."

"You don't want to be here, do you?" Gil tried not to sound so accusatory, but Barnaby looked at him like a kicked puppy all the same. "Did someone dare you to go through with this?"

"*What*? No!"

"Then why'd you show up, dude?"

"*Because!*" Barnaby hunched over, burying his face in his hands. His shoulders rattled, and Gil could tell he was having trouble breathing.

Just his luck.

In the silence, he made his way over to the blond, sitting beside him. He rubbed soothing circles along his back, and minutes later, Barnaby was relaxing to his touch, his breathing less ragged. "Better?"

Barnaby nodded, starting to lean into Gil's side. "Thank you."

Gil didn't have the right words, but he knew the right moves. He draped an arm around the boy and squeezed his shoulder.

"I wasn't dared to come here," Barnaby said, sniffling. He started to crack his knuckles. "If I tell you the real reason, you'll think I'm even more pathetic."

Tilting his head, Gil could spot the blush creeping back to his face. "You weren't dared *and* you're sober? C'mon, it can't be that bad."

6

Barnaby shook his head. Another minute passed before he collected himself and spoke, "I want to be touched. *Intimately*. It's all I've thought about lately. I'll take anything at this point, I just need...*someone*."

"Anything, but you decided on me?"

Lifting his shy gaze, Barnaby said, barely above a whisper, "You're....*You look good*. And you look like someone who'd know what to do. Not that I...actually expected you to like me back."

Gil was almost flattered.

Barnaby was strange, but he wasn't any stranger than Gil. Just nervous. Gil could work with nervous. Maybe a part of him was nervous, too.

He offered a tender smile, using a voice that was just as sweet, "Well, I do like you. Enough that I wanted to spend the night with you." He reached for one of Barnaby's hands, taking it cautiously in his own. It was sweaty, but he didn't mind. His were always too dry and ashy, anyway. "If being touched is something you want, I can definitely help with that. Not that we have to go all the way. We can just...have fun."

Relief dawned on the blond's innocent expression, and his hazel eyes softened with hope.

"Besides," Gil added, winking, "I like to be touched, too."

Barnaby's lips were slightly parted, and he was tempted to kiss him right then and there. All he had to do was lean in.

But Gil held back, squeezing the boy's hand instead. "Let's take it slow."

Chapter 2

"Oh. You have freckles."

Gil chuckled. They were easy to miss, mere pencil dust on his face, but they were there.

Lucky Barnaby for being close enough to spot them.

"You like 'em?"

The boy gave a meek nod, resuming the laborious task of unbuttoning Gil's top. "They're cute."

The last button popped open, and Gil slipped his shirt off the rest of the way, revealing a pale, toned torso with a dark trail above his navel. Leaning forward, his abdomen pressed right into Barnaby's palms. "No way they're cuter than you."

The blush on the boy's face spread all the way to his ears. "I'm not cute."

"I beg to differ."

Barnaby bit his lip, moving on from Gil's abs to trail his fingers along his arms. Starting at the leather bracelets around his wrists, he worked up to his— "Are these tattoos?" From the front, they were indiscernible markings that peaked around his biceps. "Can I see?"

Gil turned around, giving Barnaby the full view on his back: anatomical angel wings that extended from his shoulder blades to just above his elbows.

A soft gasp accompanied the gentle grazing of inked-on feathers. "They're beautiful! The detail is incredible!"

The sincerity in his voice made Gil's heart flutter. "Thank you." He slumped forward, savoring the delicate type of touch that had become so foreign to him. After a minute of indulging, he faced Barnaby again, tugging at the collar of his shirt. "My turn?"

The boy shrank back, avoiding his gaze.

Before Gil could rectify it with space or suggest a different direction, Barnaby mumbled, "I guess so."

"*I guess so*" wasn't "*yes.*"

The raven-haired inched closer, hip to hip, and brushed his nose against the other's. "If you change your mind," Gil said, hushed, "speak up."

His glimpse of hazel was brief, a glance, but Barnaby nodded his understanding. Grateful lips thanked the boy's cheek, and soon, his polo was on the floor, his muffin-top exposed.

"Guide me," Gil insisted, offering up his hands.

Barnaby took hold, playing with his fingers as he seemed to consider where to place them. "Uhm..."

Though he was undeniably curious, Gil remained patient.

He didn't expect Barnaby to be the one to ask, "Can I, if it's okay...kiss you?"

Gil nodded, biting the inside of his cheek to avoid grinning too wide, and closed his eyes.

The air was still, the room was silent. Time itself seemed to stop.

He wondered if the boy had changed his mind.

Then, warm, plush lips pressed against his own, and time went on with Gil's heart skipping a beat.

His hands landed on baby-soft skin. Splaying his fingers, he found two nubs.

Barnaby's breath shuddered, and the flesh pushed into his palms.

Gil was cupping his chest.

He smirked and continued groping, lightly slapping his small breasts and rubbing his nipples until they were nice and perky.

Barnaby squeaked and squirmed. "Feels good..."

Their lips met again and again - each kiss becoming gradually more deliberate.

The second Gil sensed Barnaby's lips part, his tongue flicked out to fill the space.

Barnaby whimpered but didn't pull away. Rather, he raised a hand and held Gil's cheek, keeping him in place presumably so he could lap at his mouth.

Maybe he'd never had a one-night stand, but it wouldn't surprise Gil to learn he'd had plenty of practice with whoever the boy was with previously.

Their tongues danced together, and Gil was tied up in it, barely able to register one of his hands being lowered to Barnaby's leg. Before giving him a chance to map out the area, the boy must have changed his mind; the hand was moved, and Gil was quicker to recognize it being trapped between a thick pair of thighs.

Barnaby all but jumped off the bed, moaning into the kiss.

One squeeze, and Gil realized his palm was directly on top of the boy's bulge.

"God *damn*." He traced the outline through his pants, already hard from what he could tell. Gil would soon be facing the same Problem. "Starting to think you're not so innocent after all."

"N-No— *Wait*—"

Gil was ready to retract his hand -

But Barnaby was bucking his hips, his thighs squeezing together. "I am," he whimpered, "b-but...*Oh*—" He hid his face in the crook of Gil's neck, the heat of embarrassment radiating off of him. "That feels so good. How does that feel so good?"

"Someone's sensitive," the man snickered, easing up with a single fingertip along the zipper. "You make it sound like no one's ever touched you before."

At first, the boy was silent; he circled his arms around Gil's neck and swallowed his pitiful sounds.

With his hand still trapped, the raven-haired made a path for the button of his khakis.

And then, Barnaby peeped, "I haven't. Not like this. Not there."

Gil froze, and suddenly, it all made sense - his reactions, his nervousness.

11

He tried turning his hand away from the boy's crotch. "Don't tell me this is your first time."

Barnaby's silence was all the answer he needed.

The corners of Gil's mouth pulled downward, and he sighed, "You really want to do this with a stranger?"

"I don't, uhm—" Barnaby inhaled, wavering, but corrected his posture to meet Gil's gaze— "It doesn't matter," he admitted, "I just want to get it over with. Seriously. I'm trusting you. Okay? You can do whatever you want, and I won't say anything if you don't want me to—"

Gil narrowed his eyes. "If all I did was treat you like a sex doll, there'd be no point." Unless Barnaby was kinkier than he let on. "Do you...*want* me to degrade you?"

A frown deepened on the boy's lips, and he looked down, shaking his head.

Gil was used to being used for sex. Those he took to bed probably didn't see him as anything more than a toy either, and he didn't see them as anything less, but at least there was a level of performance. They pretended to see each other as people, praising and encouraging one another the same way, too.

He assumed that was the bare minimum everyone wanted.

He rubbed along the boy's thigh. "Think about why you're doing this," Gil urged him, "If you don't expect to enjoy it, I'd rather you go home. I won't hold it against you."

Barnaby, once again, began cracking his knuckles. He mumbled, "I'm already enjoying it."

Gil raised an eyebrow. "*Really*?"

The blond gave a swift nod. "You're being gentle. And it...it did feel good when you touched me, uhm..." The red tint returned to his face.

He was cute. And Gil didn't necessarily *want* him to leave.

He kissed Barnaby's cheek and prodded his bulge. "Here?"

The boy gave a sharp gasp. "*Yes.*"

Barnaby supposedly trusted him, meaning Gil had to trust him, too. At least, he saw it that way.

He abandoned his groin to tug at the hem of his khakis. "Should we take these off?"

Barnaby gulped, nodding slowly to answer.

"Stand up."

He got to his feet and stood awkwardly in front of Gil, just for the raven-haired to grab him by the hips and spin him around. Barnaby hugged himself, and Gil unfastened his pants, pulling them down along with his briefs.

He watched in awe as the fattest ass he'd ever seen on a man poured out of Barnaby's khakis, pear-shaped and perfect. He couldn't resist leaning forward, peppering kisses across one the sizable globes. "Are you *positive* you want me to have this?" Gil asked. His hands swept down the boy's sides, memorizing his curves. "Because I'm thinking this would be the ultimate Wedding Night present."

Barnaby scoffed, shifting in place. "It's not like I'll ever get married, so..."

"No?"

"I mean—" The boy shrugged— "you see what I'm like. This isn't even the worst of it."

Gil rolled his eyes. "I'm sure you're not that bad." But they weren't there for a therapy session, and he wasn't going to linger on it. His purpose was to make him feel good.

He grabbed his ass with both hands, making it jiggle and imagining how it would look bouncing on his cock. Pulling it apart, he found Barnaby's little, pink pucker. "Fuck, I'd love to bury my face in there."

The blond peeked over his shoulder. "You would?"

Gil hummed, pressing his thumb against the rim and watching it clench in response. "Have you ever tried any toys?"

"I, uhm..." Porcelain thighs rubbing together, Barnaby bit his nails and mumbled, "Have a dildo that I use sometimes."

It wasn't hard to picture him, alone in his bed, legs spread as far and wide as they would go as he struggled to aim his dildo, desperate for pleasure.

I can do so much better.

Gil patted the bed beside him. "On all fours. Get comfy."

While Barnaby slipped out of his shoes and obeyed, Gil grabbed a condom and strawberry lube from the nightstand. When he turned around, he saw the boy holding a pillow under his chin.

His ass was high in the air.

14

"If I didn't know any better," Gil mused, kneeling behind him, "I'd think you knew exactly what you were doing."

"Is this right?" the boy babbled, "I've seen it done in porn, but..."

"You're exactly how I want you—" Gil poured a glob of lube directly onto Barnaby's pucker, making him tremble— "Now, relax." Fixing his hair behind his ears, he spread Barnaby's cheeks and dug in. All it took was a few careful licks over the rim to have the boy writhing and whining; mere seconds, and he was pressing back against Gil's face.

Closing his eyes, Gil let himself revel in the warm, eager cushion of Barnaby grinding against his face. He lapped hungrily, moaning with him and making every sort of motion to get his best and loudest reactions.

Easy when he tasted like honey.

"*Please*. Oh my God," Barnaby begged, "Please, don't stop." He buried his face into a pillow, muffling the sounds that came from Gil dragging his tongue to his balls.

He rolled them into his mouth, sucked carefully, and licked a long strip back to his rim. "But...*Bee*," Gil said, wiping his mouth, "Don't you want to feel even *better*?"

Twitching from head to toe, Barnaby echoed, "Better?"

Gil smirked and savored a few more licks, ending with a kiss, before lifting his head. "You were hoping for my dick, weren't you?" Taking the lube again, he coated his fingers slick. "That's why you're here, right? To feel a real, throbbing cock inside of you?"

He caught the tepid nod of Barnaby's head behind the tantalizing sway of his rump.

He was fucking precious.

Unfortunately, Gil knew that shoving himself in, for someone who never experienced the real thing, wouldn't feel very good at all. He needed to be careful.

Rubbing one of Barnaby's cheeks, Gil tapped a digit to his entrance. "Tell me when."

A minute or so passed before the boy was raising his ass just a bit higher. He muttered, "Okay."

Gil's expression softened, and his finger slid in with ease. He watched as Barnaby's nails dug into the pillow, face hidden while his rim contracted around the finger. "Don't forget to breathe."

"Sorry," Barnaby rasped, shifting his knees to adjust, "I just...can't believe you're *inside* of me."

A chuckle rumbled in Gil's throat, and he slowly began moving the digit in and out. "Remember, it's only a finger. Not worth getting too excited yet."

Barnaby nodded again, drawing out each exhale until Gil felt he was loose enough to add a second finger.

He took his time scissoring the boy, listening to his restless mewling, before he heard him say, "I'm sorry if this is, *mmm,* weird for you."

"I promise it's not," Gil assured him, giving his ass an appreciative squeeze. "You're taking it so well, you're beautiful, and I've got the best view." With that, he worked in a third digit, pausing the moment he heard Barnaby groan.

The muscle flexed around him. "Is this about the size you're used to?"

"Y-Yeah? *Oh*— Aaahh—"

When he was the least bit looser, Gil pressed in further, wiggling his fingers within. Soon, he was thrusting his hand in and out, a slow pace, but aiming deeper each time.

The boy panted below him, rocking his hips back and forth; it was as if he couldn't decide how much he wanted to take.

With each thrust came less effort on Gil's part, and thankfully, it wasn't long until he could pump his fingers with minimal effort. The wet, sloppy sound of lube filled the room, and combined with Barnaby's voice, it was music to Gil's ears.

Another minute passed. Barnaby had backed up so much, he was practically grinding in Gil's lap. He muttered something that sounded like words, and Gil paused to hear him clearer - "What did you say?"

Barnaby struggled for air. "I said," he wheezed, licking his lips and looking back, "I want your cock. Please? I think I can take it."

Gil's lips curled, and he huffed, carefully removing his fingers. "Alright. But not from this position." He stood up and finished stripping down. On his way back into bed, he caught a glimpse of Barnaby's wide-eyed stare, honed directly on his crotch.

"Oh my..."

Gil resisted the urge to roll his eyes again. His wasn't the first reaction of its kind, though it was far from being as dramatic as some others. He just never really understood. For Gil, it was a regular penis, but according to the general consensus, he was "hung."

He stepped closer to where Barnaby rested his chin on the pillow, letting his boner poke the boy's cheek. "Still think you can take it?"

Barnaby's lips parted, and his gaze flickered from Gil's eyes to the cock right in front of him. His eyelids drooped close, and to Gil's surprise, he trailed his lips along his shaft without being told. Reaching the tip, he gave a few kitten-like licks.

Gil rewarded him by stroking his hair.

"I want to try—" Barnaby's breath flowed out over Gil's cock, tempting the man to penetrate his mouth. "I really want you to have me. Please."

Well, if that was all he wanted—

Gil sucked in his own breath and patted Barnaby's head. "Sit up."

He complied without question, and Gil laid beside him. He propped himself up with the pillows behind him, reaching for the condom, unwrapping it, and sliding it on. With another grab for the lube, he made sure his member was sufficiently coated and placed the bottle on the nightstand.

"Should I—" Barnaby cleared his throat— "You want me to sit on you?"

"It'd give you the most control."

Initially, all Barnaby did was stare at Gil's cock; the more he stared, the less confident Gil felt about it.

He didn't know what brought the switch, or what he was thinking, but eventually, the boy climbed on top of him, straddling his waist.

"I'm sorry in advance," Barnaby mumbled, attempting to align his entrance with Gil's tip.

Gil thought he'd collapse the instant he succeeded. "For what?"

Barnaby held onto his shoulders for purchase, his chin quivering. "For the way I look. Or sound—" He seemed like he was trying to smile— "I know it's not sexy."

"Barnaby," Gil purred. His fingers wrapped around the boy's cock, earning a hiccup in response. It was a tad strange, but that made him all the more endearing. "Trust me. You have *nothing* to apologize for."

He pumped his full length, and Barnaby sighed, shivering - slowly, *carefully* lowering himself onto Gil's lap. "Aah...*Aaahhh—*"

His nails dug into tattooed shoulders, and Gil froze as he felt the tip of his cock sinking into him. "It's okay," he whispered, "You don't need to rush—"

He'd barely uttered the last word when all the wind was knocked out of him.

In one, swift motion, Barnaby had plunged himself the rest of the way, crying out with him as he trapped Gil in his packed heat. "*Fuck!*"

Tears filled his hazel eyes, and Gil's heart plummeted to his stomach. "Shit—" He held onto Barnaby's hips, ready to help him off. "You're not bleeding, are you? Do you want to stop?"

The poor guy was shaking worse than a leaf. "I, I don't think so," he sniveled. He laid right on top of Gil, hiding his face against his neck. In a weak voice, he asked, "I didn't ruin it, did I?"

Gil frowned, stroking his hair. "No, you didn't ruin it—" He pressed a kiss to his temple— "but I would like to know what the Hell you were thinking."

"I thought," Barnaby whimpered, "the quicker I did it, the less it would hurt."

Gil's brows furrowed, and he blinked, as if that would somehow make it clear in his mind. "What, like a bandage? Barnaby—"

"I'm sorry. I'm so *stupid*."

He knew he couldn't fault him. He didn't have the experience, and if he was taking lessons from porn, Gil could see where he'd get the wrong idea.

"You're not stupid," he insisted, "you're just...an outcome of America's school system, refusing to teach queer kids how to have safe sex."

Barnaby looked up, a stunned expression on his face. "I," he sputtered, "Maybe? Did they go into that much detail for straight people?"

Gil attempted a smile, for his sake. "Doesn't matter—" He stole a kiss while he still had Barnaby's attention— "What matters is if you can move."

Barnaby seemed to consider it, though there was a hint of doubt in his eyes. He pushed up on wobbly arms, wincing as he rocked his hips. "I-I'm sore, but I think so."

Gil gritted his teeth, unable to ignore how fucking tight the guy was. "Give it a minute," he suggested, rubbing his hands along Barnaby's thighs, "let your body adjust."

Barnaby exhaled deeply, staying perfectly still while Gil's hand returned to his cock. "You're really good at that," he commented, fixated on the languid motion, "It's...a lot nicer than doing it alone."

Gil wasn't doing anything special, and he knew it. He did, however, remember the first time someone else touched him, how that was a game-changer.

He couldn't deny there was a slight sense of accomplishment that came with knowing he'd changed the game for Barnaby.

"I bet you give great handjobs, too," Gil humored him, "You've been a natural with everything else."

He caught the beginning of a smile on Barnaby's lips, one quickly hidden by a small hand wiping his face. "Apparently not if I almost ripped my own asshole."

Gil chortled. "Well, your body did what it wanted to do." He leaned in closer, tracing a finger along the boy's jaw, hoping to draw his gaze. "Your kisses felt natural–" He swept across his lower lip— "but I'd love to try again. To double check, of course."

Their eyes locked for a moment, and Gil saw himself in Barnaby's hazel gems.

"O-Of course..."

With some hesitation and patience, their lips connected, and the kiss that followed was even sweeter than the firsts. Both were grinning into it, their noses bumping; they mapped each other's faces and combed through one another's hair.

In time, Barnaby was rolling his hips once again; his gentle kisses became cautious bites while whimpers spilled from his lips.

As a test, Gil gave a careful thrust upward, and the boy squeaked automatically.

"Still hurt?"

"N-No—" Barnaby arched against him, and his hips began lifting, moving up and down Gil's shaft. "It feels...*really* nice, wow—" His breathing was heavier—"Thank you so much for this."

Gil brushed a few blond wefts into place, admiring the sight of him coming undone, of glossy lips, bright red cheeks, and shimmering hazels. "Thank you for letting me have you," he muttered, "I have to be the luckiest man alive right now."

Around campus, he may have only spared Barnaby a second glance, but in his bed, he was one of the most beautiful men he'd ever met. He was certainly the most grateful.

It'd be a shame when their night was over. Might as well make the most of the time they had.

Barnaby avoided his gaze, bashful, but moved in waves on top of Gil's body, fluid.

Gil waited for him to plunge down in his lap again, and in one sharp thrust, met the boy's rear.

His eyes shot wide open, and his jaw dropped in an instant. "*Oh!*"

"Did you like that, babe?" Gil clutched the sheets to restrain himself. He'd put Barnaby on top to give him control—

But holy fuck was it tempting to claw at his hips and use him like a Fleshlight.

"So much," Barnaby panted. Thankfully, he was a fast learner, attempting to mimic the intensity on his own.

Gil wondered if he was waiting for him to do his part.

The sound of Barnaby's ass clapping against him mixed in with his moans, and soon, Gil's groaning was part of the symphony.

His small, boy breasts bounced hypnotically in front of his face, and the next thing Gil knew, he had his mouth pressed between them, biting the soft flesh, licking and sucking his nipples.

"*Fuck*," Barnaby cried. He hugged Gil's head, practically smothering him with his chest. "Don't know...if I can last!"

Neither did Gil.

He crept a hand under Barnaby's gut for the last time, stroking his cock the best he knew how, wringing the shaft and circling a thumb around his tip. He could sense the boy's walls clenching around him; his limbs convulsed, and his hips jolted erratically.

He was gasping for air and nuzzling his face in Gil's hair, weeping, his voice thin, "So good...Thank you...My God...Please, please...I'm so close—"

"Come for me." It was an invitation. An encouragement. Tilting his head, Gil pressed a kiss to Barnaby's neck, breathing hot against it. "Show me how good it is to finally be *fucked*."

"I'm coming!" Barnaby warned, "Oh God, I'm coming!"

One, final plunge, and the boy locked up, squealing with pleasure as he unloaded onto Gil's hand and stomach.

"Good boy," Gil purred, continuing to pump his fat, little cock until he was milked dry, "Good, *good* boy."

Chapter 3

He could've sworn the bed wasn't nearly as soft when he had his face stuffed in the pillow, ass in the air.

When did it become a cloud?

Wrapped in a black blanket, Barnaby watched Gil return from the bathroom that separated his dorm from the next.

He had a wet washcloth in his hand and a fond smile on his lips.

Sitting gingerly at the edge of the bed, he pressed the rag to Barnaby's forehead and swept it down the side of his face.

It was cool to the touch, and Barnaby tilted his head to get as much as he could out of it. "Thank you," he whispered, "you don't have to do this."

Gil bent down, placing a kiss on his cheek. "I know—" He continued wiping sweat from the boy's chest— "but I want to." Pulling the blanket back, he gestured below Barnaby's waist. "May I?"

The boy nodded, heart skipping beat after beat as Gil revealed his bare body. His legs spread to be more accessible, and he shivered from the sensation of lube and cum being cleaned off his thighs and hole.

Judging by the amount of time Gil took, it must've been quite a mess.

He cradled Barnaby's balls, applying a slight pressure, and the boy gasped.

"Still sensitive?" Gil asked with the faintest hint of concern.

Barnaby gulped, struggling not to squirm or wish that the man would continue fondling him. "I'm fine," he said, "it's just kinda...cold."

Gil's grin widened, and he finished the task with a quick swipe up Barnaby's shaft, making him shiver. "Should be all good to go." Fixing the blanket over him again, he headed for his fridge.

Go.

Barnaby supposed it was time - they'd done what he used to think was impossible. What else was there to do?

He tried to stand up, only for an ache in his core to keep him at the edge of the bed, gritting his teeth.

He would definitely be sore in the morning.

"Here."

A water bottle was held in front of his face, and Barnaby took it without hesitation. "Thank you." He downed half of it in a single gulp, breathed deep, in and out, and forced himself the rest of the way.

Finding his pants and briefs, he began dressing himself.

"You know you can borrow my clothes," Gil said, juggling his own water bottle.

Unsure if he'd heard him right, Barnaby paused mid-putting on his shirt. "Huh?"

Gil blinked, looking just as uncertain. "I can give you something else to wear to bed if those aren't comfortable."

Barnaby furrowed his brows. "I'm sorry, I don't—"

"You're sleeping over, right?"

"*Sleeping over?*"

"Aren't you tired?"

"I..." He was, a bit. Perhaps that was why Gil wasn't making sense. "You said I was good to go."

The man's bewildered expression deflated with realization. He said, "I wasn't being literal. You can stay."

But Barnaby was already dressed and standing.

Their moment was over. They'd both gotten what they wanted out of it.

"Thank you, but," Barnaby stumbled, slipping into his sneakers, "I have class tomorrow, so I should probably get going anyway."

The only thing standing between him and the door was Gil.

Gathering the man's boxers from the floor, Barnaby stopped in front of him to hand them over. He smiled and said, "Thank you for helping and...being so nice about it. I didn't expect to have that much fun but..."

A grin was creeping its way back to Gil's lips, and Barnaby almost forgot what he was saying.

"I did. You made it...*so enjoyable*, and I really appreciate that. Uhm—" A parting kiss seemed too sentimental. Their moment was over.

Barnaby held out his hand for Gil to shake instead. "If I meet anyone else looking for...*this*...I'll send them your way?"

Gil laughed, shook his hand, and put on his boxers. "You don't have to do that—" He walked Barnaby over to the door. "Besides, I'll probably be a little pickier from now on."

Heat washed over Barnaby's face, and he bit his lip, fidgeting with the buttons on his collar. Suddenly, it didn't seem quite so scandalous to leave them all undone. "If you say so—" He stepped outside of the dorm, cleared his throat, and gave Gil one last look. "It was nice meeting you. Maybe I'll, uhm, see you around?"

"I hope you do—" The man scanned him from head to toe and back up again. "Goodnight, Barnaby."

"Goodnight, Gil."

A final nod, and the door between them was closed.

Barnaby's Walk of Shame wasn't anywhere near as shameful as he anticipated.

He might've walked with a spring in his step if not for the limp he'd gained - not that it bothered him much. It was a bit like a prize he got to take home with him for a job well done.

I lost my virginity, and all I got was this lousy limp.

He snorted and felt himself grinning wide. Despite how fresh the memories were, he could hardly believe any of them.

Had he *really* put himself in someone else's dorm? Had he truly and honestly kissed a stranger, let them see him

28

naked, and make all sorts of embarrassing noises for them? Had they actually *praised* him for it, gently encouraging him every step of the way?

If pacing outside of his dorm building to cool himself down was the result, maybe, *just maybe*, the answer was yes.

He went inside, up to the second floor, when he was finally able to force his lips into a straight line without cracking.

Opening the door to Room 208, Barnaby was greeted to pitch blackness, save for a faint beacon of light - the glow of a laptop screen, illuminating a pale face framed by the most unironically dorky glasses imaginable.

"Perfect," Barnaby chimed, flicking the lights on, "you're awake."

The other boy in the room hissed from his bed, squinting. "Where the Hell were you?"

"Out—" Crossing over to the brunet, Barnaby stationed himself behind the laptop and held out his hand. "$100, please."

His roommate's head snapped up from whatever he was working on, and he sneered, eyes widening to the size of his lenses. "For what?"

Barnaby shrugged, as if he wasn't totally smug about his victory. "Our deal."

The brunet blinked once, then twice. His brows knitted together, and his lips twitched, as if he had a dozen different smartass remarks to choose from but couldn't decide which one was good enough. He gave up when he sputtered, "No fucking way— *with who*?"

Barnaby inhaled and made sure his head was held high, standing his ground. "Gil."

"Gil *who*?"

"I don't know his last name, Seth," Barnaby sighed, "I met him on Gaydar."

"Oh, my fucking—" It was his roommate, Seth, who had his palm out next. "Show me. I need proof."

The blond pouted and pulled out his phone, opening the app with Gil's profile. He held out the screen to show him, though he'd refuse to let go. He knew better than to let him have access to their messages. "There."

Seth raised his glasses, and his jaw dropped. "Holy shit. Gil *Connolly*?!" He crossed his arms, leaning against the wall behind him. "He doesn't count."

Barnaby's heart dipped, and he demanded, "What? Why not?"

"Because Gil Connolly will sleep with anyone with a dick! It was supposed to be a *challenge*."

"*Well—*" Barnaby knocked on his chest, beating down the sting of Seth's words. It didn't surprise him; why else would they have matched if not for Gil swiping right on every picture he saw? Maybe Gil wasn't paying attention at first, but he made up for it in their time together. At least, he acted impressed, and Barnaby would've liked to think there was more than his dick that he could've given that most people

30

couldn't. "You didn't say that. All you said was whoever loses their virginity first."

"I know what I said," his roommate grumbled. There'd be a moment of awkward silence before he added, "I'll go to the ATM later. *God*, you couldn't wait until next week?"

No. And that was exactly the point.

With how often Seth had mentioned an upcoming party, Barnaby had an idea of what he was planning. He had little doubt after their trip to the local Halloween store; Seth had left with a Sexy Quarterback costume, padded in the shoulders and the rear (jock strap included). Barnaby bought a deer onesie, and even he wasn't sure if he was going.

With nothing else to say, he was ready to turn to his own bed when Seth threw out another question, "How big was his dick?"

Barnaby's face flared up in an instant. "I—" He didn't hesitate to turn off the light switch then— "I don't know."

"You don't *know*?"

"He's bigger than you," Barnaby snapped. He changed into his pajamas, retreated to his bed, and flinched somewhat when he laid on his back. "So...eight inches, maybe?"

"*Jesus.*"

Barnaby scoffed, keeping his phone in his hand. Leaving Gil's profile with a lingering glance, he opened the app for his bank and checked his balance for the second time that day. He was still in the negative, but he had twenty-four hours left to correct it.

As long as Seth went to the ATM by then, he'd be in the clear.

A string of lights appeared above his head, interwoven with the artificial vines he'd used to decorate his headboard. It was time for bed.

Looking over to Seth's side of the room, Barnaby watched him, wide awake at his keyboard. "Hey," he called over, curious, "how do you know about him?"

"We had LGBT History together last spring. Shocking, right?" his roommate answered, "Honestly, I forgot he was there half the time. But from what I've heard from The Gays, he's a fucking freak. Handcuffs, whips. The whole nine."

Barnaby's heart stopped for a moment.

He thought about the way Gil stared at him, hungry. His touch had been gentle, but that was what *Barnaby* wanted.

And he'd offered Gil to have his way with him.

"He didn't do any of that to me," the blond murmured, "Those could just be rumors."

Evidently, Seth didn't care enough to continue, unfazed as he focused solely on his screen.

Barnaby sighed and rolled over to face the wall. His bed wasn't anywhere near as warm or comfortable as Gil's, but it was where he was meant to be.

Chapter 4

He'd managed to get through the day.

He went to class as usual, took notes, and never mentioned Gil Connolly's name. At least Seth had the decency not to ask any more questions. No one pointed out anything different about him, and for once, he was grateful for the lack of attention. No one else knew what he'd done.

But then, it was time for his night shift at the cafe. He was the only person on duty, and once midnight hit, there wasn't another soul in sight. He put on the radio, did some homework, scrolled through his phone - anything he could to suppress *those* memories.

Although—

Barnaby huffed, putting his phone down, and pressed his face against the marble counter he sat behind. He could push the imagery to the back of his mind as much as he wanted; his body, on the other hand, seemed to have a much more difficult time at forgetting.

Hoping to reach some kind of relief, Barnaby rubbed his thighs together, only to make himself whimper.

Fuck.

It might have been a safe spot - his back to the security camera, a full view of the entrance in case someone *did* decide to come in. The counter was high enough that, if he stayed sitting on his stool, he could hunch over and hide himself well.

But Barnaby, being Barnaby, had too many doubts. What if someone watched the security footage and recognized the motion his arm was making? What if, one way or another, he contaminated the register? *Worse,* the pastry display beside the register?

He stared ahead, looking long and careful through the windows. He didn't notice any headlights from any cars or any shadows creeping in from under the streetlamps. Surely, he'd seen the last of his customers.

Breath bated, Barnaby convinced himself to get out from behind the counter and hobbled to the bathroom.

It was small, having a single toilet, but it was clean, and in that moment, he figured that was all he could ask for. He quickly did away with his work-apron, letting everything below his waist fall to his ankles.

A relieved sigh left his lips as Barnaby took himself into his hands, closing his eyes.

Gil waited at the forefront of his mind. Silver eyes pierced his soul, making silent commands that the boy was powerless to resist.

Gil's fingers were slender, graceful; he started his strokes slow and feather-like, hoping to imitate that.

"*Good boy,*" he could practically hear him whispering.

Barnaby shuddered, his knees already going weak below him.

"You're taking it so well."

With how warm the simple memory made his face feel, it was easy to believe the man was right there over his shoulder, breathing onto him. His head tilted to the side, expecting to press against a chiseled jaw; he bent slightly forward, hoping he'd make contact with a bulge somewhere behind him.

He didn't, but he continued hunching over awkwardly, gradually pumping himself faster.

He became consciously aware of the cramp lingering between his legs, remembering how it felt to be stretched and split open, heated by Gil from the inside out. To be so *very* full—

Barnaby could swear something was pulsing *deep* inside of him, throbbing in that instant. He wanted to bounce on it, to be able to show how appreciative he was.

He didn't realize how much he'd built himself up until he was biting his lip, muffling a moan he couldn't swallow. A few more wrings around the head of his cock, and Barnaby locked up entirely, dumping his load out in front of him.

He was still trying to catch his breath when he blinked his eyes open, staring down into the toilet.

No Gil. No pillowtalk or tattooed arms to cradle him. Just himself in a public bathroom.

He wondered, in an attempt at keeping shame at bay, how many other guys had performed the same act there before him. He redressed and washed his hands.

He wondered if it was more or less than the number of men Gil had slept with.

Barnaby sighed, fretting with the front of his apron once he'd tied it.

He was ashamed for thinking about it. It wasn't any of his business, and it wasn't as if he'd expected Gil to have a clean history - he'd picked him specifically due to the fact he exuded experience.

It didn't matter if all the man saw him as was another notch in his belt, he'd brought that on himself.

Trying to keep that in mind, Barnaby flushed the toilet and left the bathroom.

He stopped almost as soon as he exited, his gaze drawn to the entrance.

Someone stood, inside the cafe, with a hand on the door and their back to him, their shoulders hiked and tense under a black denim jacket.

He'd neglected a customer at the cost of jerking off.

"I am *so* sorry to keep you waiting." Barnaby scrambled to his post behind the register, the words tumbling out of his mouth, "Is there anything I can help you with? Anything I can get for you?" He rushed to hide the textbook and notepad he'd left lying on the counter when something else caught his eye: a card, with *Groundwork*, the name of the cafe, printed above his own name. His name tag. He hadn't seen it since he'd left for Gil's dorm.

The stranger turned around, and Barnaby's heart stopped at the sight of a familiar face. He blinked a few times to make sure he wasn't hallucinating.

"Where, uhm—" He picked up the tag and pinned it to his brown button-up. "Where was it?"

"Under my bed," Gil said, scuffing an old boot on the floor and taking a few steps toward the counter. "Hope you didn't get in trouble for not having it."

"No. *No*," Barnaby assured him, "I don't think anyone even noticed, ah—" He stole a quick glance to the clock on the wall behind him - a little after two in the morning. "Why did you—" He swallowed his words and reconsidered, not wanting to sound accusatory— "You came out this late to give it back? I mean, I'm grateful! I am, but, wouldn't you rather be...asleep, maybe?"

Gil scoffed, "Wouldn't you?"

Barnaby shrugged, avoiding his gaze to scrape imaginary dirt off the register. "It'll only be this late for the rest of the week. Midterms, y'know? Did you...not finish yours?"

"I did," came the confident answer. "Wouldn't have gone for a walk otherwise."

How convenient. "And you usually go out for walks after midnight?"

"Sometimes. If the work's done and I don't have to be up too early."

Barnaby wanted to believe it was that innocent, but he couldn't help but be skeptical. No one had ever looked for him that late before.

The suspicion must have showed on his face, because the second he looked up again, Gil was stepping back, admitting, "I was around earlier, but I saw you had customers, and...I didn't want to embarrass you or anything. I thought I could catch you on your way out, but it just kept getting later and later, so..."

He had his hands stuffed in his pockets. From the angle his head was tilted, Barnaby spotted dark bags under his grey eyes in place of freckles.

The blond sighed, cracking his knuckles. "It's alright," he assured him, "Thank you."

"Alright," Gil repeated, taking another step back, "Cool, uh—" He pointed to Barnaby's nametag. "Keep your eyes on that thing."

Barnaby managed a smile and waved. "I will."

Of course, Gil didn't want to be seen with him in public. He had other options, Barnaby was only a notch in his belt, and there wasn't any other reason for them to see each other ever again, especially if the man had to hold himself back for him. And then it occurred to Barnaby—

Was he sure Gil enjoyed it as much as he did?

Were his compliments said merely to ease the boy's mind? Did Barnaby give him more grief than gratification? Would he be "pickier" because he didn't want to get stuck in the same situation in the future?

Was there something Barnaby had done wrong?

Was he a masochist for needing to know?

"Hey!" he called out, and Gil halted, one foot out the door.

He didn't want it to be an interrogation or make the man feel confronted.

Swallowing what iota of dignity he had left, Barnaby tried to phrase it as simply as possible— "Was I boring?"

Gil looked over his shoulder, his lips quirked. He was silent for a moment, waiting perhaps - for Barnaby to answer his own question? For permission to leave uninterrupted?

He asked, "What the Hell made you think I was *bored*?"

Barnaby cringed, his resolve fleeting fast. He became very interested with a coffee stain on the floor. "I just—" Was there an unspoken agreement that he had to be silent about it? Would Gil be mad he told a friend? "I *heard*...that you were a, uhm..."

The raven raised a brow, and Barnaby blurted at last, "*A freak*."

It came as an echo, incredulous - "A *freak*?"

"Yeah, like—" He didn't mean to speak - he didn't particularly want to after that - but Gil's tone had him spooked into explaining, "You know the saying...*a freak in the sheets*, I guess." His face heated up the more he went on rambling, "Because if...if what we did wasn't what you were used to, or, or you weren't satisfied with it, you can just say so."

When Gil didn't respond right away, Barnaby dared a quick glance, finding the man a few paces closer.

He chortled, and a smile broke out across his face. "Kid, I don't know what you heard, but just because we skipped the rope and you didn't call me Daddy doesn't mean it was bad sex."

Barnaby had to be as red as a tomato.

He didn't know whether to be relieved or...embarrassed? Was he embarrassed for Gil? The man was bold, as far as Barnaby was concerned, but he didn't know any other way to respond other than to match his tone - "M-Maybe if your profile had said *Daddy* instead," he cautioned, "I would have?"

The man shrugged, crossing his arms over his chest. "Truthfully, I'm more glad you didn't."

"Oh?"

"Sure," Gil continued, another step forward, "People will call anything Daddy nowadays. Kinda lost its spark for me."

A nervous chuckle bubbled from Barnaby's throat, and he pursed his lips. If he was taking the man's word for it, then, without meaning to, perhaps he'd done something right.

Having that crumb of accomplishment, he gulped and persisted, "So, what about the rope? Or handcuffs? Do you actually use those?"

Gil nodded confidently. "If the other guy says he's interested, absolutely. But I didn't get that from you." His eyes narrowed, though his smirk remained. "If I remember correctly, *your* profile was the one that mentioned being vanilla."

"Okay, but that— *that* was me protecting myself," Barnaby retorted, "from...from people like you."

Gil snickered, scrunching his nose, and the blond felt a more natural smile forming into place.

"Well," Gil said, "allow me to apologize for not being more open about my kinks."

Barnaby snorted and wiped at his face. Rocking on his heels, he replied, "I'll accept your apology if you can accept mine for being boring."

Gil rolled his eyes and unfolded his arms.

The next thing Barnaby knew, he was marching right up to the register, landing his hands on the counter.

The boy's breath caught in his throat, and he almost stumbled back from the man looming over him, his gaze hooded with hunger.

His voice dropped to a husky murmur, "You really think I found the way you rode my dick and screamed like a girl *boring*?"

Barnaby felt the hairs on the back of his neck stand on end. Goosebumps prickled along his arms. He hugged himself, rubbing them. "I—" He wanted to shrink away, hide from Gil's eyes - that may or may not have been mentally undressing him— "You might've liked it better if I wore handcuffs. I don't know."

Gil's expression softened, a flimsy mask for the devil. "If you were handcuffed, you wouldn't have been able to hold onto me the way you did." His fingers drummed against the marble. "But the important question is, would *you* have enjoyed that?"

Barnaby's instinct was to say "no." Tied or handcuffed in a stranger's bedroom, surrendering his control? It would have been terrifying.

So, why did thinking about it in that moment make his cock twitch?

"I don't know..."

"There must be a lot you don't know, hm?"

Barnaby pouted. As if it weren't obvious?

He watched the man run his tongue across his teeth, and a shiver coursed through his spine.

He realized he was shaking his head.

Gil tutted and reached into his jacket, producing a pen. "There's no shame to being vanilla, but there's a lot more to being kinky than handcuffs." Finding a stray piece of receipt paper, he started scribbling. "If you're curious, I do have a *collection*. I can show you what I mean. Maybe something will catch your attention."

He slid the note to Barnaby, revealing a phone number.

"And if it's not your thing," he finished, winking, "I wouldn't mind having you back anyway."

Barnaby rubbed and pinched his wrists, checking to see if he was dreaming.

In real life, Barnaby Hirsch didn't get hit on by handsome boys. They didn't offer him their number, and most people had their fill of him after the first time hanging out together.

Then again, Real Life Barnaby wasn't supposed to sleep with anyone, either.

He took the receipt paper, placing it directly into his pocket. "I do," he blurted before he could tell himself No, "want to come over, I mean. I'd like to see your collection."

If a wolf could smirk, it would wear Gil's grin, and if a fireplace on a cold winter's night could speak, Barnaby believed it would have his voice, asking him, "When are you free?"

Chapter 5

He didn't originally have the night off.

But he didn't want to wait. Waiting meant overthinking it. And overthinking it meant a heightened possibility of chickening out and never taking Gil's offer.

So, Barnaby called out of work sick and went straight from his last class to the man's dorm.

When he mentioned showing him his "collection", Barnaby wasn't exactly sure what he'd meant. A collection of porn, maybe? Of handcuffs?

He didn't have to wonder for long; Gil had everything set neatly on the bed for the moment he entered: a remarkable assortment of sex toys and accessories.

There were so much more than handcuffs (though he had several pairs). There were butt plugs, vibrators, anal beads, creams and oils, blindfolds, rope, a ring, a flog and a paddle, to name a few. They were in better condition than Barnaby would've assumed - like Gil hadn't unboxed them until that day. If the blond didn't know any better, he might've suspected the toys were bought just for him.

He picked up a bundle of synthetic rope and rubbed it between his fingers to familiarize the texture. There didn't appear to be any wear to it, so perhaps there was a chance the piece had been cut for him specifically. He tried to imagine how it would feel against his skin. Would it hurt?

What would it give Gil the power to do that he'd be unable to stop?

"If I let you pick something for me," Barnaby fought himself to speak (because he didn't want to waste the other's time more than he likely already did). He set the rope down, too timid to turn around— "What would it be?"

The floor creaked behind him, and in an instant, the man was pushing against his back. Warm breath tickled his ear as Gil reached around him, his hand hovering briefly over the display.

Barnaby watched as he picked up a black, vinyl collar, accented with a cowbell. He gulped, his face feeling hot.

Gil purred, "May I?"

Barnaby nodded.

The collar was fastened around his neck, and the bell rattled as Gil spun him around.

One arm circled Barnaby's waist, and with his opposite hand, the raven thumbed over the vinyl. "Perfect."

The boy smiled sheepishly. "You...think I'm a cow?"

"It's not that. As much as I'd like to milk you," Gil explained, flicking the bell, "This comes off. It's meant to be a pet collar."

Barnaby raised a brow, the synapses gradually coming together. Did Gil see him as an animal?

The man must have read his mind, because then he was ruffling his hair, stepping toward the bed as he spoke, "You

45

listened to my orders so well last time—" He bundled his collection inside of his blanket, dumped it onto the floor, and sat on the bed— "you might as well have been a dog."

Barnaby hadn't been aware he was following "orders", he'd simply trusted Gil's direction.

He was ready to join him, maybe even sit in his lap - but Barnaby had barely taken a step forward when a palm was raised in front of him.

A once over, and Gil's order came clear and compelling, "Strip for me."

Barnaby's heart caught in his throat. Was he totally unprepared - visiting the man's dorm with the intention of gaining some sexual knowledge and then *not* expecting sex?

Even if half of him did expect it, or at least hoped for it, nothing ever prepared him to handle stage fright. He couldn't put himself in front of a classroom without stuttering to incomprehension, and this man expected him to be, what? *Sexy*?

"Alright, but I'm warning you," he sighed, gathering up his nerve, "I've never stripped for anyone." Barnaby removed his polo without a shred of grace, just to take his time. Stripping was supposed to be a slow thing, right? A tease?

Gil's expression was smug, amusement dancing in his eyes as he fixated on the boy's torso. "You don't say."

Barnaby pouted, slipping out of his shoes and pants. He was dawdling with his boxers when he mumbled, "I think I preferred when you did it."

He decided he had to turn around to take his underwear off, but—

Fine. Barnaby shook his ass as it was exposed, remembering the other's initial reaction to undressing him.

Although, he might've been too subtle about it. Gil didn't laugh or comment, but Barnaby did hear rummaging.

And then he heard, "Turn around."

Hands clasped over his groin, Barnaby faced the man.

Gil was on his feet again, holding a slim, black vibrator in one hand and a small bottle in the other. Lube, Barnaby could only assume.

"Lay down—" It sounded more like a suggestion than a command— "on your stomach."

Barnaby dipped his head and did as he was told, reacquainting himself with the bed.

A weight settled between his legs, and he held his breath - pointless when a cold, wet finger circled his hole, making him gasp into the pillow.

His heart began racing, and he had to remind himself to *breathe.* He'd lost his virginity - he had some idea of what to expect. He'd never had a vibrating dildo before, but he imagined it would make stretching him easier. Maybe it would relax his muscles. Heaven knew he'd need all the help he could get.

The finger slid in and out of him, and a whimper fell from Barnaby's lips. That mere digit held so much power over him - determining his breathing, his sounds, his pleasure. He didn't need to be collared or handcuffed; as long as Gil was inside of him, invading his body, Barnaby was under his control.

The finger gave one last thrust, and Barnaby froze as something thicker and smoother pressed against his rim. The vibrator.

Gil wasted no time sliding it deeper and deeper, earning a whine from the boy, a twitch.

It settled right against his prostate, and Barnaby's hips wiggled to adjust. A hand patted his ass; the weight behind him lifted.

Looking over his shoulder, he saw Gil sitting down at his desk chair, swiveling to face his laptop.

"G-Gil?"

"Hm?"

"What're you doing?"

"I forgot to mention," the man said, nonchalant, "I've got an article to review by midnight. It shouldn't take long, but that isn't a problem, is it? This is for *you*, after all."

For me?

Maybe Barnaby was the one experimenting, but he didn't expect to do it *alone*. He needed Gil's guidance. He needed to understand what the point was.

The boy opened his mouth to speak, only to lose his words to a rhythmic pulse between his legs. It was pleasant from the start, and he hummed, nuzzling into a pillow. It smelled faintly of smoke and musk.

Barnaby thought, maybe that was the point - to relax and feel good. He sighed, wistful, "Thank you."

Willing to accept that, he closed his eyes and settled in. He became aware of the bed sheet, like satin, and it felt *so nice* when he gave into the urge to roll his hips down. It felt natural. Casual. Gil typed away at his laptop and Barnaby, nude, lazily humped his bed. No big deal.

Click.

Barnaby shuddered from head to foot. "*Uhm—*" The vibrator beat faster, stronger, and it was difficult to keep still. It didn't take him long to figure out that it felt better to keep his hips lifted, tilted at a Ready For Entry angle with his toes pushing into the mattress.

His bell began to rattle.

"Is there a problem?" Gil asked, peeking over. He tossed a tiny rectangle in his hand.

Barnaby had to squint to make out what it was: a miniature remote with two big buttons. "Did you—" He gulped, lowering his butt once again. He didn't want to provoke him just yet. "You did that?

"Do what?"

He watched him do it that time. *Click. Click.*

Barnaby's eyes widened, and his thighs quivered as the toy hammered against his prostate. "Th-That!" he rasped.

Gil smirked. "Huh. Guess I must've—" And then he turned back to his computer to continue typing.

Even without being inside of him or laying a hand on him at all, Gil was still in control.

As pitiful as he might have sounded, Barnaby couldn't keep his mewling at bay. He fed his cries to the pillow, not wanting to disturb Gil's concentration, and without the man's eyes on him, pulled his knees up to put his weight on them, keeping the vibrator angled and secure.

Did it help his composure? Not a single bit. But it sure did feel good.

The sensation surged directly to Barnaby's dick, and he had to wonder if his member was vibrating, too.

He experienced an eternity in the course of several minutes. He might as well have been timing himself underwater.

Finally, he gasped for air, "How much longer?"

Gil spun his chair around a second time. "As long as it takes." He tilted his head to the side and demanded, "You're not rushing me, are you?"

With the tone of voice he was using? "N-No—" Barnaby wouldn't dream of it, "I'm just— I don't know how much longer I can last..."

"Poor thing."

There was another merciless click, and Barnaby yelped, bell clanking, hips jolting, muscles clenching around the vibrator. The sensation reached his tail bone, traveled his spine, and buzzed into his skull.

As if he wasn't dizzy enough.

Gil walked up beside him, and Barnaby didn't even have the strength to nudge his hand when it swept through his hair.

"Don't hold it, then."

A haze of lust fogged Barnaby's vision; he could hardly define Gil's silhouette on the other side. "But," he panted, "aren't you going to..." He trailed off with a brief glimmer of clarity. Reconsideration. *Aren't you going to fuck me? Sleep with me?* They sounded equally pathetic. He twisted the fabric beneath his fingertips. "I thought we were doing this together."

"Of course, we are," Gil said like it was obvious. "What would you call this?"

Click.

Barnaby squeaked as the vibrator reverted to its original setting. He would call it Giving Gil Control. Not that he minded. But even then, *he* was the one experiencing all the pleasure. The blond huffed, "Can you come from that?"

"*Boy,*" Gil scoffed, "I could come just from watching you."

Oh.

Gil's form loomed closer before covering Barnaby, and the man's weight fell behind him.

He was trapped.

Dry lips trailed his shoulder. Denim fabric grinded against his ass, coarse, the friction inviting.

Barnaby bit his lip and rubbed against the other's bulge, feeling the outline between his cheeks. How did Gil even hide that Gift of his?

An arm hooked around the blond's waist, and his moans flowed free while nimble fingers began working his dick.

"Do you want me to fuck you?" Gil whispered, guttural in his ear.

Barnaby's heart leapt. He nodded without hesitation.

But one swipe over his tip, and his body locked up.

Gil snickered, lifting his hand from Barnaby's cock to his face. A single finger was splattered with liquid pearl.

He'd leaked.

Barnaby's skin *burned* with embarrassment.

"Doesn't seem like you'll last long enough for me to be able to."

Before the boy could apologize - before he could untie his tongue and insist he'd hold the rest in - he was weightless, his world was flipped, and he was sitting in Gil's lap, back pressed against the raven's chest.

Maybe he didn't get to sit on his cock, but at least he had the vibrator giving him the illusion, pushing him even closer to the edge.

He spread his legs wide to make himself available, and the man continued jerking him off.

For as wonderful as it all felt, he only hoped Gil would feel the same.

"I'm sorry," Barnaby finally blubbered, scrambling for something to cling to.

An arm hooked under his thigh, preventing him from slipping, and the hand fondled his balls. He was sure he was shaking from restraint.

"Don't apologize," Gil cooed, "You're *so* new to this. I bet you're overwhelmed, hm?"

Overwhelmed. That was the right word.

Barnaby nodded along, his eyes falling to the fingers around his cock. Like an artist skillfully forming a vase. "It's a, uhm...*good* overwhelming, though." He sucked in a futile breath. "I wish I could do the same for you."

"You take me pretty close." The man nuzzled the side of his head, and Barnaby nuzzled back. He was sturdy. "Can you rub down a little for me? That might help."

It took a moment for his mind to catch up, but soon, Barnaby was grasping at Gil's thighs, gyrating down into his lap. Maybe it wasn't the buzz of the vibrator beneath him - maybe it was the man's cock, pulsing, longing to be inside of him.

Gil groaned in his ear, and that made it all the more believable. "*Good boy,*" he purred, pumping Barnaby faster. Faster.

Barnaby's breathing grew faster. He pressed a kiss to the man's jaw. "You— aaah...You really th-think so?"

"Absolutely."

Their eyes locked on incident, and Barnaby was transfixed, hypnotized perhaps, by hooded greys.

A sly smirk reappeared on Gil's lips. "And what a beautiful boy. Big ass like this *deserves* to be fucked every night."

Barnaby's face had to be as bright as a supernova; it was a miracle he hadn't erupted. "You should've fucked it, then," he giggled, whimpers slipping through the cracks. He grinded against Gil's bulge as intently as he could - a subtle way of reminding him what he was missing.

A squeeze around the head of his cock and a growl in Gil's throat let him know he'd succeeded.

The man thrusted abruptly, and Barnaby's eyes nearly rolled to the back of his head.

"Come prepared next time," he grunted, "It's not like I don't want to fill that tight, hungry hole of yours. Are you fucking kidding me? I haven't stopped thinking about it. And your *face*—" He teased Barnaby's tip.

The boy's hips twitched; he squeaked, gasped, moaned. *Oh. Oh. Oh!*

His mouth hung open, he felt sweat beading down his temples, and he was going cross-eyed.

Still, Gil stared him down. "Like that. Fucking gorgeous."

He wanted to tell him, *I've been thinking about you, too. I think you're hot and handsome* - but no matter how much he licked his lips, swallowed, and tried to clear his throat, his mouth remained a desertscape, inhabitable for words.

So, he pulled the man in to find salvation from his mouth, stealing the words straight from Gil's tongue while his fingers tangled in lush, raven hair.

Gil was quick to match his passion, his own apparent hunger competing with Barnaby's thirst. The boy could lap him up forever, drinking his groans. At least until he feared Gil might bite too hard, and he retreated. Then, Barnaby kissed all around his mouth, connected their lips over and over, and only stopped when his body became too tense to move.

The words finally flowed, and even Barnaby was startled by the sound of his own voice, "Fuck yeah! Oooh, don't stop. Don't stop! C'mon— *please*? Pleasepleaseplease, Gil, I'm so close! I'm— *aaah*—!"

One more loud, strangled moan, and Barnaby reached his limit.

Kisses instantly rained all across his face, and Gil controlled his hand as he made sure to get every last drop out of him, coating his palm in the process.

Barnaby took a minute longer to check the damage when he realized his dick was being slicked in his own cum. Glancing down, he noticed a faint spot on Gil's jeans. He sniveled, "Sorry."

"Nothing to be sorry for." Inching back on the bed, Gil guided Barnaby to lay down, removing the vibrator for him.

He continued trembling from the aftershock.

There was a box of tissues on the nightstand, and the man was quick to utilize them as well, wiping off his hand, the spot on his pants, and then Barnaby's cock.

Unable to focus on anything else, Barnaby studied the look of concentration on his face, almost shying away whenever the other glanced back, grinning.

"Was that good enough?" Gil asked.

Barnaby simpered at him, a lingering heat still in his face. "M-More than enough," he peeped, "but I, uhm..." It was hard to lay comfortably on his back with the bell of his collar in the way. He started fidgeting with it. "If you still wanted to meet up again, in the, uhm, future...I'd like that. A lot. But only if you want to."

Gil chuckled, "You *just* came, and you're already thinking about next time?"

Barnaby shrugged, wondering if he'd ever stop blushing. "I-Is that bad?"

Throwing the tissues into a bin, Gil climbed on top of him. Taking hold of the cowbell, a bit of wiggling was all that was necessary for him to pop it clean off. "Not for me." The bell was placed on the nightstand, and kisses were placed on Barnaby's cheek and lips, soft and slow. "Maybe you're a little needy, but I guess that's my fault, hm?"

Barnaby bit his lip and shrugged again. He couldn't say he disagreed.

It was, apparently, a good enough response that the raven settled onto him without another word, resting his head on the boy's chest.

Barnaby draped his arms around him, and for a minute, the world was still. Peaceful, even.

Gil rose and fell with his breathing, his eyes closed, and Barnaby wondered how he *wasn't* so needy.

Cautious, he nudged a knee between his legs. "Are you sure there isn't anything I can do for you?"

The raven pursed his lips, his brows furrowing as he tried to nudge the knee back down. "Don't need to," he grumbled, "you did plenty."

Barnaby blinked. "I-I did?"

"Yeah, you—" Gil pushed himself up, and the boy noticed another spot on his crotch - one much more prominent than Barnaby had made. "You helped. Don't worry."

He couldn't help but giggle. He'd done *that*.

He waited for Gil to fall into his arms again, but instead, the man got to his feet, gathering Barnaby's clothes from the floor. "I don't want to kick you out," he sighed, "but I do have a paper to finish."

"It's fine," Barnaby assured him, "I have stuff I should work on, too." He sat up, took his clothes, and dressed himself without complaint.

And it still felt casual. Comfortable.

He looked up to find the man already staring at him.

"Text me when you get back to your place," Gil said, "so I know you get there okay."

"I will." Barnaby crossed over to kiss his cheek, a small exchange for the hope of his safety. "Thank you for having me." He retreated a step, only for the man to grab his wrist.

"Before I let you go," Gil proceeded, "would you mind if I walked you outside?"

Barnaby bit the inside of his cheek, sensing a ditsy sort of grin coming on.

No. He didn't mind at all.

Seth had yet to arrive to their dorm, but with what Barnaby was seeing on his phone, he felt the need to hide under his covers, nonetheless. For the longest time, he thought dick pics were an unwanted thing. That they were sent specifically to unnerve the recipient, because really, what could anyone do with that?

But then, after texting back and forth for a while, discussing Future Plans, Gil offered to send one to Barnaby, and for some reason, Barnaby accepted.

So now he had a picture of Gil's very erect penis, and it absolutely was not the worst thing in the world.

> That hard again already?
> ♥

Doesn't take a lot when I'm thinking about you.

> Really? What are you thinking about me?

You in your collar.

Taking my cock like the good boy you are.

> My collar? Are you letting me keep it?

He'd left Gil's dorm without taking it off by accident. He'd been too busy texting to remove it.

Minutes passed without an answer, and Barnaby might've started to worry if not for the picture reminding him what Gil had to deal with. So, he breathed in, putting his phone aside, and his eyes fluttered shut while his hands slid into his briefs. He thought about Gil between his legs, teasing him with his cock. About it throbbing hot and thick inside of him, pounding into him with twice the intensity of the vibrator.

Would he get to ride in the man's lap again? Would he simply be bent over, fucked like the animal Gil imagined him to be? Or would his legs be forced over his head?

What was there that Barnaby couldn't imagine, and what kind of person was he becoming if maybe, *just maybe,* he'd be willing to let Gil do whatever he wanted?

He heard the door open.

Staying hidden beneath the covers, Barnaby rushed to take the collar off.

Someone sighed loudly, obnoxiously, and wandered to their side of the room.

It wasn't the first time Seth had walked in on him helping himself. At least, that round, he chose not to say anything.

Holding his breath, Barnaby tried to slow his racing heart.

His phone lit up beside him. Another text.

If I can keep you.

Chapter 6

The next time they met, they did not have sex. Barnaby didn't even know he'd be seeing Gil.

It hadn't been a very good day, so he wasn't particularly in the mood to begin with. Hadn't so much as texted his Friend yet. (Were they friends?)

Gil didn't need to hear about the potted plants he'd dropped in front of his entire class, because he didn't stop to think to balance them in his arms first. Or about his class watching as he scrambled to pick up the pieces, apologizing to everyone and no one, until his professor came over with a broom. He didn't need to see the way Barnaby hunched at the counter, nearly doubled over under the weight of customer complaints. He'd gotten two drinks wrong from his already lingering shame, and he'd hesitated on several orders after that.

People weren't very happy with him.

If nothing else, Barnaby didn't exactly feel attractive. His cheeks were wet, there was a lump in his throat, and his eyes were raw from rubbing.

But at just about midnight, Gil came in anyway. He wore a grin that faded the closer he approached Barnaby. "You alright?"

"Yeah, I'm—" Barnaby wiped his face and sniffled, standing up from his stool to force an awkward smile— "I'm fine. Just *midterms*, y'know?"

Gil huffed, and he might've been trying to laugh, but wasn't that more effort than Barnaby deserved?

He rushed to make up for it, "Can I get you anything?"

Gloomy eyes analyzed him a moment longer before an answer was given, "Black coffee. Thank you."

Once the money had been transferred, Gil strayed from the counter, scoping the room. Paper bats dangled from the ceiling, zombies climbed out of posters on the walls, and cartoonish, wild eyes peered through every window.

"What're your plans this weekend?"

Barnaby finished pouring his drink and left the mug at the register for Gil. He was hesitant to tell him. He didn't even want to *plan* for sex in that moment.

He sighed, turning to wipe down the coffee machine while telling him about the Halloween party he and Seth were supposed to go to instead. He ended with, "but I probably won't go. I'm not really a party person."

Gil perked up.

"That makes two of us." He leaned against the counter, sipping his coffee. "I know it's probably not *much* different, but I was going to go check out the haunted house they put up at that old factory. The school's running it, so it's probably going to suck, but I figured it's something to do." He shrugged. "Only problem is I'll probably look like a loser if I go alone."

Barnaby felt his lips curl. "I'm sure there's someone who'd love to join you, Mr. Popular."

"Except," Gil quipped, "the one person I'm actually interested in taking might already have plans."

"Oh?"

"Yeah," he mumbled over his mug, "something about a Halloween party with his roommate that he may or may not go to."

Barnaby paused. "Wait—" He glanced over to spot Gil smirking at him. "Do you mean—?"

Steel eyes swept over him. "Do I have a shot?"

Yes. As a matter of fact, he did.

Suddenly, it didn't matter what happened the next day because, that following night, Barnaby had something to look forward to other than sex.

He had a reason to wear his deer onesie with its little plush antlers on the hood. As silly as he felt wearing it, in his humble opinion, Seth's costume looked sillier when he left for the party. Though, rather than make him feel insecure and mention the shoulder pads were likely meant for a taller individual (in contrast, giving Seth the appearance that he was constantly shrugging), he simply told him to have fun.

They had already been through it: "Halloween costumes at our age are either stupid, scary, or sexy, *Barnaby*."

Well, Seth, you certainly marked all the boxes this year.

I'm here.

Hardly a moment after the message popped up on his phone, Barnaby hurried out of the dorm, down to the building entrance.

Gil had said he'd drive them to the haunted house, and sure enough, he was ready and waiting, leaning against a shiny black Range Rover with tinted windows.

"Hi."

"Hi, yourself." Gil stepped closer and beamed, "You look *really* cute. I love it."

Barnaby shrugged and folded his arms; his face felt warm despite the autumn chill. Scanning Gil's body, he raised a brow. "Where's your costume?"

Grey eyes widened, then blinked. "I'm wearing it."

Barnaby grimaced, and he reconsidered the man's camouflage-print sweat-clothes. "You're...a soldier?"

Gil's jaw dropped, and he flailed his arms. "I'm *invisible*. Like the *Invisible Man*. Get it, 'cause I'm—"

"The camo!" Barnaby gasped, remembering that the joke was very much A Thing. "Sorry, I'm— *it's clever*. I'm dumb."

"You're not dumb." Gil grabbed him by the shoulders, pulling him closer.

Before Barnaby could try to convince him of the contrary, the fabric of his onesie was tugged away from his neck -

And the vinyl collar he'd taken from Gil was revealed.

"You're wearing it," the man noted, sounding surprised.

For a second, Barnaby wished he could be invisible, too. He hid his face away in Gil's chest, mumbling, "You said I was like a pet...and I guess I have an animal costume...So..."

"So, a pet deer, hm?"

Fingers carded through his hair, and an arm draped around him. It certainly made him feel coddled like one.

"Is that what you are?"

In truth, he would've worn it without the costume. But because he had spots down his back and antlers on his hood, he nodded.

His fingers curled into Gil's sweater, a particularly soft fabric. A bit underwhelming to sell as a costume, not exactly something he'd picture for partying or Trick or Treating.

"Are these," Barnaby asked, trying to change the topic, "your pajamas?"

The hood of his onesie was promptly pulled over his eyes, but before the boy could shake free to fix it, Gil had pulled away.

"Get in the car."

Probably, the most alluring of Gil's features was his voice. It was his rich, husky way of speaking that drew Barnaby to follow his commands, and yet, somehow, he sounded so young. He sounded *relatable*. He'd trail off, pause, and for the first time, Barnaby noticed that Gil was capable of being uncertain of himself.

It stood out in the car, while Barnaby listened to him talk about the spirit of Halloween and how it seemed to be fading in recent years. He sounded average, maybe even a bit passionate. Disappointed.

And that stuck to Barnaby more than he realized, apparently. Because that was what he remembered about Gil inviting him out: that he had a life beyond being a Casanova. That he was human.

Not that Gil was inviting him to a haunted house.

Because, clearly, what Barnaby *didn't* remember, up until that point, was that he was *terrified* of haunted houses.

He'd only ever gone through one once, years prior, when Seth dragged him through (literally, dragged him by the arm while boardwalk-budget animatronics popped out at them).

The threat of tears had always managed to dissuade his mom as a kid, but Seth insisted it was time to "man up."

Man *down*, more like it.

Barnaby still carried the shame of coming out that other end *sobbing*. He had no doubt Seth was twice as embarrassed to be seen with him.

He bit his nails and fiddled incessantly with the zipper of his onesie as they joined a long line of people. At the end, the once-vacated factory was decorated for a zombie outbreak theme, bathed in flashing red and blue lights, blasting screams and EDM.

In attempt to prepare himself, Barnaby clung to Gil's arm.

He would stare at the ground the entire time they were inside, staying as close to the other as possible. If anyone came up to him, he'd shut his eyes tight! He could do that.

Couldn't he?

An elbow nudged his side, and Barnaby snapped his head upward.

Gil simpered down at him. "Scared?"

An all too wide smile split across Barnaby's face, and he quickly shook his head. "*Me*?" he wheezed. "No way! I used to do these, like, all the time. Are you?"

It would have been nice of Gil to humor him. Considerate, even. But since he was six feet tall, fit, and probably watched horror movies in his spare time, he scoffed, grumbling, "I wish."

"Excuse me?" A woman's voice cut through from behind, and Barnaby felt a tap on his shoulder.

Turning around, he came face to face with a girl, short and stout. Antennas poked out of her block bob, and she wore the fuzziest sweater Barnaby had ever seen.

"Hi!" she squealed, "Sorry to *bug* you, but would you mind taking our picture?"

Barnaby didn't mind at all. He took her phone with caution, and she spun to her partner's side, wings of wire and cloth flapping on her back.

Her companion was a lanky young man, and he wore what must have been an umbrella hat on his head, lined with LED lights. It did not make taking the photo easy.

"Ahh...Okay—"

They put their arms around each other, and Barnaby snapped two pictures. In the first, the boy was clear but everything else was covered in shadows. In the second, most of the image was visible, but the boy's face had been whited out, as if replaced by the moon.

"I'm sorry. I tried," Barnaby apologized, giving the girl her phone back, "Maybe if you turned off the lights on the...?"

"This is perfect!" To his amazement, both of their faces lit up at seeing the second picture. The girl cheered, "Thank you!" Then, she was jutting her hand toward Barnaby. "I'm Diana, by the way!"

"Barnaby," he replied, shaking her hand. Her partner introduced himself as Jason, and Gil, who Barnaby didn't realize was paying attention, gave his name, too.

"*Oooh*, a little *Hunter and Deer* action," Diana commented slyly, "I'm here for it!"

Barnaby expected Gil to correct her on his costume, but all he said was, "Respect to the moth-lamp combo." He elbowed Barnaby in the side again. "Why didn't we think of that?"

Barnaby could only stare at him, at a loss. *Because we never planned to coordinate*?

Jason chimed in, bragging about how Diana made the costumes herself. Beyond that, she had apparently made half of the costumes being used in the haunted house, as well.

The girl, frazzled by being boasted, cut him off, promising them, "It was nothing!" and, "All I did was hold a hot glue gun!" The line moved further along, and she interrupted herself, "Gil, if you could—"

Barnaby pressed closer to the raven, and Diana bounced beside Jason as two ushers in gas masks came into view. She asked, "Are you boys ready to be *shooketh*?"

"*Oh yeah*," came Gil's flippant answer.

Barnaby must've been stalling, counting the number of people ahead of them (a handful), because then the man was nudging him a third time. It surprised the honesty right out of him, "Not really? I mean, I bet it's great, but— I'm not...*good* with jump scares."

"You know, I've yet to meet someone who is," said Diana, having a sympathetic look about her. Barnaby decided she was nice the instant she added, "I know I'm not!"

"If you guys want," Jason offered, haloed in Lamp Glory, "you could stick with us?" He sucked in his breath and puffed it back out. "They've already got a target on me, I know that much. They could be less likely to bother you if I'm in front."

"What made you so lucky?" Gil asked.

Jason flashed his teeth, not quite a smile. "I'm friends with them."

Barnaby snorted, and Diana rubbed her partner's arm, looking up at him like he was (pun unintended) the light of her life. Gil stepped aside, gesturing ahead, and allowed the couple to cut in front of them.

They continued talking with the time they had - or rather, Diana refused to let the conversation die. She talked about zombie-killing video games that Jason had been teaching her to play, so if it came to it, she felt she could "take them on." According to Jason, she was, in fact, surpassing him.

Barnaby tried to contribute. Self-conscious as he was, they seemed eager to connect. He admitted that, while he never had a zombie phase, he did read *Warm Bodies* in high school. He preferred the more romantic spin on the genre, where love triumphed even in the face of death. Perhaps it was cliche and unrealistic, but he'd never turn down a happy ending.

Apparently, the movie adaptation was the first zom-flick Jason shared with Diana, thinking it had elements they both would enjoy.

Gil didn't speak up until the group found themselves at the front of the line, and everyone reached for their wallets.

"I've got it," he insisted, urging Barnaby's hand away.

"*But*— Are you sure?"

"It's...$5 each? It's fine."

A swift payment later, and they followed Diana and Jason to the entrance.

There, they were greeted by two men in army costumes, geared with modified Nerf Guns. Flashlights were shined in their eyes, and someone shouted, "*All clear!*", before herding them through the front doors.

Barnaby maintained a white-knuckle grip on Gil's arm.

He couldn't guarantee he would still have circulation in it by the time they reached the end.

Chapter 7

He'd braced for terror.

For helplessness - but entering the factory meant he'd consented to being scared.

He expected the narrow walkways, the animatronics, timed to pounce, and the actors, gored and eerie as they prowled about.

He got that.

He just hadn't expected it would be in the form of laser tag.

Jason was the leader of their "troop." He was singled out immediately by the first actor they were introduced to, "General Mell", who informed them from a rafter above the factory floor that there was a "breach in the colony." That their group was their last line of defense; that the future of the colony rested on their shoulders, and that if Jason's apparent leadership was any indication to the rest of the troop's abilities: "We gave it a good run, guys."

They were rushed to The Armory next. It was the only place Barnaby felt safe enough to detach himself from Gil. There were "bullet-proof vests" that were meant to help count their scores, and the raven helped put his on, handing him his laser gun in the process. Not that it would get much use.

Once Barnaby was latched onto Gil again, it was impossible to break free enough to aim the damned thing.

Jason reluctantly headed the charge into the Breach Zone, and Gil, thankfully, hadn't forgotten they were meant to trail behind.

Walls and curtains and bloody drapery were set up to create a maze. At first, it seemed like they were retracing their steps at every turn. Flashes of neon lights overhead made it that much more difficult to determine what were shadows and what were genuine barriers. The music wasn't any less disorienting, either. The bass was so strong it shook Barnaby to his very bones.

Giant spiders and snarling, animatronic dogs leapt out of the shadows, but they were hardly scary. Barnaby thought that, for sure, but they still made his heart race. They still had him pressing his face against Gil's shoulder each time.

He'd tried to laugh it off and apologize, but with everything else, he doubted the man heard him.

The Zombies themselves weren't all that creepy, either. But knowing their group was being stalked - bones already shaking, heart already pounding - had Barnaby's stomach churning. He probably could've handled their growls and over the top stage make-up, but when they started charging at them with lasers of their own? Barnaby wanted to turn his little deer tail and run.

However, the zombies weren't after him. They were after Jason.

Gil must've noticed it, too, since the next moment, he was dragging Barnaby down another corridor.

Out of the corner of his eye, Barnaby watched everyone disperse with Diana frantically yanking Jason along.

There were screams and cries of laughter at every turn. It sounded like fun.

Gil had a much better sense of direction than Jason. They didn't box themselves in as much, and in hindsight, Barnaby would wonder if, when they did, it'd been on purpose. Rather than retreat, Gil would wait for a zombie to round the corner, aim his laser and recoil victoriously when they sunk dramatically to their knees.

He had a number of successes, and Barnaby strained his ears to listen once he realized Gil was muttering "*Yes!*" and "Got *'em!*" under his breath.

He'd lost sense of time, but at some point, the walls began opening around them.

Moonlight flooded in through a rising truck door, and Gil rushed them out.

On the other side, more volunteers waited to collect their equipment and tally up scores. Gil wanted to wait for the rest of the group to see where he ranked, and Barnaby was more than willing to stick with him. He wanted to see Jason and Diana, to have a chance to tell them "thank you" and "goodbye."

But then his knees were weak. His stomach hadn't settled, and he felt himself paling from head to toe. As fast as they could outrun zombies, he couldn't outrun his anxiety.

Leaning against Gil, Barnaby closed his eyes and focused on filling his lungs with cold air. He pictured knotted rope in his brain and stomach, and with each breath, he tried to imagine a knot undone.

"*Barnaby—*" Gil's voice was quiet but urgent enough to make him lift his head. "Are you okay? You're shaking. A lot, dude."

He pulled back to find that his hands were, in fact, trembling tremendously. "*Sorry,* I'm—" Barnaby started, waiting for them to stop to give an excuse. They didn't, and he tucked them under his arms, hoping that what Gil didn't see, he could forget. "Sorry."

The man knitted his brows and eyed around for the rest of the group.

Jason and Diana finally ran out, still being chased by General Mell and another zombie. The collecting volunteers looked on tiredly.

"C'mon." A firm hand pressed between Barnaby's shoulders, and he realized he was being led again, to a pathway around the factory, back to the parking lot.

"But," Barnaby peeped, "what about your score?"

He watched the wheels turn in Gil's head as he spared a glance back. He ended up shrugging, though, and a kind smile almost proved warm enough to end the blond's shivering. "How do you think I did?"

Barnaby considered it. How Gil protected him. How he barely flinched and stood his ground against gun-wielding zombies, the number of times he caught his quiet cheers, each a result of victory. He hadn't seen that from anybody else.

He smiled back at him, hoping, wistful that Gil would think him just as kind. "I think you're the winner. No contest."

"Thank you."

Barnaby rolled up his window, and Gil turned off the car. It'd been a quiet ride, but at least his nausea had subsided. No more shaking.

Gil still had that pleasant expression on his face. "Did you have a good time?"

Sensing a glow wash over him, Barnaby dipped his head. "Yeah. I had a lot of fun. Sorry, if I didn't, uhm, act like it. But I enjoyed it. Thank you."

Gil's hand left the steering wheel, and Barnaby's breath stuttered as his chin was tilted up. "Well—" His voice barely above a whisper, Gil leaned in.

Barnaby studied how his lips formed each word -

"I'm glad for that. Would hate to find out I traumatized you."

"*What*?" Gil's eyes were twinkling, but no amount of charm could prevent Barnaby's habitual rambling, "*No, nothing like that. God, I know I'm like, a coward, and I'm, sorry if I did do anything to embarrass you or act ungrateful, but I swear I had a great time, and if you ever need the money back, I can totally give that to y—*"

The rest faded into Gil's mouth, a point forgotten as Barnaby's attention abruptly shifted to kissing the man. He made a grab for his sweater, something to use for purchase in an attempt to match Gil's sudden heat. It was the least he could do.

The man's lips were quick to travel to his ear. He muttered, "It's hard to think of you as a coward with that collar around your neck."

An involuntary whine slipped out, and Barnaby tucked his head under Gil's chin. With cheeks beginning to burn, he mumbled, "That's different."

"Different how?" Gil rubbed his arm, and the boy melted to the touch.

"You know..."

"Maybe not. Explain it to me."

Barnaby huffed. He would have rather done *anything* else.

"I didn't...*think* about putting the collar on," he admitted, "I knew I would see you, and...I guess I thought it made it personal? Like, I thought if I wore it, it would make you happy, and well, I wasn't scared by that. I'm scared *now* because that's probably a weird thing to say."

It was silent as he tried to think of more to include. Gil was motionless.

To quell his curiosity and ever-present anxiety, Barnaby forced himself to look up.

The man had raised a brow at him. "You think it's weird that you want me to be happy?"

Barnaby shrugged. "Is it?" He shrunk away into his seat, fidgeting with the cuffs of his sleeves that seemed to be a little too long. "I don't even know if we're friends. You're nice, and I'd like to be, but with where this is going, if we're still having sex..." He could feel his brain starting to fizzle and decided not to push it. He sighed, "I don't know. I don't know how these things are supposed to work - if you're comfortable with me being around you, or if you only want me around for sex, which...I guess I don't mind..."

He flinched at the sound of keys spilling into a cup holder. Relaxed at the sight of Gil slumping in his seat.

"Where do *you* want this to go?"

Barnaby blinked, straightening his posture somewhat. "L-Like I said—" He cracked his knuckles— "I want to be your friend, and I don't mind if we keep having sex, but if I had to pick, I think I would rather hang out with you than sleep with you. No offense. It's just...I don't really have any friends."

Gil chuckled, "It's fine. I don't either, honestly." Meeting Barnaby's gaze, he offered up an open palm.

Barnaby slid his hand into it.

Weaving their fingers together, Gil spoke, "We can do both. Friends with benefits? I'm cool with that. But I do have one condition."

Barnaby squeezed his hand. "Go on."

The raven bit his lips, his eyes like storm clouds drifting briefly before striking him with lightning. "It doesn't go further than that. I'm not interested in a relationship."

Well, that wasn't a problem for Barnaby. He didn't even know how to be in a relationship. "Sure," he agreed, "I'm not either."

A sweet smile returned to Gil's face. "But I am very interested in having a new pet." He released the boy's hand in favor of scratching under his chin, behind his ear.

Barnaby was all too inclined to lean into his touch.

A pet.

They had the easiest lives, didn't they? Getting to laze about while their masters ensured they were happy, safe, and fed. Little was expected of them beside companionship.

And Barnaby was more than happy to provide that.

"Sh-Should I call you Master?" he asked, kissing Gil's palm.

Once more, the man was closing in, practically climbing out of his seat to tickle Barnaby's jaw and neck with his lips. "You absolutely should, little fawn."

Barnaby giggled, biting back a moan when those wonderful lips grazed a tender spot right above his collar. "Master..." he cooed, testing the word out. It came so easily.

In an instant, Gil was flicking his tongue out, a hand gliding down Barnaby's body to rub his inner thigh.

The boy gasped, clinging to his shoulders.

"Say it again, fawn."

"*Master.*" He was still a coward, afraid of haunted houses and disappointing a man he'd known for less than a week—

But those teeth had sunken into him before. He welcomed the hand that crept toward his crotch.

He wasn't afraid to make Gil happy. Especially since doing so made him happy, too.

"Stay," the man ordered, hot and honeyed, "another hour. That's all."

He was officially his master. Who was Barnaby to deny him?

"I-In your car?" he squeaked.

"Would you rather take it outside?"

Barnaby pouted. "I'd rather not get caught."

"That's what the tinted windows are for." Gil broke away, snatching his keys from the cupholder. "I can drive us to the back of the parking lot. Unless you want to wait and go all the way to my dorm."

Barnaby debated it. On one hand, he'd daydreamed about Gil's bed, being cradled by the mattress, snuggled up in his blankets. On the other, he'd have to *wait*. And if he waited, that gave him more time to be a coward.

Barnaby didn't *want* to be a coward.

"If we get in trouble," he puffed, fidgeting with his seat belt, "I'm blaming you."

"That's fair," Gil snickered, messing up the blond's hair, "Now, get your sexy ass back there, Bambi."

Barnaby gawked. "You— *Oh my God.*"

A bold smirk decorated Gil's face as the car's engine purred. "What?"

"You can't use *Sexy* and *Bambi* in the same sentence like that!"

"My mistake—" The man rolled his eyes. "Get your sexy ass back there, *Barnaby*."

He hoped Gil didn't flatter himself too much - he didn't climb to the backseat because he was ordered to.

He did it to hide his blush before the other could take pride in it.

While Gil brought them to the last row of the lot, Barnaby wrestled to get out of his onesie. He'd managed to get it tangled around his ankles, laying on his back, when he caught a glimpse of the other reaching into the glove compartment.

Seconds later, Gil was opening the door where Barnaby propped his feet. Placing a wrapped condom and small bottle aside, he helped him down to his briefs.

An Autumn breeze rushed into the car, and Barnaby whined, shivering, "Close the door, it's cold." He yelped when the response was a heap of camo to the face. A topless Gil climbed in between his legs, shutting the door behind him, while Barnaby hurried to put the sweater on.

"You weren't wearing anything else underneath that?"

"*Well—*" Comfortable from the waist up, the boy tried to angle his legs to give Gil optimal space and to hopefully avoid kicking him. "No?"

Gil scoffed, tucking his hair behind his ear, and lowered himself onto his pet.

Barnaby craned his head for him, and he continued decorating the boy's neck in kisses.

It didn't take long for the raven to put all his attention on one area, right near his shoulder, where he tugged the sweater a bit to the side. He kissed and grazed his teeth, and when his tongue finally dragged over it, heat pooled in Barnaby's core.

"*Yes*—" He wove his fingers in Gil's hair, hoping to keep him there. Not that it was necessary, though.

The man licked the same spot, over and over, and then, without warning, clamped his teeth down. He nibbled carefully, at first, and Barnaby struggled not to squirm. Little by little, he became more deliberate. More intense.

Soon, Barnaby was hissing, scratching at Gil's scalp and pulling his hair. "*Ow*. Oww!"

Gil stopped in an instant, soothing the bruised skin with his tongue instead, giving the boy a chance to recover.

Barnaby's grip loosened until he was combing through raven locks, sighing, content.

Switching to the other side of his neck, Gil tried again. Less harsh, more frequent bites.

It was the perfect amount to keep the boy feeling claimed.

It nearly distracted him from Gil's touch, too, returning to his thigh, featherlike against his bare skin.

Every last hair stood on end, and Barnaby became stiff between his legs. He waited for contact, for relief.

He was touched everywhere but where he needed Gil most - his hips, the fold where his inner thigh met his groin, his briefs, played with, the hem traced across his waist.

Gil even outlined the tent in the fabric without any other sign of acknowledgement.

Barnaby could only take so much teasing.

The next pass Gil made over his bulge, he lifted his hips, ensuring it would be cradled in the other's palm. "*Please.*"

"Someone's getting needy," came the gravelly response, not without a delicate squeeze to Barnaby's package.

There was a haze on the horizon of his mind. He mewled, weakly rocking his hips for more, "Aren't you?"

The raven lifted his head, and the two shared a smile.

In minutes, they were both nude from the waist down. Barnaby refused to give up Gil's sweater, wondering how the other wasn't freezing.

Legs spread wide, he assumed Gil's next move would be to reach for the lube.

He blinked when three fingers pressed light against his lower lip instead.

"Open."

Hesitant, Barnaby gradually accepted them, one at a time. He greeted them with his tongue, wetting them thoroughly with Gil's eyes locked on him, adding fuel to the fire under his skin.

There were murmurs of "*Good boy*" and "*Fuck yeah, that's it*" as those fingers pressed deeper.

His eyes half-lidded and his lips curled into a smile around them, Barnaby began to suckle, swallowing them further and further.

He was almost disappointed when Gil retracted them, without leaving a trace he'd ever given his pet anything to suck on.

Thankfully, that disappointment quickly aided to bliss as those same fingers, one by one, filled up Barnaby's other hole. He groaned and whimpered until the raven stole his sounds with a fervent kiss. It was enough to distract him from the discomfort, although, nothing could make him oblivious to the motion of Gil fumbling with the condom.

Minutes passed, and the discomfort faded altogether. His fingers slid in and out with ease, only to come to a stop, sliding out for good.

Evidently, Gil needed both hands to hold onto Barnaby's legs, positioning them as needed while pushing something much thicker into him.

"Slowly," Barnaby begged.

"I know." Gil's jaw was clenched so tight, the boy could make out the veins in his neck. He was patient.

He leaned down, and their lips connected again, each kiss equally as patient. They nuzzled their faces together, and Barnaby tried his best to mark his master's neck in return.

Before he knew it, Gil's hips were flush against his own. He was all the way in, and as they paused, Barnaby succumbed to the gratifying sensation of being stuffed.

"I'm okay," he whispered, "you can move."

And Gil did, dutifully.

Everything seemed so in sync. From the way they looked into each other's eyes, to the simultaneous rise and fall of their chests, to Barnaby's hips lifting to meet each thrust. They moved as one. Even when Gil picked up the pace, Barnaby did everything he could to match, eager to play an active part.

At least until he was left panting, and nearly all of his energy was spent while Gil moved like a well-oiled machine.

"Still doing alright?" the man asked, smoothing his pet's hair back.

Barnaby wheezed, breathless but with a smile on his face, "Yes. Thank you. Keep going, please."

Gil's own grin widened. "That's my plan." As if to prove a point, he gave a particularly direct thrust that had the boy seeing stars and crying out.

Another passionate kiss pursued, one where Gil still had to put a hand to Barnaby's cheek to guide the mess that was his tongue and lips. There was biting and sucking until Barnaby's mouth felt swollen. There was pride in his chest when he raked his nails over the man's inked shoulders, beckoning a vocal groan.

The more he did it, the rougher Gil pounded into him. His head was spinning from it all—

And then it was colliding with the door behind him. "*Ow!*"

"*Shit*," Gil grumbled, failing to hide his laughter, "sorry."

Barnaby huffed. Luckily, the pleasure was quick to replace the pain. "Be careful..."

"I'm trying, baby, I promise. You just feel so fucking *good*."

Judging by the increasingly reckless motion of Gil's body, Barnaby had to wonder if that first part was true. Although, that wasn't the only thing that he observed. "Gil, the car—"

It was moving along with them, rocking with the man's thrusts.

He paused briefly, looking a bit like a kid caught with his hand in the cookie jar, before shrugging and decidedly picking up where he left off: breaking in his new pet. "So?"

"*Gil!*"

There was laughter. Not Gil's. Not Barnaby's. A group of voices, laughing. Hollering. Unmistakable on the other side of the door.

Barnaby's blood turned to ice with the realization. *Someone* was outside. His body began to go numb.

Again, Gil stopped, his eyes like daggers as he glared out the window. Barnaby tried to pull him down, but the man wouldn't budge. Instead, his expression turned smug, and he was calm when he spoke, "They can't see us, remember?"

"But—"

A faint, lingering kiss took away Barnaby's opportunity to finish, along with some of his worry, but even that wasn't enough to keep him from trembling.

Gil's arms wrapped protectively around him, and he rolled his hips once again, grumbling into the boy's ear, "They want a show? Let's give them a show. Let them hear what they're missing out on."

With how Gil continued, with how he held Barnaby, aiming deep inside of him with every thrust, it was impossible to stay quiet.

There might have been cheers and knocking against the car, but it was hard to tell over Gil growling in his ear, "*You're such a good little fawn. You're so tight. If only they could see how pretty you are.*"

It was even harder to tell over his own wailing.

It was all so *much*.

He couldn't tell if their sounds were drowning out the intruders, or if their audience had left to find another show, but there came a point that it didn't matter. Nothing mattered when he was given such praise, fucked as if it was Gil's own life that depended on it.

Eventually, the man wrapped a hand around Barnaby's dick, and it became *too much*.

He moaned and babbled, fighting to say "Gil" and "Master" while his hips jolted erratically.

It took little effort for the man to milk him through, and Barnaby thanked him over and over again, even when he had nothing left.

Even when Gil was the one reaching his limit inside of him.

Everything after moved by in a blur.

He must've cried tears at some point because, there Gil was, wiping his cheeks and kissing his eyes. Somehow, Barnaby ended up back in his onesie with his collar removed. He was sweaty and sticky, but it was soft and cozy to cuddle up to the man in the backseat.

The window was cracked down, allowing Gil to blow out smoke from a cigarette, and the world outside was quiet. Did they ever have an audience, or had it been the sound of chirping crickets all along? Perhaps it'd been the voices in his own head.

Still without his camouflage sweater, Gil sat with his chest exposed - a canvas that Barnaby's fingers inevitably occupied, painting invisible designs.

He wondered if he'd ever tattoo the rest of his torso.

"You're sure you're okay with this?"

Barnaby perked up. "Hm?"

"Meeting up like this—" Gil gave a few more puffs and flicked his cigarette out the window. "Obviously, you could always call it off, but—"

"Yes," Barnaby interjected, causing grey eyes to collide with hazels, "Yes, I, I'm okay with this. I want this."

Gil studied the blond for a moment, then ruffled his hair. "I guess that's what happens when you repress everything for so long, huh? Makes you wanna dive right in."

Barnaby hummed, burying his face into Gil's chest. "Guess so."

The raven had a steady heartbeat. His skin was cool, perfect for preventing the boy's mind from overheating.

He wondered if it was normal - if it was easy for Normal People to bond so seamlessly through sex. He could understand how it would be, since, as he discovered, it was such a nice thing to be touched. He realized he'd never be able to achieve the same effect on his own.

With someone else, chasing that high had become *fun*.

Barnaby thought about how much fun he had with Gil. How kind he was. How gentle.

Slender fingers continued to stroke through his hair, calming his nerves with each sweep.

He memorized his pattern and tingled with satisfaction each time Gil's nails grazed his neck.

His eyelids felt heavier, his breathing was slow.

Gil spoke, as soft as the night wind, "Tired?"

"Mmhm."

"C'mon, then. Let's get you home."

Barnaby thought he could earn a little bit of time by choosing not to move, but as it turned out, Gil didn't need him to.

He simply wriggled out from under him to climb to the front, grabbing his sweater on his way into the driver's seat. He drove them back to the entrance, and Barnaby mentally prepared himself for the trek he would have to make to his dorm.

"Good night," they told each other, and a final kiss was shared between them.

Barnaby dragged his feet out of the car, into the building, stumbling, likely matching the steps of his drunken peers. He wanted nothing more than to flop on his bed.

But then, right at his door, his heart jumped, and he became a bit more alert. He felt ashamed for forgetting.

He'd left his collar in the car.

Chapter 8

"—so, *heh*, there may or may not be a video of me going around where I'm moaning in the back of a car, but the thing is, I don't know if I care? Because how would anyone know it was me? I don't even think I sound like myself when I'm *In The Moment*."

At least, that was what he kept telling himself.

So far, Barnaby had spent the morning rambling to Seth about the night before. He'd woken up grinning, a rarity in itself, thinking, *that actually happened*. Perhaps he was oversharing, but he had no shame.

He bragged about laser tag, how he made it through; sure, he didn't see half of what was going on, but wasn't Not Crying an improvement?

He painted Gil a hero, the victor that could outsmart zombies *and* calm his nerves.

"He's so down to Earth," Barnaby added, "and so sweet with me. Like, I'm still wondering, *is this actually a dream? Am I hallucinating?*"

Seth had been scrolling through his phone, humming when appropriate. It was only at the mention of hallucinating that he interjected, "No, it's real. Or else I wouldn't have to listen to this."

Barnaby rolled his eyes. *Always supportive, Seth.*

At last, the roommate put his phone aside, took his glasses off, and rubbed his face. He asked, monotone, "Does this mean you'll be over his place more?"

"I think so?" Barnaby hesitated, "We haven't really talked about it in depth yet."

He watched as the other struggled to sit up. The blankets shifted, and a split-second too late, he realized Seth was naked.

He turned away but couldn't resist sparing a glance when the rest of Seth's appearance registered a split-second later. He had to make sure his mind wasn't playing tricks.

It wasn't.

Marks he'd never seen before covered his roommate's neck and chest. They were more than the small, purple spots Gil left on Barnaby. They were *ugly*. Long, red lines, disconcerting impressions on either side of his throat.

He limped his way to a pile of clothes. "You're not thinking that someone's gonna notice? On the chance it gets out, and you're the bastard in and out of his dorm all of a sudden?"

Barnaby scrunched up his nose and pulled his knees closer to his chest. He hadn't thought of that. He didn't want to. And what good would it do? What were the chances?

Seth had said it himself: Gil got around. By the time anyone noticed Barnaby's presence (and really, how often did *anyone* notice his presence?), there could be any number of potential partners the voice might have belonged to.

He shrugged and answered simply, "No."

Seth scoffed. He finished dressing but stayed pressed to the wall, as if using it as a crutch.

"Seriously, are you okay?"

"Fucking great," he spat, grinning sarcastically. He sucked in his breath, hobbled back to bed, and flopped onto his stomach.

A frown became deep set on Barnaby's lips. "Maybe you should go to the nurse."

"I'm *fine*, Barnaby." Seth went right back to his phone, tapping aggressively. "Just *enjoying the afterglow*."

Barnaby paled. He could forgive his criticism; he could forgive his tone. He'd grown up with it. He'd gotten used to it.

He couldn't forgive anyone who hurt Seth.

"Who was it?" he demanded, scurrying to his roommate's side. He placed a hand on his shoulder, despite his better judgement. "We can report them."

Seth immediately brushed the hand away. "Alright, chill the fuck out. It wasn't anything I didn't ask for, just—" He sank further into the bed, further away from Barnaby. "Not what I expected. Don't know what the big deal's supposed to be."

Why would you ask for that?

But Barnaby couldn't even ask Seth. He could only stand there, doing what he did best: being too scared to confront anyone. Being useless.

Probably there wasn't a big deal. If anything, the biggest change Barnaby got out of being with Gil was gaining a friend, and if that was something Seth missed out on, he would gladly be twice the friend moving forward. He didn't intend to back away.

Except there wasn't anything friendly about the way Seth's gaze flickered back and forth between Barnaby and his phone, each glance more annoyed than the last. It wasn't long before he snapped, "Do you mind?"

Only then did Barnaby feel obligated to retreat a step, not letting himself be hurt. It wasn't about him. "Sorry," he said softly, "You know I worry."

"Yeah, well, *don't*," Seth grumbled, "It's over. It's done with. I'm fine. Go see your new boyfriend or something."

Barnaby bristled, quick to correct him, "He's not my boyfriend."

"*Right*," said Seth, "You're his prostitute. Whatever."

It was so sudden. So...*absurd*. Barnaby had to laugh. "Okay, that's— I'm allowed to sleep with someone, Seth. If I was...*that*, you would be, too."

"*No,* actually—" There was an audible *thump* as the boy slammed his phone back into his mattress. He whirled around to face Barnaby, glaring him down— "because *I* didn't get any money out of it. Can you say the same?"

The blond shrunk in front of him, not fully understanding what he was hearing. "But that's," he blubbered, "that's not fair. If I'd waited, it'd be the opposite."

"You really think I'd ask for your money?" The sincerity in his voice weighed like a stone. Or maybe Barnaby's heart was plummeting off its cliff, and Seth's words were jagged rocks at the bottom. "You actually believed I thought you had *anything* to give me?"

A lump was forming in Barnaby's throat. He couldn't speak if he wanted to.

Seth brushed right past him, making a grab for his backpack. "Does he know?"

It was too much for the blond to process at once. He looked to Seth for clarification.

"That you slept with him for money?"

He fought to swallow the lump in his throat. He really did.

He nearly choked on it, shaking his head.

"Of course not."

With that, Seth exited the dorm, and Barnaby was left alone.

He waited a little while before gathering the courage to text Gil, hands shaking.

> Can I com ovr?

> Not to b clingy

> but I could use compny, but if nto that's fine just hope ur ok

He received a reply in minutes:

Sure.

Not the most heartfelt response, but what more did he expect?

He put on a turtleneck to ensure his hickeys wouldn't show and headed for Gil's dorm, Talbot 239.

Walking up to the room, he noticed the door already cracked open. He knocked, peeked inside, and found Gil in his desk chair, swiveling around to face him.

"Long time, no see," he chimed, discarding the headphones he'd been wearing. "You barely gave me time to miss you."

Barnaby stepped inside, forcing a twitchy grin. "Sorry, I—" He closed the door and slumped against it. "My roommate and I kind of had an argument—" *Argument* seemed like a safe way to word it— "and I didn't want to be alone so—" He gave a weak show of Jazz Hands— "*here I am.*"

The hopeful gleam in Gil's eyes darkened, overshadowed by pity.

Barnaby would have been better off keeping his mouth shut, he *knew* that. Why did he even try?

But Gil didn't know better. He didn't know enough. He asked, kind but clueless, "Do you need to talk about it?"

"I'd rather not—" Barnaby shook his head, fisting the fabric of his turtleneck. "I, I could use a distraction, I think. And I don't mean like, *you* need to distract me. You can

94

literally ignore me. I think...as long as I have something to take my mind away, I should be okay?"

Gil sighed, holding his gaze, "You came all this way. You're not staying just so I can ignore you."

Barnaby would've taken that as not being able to stay at all if not for the man patting his leg, beckoning him over.

He stepped forward, stopping in front of him.

The man wasted no time grabbing him by the hips, pulling him into his lap. Or, he tried.

Aware of his weight, Barnaby held himself up with an inch between them.

Gil, evidently, was aware of it, too. "*Relax,* will you?"

"I...don't really know if I'm capable of that, actually."

"*Sit.*"

"Gil—"

Another tug, and Barnaby involuntarily made contact.

He winced, but by some miracle, the chair didn't tip or break. Still unsure, he asked, "You're sure I'm not too heavy?"

"You're *fine.*" At least Gil seemed eager to stroke his thighs.

As hard as it was for Barnaby to relax, it was twice as difficult to resist the man's touch. He pressed close to his chest while graceful hands continued up his sides. He sucked in his stomach when they passed over his curves.

"But even if you were," Gil went on, "I wouldn't consider that a bad thing."

Barnaby scoffed, "You wouldn't consider losing circulation in your legs a bad thing?"

"Kid, you could sit on my face and suffocate me, and I would die happily."

The boy puffed his cheeks, preparing himself for a rush of warmth as he cupped Gil's face in his hands.

His irises were tinted blue from the lighting of a nearby window. It broke up the pity from earlier, revealing what might've been a hint of infatuation.

He smiled up at him, and Barnaby found it impossible not to return the favor. "No," he huffed, "I'm not going to suffocate you."

Gil kissed his teeth. "That's a shame."

The boy rolled his eyes, and in doing so, caught a flash of motion.

Gil had left his phone on the desk behind him, still playing whatever video he'd been watching.

There was a woman on the screen. One proudly brandishing a dildo.

Barnaby reached out to pause it, and the title showed up on its own: How to Deepthroat.

If he wasn't blushing before, that certainly was about to change.

"Were you...trying to learn?"

"Hm?" Looking over his shoulder, Gil noticed the screen and promptly flipped the phone over. "*No.* That— Ignore that."

Why ignore it?

What better distraction was there?

Barnaby leaned back, locking eyes with Gil once again. "Did you...want to give me one? A blowjob?" Asking made his dick curious, too. He could only imagine how it would feel. How it'd *look*.

But the man's brows furrowed, his lips parting wordlessly. In that moment, he looked apologetic. He said, "I mean...*yeah*. I do. But I was kinda hoping to get one from you—" He cringed and covered his face with a hand. "God, I'm sorry. I didn't know you were gonna be upset. We don't have to do anything like that."

"Gil," Barnaby cooed, trying to urge the hand away. He wasn't being shy in front of *him*, was he? "It's fine. I'd, I'd be happy to do it." To prove it, he rocked his hips downward, whispering, "Please? Can I try, Master?"

"*Fuck*," the man groaned, tilting his head back. Barnaby could already feel his body going slack beneath him. "Are you sure?"

"*Mhmm*." That chiseled jaw was practically calling to him, and Barnaby was all too inclined to worship it with his lips. "I'm all yours, sir."

For a moment, all Gil did was massage his hip, his bulge growing more prominent between the boy's legs. Finally, he muttered, "Alright. On your knees, fawn."

Barnaby was all too giddy to slide onto the floor. "Even without the costume?"

"It's fitting." One hand combed through his hair, and the other, Gil used to unzip his jeans.

In seconds, a semi-stiff cock was aimed inches from Barnaby's face. His mouth all but flooded with saliva at the sight.

"No rush," his master insisted, "Do whatever feels right. Just don't use your teeth."

"I won't," Barnaby giggled, wrapping his fingers around the base of the cock, "I can't imagine that would feel very good." A few pumps was all it took to get the raven's eyes fluttering.

Letting his own eyes close, Barnaby took his time placing delicate kisses along the shaft. It brushed against his cheek, and he nuzzled it adoringly, breathing Gil's musk in deep. As if triggered, his tongue flicked out on its own, licking the admirable cock like an ice-pop.

Gil continued to pet him, vocalizing his approval in quiet moans. It became Barnaby's job to wet the member from base to tip, sprinkling kisses here and there. Even if he couldn't fit it all down his throat, he wanted to be positive every inch received due attention. The man had used every inch to please him, after all.

"*Fawn*—" It sounded firm. Commanding.

Barnaby blinked up at him, discovering Gil had already been smirking down at him.

He thumbed over his cheek. "Look at your master when you're blowing him."

The blond gulped, feeling very small there on his knees. "Won't that be weird?"

"What's weird about it?"

"For you, uhm—" While his mouth fumbled with what he wanted to say, he let his hand continue stroking the cock. "Don't I look weird? If I'm looking up at you, that might be...I don't know, *awkward*."

"Barnaby—" Gil's hand wrapped around his own, guiding him up and down his length. "You're stunning. I mean it. I want you to look at me."

Stunning?

Barnaby certainly didn't agree with that.

But it didn't matter, did it? It wasn't his place to agree or disagree. He was a pet. A fawn, apparently.

It was only his place to obey.

With eyes open, he breathed in and sheathed the head of Gil's cock with his mouth.

"That's it," the raven murmured, melting into his chair. His greys glazed over.

Barnaby was lucky to be a witness.

His lips slid further down the shaft. His stage fright was pushed to the back of his mind, and at the forefront, he concentrated on opening his throat up. He wanted to fit the entire length into his mouth.

He hardly got halfway when his breath began to quicken. A test, a little bit more, and he nearly gagged.

"That's okay," Gil told him, rushed. He gave his shoulder an encouraging squeeze. "That's enough. Keep going."

Knitting his brows together, Barnaby breathed through his nose and slowly bobbed his head. He gave his all to the half he could take, keeping his lips full, his teeth undetectable, and his tongue slick, gradually making the task more and more seamless. He didn't realize he was actively sucking him until the raven chewed his lip, uttered a few helpless swears, and hooked his hand in the boy's hair.

Correction: *Gil* was stunning.

His cock felt like it was weighing heavier with each pump, its veins becoming increasingly prominent whenever Barnaby traced them with his tongue. Suddenly, it was a struggle just to worship half as it pulsed against the back of his throat.

Breathe, he reminded himself until it became natural. Until everything fell into a rhythm.

He bobbed his head faster, saliva dripping down his chin. His lips swelled from sucking, and when Gil flashed his teeth, he wished they were devouring him.

His pants were growing tighter. He needed relief, too.

Fixing his hands below him, Barnaby unbuttoned his khakis, taking hold of his own cock.

He'd barely given it a single stroke when Gil narrowed his eyes, growling, "*Stop.*"

Barnaby froze.

"What're you doing?"

Confused and afraid he'd done something wrong, the boy slid off, his mouth hanging agape. "I'm sorry? A-Am I doing it wrong?"

"*That's* wrong—" Gil's finger pointed directly to Barnaby's crotch. There, his hand had also frozen around his shaft. "Don't you trust me to take care of you?"

Barnaby hadn't thought of it that way.

He scrambled to fix his pants, tucking himself in. If not for Gil grabbing him by the chin, demanding his attention, he might have even retreated.

"If this is the game we're playing," the man explained, "I have a few rules. Rule number one: *I'm* the only person allowed to get you off. No one else, including you. Sound fair?"

Barnaby wasn't sure if "fair" was the word he would use, but it certainly didn't sound negotiable. It sounded possessive, and he'd never experienced that before. Never suspected he'd be worth the trouble.

But what was a pet if not a man's possession? What was a fawn if not curious?

He decided to go along. To submit. "Yes, Master."

Gil's smirk returned full force, making Barnaby question if it ever faltered to begin with.

"That's what I like to hear." The man patted his cheek, urging him closer to his cock.

Not that he needed to. Barnaby was glad to take him in again, sucking and bobbing his head with twice the fervor.

All the same, Gil's hand rested on the back of his neck, guiding him through the motion and preventing him from pulling too far away. And that was fine - because all Barnaby wanted to do was get him off.

He couldn't look away. Even when he was sure he looked ridiculous, Gil hypnotized him by licking his lips, slicking them for his grunts and moans to stream out of.

His hips started jerking, and the hand on Barnaby's neck turned stiff.

By the time he registered it, it was too late. He was stuck.

He gulped for air—

He was treated to a thick stream of cum instead.

He swallowed without thinking, but the moment he was released, sat back, coughing. His jaw ached a little.

"Sorry," Gil panted, "I should've warned you."

Barnaby wiped his mouth, offering a smile of assurance. A warning might've been nice, but he wasn't going to be offended that Gil was so caught up in the moment that he'd forgotten to speak. Knowing that he'd caused that made him feel kind of proud, actually. "I hope it was okay," he said, getting to his feet.

"*Okay*?" Gil chuckled, "That was better than I expected. Was that your first blowjob?"

Barnaby was blushing all over again, too comfortable to shy away, though. "Yes, sir."

The man beamed. "I'm surprised you swallowed. But I think that warrants a reward. Don't you?"

"A reward?"

Fixing his own jeans around his waist, Gil stood up and led Barnaby to the bed, telling him to lay down.

The boy complied, at home above the blankets - in heaven when the raven settled between his thighs, pulling his shoes off, his pants and briefs down.

Gil settled onto his stomach, and Barnaby's legs hooked over his shoulders, giving him plenty of space to work with.

He tried to keep eye contact, assuming that was what the man still wanted—

But all it took was one blink, and the next thing Barnaby saw was Gil's mouth covering his cock entirely.

"*Mm!*"

Piercing him with an intense, predatory stare, Gil mimicked the treatment Barnaby had given him, seemingly with much less effort. He added a hand, so even when he pulled back, focusing on the boy's tip, there was something to occupy his length.

Barnaby didn't have a prayer. Nothing could stop him from squirming or keep him quiet. Not when he felt Gil's tongue *everywhere* on his cock, swirling, dragging, and tracing over invisible patterns. Slim fingers twisted and prodded, creating a sultry massage that drove Barnaby's hands to Gil's hair, holding on for dear life.

The boy barely had the sense to register the words he was rambling - something along the lines of "*Please don't stop*" and "*Thank you*" and "*Oh my god, your mouth*", he imagined.

Whatever the exact phrases, it wasn't long before they devolved into one word: "*Master.*" He repeated it over and over again. Moaned it. Begged it. *Cried it* while his hips thrashed against Gil's face.

In that moment, he understood his urgency. He understood the inability to give a warning.

Strong hands held his waist down, bruises in the making, as Barnaby arched his back, giving out one, final cry.

Gil didn't need to retreat the first chance he got. He swallowed and kept himself in place, swirling his tongue around and around Barnaby's tip to lick up every last drop.

The longer he persisted, the more the boy's core ached - the more shockwaves surged through his dick.

There came a point that Barnaby had to push away at Gil's face, legs flailing to pry him off. "Please. *Stop,*" he whined, "it's too much."

Gil popped off before he could be kicked off, snickering to himself. "Sorry," he purred, still licking residue from his lips, "wanted to make sure I got it all."

Barnaby didn't have it in him to be mad or bratty. Not when he was still racked with chills coursing through his spine. Not when he was still seeing stars.

Gil was collapsing beside him, pulling him to his chest, and in that moment, all Barnaby wanted to do was snuggle close.

"How're you feeling?" the raven asked.

Barnaby hummed, "Amazing. Each time feels better than the last."

A chuckle rumbled low in Gil's throat. "I meant compared to your mood from earlier, but that's good to know."

"*Oh—*" It was considerate of him to ask, but it reminded Barnaby of what brought him there in the first place: to be distracted from his encounter with Seth. "Yeah."

He started biting at his nails, and maybe that gave him away, because then, Gil was asking, "Shit, did I ruin it?"

"No!" Barnaby abandoned his nails to assure him, "No, you're wonderful. It's just..." He drummed his fingers on the man's chest, trying to decide what the questions he wanted answers to were. He went with the first that came to mind— "You've had rough sex, right?"

Suspicion skewed Gil's expression, and he said, "Depends on what you're talking about."

"Like— where you were scratched or choked?"

He scoffed, "Normally, I do the choking, but...why are you asking?"

Barnaby's blush turned white. He already knew how powerful his hands were on his hips and the back of his neck. What could happen if he squeezed around his throat? "Does it...feel good?"

Gil hesitated, grimacing as he answered, "For some people it does, for others it doesn't. Again, that depends on tolerance and what you consider to be *rough*. Giving you commands? You calling me Master or wearing a collar? Some people consider that rough." Brushing Barnaby's hair away from his face, he locked eyes with him. "What are you asking? That you want me to try to be rougher?"

I'm asking so I can understand what my friend was thinking, maybe.

But if he said that, the conversation would be about Seth, most likely. And that didn't seem right. Not while he was in Gil's bed, in his arms.

He'd seen enough of how *thrilled* his roommate was that morning to know he probably wouldn't enjoy it for himself anyway.

"Not really," he sighed, sinking deeper into the space between Gil's arm and his side. "I like what we have now, uhm...I like being your pet."

The man continued to stare, but fortunately, it wasn't long before a warm smile graced his lips once again. "Y'know, if you're open to it, there is more to petplay I'd like to try with you. Nothing too rough, of course."

Barnaby clung to his words. Another distraction. "What would that be?"

Kissing his forehead, Gil got out of bed, retrieved his laptop from his desk, and came back.

The blond propped himself up, watching as he opened the browser and typed into the search bar: *PetSuperStore.com*. The corners of his mouth turned up. "Wait, are you serious?"

Gil scoffed. "*What*? Is it too weird?" He clicked on a page that showed rows of dog beds that, admittedly, did look comfy. "You don't want to have your very own spot in the corner? A little deer nest? Maybe your own little food bowl?"

Barnaby giggled, his cheeks going red. Maybe it was a bit weird, but it seemed harmless enough. "What's next?" he teased, "A fursuit?"

The man elbowed him. "*No*. I'm not into animals." He looked down at his pet, smirk broadening, "I'm into the idea of treating *you* like an animal."

Well—

Barnaby didn't exactly have a very good comeback for that.

Besides, he'd already decided he wasn't against the idea.

Without any further qualms, he joined Gil in perusing the website. They found a large, fleece pet bed and plenty of bowls (it'd have to be a plain one, they decided; unfortunately, there weren't any designed ones related to deer).

They browsed through collars, and Gil asked what his favorite color was.

"Yellow."

They searched for yellow collars with surprisingly no results.

There was, however, something else that caught his eye: a collar made of brown leather.

It seemed befitting of a deer.

And it was something he could see himself in.

He pointed it out to Gil on the screen. "What about that one?"

His master approved.

They'd go to the physical store later in the week to buy everything - or, *Gil* would buy everything. He insisted.

In the meantime, the laptop was set on the nightstand, and the raven sat up. "Well, if you're willing to commit to the part," he said, leering, "I think it's time to learn some tricks."

Barnaby snorted, raising a brow. *"Tricks?"*

"Sure. Every good pet knows at least one—" Gil tousled his hair— "and I might even have an incentive for you." He left the bed to walk to the kitchen area, reaching into one of the cabinets. He returned a moment later with a sleeve of chocolate chip cookies, showing them off— "Treats."

Seeing them reminded Barnaby that he hadn't eaten yet (if he wasn't counting the mouthful of cum). His stomach rumbled.

Gil chuckled, "I won't make you do too much. Wanna try it?"

He wanted to eat, mostly, but he also wanted to make his master happy.

Barnaby nodded.

"Good boy." The man readied a cookie. "Now, be a deer and kneel for me."

Barnaby obeyed, kneeling on the bed in front of him. He smiled as the snack was held to his lips. "Already, sir?"

"You earned it."

For such a simple task? Well, he wasn't going to complain. He nibbled away, eating right from his master's palm while gazing up at him.

Gil's eyes seemed to sparkle.

In seconds, the cookie was gone, and Barnaby was licking the remnants off the man's fingers. "What's next?"

Gil pointed to the floor, and he got down on all fours while his master sat at the edge of the bed. He gave the order to squat, and Barnaby shifted to position. Then, Gil added, "Hold your hands behind your back."

He did just that while Gil used a hand to tilt his head, pointing his nose to the ceiling. Next, the man broke off a chunk of another cookie, placing it on the tip of Barnaby's nose. "*Hold.*"

He began counting down from ten, and the blond quickly realized it was a balancing act. He clenched his thighs, trembling as he fought to keep his head still, determined not to let the treat fall.

He really did need to exercise more.

"*Five—*"

Without fail, Barnaby fell on his ass. The cookie piece followed, dropping to the floor and rolling under the bed.

Five simple seconds, and he was too heavy to carry himself.

He shied away from Gil's gaze, face flush with embarrassment. "Sorry..."

"You'll get it next time—" The raven scratched Barnaby's head and behind his ear. "Practice makes perfect."

Barnaby hummed, tilting to the touch that was swiftly putting him at ease. He could understand why most animals were so receptive to it.

"Can you roll over for me?"

Surely there wasn't any way he could mess that up. Right?

He couldn't help but be wary as he laid at Gil's feet, rolling over once to the left, then once to the right. It felt almost too easy—

And yet Gil seemed so pleased. "Again."

Barnaby repeated the motion, and another cookie was handed to him whole. "Thank you, sir—" He chewed graciously, swallowed, and almost choked as his shirt was lifted.

A hand was placed on his belly, rubbing wide circles.

"M-Master?"

The man grinned, as if oblivious, while lightly dragging his nails. "What is it, fawn?"

"Uhm—" Barnaby shivered, tingling from the unfamiliar sensation. It felt like something that should be enjoyed, something that would warrant the wag of a tail. But it was too much to notice *how* wide Gil's circles were. How wide his own stomach was. "C-Can I keep my shirt on?"

Confusion dashed across Gil's face, but he didn't complain, simply fixed the fabric around Barnaby's torso.

Barnaby sighed, relieved.

"Kneel."

Happy to hide his stomach again, the boy returned to his knees, treated to yet another cookie. While it may not have made him any thinner, he was too hungry to refuse.

"You're so well-behaved," Gil purred, tickling under his chin, "Show me your paw, and if you want to stick around, we can see if there's anything on Netflix."

Barnaby perked up. *Netflix and Chill?*

It certainly beat going back to his dorm and watching alone.

"Don't you mean *hoof*?" he asked, raising a hand.

The man scoffed, taking it and placing a kiss on his knuckle. "Get up here."

Barnaby hardly had the chance to stand when Gil yanked him onto the bed. He cuddled right up to his master's side, leaving just enough room for him to grab the laptop and set it up.

They decided on *The Office* - or, Barnaby let Gil decide they would watch *The Office*. Not that he minded; he could watch his documentaries and cartoons on his own time.

He couldn't be on his own and watch Gil smile. Wouldn't have been able to feel the tremor of his chest when he chuckled, either.

Gil handed over the rest of the cookies, and with his attention already split between the laptop and his master, Barnaby paid no mind to what he was eating.

Suddenly, he was digging for the next, but when he looked down, realized there were none left.

"Sorry," he muttered, handing Gil the empty sleeve, "I owe you another pack."

Gil snickered, dusting crumbs off Barnaby's shirt. "Don't worry about it. I bought them for you, anyway."

Still flustered with himself, Barnaby went quiet while Gil kept an arm around him, content.

And like his last visit to the dorm, Barnaby couldn't help but think how casual it was. How comfortable.

Inevitably, they came to the end of another episode to find that the sun had gone down.

It was time for Barnaby to go. He couldn't let Gil get bored of him yet.

Although, just when the blond had suspected the passion had died down for the day, his master was pulling him in, keeping him in bed with tender, lingering kisses.

Eventually, Barnaby was permitted to stand, and he redressed, thanking Gil for everything.

The man stretched and spoke, watching his every move, "It's a pleasure to have you here. Text me when you have time to go to the pet store?"

Barnaby beamed. "I will—" He scurried over to place one last kiss on Gil's cheek, catching his face scrunch up, his eyes shimmering— "and you can text me if there are any tricks you want me to practice."

Gil kissed the corner of his mouth before he could get away, his grin turning wolfish. "I will."

Incidentally, their lips met again. Barnaby had to be the first to pull away before he ended up spending the night in the wrong dorm.

He waved goodbye, walking on air as he walked out of the room.

He passed an ATM on the way back to his dorm, and in that moment, Barnaby discovered the ground below him.

He withdrew $100.

He incited no greeting upon entering the room, didn't even lift his gaze from the floor - just placed the amount onto Seth's nightstand and turned to his bed.

"*Keep it.*"

He froze, and his friend heaved a sigh, closing his laptop.

"I'm sorry—"

"You need it more than I do."

Barnaby dared a glance to find Seth handing it back to him.

"Take it."

He stared until he realized the other wasn't going to budge.

He took the money before Seth would have to tire his arm out. While their hands still touched, Barnaby pulled him in for a hug. "Thank you."

The reluctance couldn't have been more clear, but Seth's arms wrapped loosely around him in return. "You wanna grab dinner? Your treat?"

"Yes!" Barnaby exclaimed, eager for an opportunity to redeem himself, "Yes! Absolutely!"

They ended up at House of Waffles.

Over diabetic-inducing food and unwashed dishes, Seth updated Barnaby on spending his day in a nurse's office. No, he didn't test positive for anything, no, he wasn't pregnant, and *no, Barnaby,* it wasn't non-consensual. He'd expected it to feel a certain way and when it didn't, demanded it harder, faster, rougher.

Barnaby apologized.

Seth shrugged, piling hashbrowns into his mouth. "No skin off my nose. Back to whacking it to hentai, that's all."

Chapter 9

> Guess who's the new bouncer of this joint

Barnaby grinned as he read the text. That certainly was an interesting way to say, "Resident Receptionist", but if it made the experience more enjoyable to his roommate, then *bouncer* he would call him.

The car came to a stop, and Barnaby replied:

> Congrats! Does this mean you're gonna start turning me away?

> Every chance I get

He expected nothing less.

A hand reached across his lap, grabbing at the plastic bag between his legs.

"I've got it," Barnaby assured the other, snatching it first, "You're bringing the bed in, right?"

Turning to him, the blond was met with Gil's usual smirk. "I suppose I am."

They both exited the car, and Barnaby waited as Gil grabbed the glorified, oversized pillow from the backseat. He had to giggle when the man walked up beside him with it tucked under his arm, taking about as much space as Barnaby would have with that arm draped around him. "Someone's going to think you actually have an animal in your dorm."

"Let them," Gil said, leading him up the steps of his building, "It'll be one Hell of a visit from the RA if you're there."

Barnaby rolled his eyes, doing his best to act cool and collected on their way to the room.

"Hiding in plain sight", as Gil had phrased it on the car ride over.

Of course, it was that point in the evening when everyone else was returning to their dorms or leaving for night classes, causing a bit of hallway traffic. There were glances, and a few people had to step out of the way to avoid colliding with the pet bed.

And then Barnaby realized how many people lived around them, watching him follow Gil to his room.

He wondered how many of them could *hear* what happened behind door 239.

He wondered if any of them were there the previous weekend, cheering Gil on as he fucked Barnaby in his car.

He was blushing before they even arrived at their destination, the raven letting him inside.

"Would you rather have it by the desk or by the bed?" Gil asked, closing the door behind him.

Barnaby considered it for a moment, looking back and forth. "By the desk, if that's okay? If you don't mind me hanging out there while you work, that is."

"Probably will make it harder to focus," Gil said, pinching his cheek, "but what the heck?" He went over, laying the bed down before going into his closet and pulling out a few extra pillows. Once he'd fluffed them, lining the bed with them, he patted the center and called to his guest, "Ready to try it out?"

Barnaby toed off his shoes and approached him. He settled right in, curling up and nestling in between all the pillows. The pet bed itself was soft and spongy below him, a cloud he could float along on.

"It's nice," he cooed, basking in the sunlight coming through the window above. "I could get used to this."

Gil's hand traveled the hills of his silhouette before finally collecting the bag from him, reaching in to produce his brand-new yellow food bowl. "I bet you're hungry."

Another trigger - just the word alone - and Barnaby became aware of that hollow feeling in his gut. "Yes, sir."

"Stay here."

He watched his master take the bowl to the kitchen and fill it with something from the fridge.

Raspberries - he'd discover when it was placed on the floor in front of him.

He thanked him and went to pluck one.

He froze when Gil chided him, "Would a fawn have hands to eat with?"

Barnaby pouted. "Guess not." He'd accepted his role as pet, performed tricks for the man, but for one reason or another, it didn't fully sink in until he hunkered down in his nest, lips at the edge of his bowl—

Gil must have been serious when he said he wanted to treat him like an animal.

Closing his eyes, Barnaby dug in.

He was hesitant at first, but it wasn't long before he felt the remnants on his chin, dabbing his nose. He wanted to raise his head to wipe his face, but then Gil rested a hand on him, petting him, urging him into the dish—

He supposed he could deal with it.

And Gil must've trusted him to.

While Barnaby filled his belly with berries, his master made another reach for the shopping bag.

His new collar, along with a matching leash, was all that was left.

He pretended not to notice the brown leather being fastened around his neck, instead, digging in deeper. He licked his bowl clean, and as soon as he was finished, sat proud in his nest. "How does it look?"

Gil's eyes were as fixed as the smile on his face. "Why don't you take off your shirt so I can judge it better?" he suggested. "In fact, why don't you take off the rest of your clothes while you're at it? We wouldn't want them in the way of anything."

Barnaby's heart skipped, and he felt his cheeks turning as red as raspberries at the idea of what would happen next.

"N-No, sir," he said, shimmying out of his shirt, "we wouldn't want that."

His pants and briefs followed, and Gil collected each of them, setting them neatly aside before inching closer. He ghosted his fingertips up Barnaby's arms, leaving goosebumps in his wake.

He was exposed from head to toe, and still, with the way Gil studied him, Barnaby felt like the man was undressing him with his eyes.

A silver pendant hung from the front of the collar: a medallion, with a cursive *B* engraved on the front.

Gil flipped it, checking his dorm number on the back: *Talbot 239*. ("In case you ever get lost," he'd told Barnaby when they had it customized at the pet store.)

"You look like a prize," he purred, "A regular trophy buck."

He kissed his cheek before getting to his feet, and Barnaby glowed up at him. It was difficult to imagine he was anything to marvel at when Gil was the one towering over him, in view of every visible flaw.

And yet he hadn't taken his eyes off of him.

He kept inviting Barnaby back, he'd made a nest for him, and he'd collared him.

He'd made him a trophy.

There was simply too much pride in it all for Barnaby to want to hide away.

"You've caught me, sir," the boy said, "Now, what?"

"*Now*—" Gil cupped the back of Barnaby's head, guiding him toward his crotch— "we're going to practice your tricks."

Without any hesitation, Barnaby nuzzled against his bulge, chills running through his spine. "Yes, Master."

Since he was already kneeling, he was given the order to lay down; from there, told to roll over.

Then, the raven ordered him to squat, but instead of placing a cookie on his pet's nose, he balanced a coin from his pocket.

He started his count down from ten. While Barnaby struggled for balance, amusement danced across Gil's dimpled cheeks and grey orbs that were anything but dull.

The blond was too distracted to care much when he collapsed into his nest at "*three*."

"Two more seconds than last time," Gil told him, "You're getting there already."

Barnaby smiled sheepishly, returning to his knees. "Gotta get there if I want to be your good boy, though."

Gil's expression softened, and he weaved a hand through honey-colored hair. "You've *been* a good boy. Which is why..." He tapped Barnaby's nose— "I have another surprise for you."

Barnaby blinked, confused but curious as fawns could be. They'd just gone shopping. "What kind of surprise?"

"Do one more trick for me," his master tempted, "and you'll find out."

Already kneeling in wait, Barnaby decided to nod his agreement.

"Turn around."

Uncertainty made him shudder, but he obeyed, shifting to turn away from him.

"*This—*"

A hand pressed between his shoulder blades, pushing his chest to the pet bed. His hips were grabbed next, positioning his ass in the air.

A fire under his skin spread all the way to his ears.

"—is how you present yourself. When I tell you to *present,* this is what I expect. And from now on, as soon as you walk through that door, the only thing I want to see you wearing is your collar. Understood?"

Barnaby's heart caught in his throat, and his hair stood on end.

Gil definitely seemed to embrace his role.

He held onto one of his pillows. "Yes, Master."

"See? You're the perfect good boy," Gil chuckled, patting his ass. "Stay here."

Barnaby craned his neck, spying on the man as he walked away to rummage through his nightstand.

At first, he thought his master had pulled out a ball of brown and white fur. But then he smoothed it out, and its shape became more apparent, baring an uncanny resemblance to a deer's tail.

There was a black bulb at the base, and Barnaby could only assume it was some kind of butt plug.

Oh, dear.

Once it'd been covered in lube, Gil brought it back to him.

"Th-That's cute," Barnaby muttered.

The man squatted behind him. "Imagine how cute it'll look on you." He rubbed the tip of the bulb against Barnaby's pucker, and slowly, *slowly* eased it in.

It didn't go very deep at all, but the boy's lower half squirmed all the same, trying to adjust.

Fur brushed against his skin as Gil stroked the tail into place. "*Adorable.*"

Barnaby caught a glimpse of it from the corner of his eye, noticing how it appeared to grow from his body.

He smiled and wagged it right under his master's nose.

Gil pinched his buttcheek in response, and Barnaby squeaked. "Playful fawn, aren't you?" Seconds later, the man had the leash in his hands, and the next thing Barnaby knew, it was attached to his collar.

With the opposite end around his wrist, Gil sat in his desk chair, patting his knee.

Barnaby hopped up, straddling his thigh.

"Y'know," Gil said, carefully bouncing his leg below the boy, "we still have to set rules for you. You're not some wild thing anymore. Can't have you thinking you can do whatever you want."

Barnaby bristled, each bounce putting pressure on his balls. "W-What kind of rules, sir?"

"Well, you already know you can't touch yourself—" As if for emphasis, Gil lazily began stroking the boy's cock, earning a gasp— "so, let's say your second rule is, no matter where we are, you *always* have your collar on when you're with me."

A collar seemed so meager when the man had his fingers wrapped around Barnaby's cock. Total control, right in the palm of his hand. As far as Barnaby was concerned, every touch was a reminder of ownership.

But, oh, it was a lovely collar. His pride, the mark of a trophy buck.

Gil had been so generous to him already, wearing it must've been the least he could do.

He agreed, "Yes, Master."

The man's smirk grew wider. "Good fawn—" He spat in his palm, slicking it to pump his pet faster. "On top of that...why don't we make it a rule to keep yourself clean for me? That way, I'll know you'll be ready for me when *I'm* ready."

Barnaby gulped. He wanted to ask, *but what if I'm not ready,* though his mouth was drying up fast. He parted his lips, and all he could manage were quiet moans.

He settled for nodding his head.

Gil leaned in, catching his lower lip between his teeth and biting gently.

Barnaby's tongue darted out, on instinct almost, to lap at Gil's mouth, begging for entry.

In an instant, the man consumed him, sending him reeling. He feasted on his lips, all but swallowed his tongue, and sucked the life out of him.

His claws dug into Barnaby's hips, pulling and pushing him along his thigh, and soon enough, the boy was breaking the kiss, gasping for air.

"*Master—*" The friction set the desire between his legs ablaze. If Gil couldn't keep jerking him off, and if he couldn't touch himself— well, he had to do *something*.

Brows furrowed and lip bitten, he chased his pleasure, grinding against the raven's leg.

"You must be desperate," Gil muttered, spoken like a spell as he lounged in the chair, "humping me like an animal in heat. I bet you'd give anything for me to breed you right now."

Breed?

Now, that had a nice ring to it.

It painted a picture in Barnaby's head: Gil bending him over, snarling, being equally as primal—

Filling him with load after load of cum. *Fuck.* It'd probably feel so warm inside of him.

Suddenly, Barnaby was desperate for that warmth.

"*Please,*" he panted, grabbing onto Gil's shoulders to steady himself, "please breed me, Master. I need you."

The man chuckled, curling the leash around his finger. "Turn around. Let me see your tail fly, and maybe I'll consider it."

Barnaby moved as fast as he could, turning around on Gil's knee before grinding with all the persistence he could muster. Unfortunately, he could only manage in quick bursts

123

of energy before losing balance, nearly falling over into his pet bed.

He didn't know what to do with his hands, really, and it must have been obvious since, a moment later, Gil was grabbing his wrists, pinning them behind his back.

"Pretty fawn," the man hummed, "I'm not sure I want you without your tail yet."

Barnaby whined, unabashed and childish. It didn't stop his humping, however.

It didn't stop Gil from grabbing onto his hair, either. "Let's set another rule—" He bounced his leg once, abruptly, beneath him— "I don't tolerate *brats*. Disrespect me, and we'll have a problem. Break any of your rules, and you'll be punished."

Maybe it was a good thing Barnaby had his back to his master. For as long as he couldn't see his face, he tried correcting his pout. "I'm sorry, sir," he whimpered, "I'm not...*aah*...a brat. I'm needy. I'm *so* needy. Fuck— I want to be good."

"And you're being so good right now—" Releasing his grip on Barnaby's hair and wrists, Gil wrapped his arms around the boy's waist instead, keeping him in place— "Just for tonight, fawn," he cooed, his gentle tone giving Barnaby pause. To savor his words. "Just this once. Show me how desperate a young buck can be for his master."

The boy sighed. He didn't fully understand. He hoped he hadn't done anything wrong to not be fucked.

But his mind was fuzzy, and it was becoming harder to think.

He didn't want to think. He wanted to *come.*

And so, he muttered, a final time, "Yes, Master."

Secure in Gil's arms, he succumbed to his desperation, practically rubbing his balls raw against the man's jeans.

After about a minute or so of concentrating on himself, Gil made another grab for Barnaby's hand, guiding it to his crotch.

The boy palmed him blindly, hopeless in unzipping him. If not for his master's help, he may not have gotten his fingers around his cock.

The moment he did, he was determined to catch him up to speed.

It wasn't difficult, considering Gil was *plenty hard.* A few strokes, and moans were already pouring out of the man, giving Barnaby a bit of a confidence boost.

He was doing something right. He was helping someone feel *good.*

He moaned with some exaggeration - being just a bit louder, just a bit higher pitched. He thought that was supposed to be sexy. He wagged his tail, swirled his thumb around his master's tip—

And then his breath hitched.

He wagged his tail again, bouncing once, then twice against Gil's thigh before he couldn't stop.

He closed his eyes, giving into the illusion of being fucked in his master's lap.

With each squeeze of his balls, the heat in his core packed tighter and tighter. He squeezed around his plug tighter and tighter.

Finally, he erupted, crying out, hips jolting - a buck caught in his rut.

His hands shook with restraint not to touch himself. His thighs trembled with the effort of climaxing. His legs struggled to hold him up.

Gil made sure he was steady.

"Don't stop, Bee," the man pleaded. Holding him close with one hand, he helped him pump with the other.

Barnaby could barely register it.

Dazed, he transferred whatever strength he had left to his fingertips, memorizing Gil's veins, the length of his cock—

He moved like silicone - a sex toy - until finally, the man bellowed into his ear.

Suddenly, his fingers were sticky.

Barnaby let himself slump into Gil's chest, catching his breath, while Gil wrapped him up in his arms, doing the same.

They sat there for a few minutes, recovering, and Gil's hand gradually found Barnaby's face, wiping sweat from his brow and brushing his hair back. They locked eyes, and an angelic smile decorated the raven's lips. It filled Barnaby with that warmth he was so desperate for, and he giggled, nuzzling their noses together.

"God, I'm so fucking lucky," Gil breathed, "Thanks for putting up with my weird kinks."

"Shush, I'm not *putting up* with anything," Barnaby insisted, "I like being your pet." He yawned— "Being a deer is fun."

His eyelids felt heavy, and the next minute, he was weightless, floating along until his back met a familiar mattress.

His blinks were slow. One moment, Gil was gone, then he was beside him, wiping him down with a wet rag. He'd stripped to his boxers at some point, and at another, attempted to sit Barnaby up so he could dress him in a loose shirt and track pants.

His leash and collar were removed, and he shivered when his plug was plucked out of him.

The last thing he remembered was Gil sliding into bed with him, holding something cold and wet to his lips. "Drink some," he whispered, "just to be safe."

Barnaby didn't hesitate. Opening his mouth, he let the cool water hit his throat. As refreshing as it was, however, it wasn't enough to keep him energized.

He closed his eyes.

When he'd open them again, he'd realize he'd spent the entire night in Gil Connolly's dorm.

Chapter 10

"Barney? Barnaby, slow down for a second. *Hey—*"

The mug was pried from his hands, and Savannah continued making the latte, having to wipe caramel off from the sides. "Why don't you stay up at the register, alright? Let me worry about making the orders. Would that work better for you?"

Barnaby swallowed a lump in his throat and smoothed out imaginary wrinkles in his apron. *He* was the one that had to call her in at the start of the unexpected rush. *She* shouldn't have had to make accommodations for *him*.

However, Barnaby was anxious and self-absorbed, and the idea alone lifted one of many weights from his shoulders. When his gentle-faced coworker glanced back for an answer, he nodded, skirting around her to place himself at the register. "Your latte is on the way, ma'am," he said automatically, "Next?"

There were more latte orders, hot chocolates, and coffees, and though shaken, Barnaby was managing. A few "*thank you for your patience*" were thrown in for courtesy, and fortunately, nobody complained.

While one customer collected their change, he turned to find his coworker moving back and forth. "How're you doing, Sav?"

"I'm fine, Barney—" Savannah bumped her hip into his as she brushed by. "Don't worry about me. Just keep 'em comin'."

Barnaby smiled and straightened his shoulders, ready for the next person in line. "Hello!" he started, "What can I get for you?"

Grey eyes lifted off of a phone to lock with hazel.

Barnaby's heart skipped a beat, and Gil smirked.

He didn't know whether he wanted to run into his arms or runaway.

"Busy night?" the raven asked, surveying the menu overhead.

"Yeah, uhm," Barnaby cleared his throat. There was a pen on his keyboard that was slightly off center. He corrected it. "I think there was a, uhm...band or something that played nearby? Were you there?"

Gil shook his head, and his attention was back on the blond. "Nope," he said, "Came to see you."

Barnaby bit the inside of his cheek and tugged idly on his ear. He glanced around to make sure Savannah was out of earshot, and when he spoke, it was only loud enough for Gil to hear, "Sorry I haven't been texting as much. I've wanted to hang out with you again, but the past few days have been...stressful."

"Hey, no worries," Gil was quick to interject, "You've got your own life. I get that."

Barnaby thought he caught a wink before the man looked over his shoulder. Two more people in line, though he didn't seem the least bit bothered by it.

"Can you do a black coffee?"

"No cream or sugar?" Barnaby grabbed his pen to write the order on a ticket for Savannah. "Coming right—" He paused in speech and in writing in a single stroke of brilliance. "Actually—" He crumpled the note, making Gil raise a brow at him, "if you're willing to wait, I can bring it to you myself?"

Barnaby braced himself against the man's gaze as it scanned him up and down. A hint of a chuckle escaped his lips, and Gil said, "Fine by me." He produced a credit card, but the second Barnaby spotted it, his hand flew to cover the card reader. He winced apologetically without Gil having to move a muscle.

"*Go*. Sit," he urged, "I've got it."

Despite Gil's skeptical stare, he returned his card to his wallet. Something about his smirk seemed that much more mischievous as he turned to walk away. "Bossy."

The next person in line came forward.

Barnaby rushed through the next few orders, scribbling them onto tickets and passing them off to Savannah. He'd hoped he didn't come off as rude, but then again, he couldn't say he cared about customer opinions as much anymore.

Not when he had his *master* nearby, studying him from a table for two.

Soon, the counter was clear in front of him, and Barnaby looked out at couples and groups of friends. They filled nearly every seat in the house, bantering, and by all accounts, enjoying themselves.

"We did it," Savannah said, clapping his shoulder. It didn't matter that her hand was dainty and well-manicured - Barnaby flinched all the same.

"Thanks to you." He patted her back weakly, gathering his nerves so he could ask, "Would you mind if I took my break now?"

"Go for it!" Savannah was swift to put herself in front of him, fulfilling the task of adding change to the register.

Barnaby thanked her again, slipping away to fill a mug with black coffee.

Even with his back turned, he could swear he sensed Gil's glare lingering on him. For some reason, he had the sudden urge to wear his apron reversed, to cover his ass.

He resisted, face flushed, and quickly filled a second mug with vanilla tea for himself.

He carried both over to Gil's table, placing the man's coffee in front of him. "I have fifteen minutes," he said, teetering with his own cup, "would you like me to join you?"

Gil gestured to the chair across from him, and Barnaby, very cautious not to spill his drink, sat down.

"This doesn't bother you?"

The boy's eyes widened slightly, and he hesitated sipping his tea. "Does...*what* bother me?"

"Me showing up here." Elbows on the table, Gil leaned forward, seeming less confident in himself. "I'm not invading your space, am I?"

"*No.*" Barnaby shifted to the edge of his seat to be sure he was heard. To be certain Gil would believe him. Out of the many things he was anxious about, only one concerned his master. He hunched his shoulders, speaking the rest to the table, "As long as you know I can't do any of that pet stuff here. I'm sorry, but I...can't risk my job."

"I get it. This is your territory."

Barnaby caught a glimpse of Gil's coffee being lifted.

"You're different up there."

Intrigued by the comment, he looked to the man for clarification.

He continued, "Not as shy as when you're out in public with me. You held your head up. Didn't stutter once. At least not that I noticed."

Surprised, laughter squeezed out of Barnaby. A wheeze. "Well, that's—" He slicked his hair back with a sweaty palm. So much for Not Stuttering— "That's rehearsed, sort of. You say the same thing so many times, it becomes...natural."

Gil nodded despite a crooked smile that seemed less than convinced.

That was fine, Barnaby supposed. Maybe Gil believing he could be "different" wasn't all that bad.

Unless, of course, that idea secretly offended him. What if he thought it meant he was uncomfortable around him?

"It's not a bad thing," Barnaby blurted.

Gil tilted his head quizzically.

Abandoning his mug, the boy picked at his fingernails. "That I'm...the way that I am around you. I think it's just, you know, an *effect* you have on me. And I don't mind it! I like it, actually."

Gil gave a faint snort, echoed by the clink of his cup against the table. "Okay," he said, sounding sympathetic, "it was supposed to be a compliment. I'm flattered, but you really don't need to explain yourself to me."

Barnaby's face grew hot with embarrassment. He forced out another, weaker laugh. "If I don't explain myself, you'll never understand a damn thing I'm trying to say."

"Bullshit."

When Barnaby looked up, Gil was rolling his eyes, his lips curling with the word.

"You—" He pointed at the blond, then traced a line that covered the room— "make more sense to me than any other chucklefuck in this place right now."

"Oh, that's...*very* eloquent," Barnaby said, not knowing how else to respond to something so absurd.

"I'm serious." Gil swigged his coffee like it was some bar drink. When he set it down again, he stared intently into what was left, fingers tapping stiffly across the ceramic. Then, he said, "I don't get how they do it. You have a group of— what? Five people over there? Where the Hell do you even get that many friends from? And listen— I'm pretty sure I can hear...three different conversations going on? And I don't think they give a shit. I feel like I'm whispering. Not to mention the fact they saw it was getting busy, and they still decided to stay!" He ended in a huff, seeming...amazed? Baffled? Vulnerable? He crossed his arms and scanned the shop, slumping in his chair. "I can't wrap my head around it."

Barnaby didn't understand it either. But to hear it from Gil—

Well, he expected the man, of all people, would be able to make sense of it.

"*You*—" The blond attempted to phrase it as delicately as he could, "invite *strangers* into your bed. You get as close as you could get to *anyone* without knowing anything about them. How do you wrap your head around that?"

Gil grinned, and Barnaby decided it wasn't the reaction he was hoping for. "What did you say about your job?" he asked, jaded, deflated, "It's rehearsed?"

Barnaby frowned. "I don't see how you could rehearse that. Isn't everyone...*different*?"

"To an extent—" Gil shrugged. "It's the same as anything else. Except, instead of repeating the same lines at the register, you find these general patterns and places to touch people that make them feel good. Think of it this way: your job is memorizing the dialogue of a play while I memorize the staging—" He paused, the wheels in his head still visibly turning, then finished, "But sure. Everyone's different."

The blond nearly jumped out of his seat as he received a light, unexpected kick to his shin.

Gil's expression softened, apologetic but affectionate. "Have to learn a whole new set of patterns for you."

Only starting to believe he could have been different than Gil's other partners, it was nice to be reminded.

Tapping the man's leg with his foot, Barnaby muttered, "And somehow I'm the one that makes sense."

Gil gave an affirming nod, correcting his posture. "On the topic of rehearsed lines—" Grey eyes squinted at him— "I don't think I ever asked what your major was."

Barnaby giggled because *How Cliche*. He wore a collar with the man's dorm number attached under his uniform, yet he'd waited two weeks to ask? He cleared his throat, answering, "Agriculture."

Not many people were aware the program existed, and judging by his raised brows, neither did Gil. "*Really?*"

Like his lines at the register, he'd explained it enough times to have a speech prepared in his head.

He began by informing him about the campus greenhouses, how most of their planting-based labs and soil-testing happened there. Then, there were the community gardens, where they practiced in teams. There were trips to parks and farms, and the inevitable, what Barnaby most looked forward to, internships. At least that was the college's term for it. Some people, evidently, thought they were too good to be called *farmhands*. But not Barnaby. He'd be proud when the time came to it.

He didn't stutter, and he didn't hesitate, and that usually meant he was rambling, often resulting in his audience tuning him out, glancing at their phones or anything else.

Gil held his gaze the entire time, his chin rested on his hand, his smile unwavering.

Barnaby didn't realize he'd been expecting that to change until he was done talking.

He settled back in his seat, and Gil remained attentive.

"You're going to be a farmer?"

"That's the goal."

"And what are you gonna farm?" He phrased it so sweetly.

"Uhm, anything? Whatever I can give—" Barnaby shrugged. "Mostly, I've thought about crops. Something like an orchard or a vineyard. But I'd really like to have animals, too. Not for their meat, though. I can't imagine raising them just to do *that* to them."

Another affirmative nod from Gil. His eyes were still somewhat squinted, his freckles gathering together, and he had this overall look about him that made Barnaby want to pinch his cheeks, *dang it*. "I like the way you think."

Barnaby thought, *I like the way you exist.*

He was about to ask what Gil was majoring in when something grazed his shoulder. Looking up, he found Savannah, utterly oblivious to the bubble she'd burst.

"I'm gonna start cleaning," she told him, gathering each of their mugs, "If you could go around and take care of refills as soon as you come back, I would really appreciate it."

"Oh..." His enthusiasm drowned with his voice, but he was quick to force a smile, praying she wouldn't notice. "Uh, yeah, I can do that. Thanks, Sav."

"Thank *you*, Barnaby." Unfazed, she trotted off with a sophisticated sway.

That left Barnaby to bury his head in his arms on the table, heaving a sigh.

"What's wrong?" Gil asked.

"It's stupid." Barnaby huffed. "I *really* don't like refilling drinks. I know it should be easy, and you'd think I'd have it figured out by now, but it's like...*ugh*— Stage fright on top of making sure I don't spill coffee everywhere, on top of having to interrupt people, and I *know* I'm overthinking it but—" But he was whining. He'd impressed Gil, maybe, but there he went ruining it. "Sorry. Can you forget I said anything?"

There was another kick to his shin, one that barely made him flinch.

"Do you want help?"

Barnaby's brows furrowed, and he lifted his head, finding Gil's expression turned serious. "No, it's...fine. If Savannah sees you trying to serve anyone, she'll yell at me and kick you out."

The man shook his head. "Not what I meant."

"Then...what?"

Gil's stare lingered a second longer before he was reaching down to his feet, rummaging through the satchel he'd brought with him. "By *help*," Gil said, "I mean something to *help you* relax."

Realization dawned on Barnaby, and it made him want to close his eyes and cover his ears, not to get involved.

Oh no, he's one of Those Guys.

His DARE Officer had warned him the day would come.

He's going to offer me drugs.

He'd never do it, of course - he *couldn't* - but for whatever reason, when Gil slid his fists across the table, Barnaby put his hands over, accepting the offer.

Except, when he brought the items into his lap for inspection, he didn't find a pipe, or a vape pen, or a needle—

Gil had given him a butt plug with a button at its base, along with a miniature bottle of lube.

Barnaby had to stop himself from throwing them back at the man. "*No!*" he hissed, "Are you kidding? That'll make it worse!" It stung a bit more to think he hadn't been listened to, but he was closer to fleeing than confronting him about it in the middle of his shift.

Gil, on the other hand, was perfectly poised. "Think about it," he said, raising a hand in defense, "you're a lot less reserved in the heat of things, and from my perspective, you've gotten braver. I'm not saying you *have* to use it, but if you're that afraid..."

Barnaby's face was on fire.

Dick.

Sighing dramatically, he shoved the items into his apron-pocket. His leg started shaking, and he bit his nails more aggressively. He mumbled through gritted teeth, "I probably wouldn't be able to hold out. I'd give it away, and I'd get fired, or honestly, I'd probably die on the spot—"

"It's not that intense," Gil interjected, "Unless you're *that* turned on by it, I think you'd be okay. And if you *do* decide to use it..."

Barnaby stiffened as the raven's foot grazed further up his leg, pressing against his thigh.

"I'll make it worth the trouble."

The audacity of that man, bargaining with him as if Barnaby would even *let him* have the opportunity.

Using that tone and those touches on him in public.

The gall.

Minutes later, exiting the bathroom, Barnaby contemplated whether or not to spill coffee in his lap when he passed by.

He decided against it, if only because he'd have to clean it up. And he wasn't about to bend over tables or get on his knees to clean anything while a plug vibrated dully in his ass.

Upon shooting Gil a final glare, Barnaby noticed the man looking all too pleased with himself. He turned away in a whirl, doing his best to focus on *not* spilling coffee on anyone else.

Fortunately, half of the patrons had left by that point while others put their coats on.

He was all the more eager to get it done and over with.

He used the same line at every table he approached: "Hi, sorry, would you like a refill?"

The first few rejected him, but that made him hopeful. The less people he had to serve, the less his chances were of messing up. When someone eventually did say, "yes, please", Barnaby kept himself composed, able to hold the decanter steady in his hand. More and more were filled without issue.

Maybe he was getting used to the task. Maybe he was simply paranoid, doubting himself as always to a point he'd forgotten he was capable.

Maybe it did have something to do with the fact he was feeling warm and relaxed, thanks to the incessant buzz between his legs. However, he wasn't about to give Gil the satisfaction of knowing that.

Before long, Barnaby was returning the decanters to the coffee machine, Savannah was scrubbing away in the sink, and they were beginning the process of closing the cafe. Patrons continued to trickle out, and soon enough, Gil was the last one seated, buried in his phone.

Barnaby was bagging unsold pastries to take home when Savannah brushed against him.

"New boyfriend?"

Barnaby fumbled with a brownie. "*No.*" Since that totally didn't sound defensive, he added, "We're just friends. Why, are you looking for someone?"

His coworker laughed, stealing a cookie from him. "Oh, no, honey. My days with the goth squad are long over."

"He...He's not *goth.*"

"*Barnaby.* Look at him again and tell me that coat and that hairdo doesn't make him look like Mr. Edgar Allan Poe."

Barnaby rolled his eyes at her (Savannah might have had a point, but like, a *hot* Edgar Allan Poe), and she bumped their shoulders together before walking away to collect garbage bags.

He closed the pastry display, intending to follow her—

He froze instead, his breath catching in his throat. Staying very still, Barnaby clenched his cheeks as his plug delivered a much more powerful vibration.

He took a careful side-step, hoping it would shift it to a different angle, if that was the problem.

No luck.

He tried walking in place, wondering if that could somehow counteract the sensation.

It only made it worse.

"I'll be right back," he told Savannah, "I have to go to the bathroom."

He barely made it around the counter when Gil called out to him, beckoning him with a finger.

"Give me a minute," Barnaby insisted, "I need—"

Gil shook his head, pointing directly at his table.

The boy groaned and dragged his feet over.

"Where were you going?" Gil asked like he already knew the answer.

Thighs rubbing impatiently together, Barnaby whimpered, "I have to take it out. O-Or I need to fix it."

"Fix what?"

"The...position?" Another spike in intensity. He bit his lip and gripped at the edge of the table for support. "I-It's getting really strong! I don't think I can handle it—"

As soon as he said that, a miracle happened: the plug resumed a dull pulse, and Barnaby sighed in relief. "*Holy shit.*"

An impish grin plastered Gil's face. "Better?"

Barnaby didn't trust that, somehow. He eyed him skeptically.

The raven put his phone down in front of him, revealing what he'd been so preoccupied with: the screen was pink, and at the bottom, there was a sparkling ball of white. At first, Barnaby didn't understand what he was looking at—

Until Gil placed his finger on the ball, sliding it upward.

The plug shook mercilessly inside of him, and Barnaby slapped a hand over his mouth to muffle a moan. *Fuckfuckfuck.*

Just like the remote paired with the first vibrator. Gil was in control.

"*Change it,*" Barnaby begged, grabbing onto the man's arm, his legs shaking. "K-Keep it low, but— *Gil...*"

His master obliged, bringing it to its original setting.

It was too late. Fighting for composure, Barnaby realized he could barely move. The damage had been done.

He was certifiably, irrevocably horny.

Gil swept him with his gaze before locking on pleading eyes.

Barnaby waited for him to whisper something lewd to him or stand up for a kiss. He wondered if, maybe, the man was hypnotizing him into letting his guard down.

If that was the case, he nearly succeeded—

Barnaby just about missed the hand already lifting his apron. "*What're you doing?*"

"I'd like to know what I'm dealing with."

You have seen me naked!

But rather than protest out loud, Barnaby bit his lip. He glanced over his shoulder, watching out for Savannah, while Gil's hand glided up his thigh. His knees buckled as the man gave his bulge a gentle squeeze.

"You're hard."

"No shit."

Gil gripped him tighter, and Barnaby gasped, hips twitching. "Watch your mouth."

The boy quickly nodded, and Gil released him. He stepped back as the raven grabbed his satchel and stood up from his chair.

"*I'm* going to wait in the bathroom," he muttered into Barnaby's bright red ear. "Look for me once she's gone."

The blond waited until his footsteps faded, listening for the sound of the bathroom door before turning around.

Savannah was already grinning at him from behind the register. "But he's not your boyfriend, right?"

Barnaby stammered the verbal equivalent of keyboard-smashing, and his coworker bubbled with laughter.

Thankfully, she didn't tease him anymore about it. They counted the money from the register, and Savannah threw the garbage bags over her shoulder like Santa Claus with his sack. She wished him goodnight, and Barnaby thanked her once again for rescuing him from the rush. He followed her to the door, insisting he'd stay behind to scrub the floor. Despite the doubt in her eyes, Savannah saw herself out.

One last wave, and Barnaby locked the door behind her.

The plug was shaking faster.

Pressing his forehead against the cool glass of the door, Barnaby wondered how long it had been at that speed - if he was finally noticing because he was alone.

With that sort of problem, he didn't particularly want to be alone.

He tried to focus his breathing, something to stay coherent, before heading to the bathroom.

Barnaby knocked on the door and peeked inside.

Gil leaned on the wall across from him, on his phone, unsurprisingly. The moment his smoldering eyes lifted to Barnaby's was the exact moment the plug increased its intensity.

The boy held onto the door for support, whimpering, "You're so mean."

"You don't mean that." Discarding his phone to his pocket, Gil closed the distance between them and guided Barnaby into the room, keeping him secure in his arms.

"Mhm. I do," Barnaby continued to whine, latching onto Gil's coat and burying his face in his chest. "Y-You were trying

144

to make me horny even though I was working. It could've been so bad..."

"But it wasn't, was it?" Gil hummed, combing his fingers through Barnaby's hair. "You got through it so well, without making a perfect mess of yourself. And now, you know what?" He nipped at his ear and breathed hot against it. "You can make as much of a mess as you want."

Barnaby couldn't take the teasing anymore. Eyes shut, he threw his arms around Gil's neck and pulled him into a passionate kiss.

The man was shamelessly receptive, shoving his tongue into Barnaby's mouth, groping every part of him that he could get his hands on, lighting up every nerve.

When two firm hands smacked his ass, Barnaby moaned into the kiss, and the plug pulsed deeper inside of him.

"You have such a nice fucking body," Gil growled, squeezing and kneading him.

"You're just saying that." The comment came without thought. Honest and instinctive.

The next thing Barnaby knew, he was spun around, his back to Gil's chest.

When he blinked, he saw each of their reflections in the mirror above the sink.

"You need proof?"

His mouth hung open as Gil tore his apron away, and he squirmed when he began unbuttoning his shirt immediately after. "*Gil—*"

The man ignored him, his strong body keeping him in place.

Even when Barnaby tried to look away, Gil pressed his chin on his shoulder, blocking him.

His blood ran cold. "No, I—" He swallowed a lump forming in his throat. "Don't...*want to*—"

Gil paused; his fingers frozen on the final button. "You think I'm lying?"

Barnaby turned his head as far away from him as he could. "Not...*lying*..."

He thought Gil was deceiving himself, honestly. That, as much as Barnaby's hormones made him abandon his reservations, Gil's led to him abandoning his standards.

The man waited for an answer but sighed when he must've realized there wouldn't be one. "Why don't you want to look?" His voice was laced with concern.

"*Because*—" Barnaby tried to catch his breath, trying to find some clarity in his mind amid all the stimulation. He hugged himself, not to feel so exposed. "Because I know what I look like, Gil, and I know it's not good—" His voice nearly gave out, cracking, "I'm sorry you have to settle for this, but if I have to watch, I'm going to hate myself more."

Hands resting on his hips, Gil's lips pressed soft against the boy's cheek, sprinkling chaste kisses. "You ever hear that saying," he whispered, "'beauty is in the eye of the beholder'?"

Barnaby scoffed but let himself relax into Gil's chest. He could be vulnerable there and still be safe.

"I don't know what your type is," Gil went on, "but I need you to believe me when I say I've been *dreaming* to get my hands on someone like you."

Barnaby couldn't help but crack a smile at that, if only for how cheesy it sounded.

He hesitated before wiggling around to face Gil, and they looked deep into each other's eyes.

"You're fat, so what?" the man said, "I still think you look great. Yeah, you've got some meat on your bones—" He fondled the boy's belly, earning himself a squeak— "but so do all the prize-winning bucks."

"Hmph, that feels weird!" Despite Barnaby's whining, there was laughter seeping through.

Gil chuckled and nipped at his neck, rubbing his stomach instead. "You're soft—" He wrapped his arms around the boy's waist— "Huggable." He squeezed his sides— "Sturdy. So, I don't have to worry about breaking you..."

Barnaby snorted, elbowing the raven in his stomach. "Okay, okay."

"I think you're *incredibly* sexy." Popping the last button on Barnaby's shirt, Gil carded the cloth through his fingers. Together, they returned their attention to the mirror. "You have every right to *feel* sexy and see yourself that way."

Barnaby considered it for a moment - where the balance between his reality and Gil's compliments lied. Could he fool himself? Could he suspend his disbelief?

He supposed if he didn't like what he saw, he could always close his eyes.

Steeling his breath, Barnaby nodded.

Seconds later, his shirt was on the floor, and Gil was running his fingers over the collar he'd kept hidden underneath. "Were you planning on seeing me tonight?"

"No, sir."

"But you wore it anyway?"

Barnaby sank further against him, pecking his master's jaw. "In case I got lost."

He only had a moment to soak in his radiance before Gil's lips captured his own, kissing him slow and tender.

He felt pretty, and he almost believed he deserved to.

His pants fell to the floor next, followed by his briefs, then Gil's coat and t-shirt.

Gently pushed forward, Barnaby stabilized himself against the sink. He tried looking at Gil over his shoulder for as long as it was comfortable, watching as his plug was pulled out. "O-Oh, God..."

"There's plenty more where that came from." Like a promise, Gil unzipped his pants, and Barnaby shivered at the feeling of a thick cock resting between his cheeks.

He wiggled his hips to signal he was ready.

Gil, however, dedicated a bit of time to teasing his pet, grinding against him.

So close and yet nowhere near close enough.

Just before Barnaby could beg him to continue, he pulled away, searching his bag for lube and a condom.

Not a minute later, Gil's tip prodded his rim. Barnaby tensed. A hand tangled in his hair, tugging gently and persuading him to face his reflection.

"*Watch.*"

Barnaby squirmed out of habit, fully aware he wasn't going anywhere.

Gil eased in, and he tightened his grip on the sink, powerless to do anything but watch his eyes go wide and crossed, mouth slack.

It was the single, most embarrassing thing he'd ever seen, and he couldn't look away.

Gil sheathed himself completely, and Barnaby held his breath. He'd only release it with a moan when the man started thrusting. "Th-Thank you..."

God, he looked pathetic - bent over in a bathroom, wearing nothing but a collar, red from his neck to his ears, his pupils blown, tongue hanging out as he panted for air—

Glancing to the side, he noticed his stomach jiggling, a sight that almost made his skin crawl until it was stopped by Gil's powerful hands, slamming onto his waist.

And then he didn't mind. It was fine to look pathetic, he decided.

At least when he had that Adonis of a man looming over him, taking him, worshiping his body.

"I-I think," Barnaby mewled, bouncing against Gil's hips, "m-maybe we look good together."

Gil didn't need Barnaby to look good.

He didn't even need to open his eyes or stare into his soul.

As divine as his reflection had been in the mirror, he was every bit as heavenly with his sleeping face in his pet's hands.

With all the hard work he'd put into making Barnaby feel good, he deserved to rest.

He looked younger, the boy realized, without his smirk or knitted brows or clenched jaw. As young as he sounded when he laughed, or talked to him about Halloween, or hummed along to the radio in the car.

Barnaby tuned in to the radio Gil had left playing. Evidently, he'd still been feeling a bit possessive, stealing him away to the backseat shortly after turning the car on.

"Just a few minutes," he'd told him.

The boy recognized the pop artist, a song that had been an earworm in his head for a while, not that he minded.

Although, Barnaby had to wonder if that was Gil's taste. Or if he'd enjoy something more rock or *gothic*.

God.

Since it'd been pointed out to him, he wondered if it'd always been so obvious. From his black, untamed hair, to the Edgar Allan Peacoat, black shirt and jeans he wore beneath it.

Even if Gil hadn't been infinitely more good-looking, it wouldn't surprise Barnaby if others thought, based on their styles, they would never match. Barnaby wouldn't have suspected it, either.

Then again, he supposed that was the point of hiding in plain sight.

He remembered the leather bracelets Gil often wore, what likely should have been the tip-off to his alternative fashion sense. Had he worn them that night?

Taking a delicate hold of his hands, Barnaby tugged his sleeves back.

No, not tonight. Go figure.

Nevertheless, he brought one hand to his lips and placed a kiss on each finger, silently apologizing for any disturbance.

Gil's hands were notably bigger than his own - and much more masculine, he'd admit - but Barnaby had to admire them for how gentle they were, how much of his pleasure and sense of safety was derived from them.

He raised Gil's right palm and flattened it, searching for his lifelines or any clues to how he made his touch so magical.

He noticed his wrist again.

Yes, there were lines. But not the sort he was looking for.

He paled, his heart suddenly in his stomach as he examined the opposite hand more closely.

No.

No, no, no.

"Oh, *Gil*..."

How long had those scars been there? Were they recent?

Was there anything Barnaby could have said or done that would have prevented them from being made?

His throat was quickly closing up, tears pricking his eyes.

Barnaby may not have known Gil for very long, but he knew enough to say the man didn't deserve that kind of pain.

Swaddling his master up in his arms, the blond held onto him tight.

"Mph..."

He froze, not expecting Gil to move.

"Shit," the man grumbled, rubbing his eyes, "what time is it?"

Barnaby did his best to swallow his tears, glancing to the clock on the radio. "A-Almost eleven."

Gil sighed, drudging away from his grasp. "Time to get you home."

"Wait—"

The man paused before he could climb into the driver's seat, meeting Barnaby's gaze.

Despite the tinted windows, streetlamps and moonlight seeped into the vehicle, draping him in shadows. They hollowed his cheeks and deepened the bags beneath his tired eyes. He reflected the moon, as if his skin had turned to alabaster. Or maybe he was translucent. A ghost.

There were angel wings etched into his skin.

Barnaby cautioned, "Are you going to be okay?"

Gil quirked a brow at him. "Yeah? It's not that long of a drive, Bee, I'll make it."

That's not what I—

But Barnaby pursed his lips, rolling the unspoken words around on his tongue.

They tasted like an accusation. Blackmail. An *I Know Your Secret*.

If there was anything he'd learned from group therapy, it was not to confront someone about their trauma until they were ready to share it.

Pets lived blissful lives. Maybe part of that bliss came from not being able to tell what their owners were going through.

"Right," Barnaby muttered, attempting a smile, "Sorry. I just worry." A hand ruffled his hair.

"I've noticed." Sliding behind the steering wheel, Gil put the car into drive.

Barnaby watched through the window as the cafe disappeared from view.

The roads to the dorms were short and empty. Less to worry about that hour on a school night.

He abandoned his seat belt in favor of leaning forward, resting his head against Gil's seat. "So," he asked, his gaze lingering on his master's hands, "when will I get to see you again?"

Chapter 11

"Bee?"

"Hm?"

"Are you okay?"

"Y-Yeah...Why?"

"You're getting soft."

Barnaby frowned, reluctantly opening his eyes to see Gil retracting a hand from his cock. The man's brows were knitted together, and Barnaby worried he might think *he* did something wrong.

"I'm sorry," he muttered, fixing the backpack-turned-pillow behind his head. He moved his foot from the seat to Gil's shoulder, still wanting to keep him close. "I got distracted."

Gil's smile was small, but he lowered himself to kiss Barnaby on the cheek. "Wanna talk about it?"

Barnaby shrugged. "Nothing really to talk about. Just..."

I've noticed you don't keep anything in your dorm unless it's for sex.

You don't have posters or decorations or trinkets, yet you have drawers full of toys.

You don't have any trash or old assignments on the floor or stickers on the bumper of your car, but you keep condoms in the glove compartment.

You have so much personality beyond being a playboy. Where is it?

He considered asking why he didn't have any stickers but realizing how ridiculous it would sound without the context to release a can of worms, settled for another shrug instead. "Guess I'm not in the mood."

A flash of disappointment crossed Gil's face, but before Barnaby could confess to his lie, the man muttered, "You could've said so."

"I wanted to be," Barnaby blurted because that much was true. Neither of them could wait to get their hands on one another between all the teasing. Cupping Gil's face, he looked into his eyes. "You did everything right. I promise. I'm just...broken, I guess. We can try again later?"

Gil's eyes narrowed, and he promptly nipped Barnaby's nose. "You are *not* broken—" He dipped his head, burying himself away in the boy's neck. "If you're not in the mood, you're not in the mood. Besides—" He kissed below his ear, "you did plenty for me last night."

Held close, Barnaby nuzzled him, as if he could rub his creeping blush away.

Gil had been completing an assignment while Barnaby, already nude, laid in his nest at his master's feet. Then, came this *hunger*.

Rather than ask for a treat, he slipped under the desk, unzipped Gil's pants, and got to work on his cock. He craved his taste, longing to welcome the creamy liquid down his throat, filling his belly.

The best feeling had been Gil's hand in his hair, abandoning his homework to guide him along. How desperate his master had been, grunting and gripping him tight until Barnaby was faster. Faster. Gagging on his cock. Oh, but it was okay. In fact, it was wonderful. What was even *more* wonderful was the rush of sudden warmth on his tongue while Gil held him in place.

He'd swallowed and swallowed, pure instinct, until his master pulled him off.

He'd barely been given a chance to breathe when the man dragged him up to the desk, ordering him to present himself. He'd bent over, spreading his ass while Gil grabbed lube and a condom.

He might've missed out on what it felt like to be stuffed with cum from both ends, but as soon as his master pounded into him, it brought every sensation of being bred like an animal. His mind went numb. Dumb. All he could do was moan and pant, dizzy with stars swirling around his head, registering so little outside of being owned.

It helped having his leash attached to his collar and Gil's hand attached to the leash.

Claimed and connected, inside and out. A kind of high one could easily get addicted to.

He told himself he could quit at any time.

Barnaby muttered, nose grazing Gil's ear, "And I might have more energy later."

The raven laughed, sprinkling him with more kisses before sitting up. "You might. Or you might need a break."

Barnaby pouted as he was tucked back into his pants, reluctantly pulling himself up while Gil returned to the driver's seat.

"Let's go to my place," the raven offered, "we can order food, watch a movie...and if your mood's any different by the time it's finished—" Gil winked at Barnaby as he joined him in the front— "I'll let you spend the night."

Barnaby giggled, taking Gil's hand and kissing his knuckles. "Did you remember the...?"

Seeing grey eyes widen told him he very much did *not*.

"*Dammit*," Gil grumbled, putting the car in motion, "We might need to make a pit-stop."

Regardless of what mood he was in, neither of them would be getting very far if they didn't restock on lube.

Barnaby rolled his eyes and rested his head against his window, trying to memorize the route they'd taken to the dead-end park. The ground was littered with snack bags and beer cans, and he thought about visiting another day just to clean it up.

Another pop song played on the radio. The default station, Barnaby had come to recognize it as.

"Do you have a playlist?"

Gil didn't answer right away. In fact, it wasn't until Barnaby said his name that he responded, "Nah. Never sat down to put one together."

"What would be on it if you did?"

More silence. A lost cause, maybe. But then— "The 1975, Bleachers, a whole lot of Stroke 9 and Marianas Trench…Billy Joel, maybe."

Barnaby nearly jumped out of his seat, ready to latch onto anything he could connect with. "I *love* Billy Joel!"

"Yeah?" That seemed to bring the lift back to Gil's voice— "What's your favorite song by him? Yes, there is a wrong answer."

The boy raised a skeptical brow. "What's the wrong answer?"

"*Piano Man*? Does not count."

"Oh my gosh," Barnaby huffed, crossing his arms. "Well, it's not…it's *Vienna*."

"Alright, that's a good one."

"What about yours?"

"Guess."

"*Piano Man*?"

"Yes. Except it's not."

Though he could say he was a fan of the artist, it didn't take Barnaby long to realize he could only name so many songs, each of which was a miss from Gil. Eventually, he dug out his phone, searching and reading off titles.

Gil quickly noticed, and it was deemed "cheating", bringing an end to the guessing game.

Their pit-stop wasn't far off from campus. At a glance, Barnaby had to wonder what they were doing at a Dental Office, but as they pulled into the parking lot and rounded the white-walled building, he spotted another entrance - a door with an 18+ sticker on it and a neon sign that read, *XXXtra*.

"Did you wanna look inside?" Gil asked, stopping the car.

Barnaby laughed, not that anything was particularly funny - but the fact that he was twenty years old, no longer a virgin, and still too nervous to willingly go into a sex shop? Yeah, that was laughable. "I'll pass." He fidgeted with his seat belt, ensuring it wouldn't go anywhere— "I think we, uhm, have everything else we need at home."

Gil shrugged, scoffed, and opened the door to step out. "Suit yourself."

Barnaby was perfectly content to stay right where he was, going through his phone in the time Gil was away.

It'd barely been a minute when he received a text from the man:

You're missing out.

Attached was a picture of a giant teddy bear. Bound in a sex-swing.

Barnaby grinned to himself and shook his head.

That's animal cruelty.

He bit his lip, catching a glimpse of their previous messages and deciding to revisit them.

I was thinking...

About what?

Would you ever make me wear a vibrator to class?

I wouldn't necessarily MAKE you but

Is that something you'd want to try?

I don't know...

You don't know. But you've thought about sitting in class with a vibrator inside you. You've thought about what might happen if I made you.

Would anyone notice?

Would they call you out or would they watch you fall apart, studying you like the class pet?

I...

What if your professor found out?

Would he fail you or would he make you show him after class?

Hmph.

I know what I would pick.

A familiar scenario in a different setting. Gil in a nice button-up and tie, and Barnaby, bent over his desk in an empty classroom, presenting himself and the man's plug of choice.

It was like he could already feel Gil tracing a ruler up the backs of his thighs, making his hairs stand on end.

He couldn't help but squirm.

He pocketed his phone, tilted his head back, and closed his eyes.

He wanted to be good. If it meant being the perfect pet, he was determined to get himself in the mood again.

He slipped a hand between his legs and let out a rattled sigh.

He tried to focus on how happy Gil would be when he found him. *I don't need a break*, Barnaby would tell him, *I need you. See? I'm hard again. Just from reading our texts. Only you'd be able to do that to me, sir. Please, Master, I need you to play with me.*

He wouldn't get distracted, either. He'd have Billy Joel playing in the back of his mind to keep him on track.

The bulge in his pants grew, and Barnaby's breath hitched as he traced the outline over and over. His legs spread so it didn't feel so tight.

He was as ready as he had been when Gil first came to pick him up.

The driverside door clicked open, and Barnaby rested his hand on his leg.

"I got a new flavor for you."

The boy blinked to find Gil handing him a small, plastic bag. Inside, he discovered, were two bottles of lube: classic strawberry and the new salted caramel. "Thank you."

He looked to Gil with a smile, waiting for him to notice his change. However, when the man buckled in and locked his eyes on him, his lips formed a straight line.

"Did you touch yourself?"

His tone rocked something inside of him, and Barnaby couldn't tell if he was genuinely shaking or if the car's engine was making him vibrate. "O-Only a little," he admitted, "But not— I didn't touch it all the way. I just rubbed myself through my pants, I—"

"But you *did* touch yourself?"

Barnaby fumbled with his words. Suddenly, he didn't feel like he had anything to be proud of anymore. "I'm sorry."

Gil sighed, tapping the steering wheel for a moment—
"You broke a rule."

"I'm *sorry*, Gil, I—"

"You know what I have to do, don't you?"

Barnaby pursed his lips and faced the window once again
to hide his quivering chin. In his reflection of the side mirror,
he could see how easily he had given himself away. His face
was deep red, and his eyes were glazed over, pupils wide.

He never considered what a punishment from Gil might
be.

The radio played, but Barnaby still felt crushed by the
weight of an awkward silence between them.

He bit his nails. "Is it gonna hurt?"

He couldn't look at Gil, and he curled in on himself more
when a hand touched his knee.

"You can tell me after I've spanked you."

Barnaby had never been spanked - not as a child and
certainly not into adulthood.

He could, however, remember his mother making
threats. He remembered being afraid that it would hurt.

But how much would it hurt as an adult, he wondered, if
it was such a popular theme on porn websites?

He sucked in his breath and stripped down to his collar,
knowing he would soon find out. "Where do you want me?"

"Right across my knee." Gil gestured, and Barnaby
approached, head down.

Before he could sit, he was grabbed, repositioned, and laying on his stomach across the raven's lap.

"I guess now would be a good time to go over safewords," Gil sighed, already rubbing Barnaby's bottom with newly revealed leather gloves, "If you need me to slow down, say Yellow, and if it feels like it's too much, say Red. If you can keep going after that, the word is Green. Understood?"

Barnaby shuddered, raising his hips higher, rather enjoying the sensation of leather against his rump. "Yes, sir."

"I'm going to spank you ten times, and you're going to count with me. If you lose track, we start over. Tell me you understand."

"I understand, sir."

He bristled as the first strike was delivered. A test. More of a tap than anything. "One—" Two more, of similar intensity. "Two. Three—"

Barnaby gasped as the proceeding strike made him tingle from head to toe. "F-Four—"

"Guess I do need to use a stronger hand," Gil muttered, massaging the sensitive skin, "You have a lot of meat back here."

"Y-Yes, sir— *Five!*" Barnaby whimpered, his thighs beginning to tremble. He could sense his flesh prickling. Whether or not he'd call it *painful*, he couldn't say for sure.

Probably, his face was just as red as his ass.

"You're doing well so far."

Two more followed in rapid procession, and Barnaby yelped, struggling not to jump out of Gil's lap from how much it stung. "Y-Yellow!"

"I hear you."

A gloved hand swept through his hair, and the boy sighed with relief as more attention was dedicated to massaging his ass.

"Not used to this, are you?" Gil purred, "You've been such a good boy for me up until now."

"I-I didn't mean to be bad," Barnaby insisted, "I, well, I wanted to get myself ready for you. I wasn't thinking that I'd be...breaking a rule..." He dared to look at the man over his shoulder— "I'm sorry, sir."

A gentle smile made its way to Gil's lips, and he patted his pet's bottom. "It's okay, fawn. At least we can say this is the first and last time you're punished. Consider it a learning experience."

He wasn't getting away with it.

Emitting a huff, Barnaby lifted Gil's shirt to kiss his side and traced patterns absently along his thigh. Just until the sting in his ass subsided. Eventually, he muttered, "Green."

He winced from a pinch to his rear.

"Do you remember your number?"

"Six?"

Another, harder pinch.

"S-Seven?!"

"Good boy."

The last three spanks were quick, but Gil did not hold back. He left Barnaby with his face buried in the mattress, muffling whimpers that continued to spill out with the aftershock. His ass was *throbbing*.

"Learned your lesson?" Gil asked. His gloves disappeared, and he used a bare touch to work a soothing cream into Barnaby's rump.

The boy sniveled, "Mhm."

"Am I gonna find you touching yourself any time soon?"

"Nu-uh."

Chapter 12

Someone (probably his mom) had warned Barnaby a long time ago that part of how people developed drinking habits was by convincing themselves that alcohol tastes good. That, apparently, is achieved through repetition. You have one sip, then another to get used to it, then another and another—

And soon, you're too drunk to forget it tastes bad.

Barnaby wasn't sure his punishment actually felt *bad*.

Sure, it stung, and sure, it was tough to sit afterward, but he'd still had a boner by the end of it.

He still liked having his butt played with.

It all made him feel very tingly, and he liked that, maybe.

But he knew if he wanted to be positive, he'd have to try again.

He'd have to break another rule.

"...two, one! What a good little fawn."

Gil snatched the gummy bear from Barnaby's nose, and the boy let himself rest on his knees. Of all the tricks his master wanted him to perform, that balancing act was the one to require the most practice. At least he wasn't falling on his ass anymore.

His hair was ruffled, and two treats were held to his mouth.

Locking eyes with Gil, Barnaby licked them up from his hand—

And promptly spat them right back in his face.

Rule #4, wasn't it? Don't be a brat.

The response was immediate. Gil grabbed him by the chin, and with one blink, his eyes had turned to daggers. "There better have been a good reason for that."

Of course, there wasn't. A Good Reason wouldn't get him punished.

So, rather than answer, Barnaby tilted his head, nipping at Gil's hand.

"Hey!"

His chin was released, but not a second later, Gil's fingers were hooked in his hair, locking him in place.

"You were behaving so well a minute ago, what's gotten into you?" The man almost sounded sympathetic.

Barnaby, however, wasn't looking for sympathy. He shrugged, and though he couldn't move his head, let his gaze drift away from Gil, humming a tune.

"If you keep it up," the raven warned, "you're going to find yourself punished."

Barnaby resisted the urge to smile. Instead, he rolled his eyes as dramatically as he could.

Then, came two magical words: "That's it."

Pulled by his hair, Gil ordered him across his knee.

Barnaby sprung into position, his ass raised high. The tail of his plug stood straight at attention.

"*Now* you listen to me?" Gil muttered, rubbing Barnaby's bottom.

The blond nodded swiftly and swayed his hips. His cock was already twitching with interest.

Smack.

"I thought you'd learned your lesson after yesterday."

Barnaby bit his lip to suppress a whimper. Gil gave him just enough time to recover and say, "You thought wrong, I guess."

Another smack. A chill racked Barnaby's spine, and he was sure there were goosebumps all over his ass. One more, and it started to sting. A moan was torn from his throat.

It was official. Barnaby Hirsch *liked* being punished.

"You're not counting," Gil growled.

"I don't want to."

Smack - right at the back of his thigh. Barnaby couldn't help but jump, yelping.

"Make it twenty and pray I don't forget."

"Yes, sir."

He shook his ass just as Gil delivered another strike. Another moan fell from his lips.

"If I didn't know any better," Gil muttered, grabbing a cheek and digging his nails in, "I'd say you were enjoying this."

Barnaby giggled, looking over his shoulder at the man. "Maybe," he said, grinding his cock against his leg, "you don't know better."

Gil raised a brow, but just as Barnaby began to suspect he'd turned the tables, the raven spanked him again and again without reprieve.

Barnaby writhed and gasped, squealing and swearing, but *holy shit,* he loved each one more than the last.

"You're not supposed to like your punishment."

One final blow, and Barnaby was dumped to the bed, scrambling to lay on his stomach while Gil dug through the nightstand.

"What're you doing?"

"You'll never learn that behavior isn't acceptable if you see your punishment as something to look forward to."

Gil faced him, and Barnaby curled in on himself, heart picking up speed.

In his grasp, the raven held a fistful of rope and what appeared to be handcuffs.

"Can I—" Like whiplash, Barnaby's resolve was fading fast— "Can I still use my safewords?"

Gil nodded, though he didn't seem to waver from whatever he had in mind. He spoke like it wasn't any concern, "Put your hands behind your back."

Barnaby obeyed, and the next thing he knew, his wrists were bound by velcroed straps. "I'm sorry, sir, I didn't—"

"Quiet, Barnaby."

The man sat him up, and Barnaby gritted his teeth against the soreness pulsing from his bottom. A shame he couldn't say he didn't ask for it.

His ankles were bound next, one to each of the lower legs of the bedframe. Elaborate ropework ensured Barnaby was comfortable but secured.

He tried for a submissive smile when Gil lifted his head, wanting at least to appear grateful for being given any attention at all.

Gil merely stared, sighing, "This isn't going to be any more fun for me than it is for you."

Before Barnaby really had a chance to question him or brace himself, a rubber ring was slipped down the shaft of his cock. It had a peculiar attachment that, when pressed by Gil, made it vibrate incessantly.

Oh.

Oooh, God.

"*Master—*"

The man slid right up beside him, kissing his cheek, his neck; he snuck a hand between the boy's legs, grazing his thigh, and his whole body spasmed.

There was nothing he could do.

"What happened to—" Barnaby whimpered, already wiggling like a captive animal to free himself, "I-It's not supposed to feel good...?"

"This?"

No matter how the boy tried to tilt his head, Gil kept his face away from sight. Though, pressed against his neck, he could sense the reason: a smirk, trying to be hidden.

"*This* isn't your punishment."

Barnaby's mouth abruptly ran dry, and worries were pushed back in his mind while he did his best to accept the unexpected gift of pleasure. Instinct, however, had other opinions. Despite his twitching and trembling, Barnaby countered with a "thank you" each time.

"Thank you" *for touching me there.*

"Thank you" *for marking me, sir.*

"Thank you" *for being so merciful.*

It wasn't long until Barnaby became putty in Gil's hands.

He didn't know exactly how much time had passed; he didn't know much of anything at all. He knew how to say, "thank you", and he knew that he felt good.

His twitching turned to throbbing, and his cock pulsed along with the vibrations.

He knew it wasn't enough to satisfy him without Gil's touch, which seemed to be caressing him everywhere but where he needed it most.

And he was nearing his limit.

All it took was fingertips grazing right across his navel to get Barnaby's hips to buck forward.

"*Please—*" he finally remembered to say, hands itching behind his back, "Please, Master, I'm so close."

Gil's hand dipped further, making a single stroke along his shaft. His fingers circled the head of his cock -

And then he squeezed— "I don't think so."

He held on, and it was as if all the blood, along with the vibrations from the cock ring, was retreating from Barnaby's dick. Nevermind a boner, he swore he felt his literal bones vibrating as a result. And that wasn't very pleasant.

Barnaby whined, his mind too clouded with lust to understand what was happening. "But...But I'm close!"

"Are you?" Gil snickered, "Because it doesn't seem like it to me."

He squeezed and squeezed, and soon enough, Barnaby was drawn away from the edge. Like he'd been reset.

Gil finally let go, and the boy stared, dazed and confused.

Without a moment to spare, he was pumping him again, working him back to his limit.

"Why did you..." Barnaby panted, "What's—?"

Was he ever actually close to begin with?

Gil chuckled as he shifted to sit behind Barnaby, his free hand scooping lower to cradle his balls. One slight press against the ring, and the boy's hips jolted forward, pre-cum leaking out of his tip.

He was close. He was *definitely* close.

But then Gil's strokes stopped, and once again, he was squeezing around the head, taking that feeling away.

Barnaby groaned. *"That's not—!"* Cheated! And his body knew it. He tugged against his restraints, and his sac was abandoned for a sturdy arm around his waist, keeping him in place. "Mah! *Mah!*"

They froze simultaneously - Gil's hold slackened a bit while Barnaby's surprise in himself left him stunned.

"Did you just...*bleat*?"

He didn't know what it was, only that it came out on its own. The most pathetic sound he'd ever made, probably, and even when given the chance to redeem himself, it was the only sound he could produce, "Mah..."

The raven scoffed, "Poor little fawn. I bet this isn't any fun, hm?" Strengthening his hold, he teased Barnaby's tip. "That's the point of a punishment," he hissed, "and if you think you can disrespect me and get away with it, you've got another fucking thing coming."

He squeezed to the point it was almost painful. Barnaby nearly shouted, "Red."

Before he could, Gil, once again, reverted to jerking him off. The cycle continued.

He hadn't meant to disrespect him. He'd meant to be a brat. To be spanked for it and to feel good.

Even though Gil's fingers worked expertly along his shaft, made even more sensitive by the buzzing cock ring, it no longer felt *good*. It didn't feel deserved.

Had Gil not been so skilled with his hand, it may have been impossible to near the edge that third time. Inevitably, though, Barnaby's legs were restless with tremors, and he whimpered at the returning heat in his core.

He mumbled to Gil as a warning, "I'm close."

He shut his eyes, holding his breath and counting down from ten while the raven's hand clamped around his cock.

Seconds later, Gil released him entirely. He rose up, removed the ring from Barnaby's cock, and busied himself with the ropes around his ankles.

Before he could move on to his wrists, Gil paused, looked into his pet's eyes, and asked, "Promise not to touch yourself?"

The boy gave a solemn nod. "I promise."

Soon, he was all untied, and everything that was used was returned to the nightstand.

While Barnaby rubbed his ankles, Gil stepped away to the fridge. He'd return with a water bottle and a carton of strawberries. The bottle was handed directly to Barnaby, and the carton was left open between them.

The boy glanced back and forth between the container and his master. "M-May I?"

"Of course," Gil said, sitting beside him, "take as many as you want."

Eyes locked on the man, Barnaby plucked a strawberry with the greatest caution, popping it in his mouth before it could be slapped out of his hand. Or something.

Gil simply brushed Barnaby's hair away from his face.

"Can you explain punishments to me?" Barnaby blurted, inching closer, "I-I'm not really sure I understand it. Are you mad at me?"

The man sighed, and Barnaby relaxed a bit as an arm was wrapped around him. "No, I'm not *mad* at you, but I didn't give you those rules to challenge you. I gave them, basically, to set up my own limits. For instance, if you wanted to be a bratty kind of pet, or if you didn't want to wear a collar and you wanted to see other people...That's fine. But then our dynamic would be different. I probably wouldn't call you my pet."

Putting a hand over Gil's heart, Barnaby gripped his shirt. "And the pet you want...doesn't disrespect you."

"Exactly."

"Do you like punishing me?"

Gil frowned, and he shook his head. "I'd much rather be rewarding you. Giving you treats—" He took a strawberry, held it to Barnaby's lips, and the boy ate eagerly from his hand. No spit-takes. "Making you happy—"

Scratching behind his ear, Barnaby hummed his approval.

"Isn't that what you want?"

"I do," Barnaby agreed, then shrugged. "I guess I just thought that...I could only be spanked if I was being punished. Or that it was like...uh, a game? I don't know. But I didn't mean to make you upset. I-I really do respect you. I'm sorry."

Gil's lips curled hesitantly, and he messed up Barnaby's hair, nails dragging across his scalp. "I could've been clearer from the beginning. That's on me."

Maybe so, but Barnaby had no intention of holding it against him. Instead, he snatched another strawberry and straddled his lap, not so much caring if he crushed him with his weight. "Well...I could've not been a brat. And then we wouldn't be here."

"That's true," Gil laughed, falling to the mattress and taking his pet with him, "Although, I think, *physically,* we'd still be here."

Barnaby beamed, kissing his chin and tracing patterns across his chest. "Reward or punishment...Anything to keep me in bed, hm?"

"Are you complaining?"

"No, sir."

As long as he was wanted somewhere.

Chapter 13

Mornings with Gil Connolly typically went like this:

First, well, Gil's alarm would go off, and Barnaby would wake up with the sinking realization that he'd fallen asleep on top of him *again*. He'd be apologizing before the man had even opened his eyes.

"It's fine," Gil would say. Or, "Don't worry about it. How'd you sleep?"

So far, Barnaby had only slept soundly with him.

They'd try to move around just to greet one another with the other's Morning Wood. Normally, they'd laugh it off and hurry out of bed. But if Barnaby was lucky, Gil would pull him close, kiss him tiredly and jerk him off under the covers.

That particular morning, Barnaby was lucky.

Next, Gil would get up and head to the bathroom connecting his dorm to another. He'd try to be quick, to spare Barnaby from having to run into his next door roommate, but it'd happened more often than not that the boy would have company while brushing his teeth with Gil's spare toothbrush - or that he'd have to shout, "Occupied!", to an opening door while on the toilet.

That morning, he noticed something bright and orange poking out of the bathroom wastebin. A prescription bottle.

Upon closer inspection, he realized that despite being empty, the label was still intact: "Connolly, Gilbert. Fluoxetine. Take one capsule every morning."

So, Gil is short for Gilbert.

Barnaby sighed, burying it deeper in the bin.

Returning to Gil's dorm, he'd find an outfit laid out on the bed, usually lounge pants and a hoodie. Barnaby, however, had already sported Gil's hoodie the day before. Although, he wouldn't have been opposed to throwing it on again, he discovered Gil was kind enough to offer him something new and camo-print.

"Isn't this what you wore for Halloween?"

The raven, rolling the sleeves of his grey, tattered flannel, flashed him a grin. "Might be."

Barnaby attempted a smirk, though his gaze was promptly drawn to Gil's wrists. He almost got nervous for him, leaving them exposed, until the man grabbed a few bracelets from his nightstand and strategically slid them on.

He'd wait until Barnaby was all dressed to ask him, "Ready to go?"

By the time they'd step outside, Barnaby's stomach would be rumbling. They'd find the nearest building with a coffee counter, order some bagels and a drink, and be on their way. Barnaby would ramble about the Secret Life of American Agriculture or pass on some stupid story about Seth between sips of tea, and Gil would be in control of the bagels, breaking off small pieces and passing them off to the boy at his leisure.

Barnaby would have to remind himself not to eat directly from his master's hand in public.

So far, Gil had insisted on walking Barnaby to his building first. Whether he actually had class as early as Barnaby did— the boy wasn't sure. But, then again, it was a routine he wasn't exactly eager to change.

A head taller on the steps of his building, Barnaby paused to face Gil. "When would you like your shirt back?"

"What shirt? You're completely topless."

"*Gil.*"

The man smiled wide, squinting up at him against the rising sun, and shrugged. "By Thanksgiving at least? Or don't give it back at all. Either way, it's fine."

Barnaby scoffed, grabbing the straps of his backpack, and tapping his foot against Gil's leg. "Does that mean you're not in a rush to see me again?"

"Absolutely not. See me with or without a shirt. I don't mind."

Of course, he wouldn't.

Barnaby felt himself leaning forward, his lips already puckering. It'd be nice, he thought, to kiss Gil goodbye. He'd almost become accustomed to it.

But he never made contact. Instead, Barnaby rocked back on his heels.

They'd done it before, but never in front of anyone. Never in view of anyone who might have anything to assume. And more and more people were passing them on the steps.

His lips pursed, and Barnaby glanced to the door. "I should probably let you go," he told Gil. "Can I text you later?"

"You better," the man replied, handing him the last complete bagel, "unless you want to be punished for ignoring me?"

"*What*? I—" Barnaby had to go to class, and, *perfect*, his face was probably blushing— "*Never*."

"Good."

An exchange of half-hearted waves replaced the Kiss That Should've Been, and Barnaby turned to enter the building, replacing his security from Gil with security by cellphone.

A text from Seth waited for him:

> Assuming you're not dead in a dumpster, can you do me a BIG favor?

Barnaby grimaced, realizing he hadn't spoken to his roommate in over twenty-four hours.

> Not dead yet. What's up?

> Damn. Oh well.

> Can you go to the room and grab the pizza from the fridge? Apparently, they want me in Abbott Hall later, not Salten.

181

> They can do that?

They can do anything they want so long as they're paying me.

So can you or no?

> I have stats...

After stats

> I guess

Thanks babe ;*

And so, an hour later, after learning about statistics that did not directly affect the farming industry, Barnaby hopped a shuttle to their dorm, grabbed a bagged Who-Knew-How-Old pizza from the refrigerator along with his own laptop, and set out for Abbott Hall.

When he arrived, he found Seth at the reception desk, his feet up on the table. He wasn't alone.

Across from him, perched on the back of the lobby sofa, was a lanky young man in a blue denim jacket, holding a cup of ramen.

Both looked to Barnaby as he approached.

"If it isn't the Pizza Man," Seth exclaimed, "Give it here."

Resisting the urge to make a face of distaste, Barnaby crossed over and placed the paper bag on Seth's desk. "Do I get a tip?"

"Oh. Yeah—" Seth reached into his pocket like he might pull out some spare change. Only to shoot Barnaby with a finger-gun instead— "Here's a tip: learn how to wear concealer."

Barnaby realized Seth was pointing to his neck.

Gritting his teeth, he fixed the collar of his jacket in hopes of hiding most of Gil's hickeys.

Seth exaggerated a sigh, turning his attention to the other boy in front of him. "Jason, this is my roommate, Disaster."

There was a quick slurping of noodles before the cup was placed on the desk, and a hand jutted out to Barnaby. "How's it going, Disaster? You can call me Loser. Most people do."

One look was all it took for Barnaby to recognize him, despite his face being dimmer than he remembered. "I know you," he blurted, shaking his hand, "You were Lamp Man, weren't you?"

Somehow, Jason (a.k.a Loser, a.k.a Lamp Man) managed to light up all the same. "Or call me that. Whatever works for you, Deer Dude."

"Wait, wait, wait," Seth interjected, chomping into cold pizza, "you nerds know each other?"

Barnaby could only open his mouth while Jason readily explained, "We met at the Zombie Break. He was on my team."

Remembered as a teammate? Barnaby might've blushed.

"Is he going to—?" Jason started, then trailed off as if to erase his own words the instant he locked eyes with Seth.

Seth shrugged, wiping his hands on his pants. "I didn't ask yet—" Perhaps obliged, he focused on Barnaby— "Asking now: do you wanna go bowling tomorrow night?"

Barnaby hadn't heard that question since high school. "Uhm—" Had he not been familiar with Jason, he likely would've reverted to an old excuse: "*You know I'm not very coordinated*", or "*I can't throw to save my life*." But then, there was the chance he wouldn't have a say. What if Gil wanted him for the night? Whatever the scenario— "I have to check my work schedule. I might be on."

"So, go to work 'til, what? *Nine*? We'll go after."

Barnaby shifted on his feet, tugging on the ends of his sleeves. "Who else is going?"

"You—"

The decision was already made for him. *Great*.

"—Me, Jason, Jason's girl, and two of our other friends."

"Diana," Jason chimed in, "You met her."

Had he not, Barnaby probably would've made any excuse to miss out right then and there.

He used to feel safe with Seth; in high school, they shared the same social presence: none. Then college happened, Seth joined every kind of geek squad, and Barnaby, never attuned to video games or busty anime women, joined those community gardens that, with all due respect, lacked a sense of community.

Sometimes, he wasn't so sure he wanted to belong to a community, though. The more people he knew, the more people he tended to burden.

He already wanted to apologize to Jason for trespassing into their circle, but before Barnaby could say anything at all, it was Seth who reiterated, "You're going."

Barnaby didn't protest - not with Jason there, and not with time running out before his next class. Instead, he swallowed his nerves, fidgeted with the straps of his backpack, and told them he'd let them know if or when he was working.

Seth let him go without any further hassle, and Barnaby's phone stayed in his pocket until he reached his second desk of the day. When he finally checked it, he noticed he'd missed a text from Gil.

:(

What's wrong??

You walked by my class earlier and I waved at you but you didn't wave back

Omg I didn't know. Where?

Outside of Reed Hall

I'm so sorry. I wasn't
really paying attention.

It's fine, lol. You looked
pretty focused.
Everything okay?

Yeah! Just some stuff on
my mind.

Quick subject change—

Wasn't it kind of chilly to
have class outside?

It was for Psychology. Studying human social behaviors.
Of course, it was.

At least it gave Barnaby's imagination something to play
with.

The professor began a lecture on geology, while Gil's
major remained stuck in his head like a mystery. Was he
going for a psychology degree? Barnaby imagined he'd make
a good therapist. Or maybe even something like Criminal
Justice, lending a hand in forensics or profiling.

Of course, it didn't take long for Barnaby to imagine
himself handcuffed to a table while Gil loomed over him,
wearing a tight suit—

He shifted to cross his legs, and when he was able to sneak it, texted back, hopeful:

> You never actually told me your major.

It wouldn't be until later that night, when both Barnaby and Seth were settled into their dorm with Chinese food, that Barnaby would see a response:

> English.

"That's underwhelming."

"What is?" Seth asked, apparently with attention to spare away from his PC game.

"Gil," Barnaby sighed, swallowing another spoonful of fried rice, "I thought he'd be into something...*cool.* I don't know. English Major just seems so...*meh.*"

Seth snorted. "Wow, Barnaby. Didn't think you of all people would be so anti-Liberal Arts."

"I'm not!" the blond sputtered, "I just...thought Gil would be a little...*more.*"

"You're valid. I'd turn down good dick too if the guy said he wanted to be a writer."

Barnaby chucked a pillow at his head, and the brunet yelped.

Writer. Now, there was nothing wrong with that. Barnaby wrote a few short stories of his own back in high school. He was sure with all of Gil's experiences, the man would have far more interesting stories to tell.

The problem though, and why it didn't immediately come to Barnaby's mind, was that Gil had nothing to show for it. He never gave any indication that the homework he was supposedly typing up was part of some creative piece, he never tried showing off, and he never talked about ideas or other books. Come to think of it, for all the time Barnaby was spending in his dorm, the only books he remembered seeing were textbooks.

He wanted to ask about it, but before he could come up with a text, flinched from his pillow landing back in his lap.

"*Are* you working tomorrow?"

Shit. Barnaby still hadn't checked yet. He referred to the calendar on his phone and - "*Wait*. Is next week really Thanksgiving Break?"

"Barnaby, focus—"

He'd genuinely lost track of the dates, but there it was, a reminder set for Tuesday night: *Freedom*. Marked all the way to the following Tuesday.

And, in fact, he was working. All afternoon the next day, Sunday night, and Monday night.

Barnaby sighed, rubbing his temple as he told Seth what he wanted to know. He didn't say any more than that though, looking right back to his texts with Gil. If he didn't stop by the cafe again, if Barnaby didn't spend the night with him Saturday— he wouldn't see him for over a week.

He started biting his nails, his fried rice forgotten.

No doubt, Seth would give him shit if he found out he backed out of bowling for his, as far as his roommate was concerned, "fuckbuddy."

"Can I invite Gil?"

He glanced over to find Seth's eyes dramatically widen. "*Pardon?*"

Abort. Abort.

Barnaby's mouth didn't get the message fast enough. "I mean— We don't just have sex. We hang out, too. It's gonna be you and your friends anyway, so...can I bring Gil?"

Seth's lips moved without sound before he resigned, shaking his head, taking off his glasses, and rubbing his forehead. "I don't care, Barnaby."

Well, it wasn't a "*no*", and he must've been reasonable if Seth wasn't arguing. "Jason and Diana already know him. We were all in that team together—"

"While I went alone to that party?"

Barnaby's heart plummeted with his confidence. "That wasn't—" he stammered, "I didn't— I'm sorry, that shouldn't have—"

"I know," Seth huffed, lifting his head despite his shoulders remaining slumped. "I'm being petty. Wasn't anyone's job to watch over me."

Barnaby frowned. Even if Seth was right, it wouldn't have been fair for him to miss out on a chance to have fun just because no one else would join him. If Barnaby was a better friend, he would've insisted that Seth came along that night, to be sure he was safe.

At least he had the present to be a better friend and make up for it. Whether Seth liked it or not.

He moved his fried rice aside and approached the other's bed.

The brunet blinked. "What're you doing?"

"C'mere..."

"Oh— Barnaby— *Don't—*"

It was too late. Barnaby shut Seth's laptop, ignored his protests, and stubbornly wrapped his arms around Seth, holding him tight. He was No Gil - shorter, non-reciprocative, and incredibly tense - but he was warm.

"I hate this," Seth grumbled, "I hate you. You're so gay."

A smile settled on Barnaby's lips, and he nuzzled closer. "This isn't even the gayest thing I've done today."

Seth gagged audibly, a prompt, "Shut up. I don't want to hear it", and Barnaby couldn't suppress his laughter.

Luckily for Seth, he had no intention of saying more. He simply closed his eyes, hummed a little made-up tune, and enjoyed his buddy's company.

It wasn't long after that Seth finally eased into his grip. Maybe, *just maybe*, some part of him was enjoying it too.

He tried again before they fell asleep.

"So, is it okay if I invite Gil?"

"I said I don't care. Unless he starts pulling any of that *I'm So Sexy and Dominant* Shit in public, *then* I'm calling the police."

"He won't!"

"Bet?"

For once, texting Gil, Barnaby was blushing without Gil being the cause of it.

He'd get his response in the morning:

Give me the details.

And indeed, details were given. Barnaby would go to work from noon to five o' clock. Then, he'd go back to the dorm and swap his uniform for a long-sleeve polo to hide his collar under. Eventually, Seth would come to get him, and at seven o' clock, everyone would meet at The Dessert Bowl, a bowling alley-ice cream parlor combo-spot.

Stepping through the door was like stepping into another era. The floor had a checkerboard pattern, barstools and chairs were accented with pastel blue, vinyl cushions, and hints of chrome glistened under neon lights. The staff were dressed like Old School Milk Men and Women, the shoe rental was adjacent to the actual ice cream serving station, and— was that a Jukebox blasting Jackson 5?

Seth grabbed his arm and pulled him toward the white, pink, and brown painted bowling lanes.

Diana, dressed for the occasion in a yellow poodle skirt, was waving them over. "We already got our lane!" she exclaimed, greeting them with hugs. "We were thinking we'd probably skip the bumpers, though. Is that okay?"

Before Barnaby could entertain the thought that bumpers might be nice, Seth laid the law down, "No bumpers. We bowl like men."

Diana puffed her cheeks, narrowed her eyes, and raised her fists as if to Square Up before turning to the men behind her.

Three of them, one of whom Barnaby recognized to be Jason, crowded the sign-in tablet.

"It's only five letters..."

"We don't have all night!"

"I'm putting it for you—"

Diana clapped her hands to get their attention, and the three perked up to welcome them into the group. Jason let Barnaby in front of him so he could pick his own nickname for the board, and someone with a green streak through his blond hair, that he hadn't met before, grabbed onto Seth and decided, "Kaplan, you're on my team."

When Barnaby looked up at their screen, he saw that the scoreboard read: LilD, JayZ, Memes, Bitch, BarnE, and Last.

He wasn't sure whether he should've been embarrassed for being the Unfunny One or not.

"Alright," Jason (or JayZ, apparently) said as he picked out his bowling ball, "Is everyone ready?"

"Uhm—" And that was when Barnaby remembered to look around.

Gil hadn't shown up yet.

Since less attention was on Diana, Barnaby shuffled over to her. "Sorry, uhm— Gil's coming. He's just not here yet."

"Oh—" And for a moment, she simply stared while Barnaby grimaced, knowing he'd thrown a wrench in her plans. "Well...Okay! We can get food first! Guys—" The conversation was opened to the rest of the group, "We're still waiting on one more. Anyone want ice cream?"

Seth and Green Streak shared an annoyed glance, but it didn't take much consideration for Jason and his Red Hoodied friend to agree.

Wandering to the serving station/shoe rental, Jason introduced the two of them (*"Barnaby, Mell. Mell, Barnaby."*). To make up for a weak handshake, Barnaby went right into complimenting the patches on Mell's hoodie since *whoa boy,* there were a lot, from conspiracy references to pride flags. He was very humble and easy to talk to, just like Jason and Diana, and Barnaby had to remember they were *Seth's* friends.

It made him question how his roommate acted around everyone else away from him.

At the serving station, Jason and Mell got cookie dough ice cream, Diana ordered strawberry, and Barnaby was barely paying enough attention to tell the cashier, "Rocky Road", while checking his phone for texts from Gil.

He traded in his shoes, nearly doubling over after he'd changed them. His skin was getting clammy, and he started to worry the night would turn out as bad as he expected it would.

Until they returned to their lane.

Lo and behold, there was Gil, clad in a leather jacket and visibly uncomfortable at the edge of his seat across from Seth and his green-streaked friend. He looked like he needed someone beside him.

As his pet, Barnaby was more than happy to fill that space.

"You made it!" he chimed, bounding over to the raven.

Gil looked to him with a start, eyes wide before a soft smile settled on his face. "Did you think I wouldn't?"

Barnaby bit his lip and gave a hesitant shrug. Between the possibility of an emergency, things he wasn't telling him, or being stood up, he wasn't sure what to think.

Sensing the eyes of those around them certainly didn't clear his judgment, either.

"Gil!" Diana joined Barnaby and squeezed the man's shoulder.

Barnaby noticed Gil's lips pull tight as he glanced down at her hand.

"It's good to see you again."

"Yeah," he muttered, "you too."

Jason and Mell walked up to shake Gil's hand next, but conversation didn't come as naturally between them as it had for Barnaby. At least, Gil didn't seem willing to continue it.

Jason must have picked up on it too, quick to eat his ice cream and turn his attention to the group as a whole - "If that's everyone, are we ready to start?"

"Hold on," Seth spoke up, "how're we splitting teams? We have an extra person."

"It's fine," Gil spouted, raising a hand in defense, "I'm not playing. I'm just here to watch."

Barnaby was ready to offer up his position. Aside from his willingness to take any excuse not to throw, it was his fault Gil had to go through the trouble of joining them in the first place.

Then, Diana suggested, "Why don't you switch off with one of us? Say we swapped. I could go one round, and you could go the next."

Good enough for Barnaby. "You could swap with me," he insisted, placing his hand over Gil's, "Maybe, together...you can help me get a decent score."

As light-hearted as he tried to make it, Gil still seemed uncertain. "You sure?" he asked.

"I'm positive."

Contemplation remained in the furrow of Gil's brows, but he agreed.

The groups were divided - Jason, Diana, Barnaby, and Gil; Green Streak, Mell, and Seth.

When Barnaby realized his (or Gil's) turn was going second to last, he let himself breathe. He pressed shoulder to shoulder with the raven and nudged his side. "Want some ice cream?"

"Chocolate?"

"Rocky road."

Gil glanced around but graciously accepted the spoon. "Yes, please."

Barnaby held the bowl for him, and for a moment, he could've believed their roles were reversed. His guard was up, if only to make sure no one bothered them. His priority was ensuring *Gil* was at ease.

"Your friends seem nice," the raven muttered.

"They are," Barnaby agreed, swiftly adding, "but they're Seth's friends. I'm just here for the ride."

"Huh—" Gil almost sounded surprised. He returned Barnaby's spoon and watched as Jason threw a gutterball. "I'd think you'd fit right in."

Except Barnaby wasn't concerned with fitting in with them. He wanted to fit in with Gil.

They leaned into each other, and gradually, Gil lost his tension while they laughed at the banter of their teammates.

Before long, Barnaby's name lit up on the roster, and all eyes turned to them.

Even his master watched him expectantly, gesturing to the lane. "After you."

Reluctant as he was, Barnaby forced himself up.

The ball he picked was too heavy, but Diana's cheering seemed too hopeful to turn back once he was in position.

At least he managed to get some pins down.

"Now—" Seth announced, replacing him, "watch how a pro does it."

Apparently, pros had a habit of wiggling their hips and sticking their tongues out. To Seth's credit, he did score a strike.

"That's your roommate?" Gil asked when Barnaby returned to his side.

"Yep," the blond sighed, "that's Seth."

Gil tilted his head, his brows knitting, and Barnaby could practically see the gears churning in his head. "He looks familiar."

It was then Barnaby remembered how *Seth* knew Gil— "He said you had a class together before."

The realization dawned on Gil's face. "We did—" The next round had begun by the time he mumbled, "I was thinking...*IT*, Pennywise. He reminds me of the kid with the glasses."

"*Richie*?"

"Yeah, the asshole."

The boy rolled his eyes, chuckling. He couldn't argue.

"What're you nerds laughing at?"

Barnaby shut up in an instant, lifting his gaze to find Seth staring right at them. "Nothing. We're just talking."

"Secrets aren't fun unless you share with everyone," Mell cut in.

Seth scoffed, and Barnaby heard him say, "Probably asked to shove a pin up his ass."

Gil heard, too. "Actually," he said, perfectly loud and clear, "I was gonna ask if you wanted to have a threesome later."

"*Gil!*" Barnaby hissed, lightly slapping his arm. If Seth's comment didn't make him blush, he was certain the other's words did the job.

Seth barely flinched. "No thanks. Not if it's as small as Barnaby says it is."

Hazel eyes widened, desperate, as the blond clung to Gil. "*What*? No! I never—!"

The "ooooh"s were already starting.

Gil merely shrugged. "Figured it wouldn't matter if it was your first time."

At that, Barnaby spotted Seth's scowl. "Okay, maybe not with the, uhm, virgin jokes—"

"Memes!" Diana shouted, and Mell jumped to his feet.

"I'm goin', I'm goin'—" Passing Barnaby and Gil, he paused and whispered, "For the record, I'm always down for a threesome." Then, with a wink, he continued toward his throw.

Barnaby had to be bright red. "Did you," he muttered, trying to keep his voice from cracking, "Did you mean that? About wanting...*that*?"

The raven scoffed, shaking his head, "No."

Barnaby relaxed somewhat as Gil's arm stretched around his shoulders.

"I'm not sharing you," he said, his gaze drifting from Mell to Seth, "but if he wants to use humiliation as a tactic, he should expect some back."

"Okay—" The slight possessiveness was sweet, but as far as Seth and Gil, Barnaby could already picture the shots being fired. He was used to Seth, and he'd learned, sometimes, the best thing to do was ignore him. Somehow though, it didn't feel right to tell Gil to take it and ignore him. Instead, he reasoned, "Just don't be too mean. Okay?"

A kiss landed on his temple.

"I won't be mean."

Barnaby let himself smile again. How could he stay upset when Gil's arm was around him, practically letting everyone around them know that the boy was *his* property?

Barnaby's sights wandered to Jason and Diana, and there was a sense of camaraderie with the way they both made it obvious they were linked.

Diana held her lover from behind, and despite being half his size, seemed blissfully content with the way he reclined against her.

Barnaby, with shame in his heart and heat in his face, wondered what they would do when they got behind closed doors. Would they have a routine similar to his and Gil's? Or did they get to enjoy that simpler, softer side more often - where they bonded over bowling and zombies and video games because sex wasn't the main force keeping them together?

"*Giiiiiil,*" Diana sang, and Barnaby turned his attention to *anyone else*. "Are you going next?"

"Yeah, I'll go." The man squeezed Barnaby's shoulder, crossed over, and readied himself with a ball. A moment to aim and— he bowled a strike!

Barnaby was so pleasantly surprised he almost forgot to cheer with the rest of the group. Excluding Seth - who, when

Gil returned to Barnaby, asked him, "I'm assuming these aren't the heaviest balls you've handled?"

"Nope," Gil said confidently, plopping in his seat and pulling Barnaby close, "I've got those *right here*."

"*Ah—*" Barnaby squirmed, suddenly conscious of what was between his legs. "No, I don't— You don't have to include me—"

Seth stopped caring. It was his turn. He went on to knock down most of his pins in two throws.

A smirk lingered on Gil's lips, and Barnaby was sure his face would be red for the rest of the night.

He was a bit surprised, too, of how little was said. Even by Seth. No one seemed to genuinely *care* how close they were. Not even Gil, who'd seemed to lose his tension completely.

Of course, Barnaby didn't want to disturb him, so he didn't move until he had to.

"C'mon, Barnaby," Seth called when he went up for his turn, "channel the strength of those handjobs!"

Barnaby glared, and Mell, sounding unamused, uttered, "Dude..."

Not perfect throws, but he managed to add to his score on the board.

And so, the rest of the game carried on. Seth didn't heckle them as much after that - if anything, he'd traded roles with Mell and Green Streak (Bitch on the roster, whose real name was apparently Colton), who taunted Jason once they realized almost all he had thrown were gutterballs.

No one paid attention to Gil lightly running his fingers along Barnaby's arm or his leg, and it was enough that Barnaby started to feel *daring*. After one of his turns, he pointed at Gil's lap and asked, "Is this seat taken?"

Gil shook his head, gesturing— "It's all yours."

Barnaby sat down gleefully, the man's arms hooking around his waist. He locked eyes with Seth unintentionally, who pointed at him, eyes wide, as if to convey some kind of warning.

But Barnaby was cheeky. Biting his tongue through a smile, he wiggled his butt in Gil's lap.

The next warning came from Gil himself. "Watch it," he breathed hot against his ear, "we're in public."

Seth and Gil became so intent on competing against one another that they failed to recognize who was actually in the lead.

Both had a look of shock on their face when the scores were tallied up.

"And LilD is our winner!" Mell cheered, and Gil was quick to applaud for her. Seth pouted, clapping along reluctantly.

"JayZ—" Mell sighed, regarding the boy with his head hanging low. With the *lowest* score on the board— "Better luck next time."

"Ten more minutes."

According to Seth, that was all the time he needed to talk with his friends before leaving with Barnaby.

And that was fine.

That was ten more minutes Barnaby got to spend with Gil.

They intended to wait outside, heading for the exit when Gil decided to take a detour to the jukebox.

"I think this is authentic," he commented, examining it.

"Really?" Barnaby humored, "I didn't take you for a historian."

"Well, you shouldn't—" He didn't study it long before shifting his focus to the music selection. "It's just an affinity. Same thing with turntables. There's something nostalgic about them, y'know? Like...it's something that lets you appreciate the *aesthetic* of the music as you're listening to it."

Stepping up beside him, the blond bit his lip to suppress a giggle. It was oddly endearing, hearing that from him, and Barnaby wondered if he was finally trusting him enough to start pulling the curtain back. "I didn't know there was an aesthetic to music."

A mischievous grin spread across Gil's face as he glanced at his pet, then to the rest of the bowling alley.

Barnaby followed his gaze, to the No One in particular. No one was minding them.

"Fuck it. I'll show you."

The song he picked was by none other than the King himself, Elvis, "*Jailhouse Rock*."

"Let's say," Gil mused, taking his jacket off, "I'm some lowly poindexter, and you're the Greaser from the wrong side of town."

A bashful smile grew wider than Barnaby knew how to speak with. He couldn't even argue that the roles would be reversed.

"And let's say—" Gil passed the jacket off to Barnaby, and when Barnaby accepted it, offered his hand, "I asked you for a dance."

"I—" Nervous laughter bubbled out of Barnaby's throat before his words could. His hands gathered with excitement, and he busied himself putting on Gil's jacket to avoid flapping them— "I don't know how to dance."

And yet he accepted Gil's hand.

"It's dumb, but it's easy." The man pulled him close, keeping his hand while placing the other on his pet's hip and having Barnaby mimic him. He started bopping him around and in seconds, the blond was stumbling.

"Oh my God," he sputtered, "I'm sorry if I step on you."

"Step on me," Gil insisted, "Maybe then I'll have an excuse to take myself out of Thanksgiving."

Barnaby rolled his eyes playfully, the last time he was able to avert his gaze.

Silver moons and constellations above the drive-in theater of his life distracted him from anything else that could've been going on.

"Do you have any plans for break?"

"My...mom and I go to my grandma's for Thanksgiving," Barnaby said, "but that's pretty much it."

"Well—" Pressing their foreheads together, Gil's voice dropped to a whisper, "tell your mom, your grandma, and everyone that I wish you all a very happy holiday."

Barnaby's heart soared.

Possibly, it was the happiest he'd ever been.

He couldn't believe how little he was sweating, too entranced to give much of a damn about the fact they were dancing in public.

He couldn't believe he was dancing! No one had ever asked him to dance before. He'd never dreamed that, if he did, it would be with someone so charming and Aesthetically Pleasing, either.

It was so much better than anything he could ever dream, and yet it didn't seem any more real.

Hiding his face in the raven's neck, Barnaby muttered, "You too, Gil."

They bopped and swayed through another song, and Gil tempted him to "dance the night away" if Barnaby went back to his dorm with him.

The boy knew if he agreed, he'd never have time to pack everything he needed to take home.

With a heavy heart, he declined.

"What the *fuck* are you gays doing?!"

Barnaby shuddered, and Gil fell out of rhythm at the sound of Seth's nasally voice.

"You wish it was you, asshole."

"Gil—"

"I *wish* I could bleach my eyes."

Barnaby lifted his head to see Seth standing across the way, feet pointed to the entrance.

As soon as the brunet caught his gaze, he sneered, "Now or never, dude."

Barnaby sighed, sneaking a kiss on Gil's chin before taking a step back, returning his jacket. "Guess I'll see you soon?"

The raven didn't let go of his hand without giving it a gentle squeeze. "Text me?"

"I will."

Seth began snapping his fingers incessantly. "Come on!"

"What a fucking brat."

Barnaby squeaked as he was grabbed at the hip, pulled back in, and kissed deeply by his master.

Circling his arms around Gil's neck, he let his nature take hold, giving the man enough passion to last through the week.

Screw whoever saw. As his pet, he owed it to him.

As Barnaby Hirsch, a lowly, awkward, poindexter Agriculture Science student, he owed it to himself to be carefree and unafraid.

He couldn't imagine a more perfect way to show it off to the world.

Chapter 14

Smile.

But not too much.

Just enough to seem optimistic.

Don't cross your arms, she'll think you're defensive.

If you shake your leg, you give it all away.

"Gil—" *She's so hesitant when she speaks. She still feels like she has to walk on eggshells around you.* "I have to ask. Have you been smoking again?"

She smells it on you. No point in lying.

"Once in a while." *Excuses, excuses.* "Just as a way to relax."

Her lips pull an even tighter smile. *Expressing her disappointment is supposed to help you.* "You know there are healthier ways to relax." *She makes it sound like an accident.*

"I know."

"What are some things you can do?"

Take a deep breath. Straighten up while you're at it. "Writing, music, going for a walk, going to the gym..."

"Have you been doing that?"

Stop fussing with your hair. Everyone knows that's your nervous tick. "Walks, I pretty much stopped because of the cold, writing I have to do for class—"

"But is it something you *want* to do?"

"I mean…" *I'm not going to waste my spare time staring at a computer screen when I could be getting my dick wet but—* "Yeah?"

"So, why get back in the habit of smoking?"

Jesus Christ. Sit on your hands if you're going to keep rolling up your sleeves like that. "Convenience? It's something I can do on the go and not get in the way of anything else."

"There's plenty to do to relax when you're on the move. Even if it means setting aside more time for yourself."

"I thought I was supposed to be making less time for myself."

Way to issue a challenge. Expect twice as many appointments for Christmas.

"You're supposed to be socializing." *She's being careful with her words now. She knows you'll twist them.* "That's how you find a support group, Gil. You shouldn't have to give up so much time that you aren't able to do what you want to do."

"But I get to."

"Okay. Then, tell me about that."

You knew from the moment you walked in it would come to this. Might as well let one person know.

"I made a friend."

Barnaby should have stood his ground.

"The mall won't be that busy," his mother had insisted, "Everyone's waiting for the online sales tomorrow, anyway."

He could have told her she was wrong - that those sales would be the same all week, everywhere, regardless - but he knew what the outcome for that would be:

"Still! We'll get to spend time together!"

And if that didn't work:

"What else are you going to do? Sit on the computer all day?"

He wanted to avoid it. In the very least, to make her happy.

And then they got to the mall parking lot. It took ages to find a spot.

He almost refused to leave the car.

If he was two years old, he would have clung to her leg. But instead, since he was twenty, he walked directly behind her with only enough room that he wouldn't step on her ankles. It was the easiest way to stay out of everyone else's way - and the quickest way to frustrate his poor mother.

"Barnaby," she said when she accidentally elbowed him for the dozenth time, "I love you, but can you please take one more step back?"

He'd barely been aware of it. He'd been too vigilant of everyone and everything happening around him. The fluorescent department store lights were starting to hurt his eyes. "Sorry."

Maybe his mom noticed something he didn't, because then she was rubbing his arm, telling him, "If you want to go somewhere else for a bit, go ahead. Just keep your phone on."

He took the offer without any question.

The instant Barnaby stepped out into the open mall was like being broken out of a trance. He could breathe again.

For a moment, at least - before being swept up with the foot traffic.

He knew he had a few options: find a bathroom and hide in a stall, go to the food court and find a spot where he could sit and ground himself in his phone, or find a store that wasn't too crowded. Maybe get some shopping done.

When the latter presented itself in the form of a tea shop, he dove right in.

No, he didn't need help from the employees, thank you. In fact, he probably knew enough about their inventory that he could pass as one of them.

He needed to breathe. And relax. Focus on one thing at a time to keep his head from spinning.

He started reading the labels on the tea cans—

"Excuse me?"

Someone tapped Barnaby's shoulder. He was in somebody's way. He apologized, stepping aside.

The pretty young woman in the corner of his eye didn't step any closer, though. Instead, she asked, "Are you Barnaby?"

His eyes widened somewhat. There was something familiar about her that he couldn't place, but damn it if he didn't remember how he'd known her. "Uh...yeah?"

She shifted and tucked a chocolate brown wave behind her ear, the knit in her brows uncertain despite the sparkling lights in her eyes. "Sorry, I just had to ask...Do you know anyone named Gil Connolly?"

Ba-dum.

Uhm.

Barnaby grabbed a random can. *Rainbow Lemonade, huh? What kind of ingredients do you have?* "Yeah. He goes to my school."

His phone started vibrating in his pocket.

"Sorry," he said immediately, digging it out, "Can you just— I have to take this."

His mother, he graciously assumed—

Before registering the name right as he held the phone to his ear. "*Gil?*"

"If a girl in a plaid dress with long brown hair comes up to you, just walk away. You *do not* have to talk to her."

Barnaby spared another glance at the girl to make sure.

Oh yeah. Her dress definitely had a plaid pattern.

"Should I be worried?"

"She's an idiot. I don't know what she's thinking."

"That's him?" the girl spoke up, sounding a tad peeved.

Barnaby nodded.

"Where is he?"

"Uhm, Gil?" he cautioned, "Where are you?" *And who is she?*

He heard him breathe in. There was rustling and other voices in the background.

The call ended.

"I'm sorry," Barnaby started apologizing to the girl, looking for a way around her. For all he knew, she could have something to tell him that he was better off not knowing. "I don't—"

And then Gil came into view.

"Leave him alone, Addison."

"Relax," she said in immediate defense, "I was just introducing myself."

Barnaby's heart leapt for him. It took everything to stay still, not to throw his arms around him and pull him close. It was all he could do to ask, "What are you doing here?"

The man's expression softened as he turned to him, pleasantly surprised, perhaps. "Same as everyone else—" He showed off their various shopping bags. "What about you? I didn't know you lived around here."

"When would I have told you?" Barnaby didn't mean to sound like he was implying anything, but he swore Gil winced.

"Fair point."

"Hey—" The girl, Addison, demanded Gil's attention by elbowing his arm— "If I go find mom, can I trust you to play nice?"

Gil sighed, and in an instant, reverted to his sharp angles and impatient tone. "*Yes.* Could've been nicer if you didn't bother." Addison rolled her eyes, but before she could object, Gil was shoving half of the bags into her hands. "Take these with you."

"A 'thank you' would be nice—" She didn't hold her breath for it, evidently. Rather, she looked to Barnaby with a smile as stunning as her brother's. "It was nice meeting you." She spun on her heels, hair cascading down her back as she exited the store, her head held high.

Left alone together, Barnaby exhaled and retorted, "I didn't know you had a sister."

"When would I have told you?"

Uhm. Literally whenever?

But rather than make a fuss about it, Barnaby asked, "Does she know anything?"

"No." Gil's shoulders slumped, and somehow, without Barnaby realizing, he'd closed the space between them. "Apparently—" It was his turn to pick up a can and analyze the labels— "when I called out to you, I must've sounded too excited."

His smile was so faint that, had Barnaby been standing at any other angle, he might've missed it.

"*Is that someone who might actually tolerate Gil?*" the man went on mockingly, "*We can't let that one get away.*"

Barnaby scoffed, "I do way more than '*tolerate*' you." His heart caught in his throat as an arm was swung around his shoulders, nearly folding under the weight of Gil's bags.

"Then, you won't mind if I stick around."

Holding himself up, Barnaby's gaze landed directly on the man's lips. *Well.* Not if by the end of the night, their smiles could meet.

"What about your sister? Or your mom?"

"They won't miss me."

I find that very hard to believe.

But Barnaby hadn't spent years with Gil. He only knew what it was like to be doted on by him - to know his patience, his wit, his charm. And to dream about his touch when they were apart. How could he not miss him?

They left the shop with Gil flanking Barnaby to shield him from the masses. "There's one place I want to check," he'd told the blond, "It didn't look too packed earlier." He wouldn't give the name, though, content to wear a smug grin until they slowed to a stop in front of a colorful little store. Only two or three families were inside.

"*Fluff-A-Friend?*"

"You're not too old to look around for a bit, are you?" Gil asked, nudging his side.

"I...guess not?" Probably yes - maybe a bit odd for two grown men to dawdle around a children's store. But compared to the rest of the mall, it was welcoming, and all Barnaby needed was an excuse to get away.

They stepped inside together.

"It's kind of funny," Barnaby commented, approaching the display wall of stuffed animals. There were bears, cats, dogs, and more, arranged in a rainbow of colors. "I've never actually gotten to *fluff* a friend here before."

Gil stopped to raise a brow at him. "You're joking."

A smile felt awkward on Barnaby's lips. "Mom always said it was too expensive."

"Even for a birthday party?"

"No friends to invite me to any."

He caught Gil's frown as the raven scanned a bin of Unstuffeds. "Me neither, honestly—" Picking up a deflated bear, he examined it in his hands. "I only got to go with Addison. She had her birthday here for years."

Barnaby inched closer, hoping to seem unbothered. Christmas music played on the store radio, and as the slogan read, *Fluff Is the Stuff That Keeps Us Together*. "Must've made you quite the collector."

That brought the smirk back to Gil's lips. "Kind of. I got the same thing every visit." Another glance, and he plucked a grey wolf from one of the bins, showing it off to Barnaby.

"*Oh no—*" Barnaby beamed, taking the plush and looking between the two, "you were the Wolf Kid, weren't you?"

Gil snatched it right back. "Because they're *pack animals*. Obviously. I had to come back for more—" Then, under his breath, he added, "Who I growled at during recess had nothing to do with it."

"Hey guys!" an employee called out to them. She wore a purple apron, round glasses, and a smile that might've appeared forced on any other children's store employee shone genuinely on her. "What brings you in today?"

Barnaby started to say, *"We're just looking"*, but Gil's words drowned him out - "We're here to make his first friend."

"We are?"

"Oh my gosh, how exciting!" the girl gasped. "Well, have a look around, and when you're ready, I'll be waiting at the Fluffing Fountain. If you have any other questions, you can let me know!"

"Thanks, Imani."

She waved, whirled around, and trotted over to some cotton-filled contraption.

Barnaby's brows furrowed, and his gaze flickered from the girl to his master. "Do you know her?"

"She's Addison's girlfriend."

Interesting.

Gil went back to scouring the bins, apparently serious about their mission, and Barnaby began seeking out the cheapest options. He narrowed it down to a few classic-looking teddies, simple and cute.

He had a cream colored one in his hand when Gil walked up to him with his own hands behind his back. Already skeptical of that mischievous glint in his eyes, Barnaby asked, "What did you find?"

With his full attention, Gil presented white spots on an umber pelt. "Part of your herd?"

An unstuffed fawn. Barnaby held it delicately. He couldn't deny it had the most precious face and ears he'd ever seen.

Even without its fluff, he had to give it a hug.

He didn't know the price, but the decision had been made.

They brought it over to Imani and passed it off to her. "Great choice! He's such a cutie!" There was a hole in the back that she used to put the fawn over a tube coming out of the "fountain."

A flick of a switch, and Barnaby watched in wonder as cotton shot up through the tube. Gradually, the baby deer got bigger and bigger until it was fully formed. Brought to life.

"One more thing, and he's all yours," Imani said. She pointed to a small container beside her, one filled with tiny satin stars.

Barnaby grabbed one, waiting for further instruction, but Imani's gaze remained fixed on Gil.

"You too, Mr. Connolly."

Barnaby turned to see Gil's eyes widen, the amusement in his face fading fast. "No, it's...just for him."

"You came in here together," she insisted, holding a star out to him, "You're part of this."

Gil bit his lip, rocked on his heels, and stared at Barnaby. All the boy had to do was tilt his head, curious of his reluctance, for the raven to step forward and take the star from Imani.

"Now," she said, holding up her own, "shake your stars in the air so they can wave at the sky!"

Gil and Barnaby looked at each other with equal uncertainty. *Okay?* A quick glance over his shoulder told

Barnaby no one was watching, so he raised his star to follow along.

Gil was more hesitant, muttering, "*Jesus Christ,*" before complying.

A few shakes, and Imani gave the next command, "Rub it on your forehead to spark your friend's imagination."

Barnaby giggled, rubbing the heart on his forehead. *Okay. This is kind of cute.*

"Rub it on your heart so his matches yours!"

They rubbed it over their hearts, and Barnaby caught Gil grinning.

"And rub it on your toes so your new friend can follow in your footsteps!"

A bit awkward, but they both managed.

"Last but not least," Imani said, "you're gonna make a wish and seal it with a kiss on the star."

That was too much responsibility for Barnaby. Rather than mull over it, he kissed it quick.

Gil had a moment's pause with his.

Both stars kissed, Imani let them place the each of theirs inside of the fawn before sewing it up for safe carry.

Once it was in his arms, Barnaby gained a rush of affection, wanting nothing more than to protect it. He kept it close to his chest. "Thank you, Imani."

"You're welcome!" she chimed, "Let me know if there's anything else I can help you guys with, alright?"

That settled, Barnaby was about to make his way over to the register when Gil swung an arm around his shoulders, directing him to another portion of the store - the clothing wall. Clothing for dolls.

"You weren't gonna let him leave undressed, were you?"

"He's—" As cute as the many sequined dresses and silly graphic shirts were, it was money they didn't have to spend. "He's a deer. He doesn't need clothes."

Gil leaned into his ear and whispered, "Since when has that stopped *you*?"

Barnaby promptly elbowed him in the stomach.

The man snorted, persisting, "It's your first time. Might as well go for the whole experience."

It absolutely wasn't necessary; he was happy with what he had.

He thought the least he could do was humor Gil, dressing the fawn up in a few different outfits.

Well. Maybe it made him a little bit happier.

He settled on a black hoodie and jeans that his new friend's tail went through. Gil had been trying to help, bringing him doll-sized polos, but the moment he saw Barnaby's final result, he chuckled and said, "Looks like something I would wear."

Barnaby's face flushed with warmth. Was that why he thought it would make the fawn all the more comforting? He asked Gil, "Is that bad?"

"No," Gil replied, patting the plushie's head, "It's cute."

When they finally brought it to the cashier, his master's credit card was the first on the counter.

Barnaby brushed up against his side, thanking him.

"Consider it an early Christmas gift," the raven muttered, squeezing his hand.

They left with the fawn in a bag and continued walking together. From the corner of his eye, Barnaby noticed Gil checking his texts, and seconds later, spotted a scowl.

"Is everything okay?"

"Yeah. Just Addison making sure I don't forget her present."

Barnaby cocked his brow. "What does she want?"

Pocketing the phone, Gil grumbled, "Victoria's Secret gift card."

He told Barnaby it could wait, that he wouldn't have to be bothered getting dragged in there because of him.

The blond barely had to consider it before shrugging. Why not? He was sure they'd be wandering around, aimless otherwise, and he'd much rather have some kind of plan. "I don't mind. Really."

Despite his doubtful expression, Gil corrected his posture and walked on with purpose. It didn't take long to locate the store, but nearly the moment they entered, they collided with the end of the line.

"Are you sure you don't want me to wait?"

Barnaby grimaced, understanding Gil's doubt. Although, while it might've taken away time for anything else, he remembered to ask himself, *what else was there to do*? Shop? He didn't want Gil to spend any more money on him. Walk around and talk? If they wanted to talk, waiting in line might've been the perfect spot. At least they could avoid the crowds.

He sighed, looking up at him with a smile. "I think I'll be okay."

The conversation went on with Barnaby asking about Gil's Thanksgiving.

"It was good," he said.

When it seemed like he'd stop at that, Barnaby prompted again, "Did anything happen?"

Several seconds passed before he answered, "Other than constantly having to kick my younger cousins out of my room? Not much." Then, of course, the question was turned back on Barnaby.

He ran with the first thing that came to mind: being on the living room couch to stay out of everyone's way, only for the other Men of the Family to gather around to watch football on TV. How they'd try to talk to him about The Game and ask about school, and he'd have to either nod along or laugh politely when they laughed Less Politely while teasing him about his quiet demeanor or about his major.

Gil interjected, "You're not alone in that. I've been there—" They advanced in line a bit. "At least you have a leg to stand on. Being a farmer— Isn't that one of the manliest things you can do? You'd literally be working the land through every kind of weather, providing for hundreds, if not thousands, of people. I *wish* I could be as proud about being a literary agent."

Barnaby abandoned his baggage right then and there, on the floor of Victoria's Secret. "Is that what you want to be?" he asked, his focus solely on Gil, "A literary agent?"

The man's expression held a hint of surprise. Like maybe Barnaby should've already known.

Or maybe he had let something slip. "Yeah?"

"I mean, that's great!" the blond offered, going along as if it made perfect sense, "I just didn't expect it. Can I ask what...inspired that?"

The answer was obvious, probably. If only Gil had felt comfortable enough to show the signs sooner— "I like reading. Figured it was the easiest way to make money off of it."

Something else they had in common, though Barnaby wasn't any better (thanks to studying, laziness, and the man himself). He didn't expect Gil to guess, either.

He was prepared to ask what he liked to read, or what his favorite books were, when the man placed a finger on his cheek, directing his gaze to a display table beside them.

"Would you ever wear something like that?"

The mannequin wore it best: a sheer, taupe lace bra with frills around the trim and a matching panty set.

Barnaby pictured himself, a Not At All Flattering sight in something so dainty, and scoffed, "I'd look ridiculous."

He felt Gil's eyes scanning him up and down.

"I respectfully disagree."

They continued down the line, and Barnaby became more aware of other mannequins and their Outfits. They were beautiful, but they couldn't have been made with him in mind. Right?

"Really?"

"Hm?"

Barnaby bit his lip and stood close. "Do you really disagree?"

"Think of it this way—" Gil's hand swept over the boy's shoulder, and his voice dropped to a whisper, "Wearing lingerie would give you total power over me."

"H-How?"

"Because all I'd do is stare," Gil admitted, "You could tell me to do just about anything, and I'd go along with it."

Barnaby shifted in place, feeling the slow bloom of blush on his cheeks. What would he even do, given that much power? Gil was already so good to him, giving him more than he knew to ask for.

The boy fidgeted with the handles of his shopping bag.

He did buy him his own Fluffy Friend.

Eventually, they neared the registers. While Gil was occupied with gift cards and his own wallet, Barnaby followed his impulse and slipped away. He went right for the mannequin with the taupe lace bra and panties, found the panties in the largest size and prayed his estimate on the bra was right. By the time he returned to the end of the line, he spotted Gil searching the store, dumbfounded, and waved him over.

"What're you doing?"

Barnaby stuffed the set into his Fluff-A-Friend bag before the man could notice— "Grabbing a few things."

Gil's brows wrinkled curiously, the hint of a smirk on his lips. "Why didn't you grab it earlier?"

"Because I had to think about it."

The raven gave a playful roll of his eyes, and once again, Barnaby realized, he was reaching for his wallet.

"*I've got it,*" he assured him, taking a step back, "Consider it my present to you."

Gil's face lit up, like he was touched, and Barnaby promised him that he'd catch up in the next fifteen minutes. They agreed to meet at the food court, and Gil was on his way.

When the time passed and the underwear was paid for, still hidden in his Fluff-A-Friend bag, Barnaby made a straight path to the heart of the mall. It didn't take long to clock Gil waiting beside a pretzel stand.

The man locked eyes with him, and he started approaching. "Bad news," he said, disappointment weighing in his voice, "Mom and Addison want to head out for the night."

"That's just news—" Barnaby prohibited himself from being let down. "It's only one more day apart. Then...we can go back to how we were."

Gil managed a slight smile, tousling Barnaby's hair. "Guess you're right."

The boy accompanied him all the way to Hallmark, where Addison supposedly said she'd be, only to find her lingering outside.

"You went to Fluff-A-Friend!" she exclaimed, all of her attention on Barnaby, "What'd you get?"

Barnaby couldn't have been more careful digging out his fawn friend, but once he did, he was proud to show it off, all the more giggly about it with Addison gushing along.

"Mom said she needs help carrying bags," Gil interrupted, dumping another of his own into Addison's grasp. "We should get going."

The brunette groaned but didn't argue. She reminded Barnaby it was nice to meet him, and Gil insisted it was good to see him - although, not good enough to hug him or kiss him goodbye.

They parted ways, and Barnaby went on to look for his mother.

He wasn't upset with Gil. He understood.

But maybe, *just maybe*, he'd be able to even the score and make him wish he *had* touched him one last time.

After twenty minutes of deliberation, Barnaby pressed the Call button.

He spent an extra minute or two out of frame, gathering up the courage for his Big Reveal.

The panties almost fit, and the bra, thankfully, wasn't too baggy on his chest. Maybe the frills were a little too feminine for him, but Gil didn't seem to mind.

He'd put his collar around his neck.

"Holy shit."

Barnaby slid his hands down his sides, as if to re-familiarize himself with his own body. If only his stomach didn't bulge out so much. "Do you like it?"

"I'm fucking obsessed." Gil had his head on a pillow, face taking up most of the screen as if he couldn't get close enough to what he was seeing. "Turn around for me?"

Any more heat in his face, and his brain would probably fry, but then, Barnaby couldn't disobey his master. He bent over, knowing it would accentuate his ass, the Already Wedgie pulling tighter between his cheeks.

"You're killing me, Bee."

The boy giggled, swaying his hips. "What're you gonna do when you see me in person?"

"Have a heart attack? I don't know."

So dramatic. "Welp—" Barnaby straightened up, faced the camera again, and sat properly at the foot of his bed— "we probably wouldn't want to risk that happening sooner than later."

Gil whined, "Speak for yourself."

"No," Barnaby chided, "If you have a heart attack..." He put a hand on his thigh, slowly gliding toward his crotch— "Who's gonna take care of me?"

Gil's eyes narrowed in an instant. "Don't you dare."

Barnaby pouted. "I won't—" He flopped back on his bed, feeling the lace hug his cock with every shift— "I just wish I could've brought you home with me."

"You only live an hour away. I could still make it."

He very well could.

225

Barnaby bit his lip, bringing his hands to his belly and absently rubbing himself. For a man, it always surprised him how smooth his skin was. "My mom would be suspicious. Plus, the walls are paper thin."

"We could gag you," Gil said without hesitation, "I'd be careful. I'd be *so* gentle."

A chill shot down Barnaby's spine, right to his dick. "Two more nights," he muttered. Better not to risk it. "Two more nights, and I'm all yours."

That earned a heavy sigh from the man on the other side of the screen— "I want to do more than touch you."

"What do you mean?"

"I want to...What's the word? *Ravish you*, I think."

Barnaby bubbled with laughter, his thighs rubbing together. He craned his neck to look at the phone propped up on his desk. "*Ravish, hm*? How very Jane Austen of you."

Gil chuckled, his smile just as sweet as the sound. "I am an English major."

"True." The angle of his neck quickly became uncomfortable. Instead, he spread his legs, gaining a better perspective of his master through them. "Sexiest English major I've ever met."

Judging by the drop of his gaze, Gil must have taken notice. His voice dropped to a deeper octave, "Could say the same about you, farmer boy."

"Yeah?" Once again, Barnaby's hands were slipping down his thighs, narrowly avoiding his crotch. "This is sexy to you?"

Gil went quiet for a moment, and Barnaby felt like whatever game they were playing, he'd won. Laying his head back, he closed his eyes and continued rubbing circles mere inches away from his bulge. His hips started to move on their own, grinding against the tug of his wedgie.

"What're you thinking about?"

"*You.*"

"And you're sure you don't want me over?"

Barnaby shook his head. "I don't want to hold back. I'm sorry."

"Shh, don't apologize—" He heard rustling on Gil's end. A belt being unbuckled— "Just keep being a good boy for me."

Barnaby whimpered. Gil was about to masturbate to him when it was against his own rules to touch himself. For the show he was putting on, it didn't seem like a fair trade.

He retracted his hands and closed his legs again, reverting to rubbing his thighs together instead. "It's hard being good."

Gil groaned, and a moment of silence followed.

Finally, he ordered, "Use a pillow."

Barnaby's eyes shot open, and in seconds, he was up on his knees, stuffing a pillow between his legs. He didn't make another move without looking into Gil's eyes as best as he could, asking first, "A-Are you sure? I don't want to break the rules."

"As long as you don't *actually* touch yourself," the raven grumbled, "It'd probably be better if you kept those panties on."

Barnaby smiled, shakily. "Thank you, sir."

It wasn't as good as riding Gil, or humping his thigh, or even jerking off, but with his mother across the hall, it was likely for the best.

Still, he did his best for himself and for Gil - chasing friction with each thrust into the pillow, breathing heavy and letting his tongue loll out. He'd tried to feel up his chest, drawing attention to the bra, but he was quick to fumble, nearly falling out of the bed.

Gil chuckled, his eyes never drifting from the sight on his screen. He wasn't much better off for coherence, grunting, mumbling swears and praises, and licking his lips.

Had Barnaby been capable of forming words, he would've asked what he would rather be using his tongue for.

Gil crumbled first, and Barnaby mentally repeated the phrase, *"he came for me, he came for me, he came for me"*, until he reached his own climax. It drained any strength he had left to hold himself up, and soon, he was faceplanting directly into the mattress, his ass high in the air.

"Hey. Barnaby."

He thought he'd only rested his eyes for a moment. But as he came to, stretching and rolling onto his side, Barnaby winced, realizing the cum on his panties had dried. A pop-up on his phone warned him that his battery was dropping below 10%. "I'm awake."

"Go get cleaned up."

Barnaby sighed, pulling himself from the bed to meet Gil on his desk.

The man looked cozy, wrapped up in a blanket, the lighting dim and warm around him. A sight of pure peace.

"Thank you for letting me do that."

Gil's voice was gentle - "You deserved it. Seriously, though, go wash off. Put some real pajamas on and get comfy. Where's your fawn?"

Barnaby rubbed his eyes and smiled. "In the bag still. I'll get him out. I'll probably have to use him as a pillow."

"*Heh*. Alright. Did you think of a name for him?"

Barnaby scratched his head, considering it for a moment. "Gi...Gidget."

"Gidget?"

"Mhm," the boy said, "Kind of sounds like...Gil Junior?"

Gil smirked. "Goodnight, Barnaby and Gidget."

"Goodnight, Gil."

I love you.

Chapter 15

Barnaby had never been in love before.

He'd never been on a date, never imagined a future with anyone, and never felt the need to put all of his time and effort into a single person. No one else had ever made him feel the way he did around Gil.

He thought, at first, that was what a real friendship was supposed to be.

So, what reason did he have to want *more*?

On their first day back on campus, Barnaby was determined to make himself all but brand new for his master.

He wasted no time kicking Seth out, barring him from coming back until he texted him, "All Clear."

In addition to his lingerie, clean and fresh from two days prior, he'd gone out and purchased thigh high stockings of the same color, completing the look. As nice as the outfit was, though, Barnaby wasn't sure he'd look like *himself*. For that, he'd picked up a headband. With deer ears and antlers attached.

His collar, of course, was around his neck, where it was meant to be.

He couldn't help but laugh as he inspected himself in the mirror. *A sexy deer*, he thought, *never thought this would be my life*.

He texted Gil:

> Salten 208. I'm all yours.

The response was immediate:

> Be there in 10.

> I'll leave the door unlocked ;)

He wouldn't be able to answer it anyway. He'd be too tied up, if he could help it.

It was a struggle, but soon enough, using an old tie, Barnaby was able to bind his wrists together and secure them to a plank on his headboard.

It wasn't exactly comfortable, but he wanted to appear vulnerable. Like a deer caught in a trap, belly up.

The minutes ticked by, his heart spiking and falling. He'd squirm, then relax, his body preparing for submission.

He heard a knock on the door, and his dick practically stood to attention.

Gil appeared in the corner of his eye, a satchel at his hip, and Barnaby's voice cracked when he squeaked, "H-Hi."

The man didn't move right away. He stayed by the door, blinking, his eyes wide.

And then Barnaby heard the door lock.

"What do we have here?"

"Your, uhm—" The boy cleared his throat, doing little to help the sudden dry spell, "Your present? I thought I could still surprise you."

"Well—" The satchel dropped to the floor, and Gil, not unlike a wolf, prowled onto the bed.

Barnaby's legs spread to accommodate him.

"Consider me surprised."

The blond shuddered from his toes to his restrained wrists as Gil's fingertips began ghosting along his calf. A trail of kisses started at his knee, tearing a whimper from pink lips.

Gil chuckled, "Does this mean you want to hold off on my offer?"

"O-Offer?"

"On Sunday. I told you if you wore lingerie, you could get me to do anything you wanted. Remember?" He seemed to appreciate the stockings, feather-like touches quickly becoming purposeful sweeps along the boy's thick legs. He took his time reaching his hip, fingers gliding underneath the frills of Barnaby's panties to send chills directly to the boy's cock.

He was sinking fast into a familiar daze. It was hard to remember anything before Gil's arrival. As far as Barnaby was concerned, the universe stopped outside of his dorm. All that mattered was his master's touch. "I, uhm— That sounds nice but— Master, it's hard to think." He tugged at his restraint, itching to guide the raven's hand to his cock.

232

"Hey—" The hand was retracted and pressed to his wrists instead, "That's alright."

Barnaby's brows furrowed up at him. "You're not disappointed?"

"*What*?" The tiny smirk on Gil's lips broadened. "Hell no—" He loomed over his pet, pressing down chest to chest, and kissed his cheek. "You look too fucking good to be disappointing. You deserve to be rewarded for this." His hips were flush against Barnaby's, and his bulge was prominent as ever.

"For...For being a good boy?"

"That's right, fawn—" His lips continued down Barnaby's neck, nipping and licking at his skin— "The best pet any man could ask for." His hands continued to roam his body, one grazing over his bra and catching his nipple.

Barnaby's breath hitched. "Nu-uh. I—" The hand made a path toward his side, and he whined, "T-Touch my chest again? Please?"

"Like this?" Gil brought the hand back, giving special attention to Barnaby's blooming bud.

His whimpers must not have been enough to feed him, because then, the man was dipping his head, hungrily licking over the opposite nipple, over the lace.

Barnaby breathed in, pushing his chest up toward Gil, and exhaled a moan. When he dared to glance down, he found silver eyes waiting to possess him, silently demanding more pathetic sounds from his pet. The boy was mesmerized, hypnotized by the circular motions of Gil's tongue that made a bump in the lace. The rise and fall of his chest became increasingly rapid— "*M-More.*"

The man didn't object. He probably didn't mean to tease him, either - but while aimlessly exploring Barnaby's body, his hand grazed a sensitive area on the boy's side, making him seize.

"Did that tickle?"

Barnaby nodded, only able to whimper in response.

"*Huh,*" Gil hummed, "Then, I guess it would be a shame if...I kept doing it?"

There wasn't any time to beg. Both of Gil's hands flew and danced along Barnaby's sides faster than the boy could wrap his head around. He laughed and shouted, legs flailing and arms aching as he pulled and pulled in effort to free himself from his bind. "Don't— Gil— *Stop!*"

"*Don't stop?* Gladly—"

Crack.

Both froze at the splintering sound.

One glance upward was all it took for Barnaby to find the source: a new dent in his headboard where the bind had been looped. "*Shit.*"

"Okay, okay," Gil chuckled, reaching over to untie him, "How about we save the bondage for my room?"

Barnaby pouted, massaging his wrists the instant they were released. "Sorry."

"Why are you sorry?" The man sat back, grabbing Barnaby's hips in the process.

"Because..." Barnaby was pulled into his lap, and he had to wrap his arms around Gil's neck to keep steady— "I wanted you to feel like you had more control."

"Barnaby, that is the last thing I care about right now." Crashing their lips together, Gil kissed him, slow and tender.

Barnaby's heart managed to slow down, but the butterflies in his stomach soared to new heights. Soon, he was cupping the man's face, intent on pursuing the kiss. Grinding into his master's lap, Barnaby's hips moved on their own free will.

It didn't take long to build to a crescendo. Amorous kisses led to entangled tongues, teeth sinking deep. Barnaby's hands moved to raven hair, tugging out of desperation and earning a growl. Gaining an ounce of confidence, he scratched down the back of Gil's neck. A light smack across the ass made for a reward.

Eventually, Barnaby was molded back to the mattress, so Gil could strip down to everything but bracelets and angel wings. After rummaging through his satchel, he returned to the bed with a condom, salted caramel lube, and the setting sun creating a halo behind him.

"You're beautiful," Barnaby mumbled, welcoming the man home between his legs.

Gil smiled, and the room was filled with the scent of caramel, his fingers glistening with liquid. "You're perfect."

Barnaby's panties were pulled to the side, and one finger after another, he was made ready for his master. Even when

Gil's member slid inside of him, making the boy feel whole, his panties stayed on. Gil's stare had never seemed so intense.

They were entirely wrapped up in one another - arms, legs, lips, and breath. They moved together, familiar with each other's bodies and taking advantage of it at every turn. Neither held back from vocalizing their pleasure - whether it was a moan, a pet-name, a whimper, a laugh, or a complete, coherent compliment.

"I feel so full with you, Master...*Mmm*...it's so good..."

"No one else can have you, fawn. You're mine."

"*Aah!* Faster, Master, Faster!"

"That's it. As loud as you can. I need to hear you—"

A few pumps of his cock in time with Gil's thrusts sealed Barnaby's fate.

While the boy scrambled for a grasp on reality, the wolf let himself loose. Carnal and frantic.

At last, he pressed his sweat-slicked face against Barnaby's neck and howled, trembling with the force of his own orgasm.

They didn't stop there.

As soon as they had their breathing somewhat under control, Gil pulled out, took off his condom to toss into Barnaby's wastebin, and guided his pet's head toward his cock.

Barnaby didn't have to think about it - he simply followed direction, drugged by the overwhelming scent of caramel, and licked his master's cock clean, sucking and stroking it back to life. His lips curled around him, enamored by the sight above of Gil tilting his head back, groaning and swearing to the ceiling while rubbing one of Barnaby's Deer Ears between his fingers.

Next, the boy was ordered to dress him in another condom, adding more lube. Before he could resume his position, he was lifted from the bed, taken to the window, and pressed against the glass.

Thankfully, the window faced the woods, and Barnaby sighed in relief, unable to find an audience. Although, it didn't take long for his breath to fog up the glass; had anyone passed by, he wouldn't see them, anyway.

His sole concern was proving how much of a Good Boy he could be for Gil - and, maybe, anyone else who happened to catch a glimpse. He didn't resist when the man claimed him all over again, pounding in deep. One hand held onto his collar while the other spanked him over and over, making Barnaby yelp and cry at the top of his lungs. It was an honor. He *wanted* his ass to be as red as his face - *needed* Gil to fill his hole as much as he filled his heart and mind.

His master came first, and Barnaby, feeling like he'd fulfilled his sole purpose in life, reached his climax with tears raining down his face.

If it weren't for Gil's arms holding him up, he likely would've crumbled to the floor.

Instead, he was swept off his feet, carried back to his bed, and wrapped up under the covers with the man.

Cool fingertips brushed his hair back before removing his antlers and placing them on the nightstand. Tears were wiped away, and Gil used a blanket to clean up the drool on his chin.

Hushed words were muttered to Barnaby that he didn't quite understand. At least, they sounded like praise. He smiled, still all aglow, and cuddled as close to Gil as he possibly could.

The world around him went quiet, and he realized the room had fallen into darkness. It was peaceful enough to tempt Barnaby to sleep, yet he fought against it. He had absolutely no plans to risk waking up without his master.

"Oh. Wow."

Barnaby blinked, recognizing a sudden, warm light coming from above. His fairy lights.

Gil stared at them, and Barnaby stared at Gil, in love with the way they sparkled in his eyes.

Love.

"Yeah," the boy mumbled, tracing hearts along his master's chest, "they're on a timer."

"They're pretty—" Gil glanced down to Barnaby. He grabbed a hold of his hand, bringing it to his lips to kiss each knuckle— "Just not as pretty as you are."

Pretty. Perfect.

No one else can have you. You're mine.

Fucking against windows and kissing at the bowling alley.

"Gil—"

How was he supposed to know where the line was?

Barnaby interlocked their fingers, holding tight. "What are we?"

Gil's expression faltered briefly before dawning a hooded, seductive gaze. "We're master and pet," he muttered, placing another kiss on the boy's forehead, "More importantly, you're my best friend."

Well, it wasn't as if that was any less significant. It'd been years since even Seth considered him his Best Friend.

Barnaby pecked his chin, hesitant, before he asked, "Will we ever be more than that?"

Gil was silent, keeping his head above the blond's, avoiding eye contact.

Each second passed was Barnaby's heart echoing louder in his head.

Finally, the man spoke, "No. Trust me, you wouldn't want that."

In an instant, Barnaby was awake and alert, propping himself up on his elbow. He felt a pit of guilt, of course, for giving that impression, but— "Yes!" he insisted, "Yes, I really would. A-And I can still be your pet— I'm fine with keeping everything the same, just...*y'know*."

Gil remained motionless, despite his gaze hardening, the corners of his mouth tugging down. He asked, monotone, "Then, why would you want to change it?"

"Well—" There was too much nervous energy building up in Barnaby's hands. Letting go of Gil, he grabbed onto the blanket, twisting and rubbing the fabric between his fingers—

"B-Because...I, I think it would mean more. L-Like I'd be able to, to say stuff that I might be afraid to now."

"What do you want to say?"

Barnaby swallowed, his throat feeling tight, and picked at a thread until it came loose from the blanket. He looked down when he said, "That I like you. A lot. And...I want to keep telling you it and show you I like you in more ways than sex. I want to learn about you. I want to be there for you and for you to be able to trust me."

"*Barnaby—*" Gil sat up, and Barnaby made the mistake of looking at him too soon - to a man who seemed utterly lost, like someone just discovering they'd woken up in the wrong bed— "I told you at the beginning that I didn't want a relationship."

"I-I know, but the way things were going—" *You kissed me in front of my friend. What message were you trying to give him?* "I thought maybe you changed your mind."

Gil pinched the bridge of his nose and rubbed his forehead. "I didn't."

For sure, Barnaby's throat was swelling.

The man breathed in, a rattled sound. "I'm sorry, Bee, I didn't mean to lead you on. I thought we both agreed on the same thing. I thought you were finally getting comfortable."

He was. Too comfortable, clearly.

Gil turned to him, managing to pry one of his hands away from the blanket, into his grasp. "I'm trying to give you my best self," he urged, "You're *incredible,* Bee, and...I've loved

240

having you around, but it's better this way. This is the most I need from a relationship, but I can't do the commitment."

"Then, why'd you say no one else could have me?"

Gil's mouth opened, though he didn't speak, hesitating - realizing he was caught, perhaps - before admitting, "As long as I'm your master. But you can call that off at any time."

For the first time, Barnaby considered taking advantage of that.

His eyes stung, and the clog in his throat had him stuffed all the way to his sinuses. "Right..." His arms might as well have been stuffed with cement; his hand dropped out of Gil's like a brick.

Something trickled down his cheek, but as soon as he caught it, another one followed.

Gil's brows furrowed pitifully. "I like you a lot, too, Barnaby...but I can't like you *that* much."

"*Please*, just...*stop.*"

Of course, you can't.

No one can.

He was an idiot to think being someone's sex slave would turn out any different.

He felt a trickle from his nose, sniffled, and balled the blanket up around him to cover himself. "I think you should go."

"Barnaby—"

"No. Really," the boy choked, pressing himself to the wall, "I know you don't want to be here right now, so I think it'd be better if you'd—"

"That's not what I said."

He didn't have to say a word.

"Leave!" Barnaby's throat was a dam, and no matter what Gil said or meant, the water was rising. He had to break, letting the flood loose and sobbing so much he shook to his core just to shout, "Get out of my room!"

He shut his eyes and grabbed blindly at a pillow, tossing it in Gil's direction. It must've had some impact since, the next moment, the weight on his side of the bed disappeared. He heard rustling and feet across the floor, and a minute later, the sound of the door opening.

"Text me when you feel better."

And then he was gone.

Chapter 16

"You have no idea how relationships work, do you?"

Gil grunted, squeezing his thighs together and finally releasing the pullies. A *clang* of weights echoed behind him.

He slumped forward, taking a minute to breathe while succumbing to the ache sprouting up around his body.

Nothing like a good ol' healthy dose of self-harm.

Fortunately, the gym had been empty.

"Are you even listening to me?"

Feeling equally as shitty as when he'd entered, he wiped his face with his shirt and dug his phone out of his pocket, glaring at the curly-haired boy on the screen. "Yes, I'm listening," he grumbled, "I *know* how relationships work. All we were was friends with benefits. I *told him* I didn't want a real relationship weeks ago."

"You and I were friends with benefits. *You* put a personalized collar on the kid."

"Part of the benefit."

"Being exclusive, hanging out and having sex, treating someone like a pet - what do you think dating *is*?"

"Being *honest* about yourself? Look, I'm not proud of it, but I told him as little as possible trying to avoid this exact thing. Wouldn't that go to show he only fell for some *idea* of me?"

Brown eyes rolled at him on the other side of the screen, and the boy rubbed his temples in frustration. "You don't need someone's entire backstory to know you're attracted and want to keep them around, dumbass. People will be together for years because they thought the other person was hot and the one thing they had in common was Harry Potter."

"Billy Joel."

"Huh?"

"Nevermind. Continue."

"Point is," the boy sighed, "it sounds like that was the exact path you two were heading down."

If that was the path, Gil had taken a wrong turn somewhere.

He didn't need a date. Hell, he didn't even need a friend. He just needed an excuse. Someone to answer his "what ifs." *What if I had something to look forward to again? What if I could trick myself into being better?*

It could've been anyone.

Leaving his phone aside, Gil buried his face in his hands, hunching so far forward he was practically doubled over.

Barnaby brought up so many "what ifs" he'd never considered.

What if I could help him feel better about himself?

What if I could be like him, gentle and sweet?

What if I looked after him? What if I could make him feel safe?

What if I can't stay away from him? What if I don't try to?

"What are you doing now?"

"*Thinking.*"

A dangerous past-time that, granted, without the other on the phone, could be potentially fatal.

Barnaby was his own fucking person. He had a life, probably much more fulfilling before Gil stepped into it. He was more than solutions to problems the man only made for himself.

Barnaby deserved someone who was stronger and put together. Someone who could give him a happy ending.

And happy endings mixed into Gil's life as easily as oil mixed into water.

"Regardless, I'd only be wasting his time," he decided, "I already told him I'm not ready for the commitment. The fact is the only reason I haven't moved on yet is because he's the only guy I've found that has the same kinks."

Didn't matter if it was true. What mattered was that the other believed it.

There was a moment of silence. Then, he heard in the most exasperated voice - "You're a piece of work, Connolly."

Bingo.

"So, is that it? You're just never gonna talk to him again?"

Of course not. That would be the sensible thing to do.

"I'll give him a few days to cool down and try to talk to him then. Assuming he doesn't tear into me first."

"God, I hope I'm around for that."

Gil scoffed, and it somehow brought a smirk to his lips. "Oh, so you can play therapist in real time?"

"I sure as Hell won't! What happened to your last therapist? You can call her."

"I see her when I go home. For everything else—" Swiping his phone, Gil came face to face with his old friend once again— "there's you."

The boy shook his head, brown curls swishing over his brows. "One of these days I'm not gonna pick up unless it's for good news."

And Gil wouldn't have blamed him.

In fact, it was probably good practice.

"Please," Gil muttered, "we both know you don't get this kind of excitement from your cooking classes. Otherwise—" Grabbing his water bottle, he picked himself up and strutted out of the gym, back to his dorm, "why else would you be visiting?"

I'll leave the door unlocked ;)

Three nights later, and it was the same message greeting Barnaby as he checked their texts for the hundredth time.

He didn't know why he expected any different. Gil had said to text *him* when he was feeling better.

He almost was.

246

He'd woken up the next morning with a pit in his gut and a new outlook in mind. Maybe he didn't love Gil. Maybe he could love things *about* him, and maybe Gil felt the same, but that didn't automatically mean they had to be *in* love.

Right?

A conversation with Seth confirmed it for Barnaby: "I'm not a health professor," his roommate had told him, "but isn't sex *supposed* to make you feel that way?"

"You mean, like...dopamine?"

"*That's the bitch.* Yeah, you're not in love. You're just not as depressed."

He was right, probably. Barnaby didn't like hearing it, but it made sense. He'd used Gil as an anti-drug. Developed an addiction, maybe.

He couldn't hold it against the man for preventing an overdose.

He wanted to apologize. Each time he went to, however, Seth would discourage him. Apparently, it was "too soon." He needed to wait. Barnaby tried - busying himself with classes, work. Though, he didn't know what he was supposed to be waiting for. He did, at least, use the time to reflect. Time to consider that once the wait was up and he could apologize, he might actually be okay with only being his friend.

On the agreement they'd stop sleeping together.

Yeah. He could handle that. Probably.

By the time Seth returned from his Friday shift, too late even for him to suggest going out, Barnaby decided enough time had passed.

"I'm going to talk to him," he said, determined.

Seth huffed. "You're still on this?"

Barnaby took a deep breath, bracing himself as he sat up in bed. "I can't just forget about it. I can get over the, uhm...the *heartbreak*, if you can even call it that, but I don't want to give up on *him*."

Exhaustion was all too apparent on his roommate's face as he toed off his shoes. "Don't understand why."

Barnaby shook his head. "I-It's not his fault that...that I got the wrong message. He probably did what anyone else would've done, and I got too invested."

Seth turned and walked over to him, reaching out to place a hand on his shoulder. Looking into his eyes, he said very sternly, "Barnaby, I didn't wanna be the one to tell you this, but he's already seeing someone else." He paused, giving him a light squeeze, and finished, "Do yourself a favor, and let it go."

Barnaby didn't flinch. He was disheartened but not surprised. "How long did it take you to come up with that one, Seth?" he asked, "Five seconds?"

Seth's brows knitted together, and he hesitantly formed the words, "You think I'm joking."

"I know you think I'm naive. Okay?" Barnaby pushed, shrugging the other's hand away, "But I'm not *that* gullible."

A smile spread onto Seth's lips, bitter and sarcastic. "Text him if you don't believe me." Then, he whirled around, starting a search for his laptop. There seemed to be an unnecessary attempt of throwing around blankets and backpacks in his wake. "Ask him why, when he saw me in the lobby, he bolted past me to wait out in the rain. Ask him who Raul is, and if he's still there since *three o'clock this afternoon.*"

Barnaby immediately swallowed the tickle in his throat and glanced down at his phone. "That, uhm—" He scratched his nose. Rubbed his face. He breathed shakily, "Just because he's spending time with someone else doesn't mean anything. He could need support, too."

"Yeah," Seth grumbled, "support for keeping his dick up."

"*Stop it,*" Barnaby snapped. Suddenly, it was impossible to look anywhere but down. He cracked his knuckles. "Seriously. He's not...*like that*. He's—"

"Well, how the fuck do you know what he's like?" Blankets ended up in a heap on the floor, and he felt Seth's gaze burning into him again. "Because you slept with him for a month? Oh! Or because he took you to *Fwuff-A-Fwiend*?"

"I know him!" Barnaby blurted, quickly biting the inside of his cheek. "H-He was the one that said I was his best friend."

"Yeah," Seth scoffed, "and clearly that wasn't enough for you."

In his side-research on deer, Barnaby discovered that they stamp their hooves when on the defensive. It was a wonder he felt inclined to stomp his foot at Seth.

He muttered with every ounce of spite within him, "If it means having a friend who's actually nice to me, it's more than enough."

"Grow the fuck up," Seth spat, and all of Barnaby's resolve was gone. He hugged himself tight while the other persisted, "I'm not *nice* enough for you, but here I am, trying to look out for your autistic ass, and all you wanna do is defend the guy. I've *asked* about him, Barnaby! Everyone says the same shit: aside from having a class together or him using handcuffs during sex, they don't know anything about him. He *fucks* and flees. What did you think would make you any different?"

Barnaby winced. Once again, his throat was so closed up, he couldn't speak if he wanted to.

I was his pet.

I spent time with him.

I know he wants to be a literary agent. He has a sister named Addison, and he used to collect wolves as a kid.

I know he likes Billy Joel and he's in so much pain he hurts himself and has to be medicated.

He couldn't say why Gil treated him differently, but he'd never had a reason to question it. He'd accepted it, and he was grateful.

Seth was ignorant, and evidently, fed up. "Fuck it—" He threw his arms up in resignation and hopped onto his bed— "do whatever you want." He put on his headphones, a clear sign he'd block Barnaby out for the rest of the night. "At least I'll get to say I told you so."

> Can we talk?

Three words. But no matter how simple, Barnaby knew if they'd been sent to him, his heart would stop. When minutes went by without a response, he wasn't all too surprised. He tried to lessen the blow—

> I'm sorry. I'm not mad at you.

Minutes became an hour.

He couldn't stay in the dorm. Seth hadn't spoken a word, but Barnaby knew they were both waiting on proof against what the other had said. The difference between them: Seth likely didn't have to hold his breath with each passing second. Barnaby was suffocating.

Being outside helped him breathe, and the cold definitely kept him awake. He imagined he could go a lap around campus before going out to the bordering woods, curling up under a tree, and falling asleep for the night.

He could just as easily picture himself taking off his jacket, hoping the temperature continued to drop, and falling asleep for much, much longer.

He shivered and shook his head, his stomach in knots.

He needed to get back inside before thoughts became actions.

Giving his impulse some control, he headed for Talbot Hall. *I talked to him in person*, he fantasized telling Seth. Seth would sneer, but Barnaby wouldn't let it bother him. He'd know he was brave - impulsive, but he'd be wearing a badge of victory in his mind. And maybe, depending on how far Gil wanted to extend his generosity - *I spent the night, and the most we did was hug*. He could sleep on the floor. He was used to being treated like an animal, anyway.

Maybe, if he was lucky, he'd get to spend one more night in his nest.

He swallowed and swallowed, trying to breathe deep and steadily, focusing on the clouds puffing up in front of his face.

He wasn't thrilled about having to make the change. About not being kissed. Or held. No more "good boy" or "you're so cute" to make his heart flutter.

But those were just sacrifices he'd have to make.

It wasn't like there wouldn't be any gain. If they stayed friends, it'd finally give them a chance to be normal. They could go bowling, maybe play video games in the lounge like all the other Cool Kids. They might even be able to meet up during winter break and visit the mall again. He could ask Gil how to pick out decent clothes.

They'd turn a blind eye to Fluff-A-Friend, and Barnaby would probably have to come up with a new name for his fawn.

The name Talbot loomed over his head like a metal detector as he stepped into the red-bricked building - as if, without his collar, it would sound an alarm, warning its residents of a trespasser.

He barely had to flash his ID to the Not Seth Receptionist to be nodded at, permitted to continue.

It was late on a Friday night, and people were still lingering in hallways, coming in and out of dorms. Plenty of doors were open.

Room 239, as Barnaby assumed usual, was not.

He was about to knock when he thought he heard an eruption of laughter over music. Unsure and disbelieving of the source, he pressed close to the door.

He heard Gil's voice, too muffled to make anything out. And then he heard someone else.

He's allowed to have other friends.

Barnaby wanted him to be happy. He deserved to have a friend that would lift him up rather than bring him down.

He wondered how generous his friend (Raul?) was. If he'd let him borrow a minute of Gil's time.

Barnaby shrunk back. He stared at the door and twisted the fabric of his jacket between his fingers. He should've written everything down first. He didn't want to waste a moment.

I'm sorry for bothering you, Gil, I just wanted to apologize for being clingy and taking it too far. I'm also sorry because I want to be your friend, but I can't do the pet thing or sleep with you anymore. You were really good but—

But you're too good. And it means too much.

I still want to see you. And hang out. I still care about you. I hope you feel the same way. That's it. Have a good night.

Simple enough. He hoped.

As long as he could get the words, "I'm sorry", out.

He inhaled and took a small step forward.

His eyes were drawn to movement, and his heart stopped immediately.

The knob turned, and the door was opened.

Barnaby was a deer in headlights.

The light came from wide, russet eyes, right at his level.

He wore a leather jacket and a dangling earring. He was slim and had a flawless, almond complexion. Unruly brown hair made for the chocolate cherry on top of it all.

He was Not Barnaby.

He was beautiful.

And he had a very big hickey on the side of his neck.

"I'm sorry."

Barnaby wasn't needed there, and he didn't need to wait for anyone to tell him.

He turned away, walking right back the way he came.

Of course, Gil could have company. And he had every right to cuddle and claim them as he had with Barnaby. They were only friends to him, after all.

A gust of wind nearly pushed him back into the building as he tried to storm out.

Fuck.

There was nowhere else to go but home. Home where Seth would ask what happened, and maybe Barnaby could lie to him except - one, he doubted he had the capacity to make anything up in that moment, and two, even if he could, he'd be lucky to get a word out. It'd be obvious what'd happened. Seth would say he told him so, and—

"*Barnaby!*"

His blood ran as cold as the air. He fought to drag his feet away from the building, his knees buckling up. He was turning to ice.

Hypothermia couldn't take hold fast enough.

The wolf caught up with him, sinking his claws into Barnaby's shoulder. "Wait!"

The boy pushed Gil away with a force that caused both of them to stumble. "Don't *touch* me."

Gil panted. He wasn't wearing a coat. "I needed you to *wait*."

"I don't *want to* wait."

"But you...you came all the way here—"

Barnaby was having no easier time breathing. He pounded on his chest and wheezed, "I was— I wanted to— apologize and tell you—"

A frown settled deep on Gil's face; his pity took the form of puppy dog eyes.

Barnaby didn't want pity. Most of all, he definitely didn't want a friend who was willing to leave hickeys and who knew what else on another friend just to forget about him.

He swallowed yet another lump in his throat and continued walking. "Nevermind."

"No!" Gil was right up beside him. If he stayed out too long, he was going to get sick. "Talk to me. *Please*, Barnaby."

"Go back to Raul," Barnaby grumbled. His eyes were bleary, and he had to crack his knuckles over and over. Was he even on the right path to his dorm? "He probably needs you."

"*Raul*?" Gil asked, and Barnaby wondered how it felt to be found out. If it was as Earth-shaking as it was to walk in on. "Did he text you already?"

"Wha— *No*," the blond croaked. Did he want to brag to him *personally*? "And he doesn't need to. I get it. I'm sure he's so much fun to be with."

He could see Gil trying to get closer.

"He's not you," he said, strained, "He's—"

"*Prettier*?" Barnaby finally stopped, arms folded as he looked up at Gil. "Kinkier? Knows what he's doing? Easier to deal with? Everything else I made you miss out on?"

One blink, and Gil's eyes widened to the size of the moon before his brows knitted together, looming clouds. "Are you *kidding*?"

"*Are you*?!" Suddenly, Barnaby's face was warm. And wet. He'd believe it was raining if every other part of him wasn't dry. "I...I thought I *meant* something, but...if you can move on *that* quickly, I—"

He should have known.

He should have expected it.

If not for the fact that Gil got around, then for the pre-destined fate that Barnaby would have almost *no* impact on anyone he encountered.

He could practically count the sinews of his heart tearing one by one.

"I didn't *move on.*"

He envied how steady the man was able to keep his voice. "He had a hickey on his neck, Gil."

Silence.

Barnaby swallowed, rubbed his eyes, and watched Gil hang his head, fussing with his hair. "I'm sorry."

He'd admitted it. That was more than Barnaby needed.

He turned his back on him, ready to walk off again.

"I thought I could distract myself," Gil spoke suddenly, "but he's not— It's complicated, Barnaby, but if you'd let me *explain—*"

He didn't need an explanation.

He needed to leave.

He needed to *not* think about Gil giving someone else the same treatment he'd given him, uttering those same praises.

"It's fine—" Barnaby stomped his feet and clenched his hands, trying to get the blood flowing in his limbs to power through. "You should go," he sniveled, "be happy. Have fun with Raul."

"I can't be happy," Gil sighed, "knowing you're this upset."

That didn't stop you before.

And chances were, if Barnaby pointed it out, the cycle would repeat itself. Gil would go back to his Distraction, and Barnaby would still be crying to Seth about it.

His roommate. Who, with a bet, led him to meeting Gil in the first place.

He could've saved himself so much trouble, laughing it off the moment he'd suggested it.

Gil could've stayed another face in the crowd.

A hand grazed his back, and Barnaby flinched.

"Let's go somewhere warm, huh?"

"I only slept with you for money."

He wanted him to stop touching him. He wanted to avoid the risk of being tempted.

And it worked.

The hand fell from his back, and Gil retreated a step. "I never paid you."

"That's not—" Barnaby sniffled, cracking his knuckles. Cracking frostbite, maybe— "*I* was paid to sleep with you."

"What the Hell does that mean?"

"It means—" Spots started popping up around his vision. He blinked once, twice. Squeezed his eyes shut again and again. A tunnel was forming, and there wasn't a light he could make out the end of it. "It means I didn't sleep with you because I wanted to. I did it because I had to."

Gil was hardly a blur. Whether the man was stumbling, or Barnaby was dizzy - he couldn't tell.

The man scoffed, chuckling, "Okay, so…*What*? Someone paid you to sleep with me, but *you* were the one that wanted to be in a relationship with me. You—"

"I don't want to be in a relationship, actually. I realized that."

For a moment, the world succumbed to the cold, everything frozen.

Then, Gil said, "You came back."

Barnaby rubbed his eyes a final time.

Yeah, I did.

He managed to gain some clarity.

Gil's face came back into view, contorted by a mix of emotions, framed by hair blown into every direction.

Barnaby's breath hitched. "And I shouldn't have—" He gave Gil a once-over, one last look to remember him by, and for the last time, continued walking. "I shouldn't have agreed to any of this."

Chapter 17

where the FUCK r u

I s2g I'm not kidding

Gil

Connolly

GILBERT

Don't play this game with me, I'll call campus security.

Gym.

One word was all he had the patience for, pocketing his phone immediately after to resume his punches. He hadn't even bothered putting on gloves.

Raul must've moved fast.

He hadn't landed that many hits by the time the brunet kicked through the double doors, taking the stares previously aimed at Gil for himself.

He made a beeline for the boxing bag, grabbing onto the man's arm right as he was reeling back for another throw. "You know you can't just disappear like that," Raul grumbled.

"Last time I checked," Gil muttered, snatching his arm away from him, "I'm an adult. I can do whatever I want."

"You're a loose cannon—" Keeping his voice low, Raul scanned the other students in the gym, all seemingly absorbed in their workouts since Gil ended his assault. "What the Hell happened out there?"

"What do you think?" Exhaustion catching up with him, the man found a bench and collapsed onto it. He doubled over, hands raking and pulling through his hair until Raul sat beside him. "He saw your hickey," he growled, "He thinks I'm over the whole thing and that we're fucking."

"Shit."

It was. Absolute shit.

And Gil felt the shittiest he had in a long time.

But Raul was so against him punching the boxing bag, taking away the mental image he had of beating himself up.

His hands twitched, his muscles tensed, and his jaw clenched.

He'd managed to alleviate some of the pressure off of his brain. Staring dead at the floor, he aimed for the tension in his thigh next, barely registering the dull pulse that derived from it.

"Can you fucking...*stop—*"

The pulse was interrupted, and his hand was caught in a rigor mortis grip. In the corner of his eye, Raul examined his bruised and bleeding knuckles.

Huh. He was bleeding.

Raul licked his thumb and made himself useful, rubbing over his knuckles to wipe it up. "Are you relapsing?"

Gil chuckled, faint and humorless. *Silly Raul.*

He never improved enough for it to be considered relapsing.

But why not leave him with an ounce of hope?

"Great. Can't even show emotion without having my sanity questioned. Good to know."

He faced him just as the boy lifted his head to meet his gaze.

His shoulders bowed with his breath, somehow making him seem that much smaller. "You're allowed to be emotional," Raul stated, massaging Gil's hand, "What I'm trying to figure out is what *for*. First, you said you didn't want a relationship with him. Then, you make out with me only to break down in the middle of it. *Not like that's a first, but*...Now, you're literally kicking your own ass, man."

It'd be bold of Raul to assume he understood it for himself.

After his encounter with Barnaby, nothing made sense.

The more he thought about it, the more he questioned his own reality.

Had he been reading him wrong all along? Had he projected a desire to mean something to someone?

Like Barnaby had?

"I think," Gil said, fingers itching to reach for a cigarette, "I'm finding out what it feels like to get a taste of my own medicine. And it's not the Prozac this time."

The details were fuzzy, but they didn't matter.

Barnaby got what he needed, and that was all he cared about.

Normalcy.

Security.

Gil Connolly.

He decided he didn't need to be his friend, he just needed *him*.

He needed to know he was useful in some way to *someone*.

He needed to feel good, and he needed to forget.

Sex was a simple solution.

The only effort that came with riding Gil's face involved holding himself up, gripping onto the man's thighs while tattooed arms kept his hips in place. He had it under control, he'd assured Barnaby. He held every ounce of control.

Instead of worrying about loyalty, friendship, or unrequited emotions, Barnaby worried about breaking Gil's nose and suffocating him. Not that it stopped him, though. He bounced and grinded as if the man's jaw was sculpted from indestructible marble. He felt every solid impression beneath his supple flesh, encouraging him to rock back, cushioning Gil's face with his entire ass. Most of all, Barnaby needed his tongue - more than air, if his panting was any indicator of that. Each swipe over his rim was another stolen breath, another shiver racking his spine. Soon enough, it was poking right through him, and the boy would've collapsed face first into Gil's crotch if not for the steady hands reeling him in.

Of course, one hand proved to be strong enough on its own; the other, unfaltering, brought him to his limit almost as soon as it started jerking him off.

One final cry of pleasure, and Barnaby's world went white.

He fell to the bed all the same, blinking and squinting to get his world back into focus—

Only to find himself in his own dorm, in bed alone, under the morning light, blinding him from the window.

For a moment, all he could do was stare at the wall, slowly processing what had happened.

It felt so real.

But thank God it wasn't.

Thank God he had some self-respect left.

His reassurance dwindled when he tried to sit up. Gil may not have physically been there, but his body, evidently, had a physical reaction to the thought of it.

He considered throwing out his briefs altogether.

Deciding to head for the showers instead, he turned, intending to stand but nearly having a heart attack when his eyes landed on Seth. His roommate sat in his own bed, laptop equipped as usual.

"I thought you had work," Barnaby grumbled, glancing to the floor.

"I did," Seth sighed. He shut his laptop close to face the blond, brows over his glasses in *We Need To Talk* fashion. "But now I'm sick." He'd never sounded clearer.

Barnaby gave a small nod and pulled his knees to his chest, preparing himself. Seth had promised an "I told you so", and he deserved it.

He'd slept for hours and still he felt too exhausted to cry when Seth walked over to sit beside him.

He was silent, at first. Of course, the instant Barnaby spared a glance at him, he opened his mouth, making him flinch - "They're having a movie night later in the Main Lounge. We don't have to go together, but I think they're playing *Wreck It Ralph* or something, so I thought you might like to know."

Barnaby perked up, curious but cautious. He'd had enough of being lured into false senses of security, thank you very much. He mumbled, "Why are you telling me this?"

Seth shrugged, his expression flat. "I thought you liked that movie. And, I don't know, in case you wanted to get out and do something."

"No. I mean—" Barnaby shook his head, grabbing his blanket to rub between his hands. Wasn't he the odd one out?

Shouldn't it be easy for everyone else to be up front? Or did they like to watch him squirm? "Why aren't you telling me off? You were right about...*him.*"

Their eyes met, and Barnaby watched as Seth's loss dawned upon him. The opportunity to bring the blond down further had been taken away.

With a pout on his lips, Seth removed his glasses and busied himself by cleaning the lenses with his shirt. "Because there's no point," he grumbled, "Reminding you and having to hear you cry about it all over again isn't going to do me any good."

Barnaby supposed that made sense.

"So instead," his roommate inhaled, "I'm asking you, do you want to watch *Wreck It Ralph* later, or would you rather be left alone?"

The idea on its own was enough to add to Barnaby's dread. He shook his head. "No, I—" He swallowed out of habit, unaware if there was in fact a lump or not. He sucked in his breath. "I don't think I should be alone. I—"

"Alright, don't start hyperventilating."

A hand touched his shoulder, and Barnaby flinched reflexively. Gil's hand had left an imprint somewhere - his aura, his soul? Somewhere that the boy had to let his brain process that the one touching him would not deliberately betray him.

Seth may not have been the most gentle or easy to talk to, but Barnaby, at the end of the day, knew what to expect.

He wasn't hyperventilating. He could breathe. He was as safe as he was going to be.

He dove for Seth's torso, wrapping his arms around him. He kept his head low, avoiding whatever look of embarrassment smeared across the other's face. "I'm sorry."

There'd been a delay before Seth began patting Barnaby's back, a few awkward thumps that made the blond *more* emotional. "Don't be, I guess."

He was nothing but an inconvenience, dumping his baggage on Seth. If he'd taken his advice, he wouldn't have had any trouble in the first place.

He pulled away to wipe his eyes, already beginning to water. Why did everything have to affect him so much? He wasn't a child, or even a high schooler rejected by his first crush. He was a goddamn man.

He tried to sniffle and swallow everything down, just for Seth to pull him back in.

"If you're gonna cry," he grumbled, "go ahead and get it over with."

Barnaby hesitated, but it wasn't long before the word *inconvenience* repeated itself over and over in his head, a broken record. *He* was a broken record. Always repeating the same cycle, never changing. Always, so obviously, broken.

He'd always been a burden to Seth and always would be, good for nothing more than being a means to an end.

Exactly how Gil had intended to use him.

How had Barnaby forgotten? How did he make himself hope it would be any different, that someone could be *nice* to him and play *fair*?

How many times did Seth have to tell him, "*People suck, and life's not fair*"?

He wished it could be. He wished so *bad* that people would be gentle. Patient. Kinder.

He wished they would be like Gil. Or at least, the Fantasy Gil he thought so highly of.

He cried out of mourning. For their relationship, for the world - for Seth's shirt that he definitely ruined with mucus.

For a while, his roommate didn't say anything. He merely rubbed his back, letting the minutes pass until, eventually, Barnaby couldn't produce another tear.

The instant the blond pulled away to wipe his face with his sleeve, Seth looked down at himself and sneered, "Disgusting."

"Sorr— *ow*."

He'd flicked Barnaby square on the forehead. "Movie or no movie?"

Barnaby sniffled one last time, nodding.

"Do you want me to go?"

He was still nodding when he leaned in again, giving Seth another hug.

His roommate sighed but didn't resist. Maybe he wasn't the most affectionate, and maybe he was only putting up with it so he could say the boy owed him later. But in that moment, he allowed it, seemingly, for Barnaby's sake.

For that, Barnaby muttered, "Thank you."

They split up when it felt right. Settled. Seth returned to his computer, and Barnaby made his way to the showers.

He soaked and scrubbed until he might as well have had a new skin, a body that was his again - untouched, unclaimed. Looking down, he saw he was clear of any markings; no leftover fluids, other than water and soap suds, to trickle down his frame, either.

He smiled faintly to himself and trailed his fingers from his chest to his stomach. At times, he was grateful for how fine his hair was, unable to deny the pleasant smoothness of his body.

When Barnaby returned, he added his briefs to the rest of his laundry. If he could be cleaned, so could they.

He spent the next few hours on Seth's bed with his own laptop, lying beside him, then sitting back to back. With a clearer mind and a bit of weight off his shoulders, he did his best to read up on study guides for his classes. Finals were only a week away, after all.

At a quarter to eight, they left the dorm and headed for the lounge in Main Hall. Initially, it was a daunting sight for Barnaby - dozens of students crowded the second story lobby, piled onto couches and beanbag chairs surrounding a projector-screen.

He'd always had a habit of sitting alone in crowded rooms, and he half-expected Seth to recognize and go off with someone else.

Thankfully, he didn't.

Together, they spotted a snack table and wandered over.

Once they had their paper plates filled with pizza and cookies, they found a spot on the floor where they could sit beneath a window (Seth offered to sit in Barnaby's lap if he wanted to squeeze on the couch, but Barnaby quickly turned him down). The lights dimmed, the movie began, and those shushing their peers to be quiet swiftly became the loudest in the room. Their efforts, however, were in vain, and it didn't take long for the Class Clown types to chime in with their own commentary on the film.

Though slightly annoying, Barnaby reminded himself that if all he wanted to do was watch a movie, he would've stayed home. The point of going was— was because that was what college was supposed to be, wasn't it? Going to the lounge, getting involved with people you normally wouldn't—

Recovering from hookups and getting your heart broken.

Barnaby scanned the room.

Maybe he wasn't alone, and maybe he was better off for it. He and Gil never officially dated, but how many people around him did? How many of them had put months or years of investment into a person, poured their hearts out and planned for forever only to discover they weren't The One? How many were rebounds?

He munched on a cookie and shifted his focus to the film. It was easier when, in the back of his mind, the thought lingered: by doing the most absurd thing he could think of, did he actually become, at least somewhat, *normal*?

"Jason and them are headed over," Seth mumbled, looking up from his phone.

Barnaby smiled and nodded, acknowledging him. Maybe he was even normal enough to belong to a group.

When they entered the lounge - Jason, Diana, Mell, and Colton - they were quick to crowd them, making room for themselves on the floor around Seth and Barnaby. There was "Sorry, we're late", and "I thought they stopped doing this", and "Shut the fuck up", and even a friendly, "Hey, Barnaby! How are you?"

Nothing to suggest Seth had told them anything about what had happened with Gil.

Greetings turned to whispers as everyone settled down, and Barnaby's eyes returned to the projector, keeping one ear open to listen to the group's commentary. Whatever he heard, he'd look to them and grin. Just to be sure they felt appreciated.

As time passed and the movie approached its finale, Barnaby started catching onto murmurs between Seth and the others, plans to head to some "Gamers' Guild" afterwards. Soon enough, he felt a poke in his side, and he turned to find all eyes on him.

Seth asked, "You up for Mario Kart?"

The offer was tempting, and Barnaby considered it an honor that they'd invite him. He didn't doubt he would enjoy himself.

But another glance, and he noticed Jason and Diana holding hands. Of course, they would - they were a *real* couple. They would probably kiss and cuddle up to each other, and they had every right to.

But the reminder was too great for a wound so fresh, and Barnaby suspected it would spare his sanity if he *didn't* subject himself to witnessing any of it.

He said, "Thanks, but I'm kind of tired. I'm probably just gonna go to bed after this."

Seth scoffed but didn't push it. Although, when the movie was over and they were on their way out, he made a point of quietly asking the blond, "Sure you're gonna be okay on your own?"

Barnaby mustered a smile and nodded as confidently as he could. "Yeah. That was pretty much all I needed, I think. It helped." He gave his roommate a hug before he could get away. "Thank you for everything."

Seth's embrace was, as usual, delayed, but when he muttered, there was a playful lift to his voice, "*Gay.*"

Barnaby watched as he joined the rest of the group, all waving as they went their separate ways.

Walking home alone, he tried to distract himself with ideas of what to do once he returned to the dorm. He could continue studying, watch some videos on YouTube, maybe even make himself a genuine, decent meal.

Although, he could have done any of that while Seth was there.

Stepping into the room, Barnaby closed the door and leaned against it, thinking.

He could barely remember the last time he masturbated, his greatest sacrifice under Gil's order. How long had it been since he'd taken charge of his own pleasure?

There was nothing to stop him. No roommate, no rules, no owner. He had complete autonomy, and *he* knew his body better than anyone; he knew the best ways to make it feel good.

And he wasn't about to let anyone trick him into forgetting that ever again.

He toed off his shoes and stripped down to nothing. He left the light switch off; the glow from the fairy lights on his headboard was all he needed to get around.

Crawling into bed, Barnaby attempted to form his pillows and blankets into a nest, something cozy to cradle him in. Something safe.

He grabbed the lube from his nightstand and hunkered in. Despite the ingrained belief that his body was nothing worth marveling at, Barnaby *felt* Beauty. He felt it radiating from his lights, from his nest, plush against his skin, and from the innate act of coating his dick in lube, stroking himself without much thought.

Closing his eyes, he let out a rattled breath. A smile spread across his lips, coy, at how vulnerable he was in that moment. Naked and lewd, and he was the only one who got to enjoy it.

He was hard in minutes, succumbing to his lust. He chased every sensitive nerve, desperate and greedy for those wonderful tingling sensations, for electricity surging through his spine, and for starting a firepit in his core.

He licked his drying lips and let his whimpers pour freely out. He had no reason to be ashamed of them. He tossed and turned and humped the bed. The fire in his belly spread to his face, and his hands moved faster and faster. He was so wonderfully pitiful that he was almost proud of it.

He was everything primal. An animal undomesticated.

His whimpers became gasps and high-pitched moans. Squeals. Settling on his back, he let his hips thrust desperately upward. He lifted his knees, legs spread, and lowered one hand to fondle his balls. With more control given to the hand on his cock, he squeezed his sac gently, imagining his load being milked out. *Closer.* Closer—

"*Mah!*"

He arched off of the bed, oblivious to the direction of his stream. His eyes rolled to the back of his head. *Yes, yes, yes!* He didn't want to stop. He wanted to follow that high to the end of the Earth. It was so *good*.

It lasted long enough that his wrist started to cramp. His member became too sensitive to touch, he was terribly short for breath, and he trembled more than he was used to.

He wiped his hand against a pillow and pulled the blankets over his head, warming up but feeling no less naked.

He was drifting. Not quite tired but not all there.

He pawed at the mattress, and it was as if his own sheets felt unfamiliar.

Shouldn't there have been weight there?

A door slammed far away, and Barnaby's heart all but flew from his chest. He gripped the covers tighter around him. Voices mumbled outside of his room. *Hunters*? Were they coming for him? Would they laugh at how helpless he'd made himself? Would they hurt him?

The young buck whimpered again. He didn't want to alert them, but with no one to shush him, what was he supposed to do? He was scared.

Where were the arms to protect him?

He rubbed his hand against his neck. No collar. He was free game. Anyone's target.

The voices faded along with the sound of footsteps, but the growing pit in his chest remained.

Barnaby was an animal. He was wild at heart, and he had his connection to the natural world hardwired in his brain.

But he had been tamed. He'd been trained, eaten from a master's hand, and slept in his bed.

He'd been a Good Boy. A pet. He wasn't fit for the wild anymore.

His sight became blurry, and Barnaby began to choke up. His trembling persisted.

He may as well have been in the middle of a meadow, surrounded by traps and men with long rifles. Or better yet, a cage, up for adoption, where he could look on while people passed him and said, "Think of how much trouble he'll be to take care of."

Barnaby hiccupped. A tear fell hot on his cheek.

He didn't mean to be so much trouble.

A clock ticked on the wall. Another minute had passed, and he was still alone. No one was coming for him. No one would get to hear his apology - how *sorry* he was for existing.

There certainly wouldn't be anyone coming to contradict it any time soon.

Chapter 18

He woke up parched the following morning with a knot in his stomach and a splitting headache.

Eyes barely open, and he was cocooning himself in his blankets, as snug as he possibly could. The air was crisp, and his skin was frost. He'd fallen asleep naked.

Heart picking up speed, Barnaby rolled over to face Seth's side of the room.

It was empty.

He frowned, not knowing if it was for better or worse. Sure, he could get out of bed without being teased, but it would've been nice having someone to distract him - and possibly, someone he could ask to hold him. Just for a little while.

Hauling himself onto his feet, Barnaby pulled out a container from underneath his mattress, taking a pair of jeans and an old rugby shirt. He had to squeeze into them - sucking in his gut, barely getting his jeans buttoned (surrendering when his shirt started riding up) - but they were among his only options.

He needed to do his laundry. Especially before work.

At least it'd be something to keep him busy.

He brushed his teeth, washed his hands, and fixed his hair trying to appear halfway decent. He heard buzzing and remembered his phone on the nightstand.

He went to find it, breathing a sigh of relief when he realized the text was from Seth:

> Check the fridge. It's for you.

Raising a brow, Barnaby headed for their mini-fridge. Inside, he discovered a new paper bag. In that paper bag: cookies, pretzels, and cheese puffs. Nothing that he'd assume his stomach could handle in that moment, but he was grateful for every future bite.

> Kind of gay tbh.

> But thank you <3

He left the snacks for later and fetched his bucket filled with dirty clothes, carrying it out of the dorm, down the hall, to the laundry room. In need of some good luck, he found one empty washing machine and began piling his clothes in—

At least, until, he held a camo-print sweater and realized they weren't *just* his clothes.

He paused, unsure of what to do with the sweater, the hoodies, and the sweatpants he had borrowed. Did Gil forget about them? Would he consider them a loss, or was he waiting for the storm to pass to ask for them back?

Barnaby breathed in deep, trying to pick up his heart as it slid. *Hold on until you get back to the room.*

Maybe, when the storm had passed, Barnaby would be brave enough to take the initiative. He could start and control the conversation: "Hey. What do you want me to do with your clothes?"

In the meantime, he continued tossing them in with his own laundry.

He booked it back to his dorm the instant the washer was set. It quickly occurred to him that, by cleaning them, there was the possibility of losing Gil's scent. That should've been his goal; he *knew* crying over another missing piece of Gil's puzzle was ridiculous, but that didn't stop the tears from flowing.

Fortunately, his sobbing was brief; a few, short hours later, and Barnaby had long since dried his eyes, finished his laundry, put on a fresh uniform, and made his way to the cafe.

He walked in on the usual Sunday crowd, immediately apprehensive - but the moment he spotted Savannah behind the counter, became a little less tense.

He clocked in and went right to helping her fulfill orders while she handled the register.

"Hey, Barnaby!" she hollered, never too busy to greet him. Her smile was as warm as a summer sun, unwavering, despite his autumn clouds.

"Hey, Sav." Barnaby sent out a few coffees, waiting until she had a moment to spare before idling close enough to mutter, "Fair warning, but...I'm not really sure what kind of headspace I'm in right now? I think I'd rather work behind the scenes...if that's okay?"

It probably wasn't okay, but she agreed anyway, her tone equally sympathetic as it could have been sarcastic.

Whether or not that was the intention, Barnaby thanked her with a promise, "I'll make it up to you. I swear."

He started housekeeping without wasting another second of paid time. He cleaned and refilled their equipment, stocked the pastry display, swept the floors, and eagerly wiped down tables the minute they were done being used. The moment Savannah needed to ring up an order, he was there - even when she laughed and told him, "Barnaby, I've got this."

"Nope," he insisted, "you're good right there."

As they approached the dinner hour, the cafe began to empty out. Barnaby finally paused beside his coworker, curious as she looked around like she had lost something. Before he could ask, she gave a playful sigh, "Did you leave *anything* for me to do?"

Barnaby chuckled, "I *was* gonna take inventory after my break."

Her topaz eyes widened, and she aimed a finger at him. "I'm taking inventory. After *my* break."

The blond flushed a touch. How could he forget? He practically barred her from moving ever since he arrived.

She didn't go for it right away though. Instead, Savannah scanned the shop and the few customers that were left. Her voice was still directed to Barnaby when she asked, "How are you feeling?"

It caught him a bit off guard, and he rubbed his arms with sweaty palms. "Uhm...better? I guess?" He'd felt productive - like he'd actually been able to *accomplish* something that day. He supposed that was an improvement.

The woman nodded in thought. "Good enough to watch the register?"

Barnaby inhaled. Maybe another customer or two would come in while Savannah was away. More than likely, they'd ask for something light. Something he, hopefully, wouldn't have to rush. All he had to do was remember his script.

He practiced his customer service smile on her. "I'll give it my best."

Savannah believed it and patted his shoulder as she passed— "Call me if you need anything." Grabbing her coat from under the counter, she headed for the back door.

His prediction was right. Minutes passed, and Barnaby was able to check his phone, respond to texts from Seth, and like his mom's Facebook posts about new recipes she'd been trying out for Hanukkah. Two separate pairs of customers came in to keep him on his toes, neither asking for much or sticking around after their orders were received, thankfully.

No, Barnaby couldn't really complain.

Still wanting to show Savannah his appreciation, he went about steeping her favorite drink, a simple Earl Grey Tea, right on his tab.

"Barnaby?"

The blond perked up, facing a voice he didn't recognize.

Suddenly, he had no voice of his own, recognizing the speaker.

His instinct was to freeze. Shut down. Dissociate out of existence. He couldn't hurt or panic if he didn't feel anything at all.

He thought he would faint, judging by the immediate pressure to his brain, the sensation that an abyss had formed beneath his feet. He expected a blackout. Longed for it.

It was an absolute wonder to him how he made it from the register to the back door, startling Savannah, still outside with a vape pen. It wouldn't be the first time he'd heard it - "*Barnaby, you can't just leave!*"

"Sorry," he blurted, "I can't."

"What's the matter?" his coworker stammered.

He blinked, and her eyes were wide with fear. He was such a piece of shit. *He* caused that, and she had nothing to be afraid of.

"*What's wrong?*"

He didn't even know how to explain it. "The—" he fumbled, "guy...in there—" Barnaby shook his head, hoping that rattling his thoughts would turn them into words— "Gil *left me for*, and I *can't—*"

"Okay. *Okay.*" Gripping his shoulders, Savannah helped ground him to reality. Her fear had faded into exhaustion. Pity. Disappointment. "Wait here. *Breathe.* I'll go see what's up."

Barnaby hugged himself and nodded, already beginning the timer in his head: *one, two, three—*

He could sense Savannah's hesitation before letting him go and venturing inside. She didn't trust him alone probably, but someone had to watch the register.

He started pacing, dragging his feet across the ground to remind himself that something was there.

Cruel vengeance, Barnaby decided. It had to be. He'd damaged Gil's pride, and in retaliation, Gil sent Raul to add salt to his wounds. Worst of all, he'd sent him to his *workplace.* That was just setting him up to be publicly humiliated!

The dragging of his feet turned to stomping. He could stop worrying about missing Gil. If the man had been looking for a quick, easy way to bereave him, he'd succeeded. He could forget about the clothes he'd let him borrow, too. As far as Barnaby was concerned, he'd never see them again.

He came to a halt as the door in front of him opened.

Poking her head through, Savannah motioned for him to come back inside.

He stayed close as he entered, practically hidden in her shadow. "What did he want?" he whispered, afraid but curious of what she had learned.

"That," she sighed, stopping behind the counter, "is something you have to discuss." Pointing to one of the booths, she directed Barnaby's gaze to the last of their patrons - Raul.

He stared at his table, fiddling with rings on his fingers.

Barnaby must have gawked, because as soon as he looked back at Savannah, her mouth was already moving, "I am not going anywhere, and if something goes wrong, I will literally wipe the floor with him, but..." She glanced back and forth between the two and shrugged— "it sounds like he has a lot to say to you."

Barnaby bit his lip. What was there to say? "*Stay away from my man*"?

It made Barnaby think. *You know, don't you? He doesn't belong to anyone.*

He uttered once more to Savannah, "Promise you'll be here?"

"Promise."

Swallowing his nerves, he pressed forward, conscious of every awkward step he took toward Raul's booth. "Hey."

The beautifully tanned boy looked up at him, eyes just as wide as when they first met, just as surprised to see him. "Uh, hey—" His brows furrowed, and a faint smile appeared on his face, as if he was trying to make himself seem nervous. As if he was trying to make himself seem like Barnaby. "How are you feeling?"

The blond's frown only deepened, and he held himself. "Could be better, honestly."

Raul pursed his lips, nodding. "I feel that. Uhm—" He gestured to the seat across from him.

Assuming his legs would eventually give out otherwise, Barnaby slid into the booth.

"About everything," Raul muttered, eyes weighing to the table, "I'm sorry."

Barnaby gaze flickered to him, unexpected. "Why are you sorry?"

"Well, for freaking you out at work, and...*the obvious.*"

Hazel eyes drifted to the window, the door - at the other tables around them. He looked for a hidden camera. A phone. He almost asked to see Raul's, to check if he was recording their conversation. He had Savannah to back him up, but morbid curiosity made him wonder how far the other was willing to go along - "Did you know?"

"About you? A little—" When Raul's gaze wandered to the window, it stayed there.

Barnaby glanced again, expecting to find Gil on the other side.

"He filled me in on the situation," the boy went on, "and by the sounds of it, I thought you two were over. He said he needed a distraction, and..." He trailed off, sighing. Finally, he fixed his sights on Barnaby. "Listen, I don't know if it means anything, but we didn't sleep together."

But he did give you the impression we were through.

Which, Barnaby supposed, he couldn't really blame Gil for, after the way he'd made him leave. He might've thought it too, but—

He scratched his head. "I just don't understand how he was able to move on so fast."

"Because he doesn't see it that way," Raul grumbled, and it didn't sound like it was his first time explaining, "Like I said, it's a distraction for him. He doesn't want to deal with the situation or know how to cope with it, so he goes back to what he *does* know."

Barnaby wondered what *he'd* been a distraction from. If he had been the catalyst for another boy's heartbreak. "How long have you known him?"

"Since high school. To his credit, he's not as bad as he used to be."

Barnaby scoffed, "What, did he have multiple guys at once?"

"No— I mean, he had *worse* ways of coping."

When spoken in such an ominous tone, it wasn't hard to deduce the method— "Cutting."

Raul's face scrunched as if he'd smelled something foul. The smell of copper, perhaps. "He told you?"

"I found out," Barnaby sighed, wishing he hadn't, "I saw the meds, too."

Little by little, it began to sink in - like the first few drops of rain before a storm. He'd be saturated by the time he reached shelter.

He buried his head in his hands, trying to rub his own tension away. "I'm sorry, I..."

He wanted to be upset and feel like he had a right to be. He wanted to stand up for himself and not be a doormat for someone else for once.

But for all the times he couldn't, all that pain and grief he'd experienced as a result— was never something he'd wished on anyone.

Not even his first heartbreak.

It was a matter of fact: had Gil not shown Barnaby so much kindness, it wouldn't have hurt so much to be without him.

And, oh *God,* did it hurt to think about.

Maybe it was dependency, but there wasn't anyone else he wanted rushing up to him in that moment, wrapping their arm around him to keep him steady. He wanted fingers combing through his hair and the faint smell of smoke in his nose. He wanted a soft, velvet voice in his ear telling him it would be okay, that he wasn't easily replaceable, that they should go back to his dorm, and he would take care of him anyway he needed. He'd be swaddled in blankets and fed cookies and wear his collar to prove someone *wanted* him.

"I just wanted—" Barnaby croaked around a lump in his throat, "*Fuck.* I wanted to mean as much to him as he did to me. I wanted *both of us* to be happy. Is that selfish? Is it *wrong*?"

"No," Raul muttered, "there's nothing wrong with that. Although—"

Something landed on Barnaby's shoulder, and he would have shoved it away if not for looking up to realize it was the other boy's hand, lightly touching him.

He was leaning across the table, about to retract, when he said, "I think you mean a lot more to him than you think you do. He's *obsessed* with the idea that you slept with him for money."

Barnaby blinked away a few tears, not sure if he heard him right— "Obsessed?"

"Yeah! He talks to me about it like *I* know what you're thinking and acts like I'm the one keeping information from him. And hey, man, I'm not judging you - if you need that coin, get it, times are hard - but as much as he could've been better about making his intentions known, the least you could've done was be honest about it."

And he would've, probably, if he'd been paid any time after their first encounter.

"It's...complicated," he admitted, twiddling his thumbs, "I exaggerated. I wanted to...affect him."

He wanted to hurt him. He wanted the guy on antidepressants with scars on his wrists - the guy who told him, "I'm not interested in a relationship" - to *hurt*.

He felt green in the face, his stomach performing somersaults. He'd have to find a bathroom very soon.

"I'd say you succeeded—" Concern knitted Raul's brows over his weary expression, calculating, perhaps, which way to lean if Barnaby vomited. He'd be smart to do so. "Look, I'll be honest, I think the best thing the two of you can do is talk. It sounds like both of you are hung up on *something,* and I think it's obvious you both had a lot more invested than sex. That said...Is going back to Normal the right answer? I don't know. All I can say about him is that he's still got a lot of work to do on himself. As we've seen."

As did Barnaby. He couldn't deny that.

But doing it alone? He never made much progress. And what better proof of that than his inability to properly communicate with *anyone*?

At least he'd been open about that with Gil - though he'd been adamant that Barnaby "made sense."

"Tell him," he breathed, tugging at his sleeves, "I'd be willing to talk to him, but I need a few more days. But if he's not feeling well or if he really, *really* needs to talk to me sooner—" Barnaby swallowed, looking into Raul's eyes, "he can call me."

Raul nodded, the faintest hint of a smile on his lips. "I'll tell him—" He glanced at his phone— "but if that's all, I should probably get going. Last thing I need today is my bus leaving without me."

"How far is your dorm?" Barnaby asked, clinging to a shift in focus.

"I don't go here," Raul said, getting up from the booth, smoothing out his leather jacket, "I was just visiting for the weekend. So, don't worry, you won't have to see much of me."

He held out his hand, and Barnaby reached for it, assuming it'd be a shake before parting ways. Instead, Raul pulled, and he found himself led to his feet.

"Th-This isn't," the blond cautioned, unsure of how to phrase it, "I don't want to compete with you - not that it would *be* a competition - but if you have feelings for him—"

"Hombre, that ship sailed years ago. I let him kiss me because I didn't get the full picture, and...it was the most harmless thing he could do—" Raul shrugged— "Or so I thought."

While it should've been comforting, Barnaby couldn't help but be skeptical. Though, he supposed, that was a result of his own bias. His ship was still stuck at port, flooding. In his condition, he couldn't imagine sailing away.

Raul held a fist out in front of him, and it took Barnaby longer than it probably should've to realize he was waiting for a fist-bump.

He stuttered an apology, following through.

"Do you want my number?" Raul offered, "In case Dumbass decides to be a dick? I'll be on the next bus back here if it means beating some sense into him."

"*I*...don't think that'll be necessary, but, uhm—" Barnaby scrambled for his phone, handing it over, "if you still want to."

He almost apologized for not having that many contacts.

Raul made no comment - simply added himself to the small list, returned the phone, and parted with an, "I'm glad I got to talk to you."

More than less, Barnaby was glad, too.

He watched as the boy left through the door, crossed the street, and disappeared down the sidewalk.

He glanced to the clock. Still a few more hours left of his shift.

"Hey, Savannah," Barnaby asked his coworker, meeting her at the register, "is there a notepad I can use?"

Chapter 19

Two nights and an awkward text conversation later, Gil and Barnaby decided to meet at the library.

It seemed like an even playing field. Neither of them would be able to control the environment, and neither would be able to raise their voice.

In the back. By the biographies.

Barnaby's bomber jacket did little to protect him against the chills racking his bones from reading the message.

The sky had turned dark - not that his peers seemed to notice. They continued walking by, presumably more concerned about assignments and finals than the space he took up on the steps. He'd rather those be his biggest concerns, too.

Perhaps he'd stalled in front of the building long enough.

Be right there.

Stuffing his phone into his backpack, Barnaby hauled himself to his feet. Another group of students passed, and he slipped behind them to enter the library, his blood growing colder despite the newfound warmth.

He slinked through the aisles, following his feet before he could have the mind to turn around.

He'd faced his fears with Gil before. He could do it again.

He spotted the plaque for Biography books and turned a corner. Three vintage-style armchairs waited, facing each other, blocking out the rest of the world.

Gil, seated in one of them, was submerged in the world of whatever book he was reading.

He didn't look up until Barnaby was in front of him, muttering, "Hi."

"Hey." Placing the book into the satchel at his feet, Gil leaned back in his chair, hands folded in his lap. Like Raul, his nails were painted black. His eyes were bleaker than Barnaby remembered, lips taut in a straight line.

The blond sat across from him, wiping the sweat from his palms onto his jeans before reaching into his backpack once again. A single piece of paper was all he needed.

He prayed it was enough. So much had been cut from his revisions with Savannah and Seth. "You're rambling," they'd told him, "You're apologizing for things you shouldn't."

But I need him to understand.

He took a deep breath in, checking if Gil was attentive with a final glance, before reading, "W-When we first met, I wasn't completely honest. While it was true that I wanted to be, be touched by someone else...I probably wouldn't have gone through with it if I wasn't in financial trouble. You see, before the semester started, Seth made a *"bet"* with me that whoever lost their virginity first would get $100...I say *"bet"* because after I told him what happened, I realized he hadn't expected me to take it seriously. That was the first and only time I was ever "paid" to sleep with—"

"Why didn't you tell me when I asked?"

Barnaby locked up. Perhaps he should have told him not to interrupt him first. He sighed, shakily, "I assumed you wouldn't let me stay. And, like I said...I *did* want to know what having sex was like."

When Gil didn't try to challenge him, he swallowed, persisting, "I was vague because I was hurting and...I wanted you to hurt, too." Saying it out loud brought him face to face with guilt, but— "I'm still hurt because you didn't talk to me before moving onto Raul. I felt betrayed. I know we were never official, I know you don't owe it to me to be loyal, but please try to think about why it hurt you to think that I'd sleep with you for money. How would you feel if I didn't stay around because I genuinely cared? Or if I was acting like a pet for someone else on the side?"

His voice nearly gave out by the second question, cut off by a forming lump in his throat. His heart grew heavier with each beat, and he knew it wouldn't be long until his head was swimming.

Gil answered with silence.

"I don't know what I'm supposed to do," Barnaby continued, "I do care about you, and I want to fix things if we can, but I can't go back to how things were if it doesn't mean as much to you. I'll be your friend, but...being physical has a lot more emotional weight for me now, I think. That's why it's hard for me to understand why...or *how* you did what you did."

Maybe it wasn't Gil's fault. Maybe it was his fault for ever saying anything. For thinking he could be enough.

Why is nothing I do good enough?

A tear fell onto the paper, and Barnaby quickly wiped his eyes. "Sorry, I—" His voice cracked, barely catching a sob. He kept his hand in front of his face and fought to steady his breath, failing to keep himself together.

He'd failed at everything to that very point. He'd failed Seth and Savannah, being their burden; he'd failed Gil, overstepping his boundaries; he'd failed himself, scaring away yet another person from his life and being so *weak*. He'd probably failed the other students in the library, too, taking up their study space just to have a meltdown.

Something touched his back.

"*I'm* sorry," Gil muttered from right beside him.

Peeking through his fingers, Barnaby noticed he'd changed his seat.

He rubbed careful circles between the boy's shoulder blades and spoke, "It's not that it doesn't have emotional weight for me. It does. Which is why I...*tried* with Raul. I think the difference between us is I didn't see it as romantic. I just saw it as a d—"

"A distraction. I get that, in a way," Barnaby sniveled, "but...*shit*, was I that easy to forget about? Was it that easy to, to get what I was giving you from someone else? Please, just be honest, Gil, I need to know how to be better, I—"

"*It wasn't like that.*"

His wrists were grabbed, both hands pulled into Gil's lap.

He locked eyes with him, ugly and unwilling, only to watch regret consume the man's expression.

It's your fault I'm ugly, Barnaby thought, *is what I would say if I hadn't always been.*

Gil released his hold. "Sorry."

"It's fine—" *It's not like I have the strength to fight back, anyway.*

But Gil sputtered, "It's not fine. None of this is *fine*. What I did was fucked up, but it wasn't because of something you did or didn't do. I *closed my eyes*, trying to pretend he was you. The second he opened his mouth and I realized he wasn't? I couldn't do it. I stopped. And I know it's a shitty excuse, I *know* it's fucked up, but Barnaby, *I'm* fucked up. This doesn't have anything to do with me forgetting you or moving on, this is about me...being too selfish to let you go."

He finished with a sigh, out of breath, and hiked his shoulders while his gaze swept the floor.

Barnaby blinked, and the man was almost unrecognizable. Smaller. Frayed. Desperate. It didn't make sense.

"Selfish?"

"Knowing you deserved better and still keeping you close. Riding on the hope that...*you* would break things off first."

"Oh."

No one had ever told him he deserved *better*.

Barnaby shifted in his seat. "I didn't think that," he peeped, tugging on his ear, "If anything, I thought it was the other way around, but...then things were going really well..."

Gil shook his head, fussing with his hair. "It wouldn't have lasted. I hate to sound like a prick, but it's probably best it ended where it did. Take it as a win on your part but...for the love of God, don't think *you* did anything wrong."

He made it sound so final, so official.

They'd reached the end.

Barnaby asked, "So, what happens next? Do you...still want to be friends?"

"You don't want to be my friend," Gil scoffed, "Truthfully, you're better off forgetting about me."

I can't do that.

Even if it was for the best. Even if he wanted to.

They'd been so intimate with each other. So vulnerable.

And Gil had been so kind.

"I won't," Barnaby muttered, "but, uhm...please, stop telling me how to feel, okay? I know there's a lot I still don't understand, but...one thing I know I'm certain of is that I *do* care about you—" He ghosted a hand over Gil's— "and I care that you're hurt by this, too."

He held his breath while the man stared at their hands, nearly going blue in the face before he heard him grumble, "Raul said you knew."

"About the...uhm—"

Gil nodded.

With some hesitation, Barnaby weaved his fingers with Gil's. "Y-Your hand is cold," he noted.

"I'm sorry."

"Don't be! M-Mine's probably still sweaty…"

"Not about my hand, Barnaby—" Dead eyes gazed through black fringe, and his voice was suitably grave— "For everything else. For hurting you, for telling you how to feel, leading you on and tricking you into thinking that I was ever worth having around…I don't even understand why you would want to be close to me. All I did was use you."

"Because even if that were true," Barnaby assured him, "you still treated me better than anyone. You acted like you wanted me around. You made me feel *important*." He squeezed his hand tight— "I…I don't want to give up on you, Gil. You were nothing but good to me…I mean, *heh*, think about it. If you hadn't been, I probably wouldn't have…fallen for you, or gotten attached, or whatever I was feeling, right?"

A cautious hand lifted to Barnaby's cheek, and Gil brushed his free thumb below his eye, unexpectedly clearing his sight.

He was still fucking crying.

"If I'd been more open, you'd be living your life much happier without me right now," Gil whispered, "Don't waste your time on me. Please? I'm positive there are…plenty of guys out there who would give *anything* to spend an hour with you. Guys who you can count on to be there in the future, romantically or otherwise." Something darker dawned upon his face then, shadowing his sympathy— "You can't count on me to be there, Barnaby."

I wasn't happy before you.

If he expected the boy to make a change, he needed a reason. "Why not?"

Gil repeated the question, barely audible, and scanned the area. Turning away, he retracted his hand from Barnaby's.

Eventually, he said, "I can't tell you. Not here."

Before Barnaby could question him, the man was up on his feet, grabbing his satchel. The boy snatched his backpack and followed, all the way to the Check Out Desk. There, Gil asked for the key to the men's restroom.

Barnaby continued trailing behind until they found the door. Once it was unlocked, Gil let him in, passing the key off to him before slumping against the mahogany.

He blocked the only exit, Barnaby realized.

"Why are we in here?" he asked, keeping his distance.

"Because I'm probably going to crack." It was so blunt and matter of fact. Looking to the ceiling, Gil sucked in his breath. "Which is shitty, right? Good people don't force other people alone with them while they're losing their fucking mind, but you wanted to know, so—" His voice wavered, and his chin shook.

Barnaby's heart sank like an anchor. "Gil—"

"I mean, look at me—"

He locked eyes with him unexpectedly, stunning Barnaby.

"I look sick, don't I?"

"S-Sick?"

"In the head. Fucked."

"N-No..."

The raven huffed, and his silver daggers aimed elsewhere. "Then, what the Hell do the scars look like?"

Barnaby gulped, wringing his own wrists. He worried he might suddenly feel something sharp against his skin. "They look...painful," he admitted, "Y-You must've been in so much pain."

With veins bulging out along his neck, Gil gave a slow nod.

"Are you...still in pain?"

He shook his head. "I wish," he said, "Most days, I don't feel anything at all. Unless I'm with you, and that's...How fucking pathetic is that? The only time I feel any kind of emotion is when I'm hooking up with some poor bastard or pretending I'm in a relationship. Except I could never actually *be* in a relationship because I know one day, I'll realize it's not enough, and whoever I'm with is going to be stuck planning the funeral, and that's not fair." He exhaled, wilting, and closed his eyes, "So, *no*, Barnaby. I don't think you can count on me."

All that time, kept hidden. Holding it in to himself.

Barnaby took a small step forward. "How does it feel," he asked, "to get it out in the open?"

Gil must've considered it, answering moments later, "Worthless. Manipulative. Kinda wish I hadn't already."

"What if...you were actually feeling hopeless, b-because none of what you said is worthless? You might think you're being manipulative, but to me, it sounds like you feel guilty, and you're venting."

If nothing else, Barnaby was almost sure his therapist would be proud.

Gil shrugged. "Maybe."

"My point is," the boy murmured, suppressing his nerves (as if Gil's life depended on it), "those are emotions. You *are* feeling *something*."

"I feel like *shit*," Gil spat, "If this is as good as it gets, truthfully, I'd rather be dead."

Part of Barnaby felt like he was entitled to it: invading his space. Gil had done it enough times.

He closed the distance between them, pausing with just a few inches left. "What if," the boy cautioned, taking hold of his hands, "instead of worrying about who *I* can count on...you counted on me? You don't need to be anything but a friend to me right now...if you even want that, but friends are supposed to help each other...or, at least...that's what I always wanted from a friend. And I want to help you. I'm here for you."

When Gil looked down at him, his eyes softened, shimmering. He looked exhausted, like he needed rest.

Barnaby frowned and dared to guide the man's head to his shoulder. "Come here..."

Gil folded over him without a fight, clinging to Barnaby's jacket. "You deserve better," he choked, "all I did was use you."

"You used me to feel good," Barnaby shushed him, stroking his hair and patting his back, "I wanted to feel good, too. It's okay."

You didn't do anything I wouldn't have done.

He only wished Gil would've told him sooner.

Out of habit, Barnaby kissed the man's cheek.

"I'm so fucking sorry."

It started, broken and restrained - a battle with himself as Gil cried through his teeth. If his lips were wardens, his sobs were prisoners, slamming at their bars.

His shoulders shook unevenly, and whimpers became groans. Hisses. The kind of sounds one might make if they were being burned.

Barnaby had to wonder if the tension on his body was reopening those old wounds.

He urged him gingerly toward the sinks.

"I don't think you're pathetic," Barnaby murmured, propping Gil against the counter, "I'm almost a bit jealous. I wish I was able to feel less." Prying himself from Gil's grasp, he grabbed a paper towel, soaked it in cold water, and began wiping down the man's face and neck.

Soon enough, his sobs dwindled to sniffles. "No, you don't," he said, "Trust me."

Barnaby pouted. "And how do you know?"

Avoiding eye contact, Gil mumbled, "Because you'll only want to destroy yourself over it."

"I already do."

That drew a brief glance before Gil looked aside again - to Barnaby's hand, cupping his cheek. To his wrist.

"Not in the same way," Barnaby clarified, "but I've been there."

Maybe he didn't leave physical scars, but even his mom had expressed that working customer service would scar his mind.

His therapist, too, had said that being friends with Seth was hurting his progress and self-esteem, implying he'd be better off alone.

But Barnaby hadn't learned. He didn't want to be alone.

Instead, he wanted to take care of Gil, causing, perhaps, the greatest self-infliction of all.

It only seemed fitting that he confess to him, "I've wanted to kill myself, too. I may not know exactly what you're going through, but I get it."

Barnaby wasn't sure what he expected, but Gil putting a hand over his own came as a surprise. He certainly didn't expect him to ask, "Whose ass do I have to kick?"

Barnaby snorted, retracting the hand. "*Wha*—I— *Mine*? No one *made me* want to kill myself, Gil, I'm just..." He sighed deep. He'd cry if the well hadn't run dry, probably— "not *happy* with the way I am. I never have been. I hate how I'm wired, but it seems like, no matter what I do, nothing ever changes. People grow and move on, and I *can't* keep up. Heh, honestly, I don't know who it's more exhausting for, me or everyone else. All I know is I'm...*wrong*. My body, my mind are all *wrong*, and there was a time where...where I couldn't take it—" He couldn't stop himself; he couldn't help but *be* himself— "I walked myself to a bridge, and, and I didn't plan on coming down alive. But people were watching, and I didn't want to traumatize them, s-so I went home, and I...*got used to it*. When you came along, I think, like you...I distracted myself. Then, while you were gone, I remembered what all of it felt like..."

Maybe Gil had been right about letting it out in the open, though.

He did feel like shit.

"So, what I'm hearing," the raven said, "is that I need to kick my own ass."

Puffing his cheeks, Barnaby stuck the damp towel to Gil's chest. "*No.* You've done more than enough self-ass kicking."

Gil's smile was small, but it was comforting to see. He hauled himself onto the counter, slid over a few inches, and patted the spot beside him.

Barnaby hopped up, sliding into place.

"Can I touch you?"

The boy nodded, and Gil's arm draped around his shoulders. Barnaby leaned right into his side.

The raven asked, "Is this selfish?"

"A little. Maybe—" Barnaby adjusted his own arm around Gil's torso— "but I don't think you're any more selfish than me."

There was silence, but it wasn't so bad. He heard Gil's breath, faint but steady, and tried to get his to match. He let himself cuddle close, remembering how his body fit so well beside the other's.

It didn't feel wrong. It felt like home.

"I don't want to be dependent on you to keep me happy. Especially if you've got your own shit."

A shallow pit opened up in Barnaby's chest. "Neither do I," he admitted, "but I still want to help."

"I don't know if there's any help for—" Gil gestured to himself— "*this*."

"*I* think there's hope for you." Barnaby bumped him at the hip. "I think," he muttered, "we can at least help to make sure the other is okay. Whether it be venting or bouncing off advice and ideas..."

Gil studied him.

There was still so much to learn about him. Why he was hurting, what he needed to heal in a way that was healthy - and could Barnaby borrow the weight on top of his own anxieties?

He couldn't imagine it would be easy, and he didn't believe he'd always be the solution.

But there was a light in Gil's eyes that needed protecting. A light that had shown itself in moments of laughter and intimacy. Maybe Raul saw that light, too, but until Barnaby could see the difference for himself, he was determined to take the responsibility of igniting it. At least until someone better came along.

Gil ruffled his hair. "What else are friends for, I guess?"

Chapter 20

"I can't believe you're making me drive all the way back by myself. You are *actually* the worst friend ever."

Barnaby rolled his eyes, keeping a smile hidden while continuing to fold his clothes. "You're the one that always complains about being stuck in the car with me, Seth."

"Yeah, but if I'm not telling you to sit still to keep myself busy, what else am I supposed to do?"

Barnaby shrugged. "I don't know. Maybe stop at one of those strip clubs you've always ogled over?"

"I'm not going to a strip club *alone*."

With the last of his clothes organized, Barnaby zipped up the suitcase and lowered it to the floor.

Everything was just about bare - his bed, his closet, his shelves - all that was left was to untangle the vines and fairy lights from his headboard.

Looking to Seth's side of the room showed a similar scene. Except, instead of fairy lights hanging about, he had another boy sitting in his bed, painting his nails white.

"If you want, I'll be your Plus One," Raul offered, "I don't mind sight-seeing. And hey, Barnaby, what if we met up at your place? I could trade spots with you once Gil drops you off."

"Y'know," the blond said, "that might not be a bad idea."

Seth had an interesting reaction to Raul, and Barnaby wasn't oblivious to it.

They'd known each other for the better part of the past twenty-four hours, and not once had Barnaby heard his roommate tease or mock the other. When he came over that morning, volunteering to help pack, Seth allowed him. They talked about Minecraft and *Yu-Gi-Oh!,* shared memes from their phones, and the next thing Barnaby knew, Raul was painting his nails.

Seth was practically hospitable.

"I mean," the boy mumbled, "as long as you don't kill me on the drive, sure."

Raul finished with the last finger and winked. "Nah. I couldn't hurt a guy with glasses."

Barnaby could've sworn he noticed a tint of color creep onto his roommate's face.

"*Alright—*" All eyes turned to the door - to Gil as he entered the room— "car's just about full." His gaze landed on Barnaby. "How much more needs to go in?"

"A suitcase and the decorations on the bed," the blond told him, "Think that'll fit?"

A fond smile graced Gil's lips. "With room to spare. *R,*" he said, tossing his keys to Raul, "make sure I didn't mix up any of our stuff. Take Seth with you."

"Wow," Seth commented, "that's not suspicious at all."

Without fail, Gil produced a bill from his wallet, crumpled it up, and tossed it at him. "Grab lunch while you're at it."

One glance at the amount of the bill, and Seth shot the raven a dumbfounded glare.

"C'mon, Seth," Raul said, nudging him on his way off the bed, "let's go crash his car."

Raul was out of the room first, leaving Seth to pause as he stood in front of Gil.

The man dwarfed him by all measures, but evidently it didn't faze the smaller, aiming a fist at him and uttering, "Hurt him again, and I'll make sure you don't come back next semester."

Gil didn't flinch. Before Barnaby could interject, he placed a calm hand on top of Seth's, guided it to his side, and patted his shoulder. He said, simply, "It was nice seeing you again, Seth."

The brunet promptly stepped out of his reach, his glare falling on Barnaby. "Tell me what he says."

"Uhm—" Barnaby wasn't sure what the other expected— "O-Okay?"

It'd been enough, apparently, and Seth brushed past Gil to exit the room.

The man closed the door behind him.

If not for his roommate's animosity, perhaps Barnaby wouldn't have had a reason to worry. But with the hollow pit it left in his chest, he needed to rub over his heart and ask, "Is everything okay?"

A sly expression crossed Gil's face.

Without a word, he lifted the boy off his feet, threw him onto the bed, and settled between his legs.

Heat rose to Barnaby's face, and despite having the wind knocked out of him, his heart picked up speed. "H-Hi?"

"Hi." The man's gaze drifted to his lips, shameless not to hide it.

Barnaby wondered if Gil was waiting for him to make a move, hopeful that if he stared long enough, the boy would get the hint.

He nearly gave in—

And then grey eyes returned to his, and Gil's lips moved, "How badly did I screw up our chances of getting back together?"

Barnaby wasn't sure if his heart rocketed somewhere into his throat or stopped altogether.

Maybe he hadn't been clear.

He breathed in, breathed out, and tucked Gil's hair behind his ear. "It's not that you screwed it up," he sighed, "It's that...I can't have sex with you and just be friends. It has to be one or the other, and I really, *really* don't want to lose you as a friend, Gil."

"No, I understand that—" Contradicting himself, he took hold of Barnaby's hand, placing cautious kisses on each of his fingers.

There was nothing stopping Barnaby from pulling the hand away. Other than the fact he didn't particularly want to.

Gil asked, "I mean, what if I wanted to be more?"

"More?"

"More than friends."

All Barnaby could do was stare.

He didn't want to believe him. He didn't want to get his hopes up.

He pressed, skeptical, "What happened to...not being able to be in a relationship? Not being dependent?"

The corners of Gil's mouth tugged down, and he rolled off of Barnaby, lying beside him instead. His answer was another question, aimed at the ceiling, "We've established that I'm selfish, right?"

Barnaby pouted, turning onto his stomach. "Just because you've acted out of selfishness in the past...It doesn't mean you're a selfish person."

The man scoffed, "Either way, I'm pretty sure what I'm thinking is still selfish."

"Well, what're you thinking?"

For a moment, Barnaby got to watch the gears whirling around in Gil's mind, perhaps clanking too loud for him to concentrate.

Then, the raven tilted his head toward him, and the loudest sound in the room was his voice, speaking barely above a whisper, "I'm thinking like I'm somebody else. Someone who...could pretend he had a future, and I think it wouldn't be so bad. Sure, hanging out over break, picking up where we left off...Maybe going out on a date or two..." He trailed off, eyes roaming the rest of Barnaby's body before finding their way back. "I thought about...sitting down at dinner with my parents, and for once, being able to avoid the question of *"have you found anyone yet"*...because you'd be there."

Barnaby stared, waiting for the punchline, or the *"but"*—

But all Gil seemed to be waiting for was a response.

"What, uhm," he tried, "Why the change of heart?"

The raven returned his attention to the ceiling, and at first, Barnaby thought it was the wrong thing to ask.

However, a moment later, Gil said, "I keep going back to the last time I was in here and how it felt. It didn't feel like just another fuck. It was like...what I assume people would consider, for lack of a better term...*Making Love*. Almost *real* and safe, and I thought, *oh, it's because I trust him*, but I have to ask myself...y'know...Is what I'm feeling the same thing you were talking about? Do I want to be closer than friends, and...does it even matter what I want? Yeah, being around you makes me want to kill myself less, but that's something I can say *now*. I haven't gotten used to it yet, I haven't decided it's not enough yet, but what if I do? What if I off myself, and your health goes to shit? What happens to you?"

Barnaby blinked, gradually absorbing it all. "You're worried about what would happen to me...if *you* killed yourself?"

"I'm worried about everything, Bee. About it going right, about it going wrong...About you finding out about everything I was, everything I can become, and being disgusted by it. Not that I would blame you, I'm disgusted, too." Gil rubbed his eyes, still dry, and added, "I'm still

311

worried about becoming dependent on you, obviously. That we'll inevitably break up, and that, no matter what I do, I'll be right back to where I started. Or worse."

It was a lot to take in one sitting.

Maybe, what they both needed - the first step - was to bring themselves back to center.

Inching close, Barnaby laid his head on Gil's chest, listening to his heart drum against his ear.

When the man didn't object, he draped an arm around him. "Does this worry you?"

Gil sighed, and Barnaby nuzzled closer as a stronger arm kept him in place. "Surprisingly, no. This feels right."

Barnaby smiled. He thought so, too.

"We think a lot alike. We fear the same things, at least..." He pecked his jaw and traced patterns across the man's abdomen— "For a while, it felt like sex was the only thing I could do right for you. But the rest of the time, where you went out of your way to get to know me and treat me like a normal person? Like you are now? That's what stood out to me the most. That made me feel *special*. And...if you wanted to date *officially*...heh, well yes, I'll admit, it'd be hard to turn you down, but...I am worried about basing my own self-worth on you, too. I'm worried about straining you, about being too much, or...not being enough."

His shoulder was squeezed, and nimble fingers found their way to his hair, stroking through and bringing an instant sense of peace.

"Guess it is similar."

Barnaby gripped tight to Gil's sweater, as cool of a grey as his eyes. "I don't know about you," he said, "but something I hear a lot is..."you can't get into a relationship until you fix your own problems." And part of me believes that, I think, but on the other hand...I'm never going to stop having anxiety, I'm never going to stop being autistic...so the main problems I do have, I'll probably be stuck with forever. If *that's* the case...what do I do? Settle for being alone for the rest of my life, or...take the risk? Maybe try to find someone to grow with?"

So far, Gil hadn't pushed him away, and he hadn't tried to interrupt him.

Taking a different risk, Barnaby pushed himself up, looking down at the man.

Uncertainty seemed to knit his brows together, his lips pursed.

His bangs were in disarray, and Barnaby took it upon himself to brush them out of his face. "I don't know if it's the right thing to do, or if it's smart for either of us, but you tell me you want to be more than friends, and...I don't *want* to turn that down. I want to try, I want to know what it's like. I want to know *you*, good and bad, and trust *you* to get to know me."

Gil's expression softened, and a smile appeared, so faint and small that Barnaby could nearly believe he imagined it.

"How much of that did you rehearse?"

"*Wha*—? None of it."

"Huh—" Guiding the boy's hand to his cheek, Gil leaned into it— "and somehow, you haven't stuttered."

How *could* Barnaby turn him down?

Cupping the raven's face in both hands, he kissed him, feeling his smile broaden against his own lips. Hands settled onto his hips.

It was every bit as sweet as he remembered.

He almost didn't want to pull away - like Gil, he wanted to continue from where they left off—

But then the man's tongue grazed his lip, and Barnaby knew the risk of putting in too much passion, too fast.

He pulled away, giggling, to nuzzle against his neck. "Maybe later."

Another kiss was placed on the crown of his head. "You'll tell me if I'm being too much trouble? Emotionally? Well, physically, too, but—"

"Yes," Barnaby hummed, "if you promise to do the same for me. And if you promise to be open with me. Let's try to communicate before things have a chance to be bad. Okay?"

"Okay. I promise."

Gil hugged him tight, and Barnaby relished in his renewed sense of affection, protection, and hope.

Eventually, though, he released him to finish taking down the decorations from his headboard.

Nothing felt more right than seeing the man recline on his bed, gaze lingering when he must have assumed Barnaby *wasn't* glancing at him from the corner of his eye.

"So," the boy chimed to break the silence, "should I be psyching myself up to meet your parents now or—?"

"Whatcha lookin' at, Connolly?"

After sliding his suitcase into the trunk like a Tetris block, Barnaby straightened up. He turned just in time to watch Gil walk away, fussing with his hair.

"Nothing," he told Seth, "Making sure he didn't need help."

Barnaby locked eyes with Seth, a brow raised, and the other gave him a once over - a reminder that he'd been deeply bent over in front of the man.

Heat sparked across Barnaby's face, and he hurried to close the hatchback.

"Barnaby!"

He jumped as Raul called out to him.

The boy emerged from the driver's side of the Range Rover, going straight for a spot beside Seth.

For someone so quick to call out other men for invading his personal space, Seth allowed him to stand pretty close.

"Both of our maps are set for your place," Raul told the blond, "Make sure he doesn't leave without me." He held out his fist, presumably to seal the deal, and Barnaby bumped their knuckles together without hesitation.

"I'll make sure."

Raul smirked. "'Til later." Parting with a Peace Sign, he headed to Seth's weathered Prius.

Barnaby couldn't help but notice his friend staring after him.

"Raul's kinda cool, huh?"

Seth spun on him, scowling. "*I don't wanna hear it, Hirsch.*"

Barnaby laughed but respected his wish, reaching out to shake Seth's hand instead. "Drive safe."

"No promises." There was a slight curl to his lips as he pulled away.

It was up to Barnaby to watch him follow Raul, long enough to see them chatting excitedly once both were in the car.

That was his cue. With a spring in his step, the blond headed for the passenger seat of the other vehicle, sliding in beside Gil.

"I tried to pick songs I thought we both would like," the man said, passing his phone to him, "Hopefully, I'm not too far off. If I am, the cord should be able to plug into your phone, too."

Inspecting the screen, Barnaby found an extensive list of titles. Gil's playlist. He recognized about half the artists, finding a name or title for almost every genre of music - plenty he knew to be rock or alternative, though.

No surprise there.

Of course, Barnaby didn't mind, and he was excited to listen to each one, whatever was there to get inside of Gil's head.

But then he read, *Billy Joel*, *"Vienna"*, and knew which one he had to pick first.

The piano progression began, coming right through the stereo, and Gil flashed him a grin as they drove away from the parking lot. "How did I know?"

Barnaby shrugged and settled in, quietly humming along as he looked out the window, another goodbye to his home-away-from-home for the next few weeks.

He couldn't help but wonder what it'd be like when they returned: would Seth still consider him a roommate, or would most of his nights be spent in Gil's dorm?

Nearly as soon as they hit the highway, they were met with bumper to bumper traffic. Barnaby expected it - everyone wanted to get out at the same time, and there was another campus not far from their own.

Gil groaned, tapping his forehead to the steering wheel, "I blame the other two for this."

"They're probably saying the same thing about us," Barnaby said. Reaching over, he fixed Gil's hair behind his ear. It was definitely getting long. He liked it. "What's wrong? Don't want to be with me any longer than you have to be?"

The man huffed, taking a hold of his hand before he could pull it away. "*No—*" Interlocking their fingers, he gave a gentle squeeze— "I like being with you, but I'd also like to see something *move.*"

Barnaby rolled his eyes. He'd expect to hear that sort of thing from Seth.

Maybe Barnaby was different - the only one who could genuinely be content with looking out the window, at the hills of trees bordering the road, a reassuring sign that nature could still thrive. His imagination would run wild with what it would be like living off the grid, beyond the woods, out to the plains, cozy in his farmhouse in the countryside.

He wondered if Gil would visit him, or even, if he'd stay.

The song on the playlist changed - Billy Joel again - and the raven let go of Barnaby's hand.

Apparently, he needed both hands to tap along on the steering wheel, as if he were playing the piano himself.

It was a melody Barnaby had almost forgotten, one he couldn't remember the title of until it was sung: "*And So It Goes.*"

He asked, "Is *this* your favorite song by him?"

Rather than answer, Gil turned to look out of the driver's window.

That was fine. He didn't deny it, and that was all Barnaby needed.

"Oh, no way."

The blond could already hear the smirk in his voice. "Hm?"

Moving his seat back, Gil beckoned him closer.

Barnaby leaned over, following the man's finger to where he pointed through the window.

Straggling near the trees, a safe distance away from the road, Barnaby spotted a group of does, grazing among the grass.

One of them looked up abruptly, flicking her ears, and it was as if she was making direct eye contact with them.

"It's odd," Barnaby muttered, slumping back into his seat, "of all the times I've seen a deer in person, it's almost always a doe. Have you noticed that? Do you ever wonder where the bucks are?"

"I don't have to," Gil said, confident. Traffic began moving along. He kept one hand on the wheel while the other fell to Barnaby's thigh. "I've got mine right here."

Chapter 21

Of all your Bright Ideas, this might be one of your dimmest.

Gil's hands gripped the steering wheel.

In his own defense, he had a different image of what Barnaby's house would look like when they were on the trip home. Sure, they'd planned for the boy to visit Gil's neighborhood, but by the way Barnaby made it sound, there wasn't much to do where he lived.

With how insistent he'd been, Gil's should've known there was more to it.

For one reason or another, he'd pictured him living in a modern cottage on the edge of suburbia. There'd be a small yard with a garden, and the place would be decorated for the season. It'd be quaint but inviting. Somewhere, in all honesty, he'd rather live.

Gil's heart nearly broke when they arrived at what he would consider a shack - a beaten box on a street forgotten by the rest of town.

The yard was a strip of grass, and the only decoration he'd noticed was an unlit Menorah in the window.

He'd cursed himself for feeling disappointed. A home was a home, right? Better than none.

A blonde, fairy-like woman in scrubs had waited for them at the front door. Barnaby's mom.

Gil adored her the moment he laid eyes on her.

He helped them carry the boy's boxes and suitcases inside. For a family of two, the house was visibly lived in. The carpets were padded down - trinkets and collectibles, tacky and full of character, crowded the shelves - and Gil could only imagine what stories the hand-me-down furniture could tell.

Ms. Hirsch possessed all the character of her collectibles - with her tired eyes, a smile just as friendly as her son's, and wrinkled hands that had no trouble lifting the heavier boxes. She had no reason to believe he and Barnaby were anything more than friends, but she welcomed Gil as if he were her own.

When he'd address her, she'd insist he call her Rachel.

Once everything had been unloaded into their tiny living room, she invited Gil to stay as long as he liked. Said it was a pleasure to meet him. Then, she left for work.

He'd considered her offer, hoping to prolong his time with Barnaby—

But several obnoxious honks from the driveway reminded them their time alone together would have to wait.

It'd been two weeks since then.

He's going to think you're a joke.

He'll never say it, but he'll see your big fucking house with that big fucking Christmas tree, and he's going to meet both of your parents, and he'll ask himself, "What the Hell does GIL have to be depressed about?"

He held his breath, flashing a practiced grin the moment that rickety front door opened.

Precious as ever, Barnaby stepped out with the same backpack he'd used for school over his shoulders. He had a plastic bag in his hand and a smile Gil could spot from the car.

His colorful knit sweater reminded him of something his grandfather would wear, patterns stretched around his added winter weight.

"Hey!" Jumping into the passenger seat, Barnaby immediately leaned over to kiss Gil's cheek. "Happy New Year!"

Gil pecked his lips before he could get away. "You're a few hours early."

"I don't want to forget," Barnaby said, "in case we fall asleep before midnight."

The man shot him a smirk. "You really think I'm gonna let you sleep tonight?"

His passenger pouted, dropping the plastic bag in his lap as he deflected, "These are from my mom. She says Happy New Year, too."

"Rachel gets a pass. I assume I won't be seeing her until next year?"

"Sadly. She left earlier."

Peeking into the bag, Gil found a container of chocolate croissants. He thanked his boyfriend (his mother, by extension) and put his hand on the gearshift.

Then, he remembered his apprehension.

With the car still parked, he asked, "Are you sure you want to spend the night at my place? I mean, I'm fine with staying here."

Barnaby's expression faltered, and he was ready to retract the question.

The blond beat him to it, his voice small, "Of course I'm sure. I'm excited to meet your family, Gil. Why? Are you worried about driving back?"

"It's not so much of that." He tapped along the steering wheel, considering how to word it. Eventually, he decided, "I don't want you to be uncomfortable when we get there."

A frown tugged at Barnaby's lips. "Why would I be uncomfortable?"

It'd be to make an excuse.

But then, he'd promised to be open with him.

Gil sighed, prying it off his tongue, "My parents are stupid wealthy. I'm not saying that to brag or imply that you're *not* wealthy, but they like to show it off to the point it makes *me* uncomfortable. If you'd rather not have to deal with that, I get it. I'm fine staying here and finding something else to do."

The boy was quick to put a hand on top of his, his smile renewed and gentle. "I don't mind," he told him, "I'd rather see this part of you. If that's okay. Besides—" He leaned in again for another kiss on the cheek— "we'll probably be spending most of the night in your room anyway, right?"

Gil searched his eyes for deceit - any reflection or twitch of a muscle that might suggest he was forcing himself to go along with it.

All he saw was his soul, yearning, bare. And money couldn't buy that.

With a kiss to his forehead, Gil squeezed his hand tight. "Right."

Their fingers remained interlocked as he drove off down the street, following the GPS that spoke over his playlist. At first, he tried to add his own voice to the mix, hoping to preoccupy his passenger with small talk ("Once they're gone, the house is ours for the night", "When was the last time you went ice skating?", and "Would you want to watch the countdown?"). Each time, however, the conversation would hit a dead end with a distracted answer from Barnaby.

Maybe he's just psyching himself up.

Holding onto that thought, Gil kept quiet the rest of the way.

They drove through highways and suburbs and, within the hour, turned a corner at a sign Gil had seen one too many times: Meadow Ridge Manors.

"*Wow—*"

The man slowed the car to a roll, glancing at his boyfriend.

As resentful as the neighborhood had made him, he'd found it hard not to crack a smile during the holidays. Every second-story rooftop was trimmed with colorful lights, some extending down the entirety of the house, some thrown onto lawn trees and hedges. The lights, of course, were mandatory. Most houses had inflatables, animatronics, and wooden cutouts to turn their wide, manicured yards into scenes straight from their favorite Christmas classics.

One manor, made of masonry, had white lights on the roof, lights on domestic pine trees and shrubs, a wreath on the glass door, and a family of caroling snowmen on the lawn.

Gil pulled into the driveway beside three other cars.

Turning off the engine, he told Barnaby, "This is it."

The boy stared up at the house, gawking, silent.

Gil gave his hand another squeeze. "Are you okay?"

Seconds of quiet uncertainty passed before Barnaby spoke up, "You're not embarrassed of me, are you? Is that why you didn't want to come back?"

Squinting at him, the raven-haired said, ""Don't even. If anything, *they're* the ones I'm embarrassed of. Barnaby—" He continued holding his hand tight, and with his name, the boy finally faced him— "I want to be seen with you."

Doe eyes. He really did resemble a helpless fawn. In his perspective, it must've seemed like entering a den of wolves.

What Gil wasn't sure Barnaby understood: he wasn't actually a wolf. He was more of a sheep in wolf's clothing.

"C'mon," he urged, opening his door and taking the bag of croissants with him, "I'll be right next to you."

Barnaby followed his lead, bringing his backpack and together, they walked hand in hand, past the snowfolk, into the house.

"We're home," Gil announced. He hung his coat in the parlor closet with each of their bags, leaving his boots at the entrance. He suggested his guest do the same.

As predicted, the boy's attention went straight to their open living room, to their fifteen-foot-tall Christmas tree, decorated in gold ornaments and ribbons.

Gil nudged him gently, guiding him, instead, to the opposite side of their garland-lined staircase, into the dining room.

Their solid oak table was prepped with four sets of plates and silverware. Bowls of mashed potatoes, salad, and dinner rolls had already been placed in the center.

His mother came in from the kitchen, carrying a tray of chicken piccata over pasta.

Gil quirked a brow at her. He wasn't quite used to her recent dyejob yet, making her hair a startling red, but at least it matched the burgundy of her long-sleeve dress. "I thought you were having dinner at dad's party."

"Well, since you were bringing a guest," his mother said, setting the tray in the middle of her presentation, "we thought it'd be impolite not to stick around for a little bit."

No, I think it's the other way around.

Clasping her hands together, she aimed her Stepford Housewife smile at Barnaby. "It's so nice to see you, sweetheart. Can I get you anything to drink?"

"W-Water's fine!" the blond squeaked, "Thank you."

Gil waited for the woman to leave the room again before putting a hand on Barnaby's shoulder. "I'm sorry," he sighed, "I thought they'd only stay for a few minutes."

The boy bit his lip while, judging by the subtle twitches in his face, struggling to smile up at him. "It's fine," he muttered, "She seems nice. And I haven't eaten yet. So..."

Maybe the fawn wasn't as meek and helpless as he seemed.

Ruffling his hair, Gil stepped aside, pulling a chair out for him.

"I'm foregoing the tie. It's a party, not a charity event."

Ignoring the chair, Barnaby took an abrupt step toward the scruffy, suited man entering the room: Gil's father.

"Happy New Year, sir," he said, promptly offering his hand.

Gil wondered how many times he'd rehearsed that.

"You must be Barnaby." His father shook the blond's hand, and Gil winced at the sound of a wrist popping. "Now, that's a name I haven't heard since *I* was in school. Old-fashioned folks?"

"Oh, uhm," Barnaby sputtered, "M-My mom and grandma are musical fans. H-*Hello Dolly*? They named me after one of the characters."

Gil's father gave a sharp nod. "Some culture, then."

Gil knew the man didn't know a damn thing about musicals.

But he passed Barnaby to grab a seat at the table, and Barnaby turned to sit beside Gil, his face noticeably red.

The matriarch returned with a glass of water for everyone in the room. "Gil told us you celebrate Hanukkah," she said, sitting next to her husband, "I'm guessing that makes tonight your second New Year?"

The young Connolly rolled his eyes, though Barnaby seemed willing to humor her— "Yes! That, uhm, was a few months ago, though."

Fortunately for Barnaby, he didn't have to be a good speaker for Gil's parents to hold a conversation with him. Many, many years ago, Gil had learned his dad in particular loved to hear himself talk. When Barnaby fumbled to follow up with an answer, he was quick with another question: "Are you working?", "What's your major?", "Any sports you like?"

While Barnaby had barely more than a shrug to offer on the topic of sports, the answers he gave to the other questions were clearly enough to impress the older couple.

"First I've heard of anyone wanting to be a farmer in years," Gil's father commented, "No one wants to do the hard, dirty work. All too busy waiting for someone to hand them fame. Good for you for putting in the effort."

On the matter of already having a job, Gil's mother spoke up, "Maybe you can convince Gil to find something, too."

"It wouldn't fit in with my schedule," her son countered between bites of chicken.

"Plenty of other students make it work," his father interjected, "No reason you shouldn't be able to."

"Even your therapist said—" His mother couldn't resist— "it'd be good to keep you motivated, being productive."

Gil stared down at his plate, piling in mouthfuls.

He'd gotten used to the issue for so long, he'd practically forgotten what his excuse for not having a job was.

Maybe it was time to start looking for one.

He felt a light tap against his shin.

"Gil does a great job of being a customer at the cafe!" Barnaby chimed, "He makes sure we stay in business, and...it's a personal help, to me and my anxiety. Having him there sort of feels like...back up."

Oh, Barnaby.

Gil flashed a grin and bumped his leg in turn.

Even when you don't pay for me, I'm still using their money.

His parents' eyes widened - maybe from the same realization, maybe from the shocking revelation that someone, *somehow*, saw *him* as their emotional support.

"Well," his mom eventually said, "wouldn't it be easier for the both of you if you worked together?"

Gil and Barnaby shared a glance, and Gil hoped, despite the other's cheerful facade, he was thinking the same thing: starting a job with someone after recently becoming "official" likely wouldn't be the smartest decision.

Fortunately, neither parent pushed the idea. They went on finishing their meals in peace - except for Mrs. Connolly insisting their guest have more.

"Are you sure?" Barnaby asked.

"Go ahead, honey. We have leftovers clogging up the fridge as it is." She was practically dumping the rest of the tray onto his plate.

Although a bit flustered, Barnaby didn't seem to mind. "Thank you," he told her, "it really is very good."

He was a fast, eager eater, and Gil took notice.

No sooner did she put her utensils on her plate did his mother open her mouth again, "What kind of charm do you have?"

Gil eyed her, confused, before following her line of sight - to Barnaby's wrist, to the brown, leather strap wrapped around it.

"Monogram," the blond said automatically, indicating the silver medallion attached, "Just the letter B. Uhm— Hanukkah gift." He tugged at his sleeve, which at some point, had ridden up.

Gil stared at him in disbelief. He thought he'd seen the last of that collar. The last place he expected to find it again was his family dinner table.

As long as he stared, Barnaby hadn't spared him a glance.

His mother, oblivious, went on about how she considered grabbing one of her old charm bracelets before leaving for the night. She had "so many when they were in style", and "for the amount each charm was" one would assume she'd wear them more often.

The rest of dinner finished up without Gil and Barnaby saying another word to each other, not that Barnaby said much at all. Once he'd finished his plate, he began picking at the rolls, taking his time with what he brought to his mouth.

Gil's father excused himself to the bathroom, and the tidy redhead took it upon herself to clean up the table.

Even in such a nice dress.

Gil stopped her when she reached for his plate. He was perfectly capable. Grabbing his and Barnaby's used dinnerware, he stood and followed her into the kitchen.

"When I get back to school," he mumbled, joining her at the sink, "I'll be more serious about looking for a job."

She swept him with her gaze, and Gil noticed a slight curl at the corner of her mouth. "You never cease to surprise me, Gilbert Finn."

The boy scoffed. "I don't need to be forced to make my own money." *I just need reasons to want it.*

"That's not what I meant." Leaving everything to rinse off, she lifted a finger to his chin and wiped off a remnant from his meal. Her touch lingered as she looked into his eyes. "How'd you find your friend?"

His first thought was poetic: *he found me.* It felt truthful. *He came to me; he drew me in.*

But that wasn't what she wanted to hear; the idea had lost its romance to her.

The last time a boy, tan-skinned, rugged, and unfamiliar, confessed to finding him, he was on life support.

"Luck," he told her instead, "Literally. Found his badge from work, went to return it, and the rest is history." The details wouldn't have made a difference; as far as he was concerned, it all had to do with luck.

The woman pinched his cheek and moved the contents of the sink to the dishwasher. "And he's—" There was hesitation in her voice as she asked, "like you?"

"*Weird*?" Gil clarified, catching her roll her eyes, "Strange? Of course, Ma, how else would we get along?"

"You know!" She grabbed a hand towel and swatted him with it. "Is he...accepting? Do you two communicate? He mentioned having anxiety—"

"We just started dating, mom," was Gil's blunt, immediate response. It left a stillness in the air, and for a few seconds, neither spoke.

Only with Gil.

He knew she'd never tiptoe the same way around her daughter.

It didn't matter if he was a man or a woman, and it didn't matter his partner's gender, either.

It'd been too long since he'd given her a reason to trust him.

Even if he could manage to convince himself he'd made a change for the better, chances were, she'd always be suspicious.

He tried to elaborate, "He knows enough. Yeah. He has baggage, too. If it's more than I can handle, I'll cross that bridge when I get to it. But so far, having him's done nothing but help."

The woman pursed her lips and folded her towel, keeping doubt in her gaze.

Gil held his head high. "I'm not exactly a kid anymore. I have a *little bit* more common sense. Not much, but some."

That was honesty his mother could accept. She smiled, natural and unwilling— "A little goes a long way." She went to pass him, pausing to smooth out the wrinkles of his shirt as she added, "Tell your father I'll be ready in a minute. I know I have a charm bracelet to go with this dress."

As soon as she'd left the kitchen, Gil went to meet the man by the front door, relaying her message.

Barnaby joined them, and he noticed the boy's "bracelet" was hidden from sight.

The older Connolly asked, "Did Gil ever tell you what I do for a living, Barney?"

Before Gil could open his mouth, the blond stammered, "N-No, sir."

Nothing his son could have said would have stopped the man from making a proud sweep of his blazer, revealing the grip of a gun in his pocket. "Chief of Police," he boasted. "Better off telling me now, if I look your name up in the system, I'm not going to find anything suspicious, am I?"

Barnaby's eyes widened to the size of the plates they'd eaten off of, his face turning equally as white. "No, sir."

"Because I'm sure that'll *totally* come in handy at your dinner party," Gil grumbled, opening the door for him, "Try to resist shooting the caterers."

The other man didn't seem anymore amused. Good. "Remember," he said, "we've got security cameras all over the place."

"And I know how to disable them."

"Good luck. We upgraded."

"What are you boys rambling about?"

All attention snapped to the approaching redhead, and Gil's eyes were swiftly drawn to the addition of beaded silver around her wrist.

"The usual briefing," her husband replied. He grabbed a fur coat from the closet and draped it around her, and for a moment, the couples mirrored each other.

"You boys have fun tonight," Mrs. Connolly assured them. Taking Barnaby's hands in her own, she gushed, "It was wonderful to meet you. I hope I can see you soon."

The boy, still rattled, managed a shaky smile. "Me too," he muttered, "Thank you so much for...having me." Then, to Gil's father, "Thank you, Mr. Connolly. For having me, and for...your service."

Service? He spends most of his time in an office.

The man reached over to pat his shoulder. "Take care, son."

"Alright, you crazy kids," Gil said, ushering them through the door, "don't party too hard."

After once again wishing him a Happy New Year, they were off to the car, Gil's mom sparing more than one glance back at him.

He waved but had no qualms about shutting and locking the door, locking himself inside with Barnaby.

Barnaby. Who had chosen to wear his collar.

"Where do you get off on calling another man *Sir*?" He faced him slowly, calculating each step he took toward the boy.

The blond pouted, his eyes still wide and innocent. "I'm sorry. I was trying to be, uhm...polite."

Toe to toe, Gil combed a hand through Barnaby's hair and made a gentle grab for his arm. When he pushed his sleeve up, however, the boy's wrist was bare. "You took it off?"

Barnaby shook his head. Released from Gil's grasp, he tugged his sweater away from his neck. There, the collar had been loosely fastened. Right where it ought to be.

Gil smirked and settled his hands on Barnaby's hips, keeping him close. He leaned in, and his lips began trailing the fawn's jaw. "What a good boy," he whispered, "letting the family know who the pet belongs to."

Barnaby whimpered, and for once, Gil noticed, it didn't sound too pleasant.

"What's wrong?"

He slumped even further into his arms. "I'm *full.*"

"You're...*What*?"

"*Full,*" Barnaby mumbled, burying his face into Gil's chest, "I ate too much."

Suddenly, Gil could imagine the strain of his pants - the hem constricting around his stomach, the seams leaving impressions along his thighs.

One wrong move, and he might rip them.

His poor, fat little fawn.

"I think I might have the cure." Despite the other's groans, Gil led him to the living room. He sat him down on their Friheten sofa, knelt in front of him, and reached for his zipper.

Immediately, the blond started inching away, a hand coming down to cover his crotch. "What're you doing?"

Gil's hands lifted off of him, realizing it probably would've been considerate to ask first. "Can I help you get comfortable? I wasn't going to take your underwear off or anything—" *Yet.*

Barnaby bit his lip, and Gil spotted the faint touch of blush on his cheeks.

The moment he nodded his consent, the man was pulling his pants to the floor, captivated by his stomach spilling out, his thighs puffing like pastries. His sweater started riding up, and Gil thought he heard a faint moan.

"Thank you," Barnaby muttered, "It, uhm...It helps. *Heh.*" He sunk deeper into the couch, and Gil sat beside him. "Th-They won't see us on the security cameras, will they?"

"Not sure," Gil admitted, "but honestly?"

Barnaby looked rounder and smoother than ever; he needed to know what that felt like. It'd been too long.

He tugged the boy's shirt up further and placed a hand on his stomach, starting to rub in small circles.

He was softer than he remembered.

"Don't care much. Unless you do. We could always go up to my room."

Another sound of discontent rumbled in Barnaby's throat. "I don't wanna move, though." His focus appeared to switch to Gil's hand, watching through half-lidded eyes.

The man licked his lips. Had Barnaby eaten so much that he didn't want to move - or that he couldn't?

A thought crossed his mind, one that wrought an ounce of shame: *what would it take to make Barnaby so full, he'd be borderline immobilized?*

Gil leaned in and kissed his cheek. "Was it worth it?"

Barnaby might've debated it, but eventually, he nodded. "Probably the best meal I've had in a while."

Gil hummed as his fingers continued to dance across his belly, tight like a drum and still soft as dough.

Dough.

Pastries.

"Hang on a sec'." Rising from the couch, he went to the parlor to grab the gifted bag of chocolate croissants. He grinned to himself, announcing as he brought them back to the living room, "You still haven't had dessert yet."

"*Gil—*" Barnaby groaned again, gripping his stomach and falling onto his side, "I don't have any room."

"Why do I get the feeling that's not true?" The man returned to his spot, lifting the blond's head and placing it into his lap. "You decided to wear your collar," he observed, taking out a single croissant, "Does that mean you're willing to listen to orders? Like, let's say...a good boy?"

Barnaby blinked up at him with innocent eyes, as if waiting for his command.

Gil chuckled, petting his hair back, "That's what I thought." Holding a croissant to his lips, he demanded, "Don't stop eating until I tell you to."

Another whimper slipped from his pet's lips, but seconds later, he fell into submission. His eyes shut, and his mouth opened, nibbling away at the homemade pastry.

Keeping that hand in place, Gil used his opposite to find the remote to the TV, turning it on to some generic network streaming some generic Countdown Concert. Mere background noise while he focused his sights on Barnaby. He continued stroking through his hair as the croissant dwindled away, crumbs piling on his chest.

The moment he finished, the man would brush them away, simply to repeat the process with another pastry.

An unmistakable moan escaped between bites.

"Are you enjoying yourself?"

Barnaby swallowed, looking up at him again. "Can you, uhm—" A delightful blush glowed bright across his cheeks— "keep rubbing my belly? Please, Master?"

He was too irresistible to deny. Especially when asking so nicely.

Guiding him further along his lap, Gil used one hand to prop the pastry while the other rubbed and kneaded his

338

stomach. He wondered if he was helping him at all, if it gave any real relief—

Or did he enjoy it for the same reason his master did? To get to feel him fattening up, rounding out?

Gil smirked and jiggled Barnaby's stomach a bit, making him whimper once more.

Gradually, he fed him two more croissants (he left the last one for himself). Despite the celebration on screen, his pet's moans and mewls were perfectly audible, and the more he nibbled, the more he would squirm, pushing his stomach against Gil's palm.

It was the perfect way to spend the holiday.

After the fourth dessert, he ruffled Barnaby's hair, signaling he was done, and the boy rolled over to watch the program with him. They were still about an hour out until midnight.

"*Oh no—*"

Looking down, Gil noticed the boy gripping his stomach again. "Too much?"

"I need to..." His stomach gurgled loud enough for the man to hear, and Barnaby curled in on himself tighter— "Sorry, can I use your bathroom?"

Gil snickered, pointing to a room behind the staircase. "Go straight."

Barnaby nodded, muttered a thank you, and forced himself up.

So, maybe it hadn't been enough to immobilize him. But it sure was fun watching him waddle off.

Chapter 22

After several minutes had passed, Gil turned off the television and went to knock on the bathroom door. "I'm heading upstairs," he told Barnaby, "Gonna be alright in there?"

"Yeah!" the boy squeaked. "Sorry. I'll try not to be too long."

Gil chuckled. "Take all the time you need. I'll leave my door open. And make sure you're clean!"

He left him with that, venturing to his bedroom.

There had been an attempt to make the occasion special.

Earlier that day, he'd cleared his nightstands to make room for candles; he'd left a bottle of sparkling cider in a bucket of ice that, to his dismay, had melted prior to his return. Fortunately, as he poured two champagne glasses at his desk, he realized it hadn't gotten too warm.

He'd finished lighting the last of the candles when Barnaby appeared in the doorway, carrying his pants in his arms and his backpack over his shoulders.

"I like it," he said, grinning wide, "I see where the English Major comes from."

Gil followed his gaze around the room, around olive colored walls mostly hidden by shelves of books - the hundreds of lives he'd lived, each one more reason not to live the one he had.

Funny that Barnaby made him less interested in reading.

"That's all you need to know about me," Gil said, bringing him a glass, "reading is my entire personality. Everything else is for show."

Barnaby rolled his eyes. "That's not true." Taking the glass, he gave one cautious sip, realized what it was, and drank again, undeterred.

Gil grabbed his own, and they clinked them together. *Cheers.* "It is. And you know what else is true?"

"Hm?"

"You," the man said, "walking around in your underwear is the eighth wonder of the world."

Barnaby bit his lip and pretended the books on his shelves had more to say than him. They did, but— "You already took my pants off, you don't need to sweet talk your way into them."

"Exactly," Gil replied, "Only speaking the truth."

He still caught those hazel eyes glancing back at him.

"Permission to continue walking around, then?"

Gil quirked a brow. There wasn't much to explore, but it piqued his interest.

He raised his glass to signal his approval.

Barnaby set his belongings - save for his cider - on the floor and approached one of the bookshelves.

His ass swayed with each step, every movement accentuating the wedge between his cheeks.

He was as quiet as a mouse, yet Gil heard drums inside of his head. *Boom, boom, boom.*

Plucking a random novel, Barnaby opened to the first page. "Last checked out...*November 19th, 2008*?"

"Oh yeah," Gil snickered, "you'll find a lot of those. I wanted to start my own library, but my allowance wasn't letting me get books fast enough, so..."

"So, you stole them?"

"Not stealing," he corrected him, "*Borrowing—*" Another sip of cider— "I'm sure they've still got a tally on me somewhere."

Barnaby rolled his eyes at him again, and maybe a more seasoned dominant would've taken that opportunity to spank him, a reminder to watch his attitude—

But then, that would have cut his stroll short, taking time away to meet the likes of Neil Gaiman, William Joyce, Mary Oliver, Robert Louis Stevenson, and Oscar Wilde.

And Gil wasn't cruel enough to do that.

Barnaby asked, "Do you have a favorite?"

He'd reached for it so many times, he hadn't seen a point in keeping it on the shelves.

From his nightstand, Gil dug out a worn book with an illustrated cover and handed it over - *Comet in Moominland* by Tove Jansson.

Every feature on Barnaby's face softened, accepting it with the utmost care. His smile resembled that of a mother's, admiring a newborn, and his voice sounded too human for his angelic appearance— "This used to be my favorite cartoon as a kid, oh my God—" He bubbled with laughter, flipping through.

"Yeah?" Gil asked, unsurprised, "Who was your favorite character?"

"Moomin, obviously."

The man chuckled, scanning him up and down. Judging by his shape and personality, he could see where the influence came from. "*Obviously.*"

Barnaby handed the book back, and Gil returned it to its drawer, ready to reach for his boyfriend when he noticed the other turn to his desk.

"This is a nice picture."

There was only one picture on the desk.

It'd been there for years and it showed - covered in dust and a change Barnaby was quick to spot, "I wouldn't have thought you used to be, uhm..."

"Pudgy?" Gil finished, standing beside him. Unlike Barnaby, he hadn't worn his weight well. He'd been a brick, his hair to his shoulders and constantly greasy, even when he got into the habit of bathing regularly.

As unflattering as he was in the photo, he kept it because it was the first of its kind: the first in which he was willingly photographed with his family. His mother smiled the widest, a star appearance in her blue cocktail dress. She must've been thinking, "*Finally, my son is cured!*"

They'd all dressed their best for the occasion.

Gil wore the suit he assumed he would have been buried in.

His father looked relieved, and his sister's smile was tight with apprehension. Their dad believed it would be the end of fights at the dinner table, holes punched into walls, slammed doors, and calls from his buddies saying, "We found him, Chief." It took Addison months to be convinced.

Raul knew better than anyone, yet he seemed the most oblivious of the group. His grin was goofy, and he had an arm around Gil's torso, and who would ever guess they were all standing outside of a rehab center for the mentally ill?

"Raul must be a good friend," Barnaby whispered.

Gil bristled, quick to find his hand. "And that's all he'll ever be," he vowed, "a friend."

The boy smiled. Why did it seem so sad?

"I know—" Barnaby squeezed his palm. "Can you be honest?" he asked in his tiny, mouse-like voice, "If you could go back in time, knowing what you know now...would you try to be more distant?"

Gil sucked in his breath.

Honestly?

"Probably not. I'm selfish, remember?"

Barnaby's smile grew with the sadness behind it.

"*Probably not*" had to be better than "*yes*," but it wasn't totally "*no*," and that couldn't have been comforting.

Gil wanted to comfort him.

He guided him toward the bed, sitting at the edge and urging the boy to straddle his lap.

Shaky hands cemented themselves on his shoulders, and furrowed brows seemed to beg Gil for reassurance.

He sighed, "It's not that I would have wanted to be distant. Honest to God, even if I did, I don't know if I could have. I can't keep my fucking hands off of you—" For emphasis, he grabbed Barnaby's hips.

A light blush returned to the boy's face.

Gil was tempted to kiss him - to smother the question by smothering Barnaby with affection and making him forget everything except his name. That would prove how close he wanted to be.

He could already see it: falling asleep and waking up, utterly blissful, going about their plans without incident.

They'd forget the question was ever asked. Even when Gil finally snapped, and Barnaby was struggling to understand him through his sobs, it would be the furthest thing from their minds - "*Would you try to be more distant?*"

Or he could help the boy understand before any of that happened.

"If I'm being 100% honest, I'm not sure," he admitted, "If I didn't think I'd be around for long...Yeah. I'd be more distant to save you from whatever pain I could."

Without warning, Barnaby grabbed his face, squishing his cheeks together. Staring directly into his eyes, he asked, "And how long do you think you'll be around now?"

His hands, like every other inch of him, were soft from the delicate way he held everything placed into them, warmed by hundreds of cups of tea and coffee.

Gil helped decorate the Christmas tree to match his eyes, and it took being that close to realize it.

"Forever," he told him. If they never left his bed, if he was always looking into Barnaby's eyes, always feeling his touch, uninterrupted, he'd have no reason to want anything else. He'd do anything to stay alive.

But sooner or later, they'd leave the safety of his bedroom. Someone would make a comment, or he'd think he was well enough to go off his medication again, or he'd be alone with his thoughts and it would set in that he never planned to live so long. No matter what he did, it was too late to change who he was. He'd read a book and think, *That will never be me. I'm too damaged for a life like that.*

Forever might become "a few years", "a year", "a month" - "not long."

His grip tightened on Barnaby's hips, fighting to anchor himself in the moment.

A finger grazed his lower lip. "That's a long time," the boy whispered, "A lot of New Years can happen in forever."

A chuckle tickled Gil's throat. "They're only worth it if they're exactly like this one."

What little hair had fallen in front of his eyes was brushed back to make way for Barnaby's lips, gracing nearly every inch of his face. "What if it could be better?"

"Better?"

"Mhm. What if—" The boy leaned in, and his lips ghosted Gil's ear.

Hairs started to raise on the back of his neck.

"—instead of New Year's with your parents, we went somewhere new? What if...we had our own place to celebrate

346

it?" His breath was summer, basking in the sun, and Gil was a bucket of ice that didn't stand a chance.

He didn't expect Barnaby to be the one seducing him that night.

Then again, he hadn't expected to see the collar, either.

Gil lowered his voice, "You're not helping me be Not Dependent on you."

Plush lips traveled down his neck, and electricity shot from his head to his toes.

"Be dependent," Barnaby sighed, "as long as it means you're not dead. Be as dependent as you want."

Gil's heart shuddered in its cage, and he understood. The spell Barnaby was putting him under wasn't seduction, it was a trap.

He flipped them around, pinning the boy to the bed.

Eyes wild, he guessed it reminded the fawn of his place.

Gil said, "That's not productive to your mental health."

"Imagine what you being dead would do," Barnaby huffed, "I could be next."

Gil narrowed his eyes. "Don't be irrational."

"Then, you admit it? Suicide is irrational?"

His jaw felt tight. He pressed a bit firmer against Barnaby's wrists. "In your case, *yes*. If I did it, I'd be doing the universe a favor."

Something dark and haunting corrupted the boy's darling, doe eyes. As if he'd seen a ghost.

It was a horror Gil recognized all too well.

From therapists and peers he could never quite call friends—

To strangers having the misfortune of crossing his path, family who didn't want to understand—

It was supposed to be his ticket to salvation. Something *selfless*, in his control—

For some reason, it was never the answer anyone wanted to hear.

With a heavy sigh, Gil apologized, reeling back.

It mustn't have helped Barnaby's fear - being pinned beneath him.

But the very next instant, the boy was sitting up, and his hands rested on Gil's legs. "Is that why you wanted to date me?" he dared, his voice impressively steady, "Because the universe would be better off without you?"

Gil chewed the inside of his cheek. Barnaby had become so much braver than him; part of him was almost intimidated. "Because I'm selfish," he grumbled, "and whether I'm here for forever or a day, I want to spend time with you which is...*selfish!* It's not fair to me or you that you're the only thing I have to look forward to, a-and if I screw up, it shouldn't fall on your conscience."

Once more, Barnaby claimed his hands. He brought them to his lips, placed a small kiss on each knuckle, and Gil couldn't bring himself to look away.

"What if you don't screw up?" he asked, soft but hopeful.

It was a big *What If,* and if looking at probability, highly unlikely.

However, there wasn't anything Gil could come up with that wouldn't sound like an invitation to a pity party, so he held his tongue.

He was pulled along, lowered as Barnaby brought him into his arms. "What if," the blond muttered, holding Gil's head to his chest, "we could keep coming back to this and, in the end...be okay?"

He listened to his heart beat like the instrumental of a song - melodic, intentional, and entrancing.

Sooner or later, like all musical pieces, Barnaby's song would strike its last chord. It would stop, and that knowledge scared Gil more than the thought of his own demise. It was a trap the boy didn't even know he was setting: the promise of heartbreak, if Gil lived to see it. They could live happily ever after, but neither of them could live forever.

Gil held tight to Barnaby's sweater. Maybe if he held tight enough, if he could transfer all of his strength to him, he could keep his heart pounding for an eternity.

God dammit.

"Okay—" He didn't want to continue the conversation. He wanted to talk to Barnaby's heart while its chorus was strong. He wanted to see the life in his eyes. "I'm sorry."

"Don't apologize." The boy's coo was a dove's.

Gil lifted his head, meeting a forgiving smile.

Barnaby went on, stroking his hair, "You're being open with what's on your mind, and I'm grateful for that."

Gil's lips curled. The beginning of a smile, perhaps. "You say that now."

"I do say—" Cupping his face, Barnaby pulled him in for a quick kiss— "and I'm proud of you."

It wasn't a fair kiss. Gil barely had time to register it.

He held Barnaby's gaze - acknowledging his words, absorbing them, and making sure the boy knew he was *seen* - before diving back in.

The boy's arms locked around his neck in an instant, preventing an escape.

Not that he'd dream of trying.

Barnaby still tasted like chocolate and citrus, kissing every bit as fervently to satiate Gil's hunger. When the man swept his tongue over his lips, Barnaby thanked him with a delicious moan. It left enough space for Gil to plunge his tongue deeper, caressing every inch of his partner's mouth just to be met with the same favor.

It was easy. It didn't require too much thought, and it didn't make him question himself. He knew how to make Barnaby feel good, and dammit, *that* was what he prided himself on. He was the one Barnaby went to when he wanted his cock hard, a hole filled; when he wanted to cry from overwhelming pleasure, and when he wanted someone to take control.

Gil was good for *something*.

He nudged the boy's legs further apart to press their hips close together. After lapping up the ghosts of his last meal, Gil's lips trailed a familiar path down Barnaby's neck, to the spot where his smile could match the curve of his shoulder.

His teeth pressed in while his hands slid below the hem of the boy's sweater, sprawling over his stomach.

His stomach shook on its own, and Barnaby's breath came out uneven.

Gil snickered, "Don't get self-conscious on me now. I've waited too long for this." He squeezed, massaged, and played with his belly, encouraging it to fill out.

Gradually, despite Barnaby's whimpers, it did. He relaxed, curling Gil's hair around his fingers while his eyes remained shut. "Do you really like it that much?" he whispered, "Me being fat?"

"All the more for me to adore—" Gil lowered himself to Barnaby's hips, hiking his sweater up further to sprinkle more kisses across his stomach. He nuzzled his face against him, like nuzzling into a luxury pillow with a built-in heating pad. "I love your body, Bee," he murmured, "I'm *obsessed* with how soft you are, if you couldn't tell."

He nipped at the supple skin, just as doughy between his teeth as he was between his hands.

When Barnaby squeaked, he continued, quick and gentle, along his navel. He mewled and squirmed, and Gil stared up at him, enamored by his scarlet glow. A sunset.

Working the boy's heavy thighs over his shoulders, he figured he would drown in them.

Barnaby was sure to keep him tethered by his hair, tightening his grip, sounding short of breath. *"Gil..."*

Gil responded by nipping those thighs - slowly at first, to give the boy time to recover from his own trembling reflexes.

It wasn't long until he was sinking his teeth in, though, growling playfully as he marked his presence with hickeys.

Barnaby's stomach curved, arching, and he felt a deliberate tug in his hair. His thighs squeezed around him, and Gil quickly realized he was trapped. "Trying to strangle me?" he mumbled.

"No," the boy whimpered, loosening his vice somewhat, "but..." He trailed off, chewing his lip.

Gil glanced down, noticing a prominent outline in his briefs. "But *what*?"

Barnaby shut his eyes, giving raven hair another tug and aiming South.

It wasn't a mystery that he wanted the man closer to his crotch.

Digging his chin into his thigh to avoid contact, Gil muttered, "If you want something, you have to ask for it."

The blond whined, evidently frustrated, and lifted an arm to cover his eyes. His legs fell apart, yet he continued petting the man, soothingly.

Gil let him contemplate it, perfectly content to knead his thighs for a moment.

At last, Barnaby mumbled something incomprehensible.

Gil rolled his eyes, brushing his nose against the boy's bulge. "What was that?"

Barnaby's hips jolted in response. "Please touch me," he rasped, "Please."

"Sweetheart," Gil purred, squeezing his tender flesh, "I've *been* touching you."

"*My cock*," Barnaby groaned, and his hips rocked again, "Please touch my cock."

"See? Now, that wasn't so hard."

Though, something else certainly was.

Grabbing his briefs with his teeth, Gil pulled down, letting Barnaby's short cock spring upright.

He was swift to catch it in his hand, greeting it with a swipe of his tongue across the tip.

Barnaby gasped, grabbing at the covers. Hazel eyes glossed over before fluttering close. His mouth hung open, moans waiting to be ripped from his throat.

A few licks was all it took, of Gil's tongue tracing along his veins, and the sounds came streaming out.

"I missed you," Barnaby mewled, "I m-missed feeling you like, *aaah*, l-like this."

Letting his saliva pour, Gil coated the cock from base to tip. He popped the head into his mouth - earning another squeak - and sucked with an audible slurp. "I missed you, too," he muttered when he could, "Couldn't go one day without thinking about what I'd do once I got my hands on you."

A giggle mixed in with Barnaby's moans. "W-Well, now I'm, *mmm,* all yours—"

Gil couldn't be more grateful. He swirled his tongue around the tip of his cock and swallowed it to the back of his throat; he bobbed his head to a steady pace until the boy's legs were shaking.

Now, now. They were far from done.

He pulled off, licking his lips, and climbed on top of him again.

Disappointment flashed across Barnaby's eyes as they were blinked open, fading to the radiance of his smile. "Th-That's all?" he asked, a tad breathless.

Gil smirked and removed his shirt, tossing it to the floor— "Barely even started." He helped the boy out of his clothes next, leaving him with only his collar. Gil paused to admire it, tracing a finger over the leather strap. "Have you been good?"

Barnaby hummed, letting his hands wander to his palm-filling chest and rubbing around his nipples. "On my best behavior," he said, "Felt right to save myself for you."

Gil was still salivating.

Some people may have looked like snacks, but Barnaby was a full course meal.

His curves gave him so much sex appeal. His eyes, his tenderness, and words - they kept Gil wrapped around his finger.

The fact he'd worn his collar on top of it all? Made him the perfect pet.

Applying the slightest amount of pressure to his throat, Gil leaned into his ear— "There's so much I've been wanting to try with you." His hips pressed deeper, intent on feeling the shape of Barnaby's cock through his own pants— "So many ways I've wanted to tie you up. Make you scream—" He licked the shell of his ear and breathed hot against it— "Take your breath away."

A pitiful moan and a rock of the boy's hips told Gil all he needed to know: Barnaby wanted it, too.

He pecked his cheek and left the bed, sinking to the floor. His nightstands were already full; he'd needed a bigger container for his toy collection.

Before he could pull it out from under the bed, however, he was stopped by a timid voice -

"Hey, Gil?"

Gil looked up to find Barnaby rolled onto his side, face inches away from his. "What's up, fawn?"

The boy raised a hand to caress Gil's cheek, inspecting his eyes for a moment. He seemed— worried? His smile was still soft.

He spoke in a cautious tone, "Can I make a request?"

Gil could sense his smirk reappearing as he folded his arms in front of him, interest piqued. "And what would that be?"

Barnaby's touch wandered from his cheek to his shoulder and all the way down along his arm. "I know this is probably boring to you, but can we...be ourselves? Just for tonight? I-I still want to be your pet, but since this is our first time as a couple...is it okay if I call you Gil instead of Master? And for you to call me Bee? Or Barnaby?"

That smirk vanished fast, and Gil slowly realized what he was asking. What it meant.

He realized it was never asked of him before. Never expected. Had he ever tried to be himself during sex?

He thought about his first night in Barnaby's dorm.

Gnawing at his lip, the boy retracted his hand, fiddling instead with the bed covers. "If you want to do something else, we can, I just thought—"

"No," Gil spoke up, and it ached to think the other was ready to give up so easily, "We can do that. I don't mind."

The blond batted his lashes, and his eyes seemed to shimmer with hope. "Can we be gentle, too? Sorry..."

If that didn't tug at Gil's heartstrings—

"Don't be sorry. We'll be as gentle as you want." He got off his knees and hurried out of the rest of his clothes, making them equal.

Barnaby settled onto his stomach, and Gil finally reached into his nightstand for something useful, a condom and trusty bottle of lube, conveniently placed.

He wrapped himself up and climbed on top of the blond again, sparing little time in coating his fingers with the gel. A kiss was placed on Barnaby's shoulder, and he grazed down along his spine, down to slipping a single finger between his cheeks and circling his hole.

A rattled sigh left the boy's lips, and he tilted his head to look up at Gil. "Thank you," he murmured, "y-you can have me however you want next time, but, I think, tonight...it might be nice for both of us to...keep it simple?"

Gil pressed another kiss to Barnaby's temple. "You don't owe me anything, Bee—" Easing a finger into him, the boy gasped, his rim flexing around him. He placed one more kiss upon his head. "I want this, too."

Barnaby nodded, seemingly focused on adjusting to his finger. It didn't take him long, and in moments, Gil was able to glide in another.

He thrusted them slowly, listening to Barnaby's coos and watching him nuzzle into the pillow.

He tried scissoring him and immediately understood why he *needed* to be gentle.

He was tight, and though Gil wouldn't have had a reason to complain, seeing Barnaby wince reminded him of their difference.

He kept it gradual. "Let me know if I need to stop."

The boy shook his head, continuing to muffle any noise he made. Clearly, he was struggling.

Gil had to admire him. Already, Barnaby had decided to take on the weight of his emotional baggage; but then, there he persisted, letting Gil put him through physical pain.

Is this what it's like to be a lover?

He wondered if he'd be better off leaving him alone, cuddling him for the night and trying some other time.

Before Gil could even suggest it, his breath caught in his throat.

Barnaby's hand had wrapped around his dick.

"Oh, God—"

"Do you like that?" Hearing a smile in the boy's voice gave him some reassurance, and Gil groaned his approval while the other stroked him. He was careful, his touch graceful.

It took everything in Gil's power not to be greedier than he was and insist on more.

He added a third finger to help him, and the grip on his shaft tightened.

In minutes, Gil was stretching Barnaby, pumping in and out with a fair amount of ease.

The boy fumbled with the lube bottle, and at the same time, prepared his partner, coating his dick. He continued stroking him for a while, his movement increasingly unsteady, before reaching around for Gil's wrist. He was trying to guide him out.

Gil complied, concern renewed as the blond turned onto his back. "Is everything okay?"

Barnaby bit his lip, though it did little to hide his coquettish grin. "Yeah," he said, "I wanted a better look at you. That's all."

Gil felt a wave of heat wash over his face. He supposed if he got to see the boy in his full glory, reactions and all, he couldn't complain. He simply inched closer, lining himself up with Barnaby's entrance, and said, "You're a funny one, Bee."

"And you're very nice to look at." Barnaby angled his hips, and his legs hooked around Gil's torso.

The man smiled, sweeping a hand through his fine, blond hair. "Nowhere near as nice as you."

Barnaby grabbed the hand with both of his own, covering it in kisses and holding it securely over his heart. "You make me feel beautiful," he murmured, "Have I told you that?"

He must not have. Because Gil would've remembered that.

He would've remembered the flutter in his chest. The tingling in his face. How ridiculous he felt for how wide his grin was growing.

And he would've corrected him sooner.

Hoping to distract from the pain, he answered while slowly pressing into him, "You *are* beautiful. All I've done is point it out."

The boy gritted his teeth, releasing Gil's hand in favor of opening his arms to him.

Gil fell right into them, and Barnaby latched around his neck, his heels digging into the small of his back. The man sucked in his breath, forcing his body to be patient while the other's eyes clenched shut. He wished there was a quicker, easier way—

A memory came to mind, and he laughed.

Barnaby blinked up at him, his brows furrowed. "W-What's so funny?"

"I still can't believe," Gil chuckled, "the first time you came over, you thought it was going to be as easy as plopping your fat ass on my dick."

The boy's face turned beet red, and he whined, "Don't make fun of me."

"I'm not making fun of you—" Gil sealed it with a kiss, lightly slapping his thigh. "Your *massive* ass is one of my favorite things about you."

"No, I mean—" Barnaby surrendered, having to close his eyes again. His blush spread to his ears, and he touched their foreheads together. *"Okay."*

Gil was nearly all in. He locked their lips together, giving that last bit of push, and stilled himself to savor the embrace of Barnaby's heat.

They were connected in every sense of the word, and Gil, for the first time in weeks, felt complete.

Padded fingertips tapped the back of his neck.

"I'm okay," Barnaby whispered, "You can move."

Gil nodded, starting a careful pace. His hips knew the motions like a pre-programmed machine, but he was far from used to the motion. Each time he met the boy's thighs, fuel was added to his flame.

With pupils blown wide and plump lips glistening wet, who wouldn't be turned on?

It was tempting to kiss him all the way through, and Gil would have, if not for Barnaby holding his face.

He stared into his soul, muttering, "Thank you for this."

Gil felt more naked in that moment than ever before. As if the boy had a microscopic view into every one of his flaws.

He could only pray Barnaby wouldn't realize how ugly he was until they were through.

"Trust me," Gil grunted, "I've wanted this as long as you have."

"More than this," Barnaby said, his voice thin, "For listening and, and for caring about me, and for being so sweet—" He leaned forward, giving him a chaste kiss—

"You're so kind, and I don't know if you believe that, but you need to— *aah— aaahh...*"

Gil didn't think he'd picked up his speed, but he slowed down as much as he could.

"I want you to be selfish," Barnaby swallowed and went on, "I want you to want me and...and I want us to be like this all the time. I want us to be happy, taking care of each other..." He planted a few more kisses randomly across Gil's face— "Please stay. For me. I'll stay for you. I'll do anything for you."

Tears brimmed hazel eyes.

It didn't feel earned. Any of it. Gil's initial suspicion was whether or not Barnaby would even say those words outside the heat of the moment. But then, he supposed, the moment itself wasn't really heated. He was barely moving, acting out of—

Out of—

Well, he wouldn't call it lust.

But he did - he *did* want Barnaby to feel cared for. Whether or not he was going about it the way he ought to was debatable.

"I don't deserve you," he croaked. "I'll stay, but I know my place."

Barnaby's tears spilled over. He smiled, nonetheless. "Your place can be with me."

Gil wasn't certain who initiated the kiss, but he knew he wouldn't be the one to end it.

Maybe he'd never comprehend how he got so lucky, or why Barnaby chose to put his loyalty in him of all people, but there were still some things he understood.

He understood that if he groaned into Barnaby's mouth, the boy would moan back, needier, in a higher pitch.

He understood he could get him to moan all on his own, *loudly*, if he angled his hips the right way.

He understood that if he pumped Barnaby's dick in time with his thrusts, he'd buck his hips in return, digging his nails into Gil's skin.

Above all, he understood that if he locked eyes with the boy and smiled, he would smile right back, ten times brighter. If he whispered something nice ("God, you're adorable", "You sound so fucking beautiful"), Barnaby would giggle or try to hide his face. When he did that, Gil would mutter in his ear ("I wouldn't want this with anybody else"), and the blond would hold onto him tighter, kissing him over and over.

He knew enough to be able to tell when Barnaby was close.

His thighs pulsed around him, and his walls constricted around the man's cock; his moans devolved into panting, his tongue lolled out - he didn't mind that Gil pounded into him just a little bit harder.

He was coming undone - the main course, the centerpiece, spilling out over the man's platter in waves. Each thrust, hypnotic ripples from his love handles, his stomach, and breasts.

Gil wanted to bury every part of himself into him.

But he was close, too, his movements more erratic. He wanted to look into his eyes; he wanted that image ingrained into his head.

He wanted Barnaby to have the same experience.

It wasn't long before the boy was crying out, pleading in squeals and moans, shouting Gil's name. One last blessed stroke of his cock, and Barnaby was gone. He arched, trembling from head to toe as he came into Gil's hand.

Gil could've climaxed right along with him.

Instead, he stopped himself, more intent on milking the boy dry before abruptly pulling out.

Tearing off his condom, he pummeled his own cock, and aimed between Barnaby's legs.

The blond graciously spread himself wide, gripping his cheeks apart. "You can do it," he purred, still short of breath, "anywhere you want, Gil. I'm yours."

Gil was utterly helpless.

A final look, a photograph in his mind, and he roared his lust, affection, and longing. Cum splattered onto Barnaby's pucker. Riding his high, he spilled the rest onto his thighs and stomach.

Both were out of breath, heaving, beading with sweat, and bleary-eyed.

BANG.

Gil froze, heart stopping.

Color drained from Barnaby's face, his eyes wide with terror.

One glance to the window, and Gil spotted the many stars raining down against a dark sky.

Fireworks.

Barnaby must've noticed, too; he sighed with relief, rubbing his face.

Gil chuckled, lying beside him. He wasted no time fixing his hair, wiping the sweat from his brow, and kissing his swollen lips. "Happy New Year, Bee."

Chapter 23

He woke up to the sound of birdsong, warmed by sunlight filtering into the room.

For a moment, he was still, believing that if he didn't disrupt the scene, it would never end.

That, and his thighs might be stuck together—

No, they wouldn't be, he remembered. He and Gil had a bath, and he was sure he hadn't dreamt it. He'd been dressed in the man's shirt for evidence, naked from the waist down - an open invitation for Round Two.

Unfortunately, despite Barnaby's best butt wiggles, the raven had fallen asleep mere seconds after cuddling up behind him.

He wasn't heartbroken about it, but since then, he realized, he was no longer in Gil's embrace.

He rolled around, expecting to nuzzle into inked-on angel wings, but all he discovered was more space. The boy tried to inch closer, reaching out to touch him, but he found nothing more than room to sprawl out.

He forced his eyes open. "Gil...?"

His boyfriend sat on the edge of the bed, facing the window, his pale skin shining. Looking over his shoulder, he smiled down at him with all the warmth of the sun. "It snowed last night," he said softly.

Barnaby blinked and shifted over, laying his head in Gil's lap.

He was right. And it was a remarkable sight from what he could tell - sparkling white blanketed the ground and iced the branches of every tree. A regular Winter Wonderland.

"Perfect day for ice skating," Barnaby remarked while Gil stroked his hair.

"I was thinking," the raven hummed, "we might want to go earlier? Since there are usually less people during the day. Afterwards, we can explore the town?"

Barnaby wrapped his arms around Gil's torso, and he rubbed his cheek against his thigh. "Would we have to leave now?"

"No—" The gentle combing became playful tousling in his hair. A kiss landed on his head. "We can wait a bit."

Barnaby beamed, letting himself get comfortable.

Gil continued petting him, and all the world was delicate.

He drifted along in a dream-like state, almost unable to discern if he was fawn or human. He felt safe either way. Whether his master saw him as equal or less than, he almost didn't mind. He was cared for, protected, and confident that, whatever the case, he was the sole receiver of Gil's affection.

Light scratches were given behind his ears and under his chin. It was simply by instinct that Barnaby thanked him with little murrs and quiet bleats.

He couldn't tell how much time had passed, if he was that deep in a trance or had fallen back to sleep, but eventually, he was shaken gingerly, a velvet voice telling him, "If we wait too long, we're gonna miss breakfast."

Straining his eyes, Barnaby pushed himself up before he could get drunk off another moment. "I'm ready," he grumbled, bumping his forehead to Gil's shoulder for balance.

The raven patted his back, already getting to his feet. "We have to get dressed first. Did you bring something to wear?"

Barnaby nodded and crawled to the foot of the bed, swiping his backpack from the floor. He didn't think he'd mind staying in his headspace and letting his master dress him. He'd nudge him, paw at his clothes, and bleat until he understood. Of course, Gil should have to put his collar on for him.

He pulled out a fresh outfit, not expecting to find the silver wrapping paper hidden beneath his fleece pullover. He gasped in realization, shocking himself back to normalcy. "I forgot to give you your present!"

Gil paused from putting on a pair of slacks, raising a brow at him. "Present?"

The silver bundle in his grasp, Barnaby held it out to the other. "It's for Hanukkah! Or...Christmas. Or whatever you want it to be. I wanted you to have something."

The raven's eyes widened, staring before he said, "You didn't have to get me anything."

"I wanted to," Barnaby reiterated. Once he'd seen it, he couldn't walk past it.

Gil had to have it.

He didn't have to look guilty, approaching with a weary smile and a worried crease in his forehead. "Thank you." He took it cautiously, returning to the bed.

Barnaby curled up beside him, a careful eye on Gil's expression as he unwrapped the gift: a sculpted wolf figurine, baying at a wooden moon.

He clung to his arm. "Hopefully, it's something you're still into?"

Gil's jaw dropped; in an instant, grey stones reflected the luminescence of the wrapping paper. He turned it over in his hands, inspecting every element. "I'm never gonna get over things that are Cool, Bee, come on." Only after a thorough examination did he look to Barnaby, a bit of contortion in his face. Like a child in disbelief. "You actually remembered."

Barnaby ducked behind his shoulder, shy but no longer doubting that he'd picked the right gift. "Well...*yeah*," he managed, "You told me when you weren't giving me much information at all—" He shrugged— "I would've hung on to anything you told me."

Gil smiled fondly, and Barnaby was hugged close. "Thank you," the raven told him, "For everything. I mean it."

Barnaby pecked his cheek. "Thank you for wanting to be with me."

There was a gleam of mischief - of excitement and magic - in Gil's eyes. "I'd say it's more than a want."

But he left it at that, getting up to give the wolf a home on his desk - in front of the picture he had framed. He continued getting dressed, asking Barnaby, "You don't mind waiting a little bit to get your gift, do you?"

Barnaby stumbled to change into his own outfit; he'd been nervous at the thought of what Gil might get him in return. "That depends," he mumbled, "Is it going to be something over the top?" He finished and went to the nightstand, finding his collar.

Turning around, he came face to face with Gil once again.

"I didn't plan on it," the man said. He took the collar and fastened it around Barnaby's neck, hiding it under his pullover— "But then again, that depends on your definition."

They passed Mrs. Connolly in the living room on their way to the front door.

"Good morning, boys," she called, over the stock music of whatever phone game she was playing, "Heading out for the day?"

"Yep—" Gil grabbed his peacoat from the coat closet, handing the blond's bomber jacket to him next— "and taking Barnaby home after, so this'll probably be the last time you ever see him."

That put a cross look on the woman's face, and she set her mug aside, getting off the couch in her slippers and pink robe to meet them. "Come back soon, sweetie," she told

Barnaby, grinning with her words, "You're welcome here any time."

Barnaby's instinct was to look to Gil. For confirmation? Permission?

The man smirked but didn't offer anything more than a wink.

He would've preferred he'd speak *for* him, but maybe— maybe letting Barnaby have his own voice meant the decision was his.

"I will," he told Mrs. Connolly, "I-I'd like to. Maybe next time...I could bring something for dinner!" *And not give it to your son to force feed me.*

She radiated - the first rays of sunrise reaching above the horizon. "I look forward to it."

A hand was placed on Barnaby's lower back, and he was gently urged toward the door while Gil bellowed, "See ya later, Ma. Don't wait up."

Barnaby barely managed to squeak out a "Goodbye!" before being dragged outside. The pathway from the house to the driveway hadn't been paved yet, and he trudged his feet through the snow.

Gil hardly seemed fazed.

As they passed the caroling snowfolk, Barnaby couldn't resist asking, "Do you think she likes me?"

The raven scoffed, opening the passenger door of his car for him. "Keep it up, and she'll let you call her Mom the next time you see her."

Feeling his face grow warm, Barnaby hopped into the chilled vehicle.

Gil was being facetious, probably, but it didn't stop his mind from running with the potential implications. Would the man object to that? Would it push pressure on their relationship? Would either of them be opposed to that pressure?

He held his backpack in his lap and breathed in deep.

Come back, he told himself, *You haven't even been on an official date yet.*

They drove off with Gil's playlist making up their morning montage. A specific location was never mentioned, but Barnaby trusted Gil's judgement, and it wasn't like *he'd* ever be able to decide on somewhere to eat.

They hadn't been driving for long when the song abruptly cut off, interrupted by the ring of a phone.

Gil pressed the touch screen on the dashboard, and Barnaby noticed Addison's name pop up.

"Hello?"

A timid voice came through the speakers— "Heeey, Gil."

The man raised a brow, glancing between the touch screen and the road. "Imani?"

"Hi," Imani went on, "sorry to bother you so early, but do you think you can pick up Addie? She's not doing too well, and my parents took the car."

A distant, sickly groan joined Imani on her end.

Gil looked to Barnaby, a scowl on his lips and what might've been an apology in his eyes.

371

Barnaby managed a smile and shrugged - trying to show he didn't mind going out of their way, if that was what Gil was looking for. At least they'd be able to say they had an interesting morning.

"Alright," the man sighed, "We're about ten minutes away. Make sure she's ready."

"Will do," Imani said, "Thank you."

The call ended.

Barnaby reached for Gil's hand, holding it between them, and a hesitant grin returned to the raven's face.

The playlist resumed, and in ten minute's time, they arrived on a quaint little street lined with smaller suburban homes. They stopped outside of a house colored sea foam green, waiting only a few moments before the two girls walked out.

They wore matching coats, Addison in pink and Imani in pastel blue, and Barnaby thought that was very sweet of them.

Less sweet, perhaps, were the sunglasses Addison wore, along with her unceremonious gait that left her relying on Imani's support to get to the car.

"How trashed did you get last night?" Gil instigated the instant she climbed into the backseat.

"*Shut up*," Addison grumbled, and Barnaby held his breath as an overpowering scent of perfume flooded the car, "You've done worse."

"Really though," Imani chimed in, barely above a whisper, "She's got a headache, so if you could keep it down..."

Whether she was finished or not, her voice was quickly drowned out by the sudden blast of music. For a split-second, Gil turned the radio up as loud as it could go before immediately bringing it back down.

Even Barnaby flinched, hands flying to cover his ears.

"Fuck you!" Addison shouted, punching Gil's seat.

All he did was laugh.

Imani, still standing by Addison's door, said matter of factly, "I see now I've made a mistake."

Addison whined for her girlfriend, and Gil rolled his eyes. "If you want to make sure she gets back in one piece, hop in," he groaned, "Mom's up, but she probably won't bother her if you're there. Plus, I won't be there, so she can't blame this *behavior* on me."

"Wait," Addison interjected, "where are you going?"

Gil heaved a sigh, gesturing to the blond beside him, "I'm taking Barnaby to get breakfast. Then, we're going ice skating."

That shot the brunette right out of her seat, propelling forward to poke her head at her brother's boyfriend. "Barnaby! I'm so sorry, I didn't even know you were there!"

People usually don't.

But he kept his self-deprecation hidden behind a smile. "*Hi—* It's fine."

"Oh my God," she said, already turning to Gil, "I want to go ice skating with Barnaby. We've been meaning to go anyway. Right, Imani? We should all go. Double date."

"What happened to your hangover?" Gil objected, "You think that'll make you feel better?"

Addison huffed, plopping back into her seat. "I'll walk it off. Skate it off. Plus, I need like...toast. Or something—" She pouted, reaching for her girlfriend.

From his sideview mirror, Barnaby watched Imani grimace.

He wondered what Gil was like when he was drunk.

Imani asked, "Is that okay with you, Gil?"

"It should be," Addison answered for him, "You remember what the therapist said? We need to spend more time together. We need to be *involved*."

Barnaby hoped to lock eyes with Gil, but the man only continued to stare straight ahead, fingers restlessly tapping the steering wheel.

He mumbled, "Pretty sure she didn't say it had to be when I wanted to spend time with my significant other."

Sensing his tension made Barnaby bite the inside of his cheek to suppress a smile.

He never thought himself significant.

"You go to the same school! You can see him whenever," Addison countered. She pushed the back of his seat with her foot. "You want to be like normal siblings, don't you? You need me to interrogate him and make sure he's good enough for you."

"Y-You don't need to do that," Barnaby interjected, "I already know I'm not."

The truth - but he meant it as a joke, too. Something for Addison to laugh at.

He didn't expect his seat to be the next kicked.

"No!" she was suddenly protesting, "Oh my God, is he telling you you're not? *Gil*—!"

"Imani—"

Barnaby was so surprised by Gil's voice, he almost didn't register that the man had once again grabbed hold of his hand.

"Are you sure you want to join this shit show?"

Imani shrugged, looking at everyone around her. She spoke with a delicate voice, "What better way to ring in the new year, I guess. Should be interesting."

Gil nodded for her to hop in, and she joined Addison in the back seat. He continued driving, and it was *interesting*.

Addison's interrogation was nothing like that of Barnaby's mom's Prime Time investigation dramas. Her head on Imani's shoulder, she asked him about his past experiences, if he'd "broken anyone's heart before."

His and Gil's hands stayed clasped, and he admitted that Gil was his first boyfriend, an answer she didn't seem to expect.

She fumbled with her response before bringing in to question possible Nefarious Activities.

He'd always worried about being seen as boring (not that he wasn't) for not drinking or drugging or getting tied up in schemes.

But his honesty lent to Addison's approval.

"Good," she said, tired words slurring together, "You'll be a good influence on him. Finally."

Gil made her take her sunglasses off before entering the diner.

Once seated at their booth, Imani asked Barnaby about his fawn. He froze up until he remembered the stuffed animal.

He'd fallen asleep with it every night since he'd been home.

Yeah. Gidget was doing well.

They ordered their food, and Barnaby and Gil both got pancakes. Barnaby didn't plan to eat much, but his were made with funfetti batter, and from the first bite, he was hooked. He was almost too busy stuffing himself to notice Gil adding more to his plate, scraps and hashbrowns that the man never took a mouthful of.

Addison went silent, slumping back in her seat as she nibbled at dry pieces of toast.

Barnaby asked what Imani's store had been like over the holidays, and she readily beguiled them with tales of unruly children and parents that insisted on speaking to the manager every five seconds.

"But we are having a 50% off sale this week," she interrupted herself, "We have *lots* of new outfits if you wanted to give your fawn something for winter."

She glanced at Barnaby's plate as she spoke. At Gil replenishing it. "You must've really been hungry," she said, sounding somewhat impressed.

Barnaby felt his face glow bright red, and he almost put his fork down for being a greedy animal. As if he wasn't already the thickest person at the table.

But then, Imani pushed over the remainder of her meal. "I wasn't going to finish it anyway."

Barnaby swallowed a mouthful and thanked her.

Setting his utensils down, Gil slipped a hand onto the boy's thigh.

He stiffened, doing his best not to betray his master even as his fingers crept closer to the button of his pants. He was tempted to let him get away with it, unopposed to the relief of an uncompressed belly.

But when he finished and it didn't seem as if they were in a rush to leave, Barnaby settled in instead. Plump and pleased with himself, he pressed against his boyfriend's arm until it was draped around his shoulders.

Addison, after staring blankly through the window for several minutes straight, abruptly snapped to attention to remind Gil of "the pit behind Costco."

"What about it?"

"It snowed," she went on, "We can go sledding there."

Gil rolled his eyes. "If we're going home for sleds, you're staying home."

"No, we don't— It's *behind Costco*."

So, they went to Costco next.

Or rather, Imani and Addison went to Costco.

Gil and Barnaby waited in the car, with Gil offering to leave them there if Barnaby wanted to be alone with him.

"We aren't leaving them here," the boy scoffed. "Though, I'm starting to think you want to be alone with me more than anything."

"Of course, I do."

A hand slipped up Barnaby's pullover, and all the blond could do was squeak and melt while Gil rubbed his bloated belly. His hand was cold, but it still threatened to revert him to his trance.

Gil purred, "You'll give me a little time alone before I take you home, won't you?"

Barnaby bit his lip, nodding. "I will."

Minutes later, Imani and Addison returned with two long, plastic sleds.

They proceeded around the warehouse, and Barnaby did his best to swallow his apprehension as a wide, white field came into view.

Dozens of people or so surrounded what appeared to be a massive crater in the Earth, sledding, gliding, and tumbling into it.

The next thing Barnaby knew, their group was among them, and he stood close to his boyfriend's side as others shouted from the slopes and snowballs went flying.

They stopped at the lip of the pit, watching for a moment, before Addison dared her brother, "Race you."

Both of their sleds hit the ground at the exact same time. When Addison crawled into her's, she smiled at Imani, who eagerly shuffled in behind her.

Seeing this, Gil turned to Barnaby. "Care to join?"

Barnaby wasn't sure there was enough room; seated, Gil's knees already jutted out at the sides. He cupped his hands over his mouth and blew for warmth, muffling his words, "I think I'll watch this one—" He gave a thumbs up— "but good luck."

Gil shrugged, and Addison counted down, "Three, two, *one*—"

They took off with the girls quickly pulling ahead. Because the slope was steep, it was over fast; Addison and Imani reached the bottom first, shrieking as their sled spun out.

Barnaby winced as Gil fell out of his sled behind them, limbs everywhere.

Watching them climb back to the top brought documentaries of Mount Everest to mind. Except in those documentaries, the climbers didn't heckle each other - which Barnaby assumed Addison had done when Gil gave her a light shove.

Imani pounced right up from behind him, pushing him to the ground.

"B-Be careful, please!" Barnaby called down to them.

"Bee!" Gil called back, scrambling to his feet, "I need you."

Aww.

Heels digging into the snow and feet angling to avoid slipping, Barnaby braced for descent.

He didn't get far for Gil to notice and hold a hand up to him, stopping him in his tracks.

"I need you to go down with me," the raven said. He only reached for Barnaby's hand when he was close enough to be pulled to the top, dropping his sled to the ground without a second to lose.

Addison and Imani matched him, waiting.

Barnaby breathed deep and examined the slope once again. It didn't look any less steep, but Gil needed him. "You're sure I won't cause an avalanche?"

"Positive. *C'mon.*"

There was a pat on his back, and Barnaby turned to everyone else seated in their sleds.

Gil had his legs fixed along the sides, creating more space in front of him.

Barnaby sighed and squeezed himself in.

With his knees to his chest, Gil hooked an arm around his waist, and Addison counted down from three.

The raven whispered into his ear, "Hang on."

"*—One!*"

He pushed them off, holding Barnaby as tightly as he had the night before.

The boy's stomach dropped as they went speeding, keeping a white-knuckle grip on Gil's legs. He didn't even see the girls as they flew by.

Right when he thought they would tip, they hit the bottom, narrowly avoiding an innocent child.

Addison and Imani landed behind them.

Gil dug his heel into the ground, bringing them to a stop, and Barnaby could hear the smile in his voice when he breathed against his neck, "We won."

"Best two out of three!" Addison called over to them.

Barnaby rolled his eyes, and Gil squeezed him before letting him get to his feet.

They scaled the hill only to make another descent, a replay of the previous. Only with that race, Gil and Barnaby didn't land as gracefully.

They were thrown from their sled at the end, and in seconds, Barnaby was feeling the bite of snow at the nape of his neck.

He opened his eyes to find Gil on top of him, inches away from his face.

"D-Did we win?"

"Mhm." Grey eyes fixated on Barnaby's lips.

Addison didn't demand a rematch after that.

Admittedly, they weren't any more graceful when it came to ice skating.

Imani and Addison took right off, hand in hand as they glided along, while Gil and Barnaby shuffled in, gripping the wall.

The rink was out in the open, at least, and Barnaby thought he preferred that to a regular arena. Something about the one he used to visit at their local recreation center with his mom always left him feeling like he was in competition with everyone else. Of course, the way he saw it, he always fell behind.

But where they were, thankfully, didn't hold many skaters at all that time of day. Gil had been right.

Although, it seemed, *he* was the one facing competition.

The two young men had barely made a complete lap around the rink when Addison and Imani passed them for a third time, slowing down ahead of them.

"Really, Gil?" Addison sneered, "Do we have to go through this every year?"

"*Yes*. Besides—" The raven shrugged— "I don't want to leave Barnaby behind."

Barnaby flushed. "Y-You could've said so." He didn't want to be responsible for holding both of them back.

He held his breath. *Moment of truth.*

With stiff legs, he inched away from the wall until only his fingertips touched. Addison and Imani continued to hover around him, as if prepared to break his fall.

One way or another, Barnaby was able to move forward. His skate caught a bit in the frost, and his heart caught in his throat, but with some flailing, he regained his balance.

He exhaled and, detaching completely, offered his hand to Gil.

Equally as stiff, the man took it and pulled away with him.

"You're both so dramatic," Addison teased, encouraged by Imani's laughter.

Dramatic, but apparently, no longer entertaining.

Linking arms, the girls went on to complete another lap.

Gil and Barnaby's hands remained locked like their lives depended on it, chuckling at themselves - at the fact they were two grown men struggling to skate on their own, leaning on one another for support.

It took them a while to catch up and get their...Sea Legs? Ice Legs? Though, eventually, they had a good pace going, and Barnaby found himself moving his feet to the tempo of the stereo music around them. They didn't say much, other than to check on one another, but then, at the right moment, all Barnaby needed to do was look up.

As uncertain as his movements were, Gil held his head high, a slight squint in his eyes from the sun and a wistful smile on his lips.

When he caught Barnaby's gaze, he'd wink down at him, and the blond would feel a spark in both his face and his heart.

Minutes went by before the pair noticed Imani and Addison had split up - Addison having a bit more speed in her skate.

Honing in on Imani, Gil muttered, "I'll be right back."

He made sure the boy was steady on his own before pushing ahead.

Barnaby merely let himself drift, better at keeping his balance when he wasn't scrambling for speed.

"Heads up!"

Without any time to move or brace himself, Addison collided with his back. By some miracle, neither of them collapsed; all he suffered was a racing heart.

"Hey!" the girl chimed, pulling off of him.

"*Hi.*"

She'd seemed to recover from her hangover, and when she composed herself, tucking her hair behind her ear, Barnaby was reminded of how much Addison looked like her brother.

He inhaled - "Did you come back for another interrogation?"

"Kind of," she admitted, glancing off in Gil's direction, "Just wanted to see how you were doing."

"I'm alright—" Although, the way she spoke, like she wasn't quite finished, made Barnaby believe she was searching for more— "I got to go sledding and ice skating with my boyfriend and two new friends. Why wouldn't I be?"

The girl gave a humble shrug. "That's fair." For a moment, that was all she said. Her gaze continued to linger on her brother, and she sighed when she spoke again, "He hasn't given you any trouble, has he?"

Barnaby quirked a brow. "Trouble?"

"Yeah. Like," Addison mumbled, "past few years, we've had to drag him to go anywhere with us. *Granted*, that might be because I'm his sister, and he could be totally different with his other friends, but...This is the first time I've seen him with *anyone* else. And that's anyone *in general*. It's weird. Never thought he'd settle on a boyfriend."

It was Barnaby's turn to fixate on the raven ahead of them, who beamed in response to something Imani said.

"It's a little strange for me, too." *It's strange because I don't think either of us intended to end up here. It's strange because part of him might still believe none of this is enough to keep living.*

He felt Addison focus on him.

Barnaby cleared his throat - "Since he's the first partner I've had, and...well, I'm probably way more socially awkward than he is, so it might just be me, but it's like having, uh...a safety net? A lot of times, it is hard to feel comfortable in public, but at least I know if he's around...I'm safe."

"Wow—" The corners of Addison's mouth tugged down, and her face was considerably less rosy— "so, I don't make *him* feel safe. That's—"

"I don't think it's that," Barnaby quickly explained, "Like you said, you're his sister, and...I'm sure there's a difference there, but I don't know the dynamic. I've never had a sibling."

The girl scoffed, and sarcasm danced on her tongue, "Consider yourself lucky then."

Who was the Gil that Addison knew? Despondent and distant, perhaps? But what did that mean to her? Did she see him the way Gil saw himself? Would she think he was more like Barnaby the more she got to know him?

If Barnaby was more like the Gil he knew, he'd ask her. He'd be daring enough to find out who that boy standing awkwardly in the picture on his desk was, the person she had known for a lifetime and who Barnaby was only beginning to understand.

It was a slim chance, but it was romantic to imagine having the rest of his life to find those answers. Only time could tell for certain.

In the meanwhile, all Barnaby could be certain of was his time with Addison on the ice.

Whatever time he had left with Gil, he had to assume his moments with her would be less. For that reason, Barnaby smiled at the girl and told her, "I think I'm very lucky. I'm lucky that my boyfriend has a sister who's as...easy to talk to as she is beautiful."

Addison glowed, gently nudging him. "I am glad he picked you, though," she said, "And I'm sorry for fourth-wheeling on you guys. I think I just needed to see it for myself to believe it. Of course, if he ever gives you any bullshit, let me know. I'll take care of it."

She proceeded to skate ahead of him, in direct line to collide with Gil.

Fortunately, he spotted her with barely a second to spare, promptly skidding to the wall.

Addison, instead, made a grab for Imani's hand, and the two danced along seamlessly.

Gil waited for Barnaby to catch up. As soon as the blond was within earshot, he asked him, "Ready for a break?" Propping his arm out for Barnaby to hook onto, he added, "It's time I show you something."

If all Gil had to show Barnaby was the park surrounding the ice-skating rink, he would've been content. Arm in arm, it felt like a fairy tale, following his Prince Charming down a brick-paved path lined with trees and old lamp posts, each connected by garland and strings of lights.

It didn't take long to end up back at the main road, a street that ran through a quaint section of town. The cars passed in as little of a rush as the people on the bordering sidewalks, heading in and out window shops with plenty to choose from on either side of the lane.

Having a path already laid out in his mind, Gil walked in long, deliberate strides. Barnaby didn't dare interrupt him until they stopped outside of a store that had cursive painted on the front window, *Classic Collections and Antiques.*

Barnaby's nose wrinkled the moment they entered. It smelled excessively of his grandmother's house and had equal amounts of dust and clutter. Before he could get a good look at whatever any of it was, Gil went ahead of him, and Barnaby decided it was best to stay close behind.

They had to skirt around a wall of trinkets, fine China, and of course, other items that were easily breakable in order to locate the register.

The girl behind the counter looked up, and the instant she locked eyes with Barnaby, he was startled into gasping, "Savannah?"

"Barnaby!" She hopped to attention, perhaps ready to hop over her station if not for the jewelry that filled its display case. "I was hoping I'd get to see you. How are you, babe?"

"Really good," Barnaby answered, feeling all fuzzy as he tugged on his sleeves and stepped closer, "I didn't know you had another job."

"*Mhm*—" She puffed her chest proudly and placed a hand on her hip— "Just because we're on break doesn't mean my tuition is."

Barnaby flushed, a bit embarrassed to not be in the same mindset.

"Do you still have that order I put on hold?" Gil asked her, leaning against the counter.

She lifted her nose at him, as if he'd interrupted a very important conversation, but was able to match his crooked grin. "Try adding a please in there, Mr. Connolly."

"Can we please see the order I put on hold?"

"Much better." She turned back to Barnaby, eyes rolling dramatically, before disappearing through a velvet curtain hanging behind her.

Gil's eyes lingered on the curtain a moment after she was gone. When it was silent, he shoved his hands into his coat pockets, took a step toward Barnaby, and muttered, "I saw this thing a few days ago, thought it'd be a nice gift...but if I'm being honest, I was worried I would like it more than you, which is why I didn't get it."

It certainly piqued Barnaby's interest, but he didn't know how else to respond with anything other than a raised brow.

Gil went on, "I figured I'd let you decide for yourself. If you like it, I'll get it for you. If not–" He looked around, gesturing to the rest of the shop– "I'm sure we can find something else."

Right as Barnaby was about to question why he wouldn't like it, Savannah came back into view.

She laid it out on the counter, and as the men approached for a closer inspection, Barnaby sensed his face heating up once again.

The item up for consideration was a fur coat, specifically, that resembling a spotted deer.

Gil elbowed his side. "What do you think?"

Barnaby wasn't sure himself.

He grazed his hand over it. Even softer than it looked.

He glanced between Gil and Savannah. "Can I try it on?"

Savannah pointed to a gold-trimmed dressing mirror behind him, and Barnaby removed his bomber jacket while Gil took the coat from its hanger.

Once the boy was standing in front of his reflection, the raven helped him put it on.

He was so used to having such a low opinion of his own image, he almost didn't want to believe it looked as good as it did. Perhaps a part of him was sinking into his pet headspace, clouding his better judgement.

"That is," Savannah commented, face full of glee, "the *dearest* thing I have ever seen."

Gil, whose eyes were still scanning Barnaby from head to toe, added, "I agree. It's...a-*doe*-able."

Barnaby giggled, turning pink and turning around to survey the coat from every angle. Although it was loose-fitting and hid his curves, it somehow made him look rounder. Fluffier, for sure. He didn't exactly feel like a dainty, young fawn. "I feel like..."

Whether or not Gil would admit it, Barnaby felt like it was another way for the man to show him off - an obvious sign of their relationship but something still so discreet.

Gil really thought he was *worth* showing off. He let him hold onto his arm in public, walk hand in hand...and he wanted to dress him up where others could see.

That, or maybe he figured Barnaby really liked deer.

Whatever the case, he nodded his approval and, meeting Gil's eyes, came to a conclusion: "I feel like a million bucks."

They left Savannah's shop with Barnaby still wearing the new coat.

He was a bit self-conscious at first, unaccustomed to the stares and second glances of people on the street. He'd always tried to make himself as unassuming as possible - less chance of being ridiculed that way.

He almost worried if that's what the passersby were doing, whether internally or whispered to their partners—

And then someone called out to him, sudden and excited, "I like your coat!"

"Thank you!" he chimed, finishing in his mind, *my boyfriend got it for me!*

Gil nudged him, and Barnaby pressed against his side.

It didn't matter what anyone else thought, really. As long as Gil was proud of him.

Making their way back to the Range Rover, they waited for Addison and Imani. Both were surprised by the sight of him; neither wanted to stop petting him once they started stroking his coat.

Gil drove them home under the premise that it was time to take Barnaby back to his mother.

Barnaby was a bit embarrassed by it, but apparently, the girls found it sweet. They wanted him to say "hi" to her for them.

Once they'd been dropped off - rather than taking the route for the hour-long drive - Gil set course for a small steakhouse not far from where they'd been ice skating.

There, they were given a booth near the kitchen, where fresh, delicious scents wafted out, right to Barnaby's nose, making his stomach growl.

The instant they were handed their menus, Gil asked the waitress if they served venison.

Barnaby fixed him with a glare.

No, they did not.

He didn't want to say their meal was *better* without Addison and Imani, though Barnaby did find himself more at ease. Smitten.

As the time ticked by, he caught himself chuckling at everything Gil said, grinning so wide that it nearly hurt.

Gil seemed to be in the best mood of his life - like when they'd been darting through a zombie maze, like when they'd danced at the bowling alley, like when they'd hung out in the mall—

Like much of the time they'd spent together, for that matter.

Or maybe it was in the way the candlelight from their table danced across Gil's face, bringing the fire of his soul to his eyes.

The man laughed along with him when Barnaby recalled all the near-mishaps that happened while sledding and skating. The fact they were playing footsies under the table the entire time went unmentioned.

Barnaby noticed a pattern from their earlier meal - Gil placing half of his food onto the boy's plate - but didn't mention that, either. With the way the raven refused to break eye contact, the boy could only interpret it as his silent demand: "Accept it."

When he'd cleaned his plates, Barnaby slumped back and sighed.

Gil rested his chin on a raised palm, smirking. "Ready for dessert?"

"No," Barnaby scoffed, rubbing his stomach. "Not yet. I need a minute. Thank you, though."

Gil nodded, sliding his other hand across the table. "Don't mention it."

Putting his own hand over the raven's, Barnaby insisted, "I have to. Today was...*wonderful*, and I'm so grateful for everything. I can't thank you enough."

Gil's expression softened, and he wove their fingers together. "The fact you put up with it is thanks enough."

Barnaby feigned a pout, giving his boyfriend's knee a light kick. "I'm not here because I put up with you, I'm here because I lo–"

Realizing what he was saying, he promptly shut up.

Barnaby had never been in love.

He'd never been on a real date before - to dinner or breakfast or anywhere with someone he could call his boyfriend.

He never thought he'd experience the luxury of a five-star restaurant, a fur coat, or the unbroken gaze of an achingly handsome man.

He never thought anyone would put up with *him*. Especially someone who related to him so deeply.

He never thought he deserved it.

Barnaby cleared his throat, shook his head, and settled for, "I'm here because...I'm *fawned* of you."

Gil chuckled, leaning in. "I get it." He brought Barnaby's hand to his lips and gave it a kiss. Then, he stared directly into his soul. "I love you, too."

Made in the USA
Columbia, SC
23 November 2020

25323580R00238